KIDDING AROUND

KIDDING AROUND

JEZABEL NIGHTINGALE

ISBN 978-0-6458061-5-1 (Paperback)
ISBN 978-0-6458061-6-8 (e-Book)

Edited by Sarah Baker, The Word Emporium
Proofread by Cheyenne Sampson, Frogg Spa Editing
Cover art by Kristin Barrett, K. B. Barrett Designs

jezabelnightingale.com

For everyone who has sat through Mother's Day and other holidays looking on in pain, wondering if it will ever be their turn.

What feels like the end is often the beginning.

Anonymous

Content Warning

This book deals with infertility, something that will affect around one in six couples, and therefore, potentially, one in six readers. I don't want to spoil things by warning about things that happen in the book, but I also want to protect those for whom certain subjects, especially around fertility and pregnancy are challenging.

More detailed warnings can be found on my website:

Before you start...

This book is set in the Southern Hemisphere where seasons are back to front compared to our European and American friends. School and university years start in January/February and end in November/December with the summer holidays happening over Christmas. There may be 'Australianisms' that make little sense to you, please feel free to reach out in my Facebook group, or via email, if you need clarification!

Playlist

My Heart Will Go On — *Grand Piano Players*
Piano Sonata No. 14 in C-sharp minor "Moonlight"— *Beethoven*
Piano Man — *Billy Joel*
Piano Sonata No. 2 in B ♭ minor, Op. 35 — *Chopin*
It's the Most Wonderful Time of the Year — *David Campbell*
Come Away With Me — *Norah Jones*
Shake It Off — *Taylor Swift*
Firework — *Katy Perry*
I'll Stand By You— *Pretenders*
Theme from Schindler's List — *John Williams*
The Rite of Spring — *Stravinsky*
Ticket to Ride — *The Beatles*
The First Time Ever I Saw Your Face — *Roberta Flack*
Never Tear Us Apart — *INXS*
Even When I'm Sleeping — *Leonardo's Bride*

Available on Spotify

Chapter 1

Boyd

I've had lots of best days of my life, but today overtook them all.

"What's this pre-graduation party all about?" Henry, the older brother up from me, asks as he and his partner, Ken, step into the kitchen at Mum and Dad's house.

"You'll see," I reply with a grin. "I'm glad you got the memo to dress nice."

"When has he not dressed nice?" Ken wraps an arm around Henry's waist and kisses him on the cheek. They've been together for a year and a bit, and it's nice to see them so loved up together. Love was where it was at, after all.

"No," Mia screams as the front door closes. At age three, it is her favourite word.

"Amelia Hillary, you need to take your gumboots off in Gammy and Gramps' house, please." My sister-in-law, Bridget, likes to pretend she is firm with her daughters, but they have both parents wrapped around their tiny fingers.

I couldn't wait until Emily and I were parents. It was something we often talked about and, sure, we'd had a few near misses over the years, but now we were getting married and had finished uni, we both looked forward to a gaggle of kids in our future. I wanted six; Emily said four. We'd probably settle on five. The thought of regular sex without condoms makes my cock take notice, but now is not the time.

Like a whirling dervish, Mia twirls her way into the kitchen wearing football shorts, a tulle fairy skirt, and a T-shirt that was adorned with bits of everything she's eaten today.

"Did you have chocolate milk, Mia?" Mum appears from upstairs wearing a cream pantsuit. "That shirt is looking quite grubby. Why don't we find a clean one in the playroom?"

Mum and Dad have turned the guest room downstairs into a playroom for their granddaughters.

Mia strips off her shirt and throws it in the air, resuming her twirling until she bumps into Henry.

"Come here, Mia-moo. Let's go and grab you a shirt. I think Gammy has one with sparkles on it."

"No." Mia keeps twirling, her hands now on her hips, and Henry pretends to chase her.

"Mia's being naughty." Millie, who, at five, thinks she's almost a grownup, weaves her arms across her chest and rolls her eyes.

Bridget leans over and kisses Mum on the cheek before greeting Henry, Ken, and me in the same manner. "How about we just ignore her for a bit?"

"They're awesome kids, Bridge. I mean Bridget. You and Gilbo should have another one." I bite my bottom lip, but I don't miss the brief look of pain that flashes across my sister-in-law's face. It was probably from me calling her Bridge, which I always forget she hates.

Giles, my oldest brother, walks into the kitchen carrying what looks like far too many bags. Kids can't need that much stuff, surely? "Are you saying my wife and I don't have enough sex?" He casts a protective arm around his wife and sounds firmer than I've heard him in ages. "Because I can assure you, we do. And just because we're only going to have two children doesn't make us love each other any less or desire each other any less. Really, Boyo, you need to stop joking about things like this."

Yeah, whatever. Giles has turned into the serious one out of the three of us boys. Val, the baby of the family and only girl, and Henry are a lot alike, but not as fun as me. Life is too short to be taken too seriously, after all. Love and laughter are where it's at, and I am full of both. I have my Emily and my family. I've enjoyed medical school and am excited to be starting as a doctor in the new year.

"Okay." I rub my hands together and look at my brothers. "Has someone got a coin?" Giles reaches into the fruit bowl and produces one before handing it to me with an eye roll that rivalled his daughter. "Henry, you're the younger one, you can call. Heads or tails?"

"Well, I don't mind a bit of head, but have you seen Ken's tail? Tails, please." Ken shakes his head as his partner taps the said tail.

"Right, it's heads. You win, Gilbo."

"What have I won?" Giles asks as he rubs the bridge of his nose.

"You'll see. Now, can everyone please gather around the pool? Dad's out there with Emily's nonna. Rosa will be out soon with Val, and I'll grab Em."

"No way." Ken's jaw drops, and I know he realises what's happening. I throw him a look that implores him to keep quiet, and he simply slaps me on the back as he walks past before grabbing Henry's hand.

We hadn't wanted fuss or fanfare, just family. Family is everything to both Emily and me. There's no aisle to walk down, and no one is giving anyone away, no speeches or dancing, but I have grabbed a three-dollar mud cake from the supermarket as a bit of a joke.

We've been together for years, and in my mind, we will be forever. A piece of paper wouldn't change anything. Emily wanted to change her surname to be free from her father. Well, that's what she said, but I also think she knows what being a Dr Hartman meant around these parts.

Mum and Dad are both cardiologists, as is Giles. Well, he will be in a couple of years when he passes his exams. Bridget is almost an obstetrician and gynaecologist. I know I'm going to be a paediatrician. I mean, I'm just a big kid myself. Emily sees herself as a general practitioner, working a few days a week in the community and raising a family. I've told her I'm going to take time off, too. I'm willing to go part-time to help bring up the next generation of Hartman doctors. We'll work it out when the time comes.

Even though I won't get to experience the sensation of watching

Emily walk towards me as I stand with the celebrant in front of our small assembly of guests, seeing her emerge down the stairs at Mum and Dad's place wearing a flowing red dress is just as special. Fuck, she could have worn a garbage bag and still been the sexiest and most beautiful woman I've ever laid my eyes on. The red highlights, the subtle golden tones of her skin, and the amber flecks in her brown eyes.

There's no anxiety, just joy. We've been together since we were teenagers. So many said we wouldn't make it, but I knew we would. We were each other's person. Emily was my always and everything. My forever. We still surprise people, though. Our graduation from medical school happens Monday, and our family knows we are flying out to spend Christmas in Italy with some of Emily's family, but they didn't realise this was going to be our honeymoon.

We never got engaged. When I was fourteen, and she was twelve, I'd told her we were going to get married. She may have been my sister's best friend, but she was also mine.

I don't know how we kept the wedding a secret. Emily's mum is an amazing seamstress, and Em told her she needed a dress for a ball. She didn't want to wear white or any variation. Em was adopted from China as a baby. For years, she ignored her genetic identity, but recently, she's been exploring it a little more. Not that we needed symbols or signs for our marriage, but red is meant to be lucky, isn't it?

"She's just told me." Emily's mum, Rosa, wipes a tear from her eye with a tissue as she plants a kiss on my cheek. She uses the same tissue to wipe off the red lipstick she's left behind above my beard. "Come on, Val. We better get out there."

"Boyo, you better treat her right, because she means more to me than my brothers, and I will defend her after I've helped her bury your body." Val points a finger into my chest as she speaks, but her tone is warm and friendly. "Seriously though, I love you both, and well done on keeping this a secret from Mum."

Val and Rosa make their way outside, and I am left with Emily in the foyer. "It's not too late to run," I joke.

"I'm only running if you're coming with me." She sounds playful, tears of joy threatening to spill from her eyes. "I can't think of anything better than being married to you. Is the celebrant here?" The look of devotion on her face does me in. I know we're doing the right thing, and we'll be together forever. I can't wait to get started on forever today.

"She's in the pool house, ready to rock and roll. Fuck, I love you. You look amazing. I can't wait to fuck you tonight as my wife." I press my chub against her thigh and love the way her pupils blow as she bites her lower lip.

"Well, we won't let Millie and Mia fall asleep, so they'll be tired and cranky then, and everyone will be gone early, so we can leave, too." Emily's eyes shine as we stand holding hands, my heart brimming with love.

"Are you sure you're alright that your dad's not here?" I stroke the purple streak in her hair, set off amazingly by the shine of the black.

"Positive." Emily offers me a confident nod and kisses me gently on the lips. "I want family with us today, and he's no longer part of my family."

We make our way outside holding hands and giggling like we were still the same teenagers who would lie by the pool sharing a deckchair, kissing each other like it was going out of fashion.

Everyone turns to look at us. "Alright, everyone. So, Emily and me, I, me? Meh, grammar. Well, I'm glad you're all here, because we're getting hitched!" A chorus of cheers erupts, and the celebrant emerges from the pool house.

"AND NOW..." The celebrant closes her folder with a flourish, a huge grin on her face. "By the power vested in me by the Commonwealth of Australia, I declare you to be husband and wife. You may—"

She never finishes her sentence, as Emily throws herself into my arms, wrapping her legs around my waist as our lips meet for the first time as a married couple. I twirl her around, and Giles has to stop me before we fall into the pool.

"Steady up, Boyo. You've got the rest of your lives." He chuckles as Emily slides down my body and places her feet on the ground.

Giles was my best man. Hence the coin toss. Val signed her name as a witness in the register and stood next to Emily as we recited our vows.

It feels strange wearing a band on my left hand. We both chose plain gold bands. Neither of us are big jewellery wearers, and Emily hadn't wanted an engagement ring. Like I said, simple and no fuss, with a laugh or two thrown in.

"Congratulations." Val throws her arms around her best friend, and they jiggle from side to side as they hold each other close. "Can you believe"—Val turns to me, still holding my wife's hand—"she didn't tell me anything, not even this morning when she dragged me along to Gloria's salon for a pedicure and haircut. You'll have to do the paper-work again, though. The celebrant had Emily Hartman as your name, and it needs to be Emily McIntyre."

Val has a year left in her law degree. Yep, unlike the rest of us, she discarded the idea of being a doctor. It was a sore point with Giles, but I could see her with a wig on telling a judge what to do.

"Um." Emily looks at me with a sly grin on her face before turning to face her friend again. "It's right. We were going to do this six months ago, but we couldn't get everyone together. Nonna was in the hospital with her hip replacement. Hills and Charlie were at that conference in Minnesota, and you were too busy with Zayn."

"Ugh. Don't remind me." Val shakes her head and visibly shudders. "Two months of my life that I'm not getting back."

"Yeah, so I changed my name so I could make sure it was on my graduation certificate and registration and stuff. It's no biggie." Emily was matter of fact about this, but it was a big deal.

Ever since her father left Cassowary Point, where we both grew up and still live, when Emily just turned thirteen, her spark had lost some of its lustre. Her signing away her father's surname was a huge step, and I've noticed how much more outgoing Emily has become over the last six months.

"Nonna." Emily releases Val's hand and throws her arms around her seventy-nine-year-old grandmother.

"You should have told me, *principessa*. I would have brought *bomboniere*." Nonna breaks her hug and launches her arms around me. "Now, you look after my Boyd." Nonna wags her finger at Emily. "He's a virile man with needs, and he's going to give me lots of *pronipote*."

"Mama." Rosa tries to take Nonna by her elbow, but the older woman is having none of it. I want to be as sprightly as her when I'm almost eighty.

"I'm kidding, Rosa. Emily tells me he's got a big rooster, and I'm sure he can use it well."

"It's cock, Nonna, not a rooster." I laugh as Emily's cheeks redden. "We'll call our first daughter Isabella after you, okay?"

"No." Nonna swats Emily's hand before leaning in and resting it on my arm. "Too much of a mouthful. Isabel is a strong and pretty name."

Rosa takes Nonna inside. We're congratulated by my parents and brothers, and Millie complains we hadn't asked her to be a flower girl, but when I tell her there's party food, she doesn't seem to mind as much.

Mum and Dad have been chatting to the celebrant, who is insisting on taking a photo of the whole family. We arranged ourselves around the large couch in the living room, Nonna sitting next to me, her hand on my thigh, Emily on the other side with Mum squeezed in next to her. Dad perches on one arm with Rosa on the other. Mia has grabbed some books she wants Ken to read to her and has, once again, removed her top, refusing to put on another one. Nonna places Mia on her lap, and Millie clambers onto Mum. Giles and Bridget, Hen and Ken, and Val stand behind us.

We manage to get a photo of us all smiling with Nonna's bony hand over Mia's chest, but the one I choose to frame later that epitomises our family has Emily with her head thrown back laughing, and Giles is rubbing the bridge of his nose as Bridget giggles. Meanwhile, Henry is planting a kiss on his partner's cheek with his hips thrust forward as if Ken had just pinched his bum. Mia has her arms in the air, knocking Nonna's glasses off, and Millie is mid eye roll with her arms crossed. Val's eyes are closed, and Rosa's trying to calm down Mia. I'm just gazing at Emily. Mum and Dad are the only ones who look normal, and that's almost scary.

But hey, best day ever.

Emily, Age 14

Mum's making me go to a therapist. Her name's Priscilla, which sounds like something you'd call a poodle. I thought we'd be sitting, and she'd ask me questions about how shit life is since Dad left and tell me that I needed to see him, but I refuse. I'm like fifteen in a few months, and I can make my own decisions.

We just did a jigsaw puzzle. It was kittens sitting in a wicker basket next to a vase of flowers. I chose to do basket pieces because it was one of the harder parts. I mean, the fur on the kittens would be harder, but I'm not dumb enough to choose that option.

Well, Priscilla said I should keep a journal. She doesn't want to see it. She told me I could hide it under my mattress or something. That would be the first place Mum would look. I figure typing it and hiding it in a folder called Advanced Calculus means no one will look. So yeah, I'm writing my thoughts down, it just doesn't have to be on paper.

Kyle O'Donahough teased me at lunch for hanging out with Val. Just because she's only twelve and in the class under us. Boyd stood up for me. I told him he didn't need to, and I wanted to fight my own battles, and Kyle joked that Boyd was my boyfriend. At least he didn't call me Slanty-Eyes again.

Whatever. I mean, he kind of is my boyfriend, I suppose. Just before Dad left, Boyd told me he liked me, and we were going to get married one day. I could cope with that. He's so hot. His blonde hair is getting longer. He likes to pretend it pisses his parents off. I don't think it does. I mean, I've grown up with the Hartmans. Mum used to look after the Hartman kids during the holidays and Val and Boyd before they started school.

My mum loves kids. It's sad that she and Dad couldn't have any, but I'm glad they adopted me. I might look Chinese, but I don't feel it. I just feel like me. Priscilla asked me about it. I told her they wanted me to learn Mandarin when I was a kid, but I refused and taught myself Italian instead, so I could talk to Nonna and Nonno in their language. Nonna speaks great English, but it's nice to be close to her. I miss my Nonno. He died last year. Dad didn't even come back for the funeral. I tried to tell him that smoking was bad, but would he listen? No. Typical. I know Nonna misses him too, though.

I've got my piano exam coming up. I hope I don't get the same dumb examiner I got last year. He told me my parents must be proud of me, and he sees lots of Asian students sitting examinations to please their parents, but I needed to do it for me. I hate it when people lump me into what they think being Asian is. I get lost in music. It's probably my favourite subject apart from chemistry. I do it for fun. I could probably practice for hours and hours a day and do recitals and play concertos and stuff, but I enjoy being able to sit on the stool and get lost in the music.

Mum grabbed me a book of popular songs arranged for piano. I think it's because it has, like, three Celine Dion songs in there, and Mum's mad for Celine. If I can play them and make her feel a bit happier, then that's good. She puts on a brave face, but I know she's as pissed at Dad as I am. I know I've got a half brother now, but I don't want to meet him. He's nothing to me. After all, Mum and Dad went through trying to have a kid and then to adopt me, and for Dad to leave Mum and have a baby with someone else, let alone her...

Shit. I promised Priscilla a paragraph, and I've rattled on. Don't think it makes me feel any better, but whatever.

Chapter 2

Emily

THE LAST FEW DAYS FEEL LIKE A BLUR, AND MY CHEEK muscles ache from smiling so much. I still wouldn't have it any other way.

It doesn't feel any different being married to Boyd. We've been together for almost ten years and have lived together throughout medical school. Charlie, my father-in-law, was the only person in on the wedding beforehand, but that's because we had to arrange someone to let in the caterers and celebrant. Even then, he only found out the morning of our big day. He still surprised us, though, with two nights at one of the luxury hotels in Cassowary Point.

Waking up and feeling that gold band on my left ring finger doesn't feel strange. It feels right.

Yesterday was our university graduation. Whereas Giles and Henry went to Brisbane to study at the same university their parents had studied at, we stayed in Cassowary Point. I wanted to be close to Mum and Nonna, and Boyd understood. He even took a gap year so we could go through medical school together.

"You right there, wife?" Boyd has raised the armrest between the two seats on the plane, and we snuggle together as the plane flies towards Rome.

"Never been better, husband." Despite the ache in my cheeks, I still smile and hope I sound as happy as I feel.

"Do you think I've already fucked a baby into you?" Boyd whispers in my ear.

I rub my thighs together and hope the slickness that pools between my legs at his dirty mouth doesn't seep through to my leggings.

"I think there's a few more days until I'm mid-cycle, but I'm not averse to practicing some more. I'm loving not using condoms."

Almost twenty-four hours in the back end of the cramped plane, and I couldn't wait to be naked with Boyd again.

"Can you put your seats upright and your armrest down, please?" The flight attendant leans over Boyd as if she wants to be as close to him as I am. I don't blame her, but really, he's mine. Boyd takes no notice of her though, our fingers entwined on my lap.

"God, I love you." Boyd's voice is breathy as he gazes at me. It's a look of adoration that both of us have perfected over the years. I reluctantly lower the armrest. I don't know if the flight attendant hears his declaration of love, but she moves on.

"I love you, too." I bring our clasped hands to my lips and kiss his fingers. "Twenty-four hours in a plane has given time for my poor vagina to heal a bit, though."

"I'd say that I'd fuck your mouth or your arse, but I'm hell-bent on coming home having knocked you up. Plus, your pussy is so inviting, and I love the way it grips my cock as I slide in and out of you." The feel of Boyd's breath across my ear as he whispers into it only adds to my arousal, and unconsciously, I press my breast into his arm. "Have I made you horny, baby?"

"You know it." I kiss him gently. "And you've crossed your legs because your cock is hard."

"My rooster, remember?" Boyd laughs.

The plane bounces as it lands. We're in the middle seats, but it didn't worry either of us, as we've spent most of the flight simply gazing at each other, not needing to look at the scenery beneath us. It's so easy to simply stare at Boyd for hours. His blonde, wavy hair has grown to his shoulders. When he doesn't wear it down, he twists it into a knot on the top of his head. He's grown a very impressive beard that's a little straggly in parts, but it suits him. But it's his pale blue-green eyes that do it for me the most, though.

All the Hartman children were born in February, as were Charlie and Hillary. Boyd wasn't meant to be, though, and he arrived six weeks early. He was much shorter than his brothers, and his sister even had an inch or two on him, but it didn't worry me. To me, he was perfect.

We grab our carry-on luggage, make it off the plane, head through immigration, and are waiting for our backpacks at baggage claim. The plan is to spend a few nights in Rome before catching the train to Florence for another couple of nights, ten days in Bologna with Nonna's brother and his family, and then our big splurge of three nights in Venice.

Throughout uni, I worked a few nights a week playing piano in either the foyer of the casino in Cassowary Point or in a restaurant in town. Even though I was paid by the hour, at the casino, patrons often left tips. It became quite lucrative, and people would often leave casino chips in my glass. With it all adding up, I surprised Boyd with an early birthday present of three nights in an Airbnb in Venice. It wasn't going to be grand by any stretch of the imagination, but spending this time with him, hopefully making a baby, was going to create memories that would last a lifetime.

"Here you go, wife." Boyd helps place my backpack over my shoulders after his finally found its way around the luggage carousel to us.

"Ouch," I yelp as Boyd pinches my bum.

"You know what they say, when in Rome..." Boyd kisses my cheek as I turn my mouth away from him, trying not to smile.

"You just wanted to touch my bum." I reach for his hand as we make our way to the train station.

"I love touching all of you and can't wait until we've checked in. Hope you weren't expecting to see much of Rome today, wife." Boyd wiggles his eyebrows.

"It's seven in the morning. I doubt they're going to let us check in." A yawn escapes, and I wish I could have slept a bit more on the plane.

"I'll find somewhere to get my hands on your skin, sneak a caress of your gorgeous breasts, and feel how dripping wet you are for me." Boyd's voice is breathy as he whispers to me so no one else can hear, and I bite my lip.

I didn't doubt he would.

MY FEET ACHE, and I could sleep for a week, but we finally make it into our room at the hostel. They hadn't allowed us in at nine when we finally arrived, but at least they let us dump our luggage.

The hostel is near the Trevi Fountain. Boyd could toss coins in it for hours. Eventually, I tear him away, and we walk to the Colosseum. Even though it's December and there is a distinct chill in the air, it's crowded.

"Can you imagine the blood and guts from all those gladiators?" Boyd's eyes are large and his feet bounce in excitement. "I wish they had a rhinoceros here now."

Boyd, being Boyd, has attached us to a group full of American schoolchildren. He fits right in, and even the guide laughs at his antics. He really is a big kid himself.

"I would have been a gladiator," Boyd declares to his new fans. "I mean, look at me. I'm obviously built for it."

Boyd looks more like a mutant ninja turtle as he raises his knee and throws his arms to the side. "This is Sparta," he yells, making everyone laugh. I just shake my head.

"That's not Roman." One kid laughs.

"They may take our lives, but they'll never take our freedom." Boyd thrusts a fist into the air.

"No, silly." A girl with a gorgeous black afro shakes her head at my husband. "It's 'win the crowd, and you'll win your freedom'."

"Ah, I see." Boyd taps his nose with his finger. "So, have I won you? Am I free to go? Can I take my wife and run? This is Emily. She's my wife. Isn't she just gorgeous?"

"Do you love her?" A boy sniggers.

"Absolutely. I've loved her since she was your age, even before. I'd go into battle for her."

"But you don't need to, husband." I slide my arm through his as he looks at me with longing eyes. "I'm free to fight my own battles, and I think that if women had run the world when this amphitheatre was built, it would have had much less blood and guts and more peaceful activities."

A girl gives me a high-five, and we break away from the group as we head through the gift shop.

Our entire walk back to the hostel is foreplay. Boyd whispers dirty things in my ear as I place my hand in the back pocket of his jeans and squeeze his bum. I make him stop for gelato and take great joy in running my tongue around the iced treat suggestively, making Boyd squirm.

When we finally get to our room, our bags are thrown in a corner, and we desperately yank at each other's clothes. We're uncoordinated, and at one stage, I have only one arm out of my jacket, jumper, and top whilst Boyd sucks at my nipples through my bra. His pants are around his ankles, his jocks down his thighs.

I push him back onto the bed, climb on after him, lift a leg over him, and sink onto his very impressive cock.

"Fu-uck." Boyd sighs, his eyes firmly shut, and his bottom lip caught between his teeth. "I have to think of Nonna and gladiators, and all sorts of unsexy things to stop myself from shooting deep inside you," he pants desperately.

"I'll tell Nonna you don't find her sexy, but those gladiators gave you a hard-on," I joke as I roll my hips.

"You give me a hard-on." Boyd opens his eyes, and as much as our bodies are joined as one, there's an invisible tether between us as well, a connection that has only deepened as the years have gone on.

We've only ever had sex with each other, but I can't imagine doing this with anyone else. It's an almost spiritual experience feeling Boyd inside me. Boyd lifts his hands from the bed and dances them up my sides. He teases the edge of my breasts before gently caressing my neck.

Dragging me down, he sucks a nipple into his mouth and bites gently. He knows I could cope with more. He also knows I could come just from having my breasts played with. I press my hands against his chest, and I run them over the smooth skin, looking down to watch him slide in and out of me.

"I'm..." Boyd gasps. "I'm not gonna... I'm gonna..."

"You're gonna squirt your seed deep inside my cunt—" I can't finish as Boyd tenses, his cock jerking inside me as he does just that. A finger finds my clit, and I tumble over the precipice, the rhythmic jerking of my vaginal walls drawing the sperm inside me.

"Fuck, you're perfect." Boyd strokes my back as I collapse on top of him.

I feel his cock softening, and small moans escape his lips as after-shocks from my orgasm pulse through my tight walls.

"So are you." I plant a tender kiss on his lips. "Actually, we're perfect together."

We are. There's no doubting that.

"*BUON NATALE!*" The shrieks from my cousins fill the villa we're staying in.

Zio Gio, as Mum refers to Nonna's brother, has organised for us to stay with members of his family. We're spending Christmas in the Tuscan countryside with Gio's daughter, her children, and their part-ners and children. We'd been to Midnight Mass at the local church, and Boyd and I had wished each other a merry Christmas in the way we knew best: with our bodies.

Boyd's phone rings with his oldest brother's number. "Uncle Boyo, Santa came, and I got presents," Mia yells down the phone, holding it near her ear, even though it is a video call.

"Mia, hold it here..." Giles stands behind his daughter and pulls the phone in front of her.

"It's Uncle Boyo and Auntie Em." Mia claps her hands as Giles holds the phone.

"Yep, and they're in bed, naked." Giles laughs as Val grabs the phone from him.

"You dirty buggers." Val laughs too as she waves at us. It's like we aren't used to doing video calls, even though we chatted regularly with her in Brisbane. "We've finished lunch, and Mia's had a nap. What time is it there?"

Boyd picks his watch up from the nightstand and rubs his eyes. "It's just gone six." He yawns. "But the kids here are awake and yelling."

"Pass her here." I hear Nonna in the background.

And we are passed from person to person. Hillary and Charlie insisted Mum and Nonna join them for dinner. Henry's friend, Christian, and his mum, Lena, are also there. Millie sits on Ken's knee, a pile of books on the table in front of them. Bridget looks exhausted, having worked the Christmas Eve night shift.

"Yeah, we're going to be on the national news," Bridget sighs as she rubs her eyes. "Naturally conceived triplets made their way into the world in the early hours of the morning. Mum was booked in for a section the day after tomorrow, but they decided to come early. Dad's nicknamed them Jesus, Mary, and Joseph."

"That's, like, super rare, right?" Boyd asks.

"Yeah. The boys are identical. They'll spend some time in the nursery, but... Jesus, I shouldn't be talking about my patients with you."

"You owe me five dollars, Charlie." Hillary beams through the screen. "I told you they'd be naked." Hillary loves having these five-dollar bets with members of her family. I don't think anyone ever pays up. "Plus, you still owe me for the ring. I bet him you'd have a ring on your finger by the end of the year," she explains.

It was madness back at Cassowary Point. I miss them, and this was the first Christmas we were spending away from our immediate family. It had been ages since all the Hartman children had been together for Christmas. Henry and Val had stayed in Brisbane over the years, having to work their retail jobs when they were studying.

"We'll have to make sure we're all together next year." I kiss Boyd's cheek as he places his phone back on the nightstand, having said goodbye to our families.

"Yeah. And there'll probably be a fresh addition there with us, too."

"Can you imagine triplets?"

"With you, I can imagine anything, my beloved."

Emily, Age 16

I had sex with Boyd. Well, I mean, of course it was with Boyd. I can't believe he waited all this time for me. I mean, he's eighteen, and I'm sure most of his friends have been having sex for years.

He's never pressured me. I know Kirsten at school's been having sex with her boyfriend for ages, and she's only fifteen, but I just, I don't know. It's not like I believe in virginity or purity or anything like that, but I wanted my first time to be special, to be memorable.

Giles flew back to Brisbane for uni last week. He's been strange since Boyd told everyone he loved me at his eighteenth a few weeks ago. I know Giles has lots of sex. He tells everyone. I suppose he could be all talk and no action, but I doubt it. Boyd says his brother's never had a girlfriend, and he's just jealous. Whatever.

So, Mum went down to Sailor's Bend to stay with Nonna, who's got a cold. It's just a freaking cold, but Mum gets worried. After school, I went and bought some condoms and had them in my bedside drawer. Boyd came over, and we were playing Mario—and I was winning, as usual. I told him that every time I beat him, I'd kiss him. I think he lost on purpose.

Well, he paused it, and Boyd never pauses a game. He told me that he'd been thinking a lot, and he doesn't want to study in Brisbane like Giles and Henry. I mean, he still wants to do medicine, like me, but he wants to stay here, close to his parents, and he knows how I want to be close to Mum and Nonna. He also said he's planning on taking a gap year so we can start uni together. I was like, well, I cried. I mean, I love him so much, and I know he's doing this for me.

Anyway, we went back to Mario. I took my shirt off and played in just my bra. We've touched each other before. Boyd's sucked on my tits, and I've tried to give him a blow job. We'd never been fully naked together, though. Eventually, I stood and just stripped out of all my clothes. Boyd's mouth dropped open, and his jaw almost hit the floor. I grabbed his hand. His was shaking more than mine. We went to my bedroom. Boyd told me I was gorgeous, and I told him I wanted to have sex. He was all "Are you sure?" and I told him I wanted it so bad. He took forever to take his clothes off. I thought he would have been quick and all, but he said he wanted to savour it.

He was gentle. We'd practiced putting condoms on bananas in sex-education at school, but his penis was bigger than the bananas they gave us in class. Boyd actually went down on me and made sounds like he enjoyed it. I had trouble getting into it because he was licking down there.

I was wet, though. He slicked some on to his fingers and played with my clit until I came. We've done that before, but this was nicer.

Then he eased into me. It hurt at first. I had to try not to laugh as he was panting away, telling me he was about to come. He didn't last long.

After, we cuddled. We tried it again with me on top this time. I could feel an orgasm building, but never got there. Boyd fingered me afterwards.

I know Val reads some of those smutty books, and I've read a couple. It was nothing like those women described. I know in sex ed, Ms Shang told us it would get better, and we needed to talk to our partners to tell them what we liked. Boyd and I will get there. We're an amazing team already.

Tomorrow, I've got my monthly check in with Priscilla. She says it's ok to be angry at my dad. Speaking with her is the last thing I want to do on Friday after school, but then it's the weekend. I'll ask Mum if Boyd can stay over. She's been open about sex with me, and she's told me before she'd rather I did it at home than in the back seat of a car. Boyd's car is tiny, and I can't see that happening. Perhaps we'll spend the weekend in bed. We've both got assignments due Monday though, so we'll have to spend some time studying.

I might bitch about seeing Priscilla, but I'm glad she got me writing stuff down. It's not like I can talk to Val about sex with her brother. I mean, she wouldn't care, but she's that bit younger than me. If I told anyone else at school, it would be spread around. I think most people assume Boyd and I have been having sex, anyway. Well, now we have.

Chapter 3

Boyd

It's been the most perfect break between finishing uni and today. Well, almost perfect. I was convinced I'd knock Emily up on our honeymoon, but her period arrived just as we were boarding the flight home from Italy. Sure, it was disappointing, as a baby conceived in Italy would have been something to boast about, but we both knew that it might take a couple of months.

New Year in Venice was amazing. We were seated in a gondola as the year ticked over and fireworks lit up the sky above. Experiencing this with Emily, my wife, was magical.

I could look back on our relationship and see where things felt just right. I didn't hesitate to take a gap year between school and university, and I ended up loving working in childcare. Sure, it was hard at times wrangling little ones, and the pay was terrible, but it was rewarding. Even if I had to put up with mums coming onto me when they picked up their kids.

Throughout uni, it's been Emily and me. Sure, we've met others along the way and caught up for drinks and meals and things, but we've done it all together. Today would be another one of those days as we start work as doctors at Cassowary Point Hospital.

Giles and Henry have been ribbing me about it because I'm starting in the emergency department and Emily has paediatrics, but both of us would have loved to have swapped. We still had a few days of mandatory training, getting our life support skills perfected before we're let loose on real patients.

"You're awake." Emily rolls towards me in bed and kisses my shoulder.

"So are you." My voice is much croakier than hers, making me think she's been awake for a while.

"I'm excited we get to do this together." She nuzzles into me, throwing her leg over mine and stroking circles around my chest. Goose bumps break out as my morning wood grows into a full-blown erection.

"There are lots of things we do together." I roll onto my side so we're facing each other, and our mouths join.

I love kissing Emily. I mean, sure, I love being inside her, but she's the best kisser. Her lips are soft and delicate, but her tongue... well, that's like a weapon. In our early days, we'd kiss for hours. This kiss is more pressing, though. It shows desire. Emily pushes me onto my back and straddles me before sinking onto my cock. She sinks onto my cock easily, as she's done it hundreds of times before, and knows what we like.

She makes the most beautiful sounds as she rides me. We've become more aware of the neighbours in our complex after one asked last week if Emily was okay when he had obviously overheard us having sex. I told him she was perfectly fine. Emily was embarrassed, though, and I know she's holding back this morning.

"Come for me, baby," I purr into her ear as she leans forward, hoping I'll take her breasts in my mouth.

"Feels so good. I love you're the only guy who's been in me." Her words are disjointed, but I get her meaning.

"Yeah? You saying that pussy's mine?" I can feel my own release building as Emily rocks her hips.

"That cock's mine as much as this pussy is yours. Now fuck me."

I want to tell her how much I love her, how much I worship her, and how much I want to pump a baby into her, but her pussy contracts around my cock, seeing me erupt, and there's no way I can form any words.

Later, as we shower together in the tiny recess that is too small for both of us, I tell her again how much I love her. Emily really is my always and forever. My everything.

"WE'RE GOING FOR A DRINK. You coming, Hartmans?" Jade, one of our colleagues from uni, and a group of others walk out with us after our last day of orientation.

"Sure." Emily shrugs, looking at me to confirm I'm okay with the idea. "Where are we going?"

Jade suggests a wanky gin bar in town. I'm not much of a drinker, preferring the occasional beer, and Emily hardly ever indulges, but we both need to decompress after our first week.

As we walk in, I know this isn't our scene. It's white and bright. Sure, it is only four in the afternoon, but even so, it lacks the coziness of the pubs I prefer. Soft jazz pipes through the speakers, and the metal stool I sit on is hard and uncomfortable.

Emily grabs us drinks as we arrive. The place is almost dead, so it doesn't take long. She hands me my bottle of beer, and I clink it against her wineglass.

"So, tell us all about your wedding," Candice, one of the group, says as she takes a sip of a fruity-looking drink in a cocktail glass.

"It was small and perfect," Emily answers as she wipes a drip of condensation away from her glass. "Just family."

"And? You're drinking?" Jade asks, leaning forward as if she is truly invested in this conversation.

"It's a glass of wine, yeah." Emily's brows knit together as she looks between the women.

"I just assumed you were pregnant. I mean, you're the only people I know who've married so young." Jade bites an olive off the stick in her martini.

"No, not yet." I squeeze Emily's thigh and am glad when two more colleagues, Gregor and Al, turn up to join us. I know them both a bit better than Candice and Jade. "Where are you all starting this year?" I change the subject.

"Gastro," says Gregor with a shrug.

"Surg," replies Al as he takes a sip from his beer. "I'm with Jaynie, which will be fun. She sends her apologies tonight, but her partner flies in, and she wants to spend time with her."

"What does her partner do again?" Candice asks as she takes a sip from her drink.

"She's a nurse who does fly-in-fly-out in one of the communities up north."

"Ew." Jade scrunches her nose. "I can't imagine being a nurse, wiping bums and showering people. It sounds ghastly."

"I thought about nursing," I add, noticing the shocked looks from the other women. "I mean, yeah, my parents and brothers are doctors, but I know how much nurses make a difference."

"You'd wipe bums all day?" Candice's eyes are wide in shock.

"I wiped kids' bums all day when I worked in childcare. Not much of a difference."

I hadn't had a lot to do with Jade and Candice during uni. We knew each other, and I had a placement with Candice on a surgical ward, but we were in different teams. I was beginning to see them as the mean girls they possibly were. Perhaps they're nervous about starting as actual doctors, but I can't help but feel judged.

"I'm off to general medicine." Jade changes the subject back to our rotations.

"And I'm off to cardiology with your hot brother." Candice looks at me with a smirk on her face.

"And his hot father. Don't forget about Charlie. And I suppose Hillary is hot in her own way. Fuck, the whole Hartman family's hot, and now I'm one of them. Yay for me!" Emily throws back the rest of her drink and smiles sweetly. "Well, husband." Emily reaches over and grabs my hand. "We've got a date with some nipple clamps and a riding crop, so we should go."

"Yes, ma'am." I bow my head, if only to hide the laughter that's dying to escape. "Will you use the large strap-on again, ma'am?"

"Only if you're a good boy, and you're always Mummy's good boy, aren't you?" I've never heard Emily use this terse voice before, and I'll admit, it's doing things to me.

The others looked stunned as Emily leads me away. As soon as we walk outside, we double over in laughter.

"That was so much fun." Emily wipes the tears from her eyes as she continues shaking all over.

"Mummy's good boy? Fuck, maybe that did something for me, after all." We make our way back to the car. I wiggle my eyebrows as Emily shakes her head.

"If you call me Mummy, that will be a real mood killer. I wouldn't mind trying the nipple clamps, though."

"That can be arranged." My smile is huge. I really love this woman.

I'VE ALWAYS BEEN A JOKER. The idea of conforming to expectations never sat right. I was the one to grow my hair the year before my senior year, even when school policy said it had to be short and tidy. I'd chosen to study in Cassowary Point instead of Brisbane like my brothers and parents before me. Long ago, I decided a day without laughter was a day lost. If I had a dollar for every time someone in my family had said "That's not funny, Boyd," I'd be rich.

Most of the time, it was funny. I'd considered doing stand-up at a local club and still planned on giving it a go one day.

It was hard reining in my enthusiasm and one-liner quips in the emergency department. I hadn't yet learnt when humour was appreciated and helped break a mood, or when it was not warranted.

My humour helped me with kids, though. Even in the few weeks I've been working in the ED, I've seen some pretty sick kids, and getting even a smile on their faces was an achievement.

As I walk through the department on my way for a break, I hear the cries of a scared child. Holding the curtains that hide the patient from the ward but do nothing to muffle the sound the poor child is making, I poke my head through.

"Oh, I am awfully sorry," I say in my poshest British voice, "I thought I heard Doctor Chicken-Dingle in here. You don't look like him, though."

The child, who is six or seven, looks up at me as if I'm crazy. A nurse is trying to put numbing cream on the child's arm so a drip can be inserted.

"C'mon, Corey, just let the nice nurse put the cream on your arm." The mum, who looks like she hasn't slept for a week, sighs.

Grabbing a glove, I hold the opening to blow into it. I take a comical breath and pretend nothing happens when I blow it out. I try again and see the glove inflate. Pretending I was out of breath, I tie off the wrist and grab the nurse's pen from her pocket. Eyes are drawn on either side of the glove.

"Brrrk, bok, bok, bok, bok. Brrrk, bok, bok, bok, bok." Sure, I may need to work on my chicken sounds, but Corey is invested in my pantomime. "I thought I heard you, Doctor Chicken-Dingle." I hold the balloon to my ear. "What's that? You want me to have some of the cream?"

I look at the nurse and tentatively hold out my arm. "Are you sure, Doctor Chicken-Dingle? I don't want the cream to hurt."

Again, the puppet comes to my ear, and I shrug my shoulders. I hold out my arm, making it shake in an exaggerated manner. The nurse goes to apply some cream to my hand, and I jerk it away.

"I think he's scared, Corey," the nurse loudly whispers in Corey's ear.

"There's nothing wrong with being scared." I grasp Doctor Chicken-Dingle to my chest. "This place is weird."

"But you're the grownup." Corey speaks in a soft voice.

"I get scared all the time." I sit on the side of the bed, something we've been told was definitely frowned upon. "We put the cream on because we're going to put a plastic tube under your skin into one of your veins to get some special water and maybe some medicine into you. If we put the cream on, it means the tube goes in easier." I didn't want to mention pain or hurt or anything. "We even put a big plastic sticker over it for half an hour or so, and you can gently poke it and squish it around if you want. Do you think Nurse Nikki could do that now?"

Corey nods and holds out his arm. Nikki places a blob of cream on his hand and covers it with a plastic dressing. She does the same on his inner arm and his other hand.

"Am I getting three tubes?" Corey asks, as he looks at the blobs of cream.

"Nah, just one." I hand the puppet to Corey. "I think Nikki was having too much fun blobbing cream all over you. Now, can you please look after Doctor Chicken-Dingle for me?" Corey nods. "Lovely to meet you, young man." I return to my fake accent and tip my nonexistent hat.

"Thank you." Nikki and I stand at the sink as we wash our hands. "Are you looking after Corey?"

"Nah, I was walking past on my way for a break. That experience was more rejuvenating than a can of Coke and fifteen minutes of daytime telly in the break room, though." I smile as I toss the paper towel in the bin.

And yes, whilst it stopped me from having to be subjected to daytime telly, it also means I don't have to stop and be with my thoughts. Emily's period has arrived again. She seems to have taken it in her stride, saying we obviously weren't having enough sex and needed more. I wasn't sure how much more my overworked cock could take. I wouldn't complain, though. It is no hardship to be joined to my wife. God, I love that word.

"What are you doing in here?" Henry finds me daydreaming about Emily.

"Um, I work here?" My sarcasm shines through.

"Der." Henry shakes his head. "I didn't think you were in this section. I've been here all morning."

"Nah, I'm not. I just heard a kid screaming and stepped in to make a fool out of myself."

"So, you're being yourself, then." Henry walks with me towards the staff room. "Just be careful around here. Not everyone will accept your humour, you know. They'll take it that you aren't serious. I mean, I know you, and I know you are, and that you hide behind laughter and jokes, but..." Henry pauses. "Be careful."

I know Henry has a point, but I wasn't about to stop being me. Sure, I'd try to bite my tongue and not come out with the "Your mom" or "That's what she said" quips I loved, but I wouldn't stop having a laugh. It was the best medicine, after all.

Emily, Age 16

I'm not sure why I'm still writing this thing. It's become something I do, I suppose. Tomorrow, I head to Brisbane with Boyd and Val. I'm excited about it and spending time with Giles and Henry, but I'm still scared I'll bump into my father. I know Brisbane's a busy place, but it would be just my luck to come across him, and I'm not ready for that. He can go to hell as far as I'm concerned.

Better finish packing.

Chapter 4

Emily

I'M SITTING ON THE TOILET IN TEARS. A DAY LATE, AND I thought that this was it, sixth time lucky. I'd hoped the cramps I felt this morning were a reaction to an embryo snuggling further into my uterine lining, but, instead, they were those that heralded the shedding of said lining.

Boyd is at work, but I have a day off.

> Disregard that last message. Absolutely no need to grab more pregnancy tests :(

I hate to think there's something wrong. I know it might take a month or two to fall pregnant, but not six months. The conclusion I draw is there's something wrong with either Boyd or me.

Last week, I started in oncology. I had to sign the death certificate of a thirty-six-year-old mother of three who succumbed to breast cancer. It was one of the hardest things I've done as a doctor.

Boyd's in gynaecology and obstetrics, but not in Bridget's team. He seems to be enjoying it. I know he surprised himself and didn't mind his last rotation in the geriatric ward. He said that a lot of older people, especially those with dementia, revert to their earlier years, often their childhoods. There was no doubt he would have been at home with that.

Our jobs remind us that bad things happen to good people all the time. It doesn't make not falling pregnant any easier though.

HUSBAND

Oh, babe. I'm sorry.

I wait for more from my husband, but that's it. Four words. I suppose there's not much else to say. He's at work, and he's probably busy, but the needy part of me wants more. I want reassurance and to know why we aren't pregnant.

Hey, I'm off today, but was wondering if you might like to catch up for lunch or a coffee before work tomorrow or something?

BRIDGET

I'm home with Millie, who's picked up yet another bug from school. Feel free to pop over if you don't mind about germs.

I'll be there a bit later. Hope she's feeling better soon.

I've got the ingredients for chicken noodle soup on hand, so I spend some time distracting myself in the kitchen. It's what Mum made for me when I was sick as a child.

The pot is still hot as I wedge it into the footwell of the rear seat in my car and take the short drive to Giles and Bridget's home.

"I come bearing soup." I hold up the pot as a dishevelled-looking Bridget opens the door.

"Oh, you are a doll." Bridget's shoulders relax, and a smile lights up her face. "Giles is in Brisbane for a course. Millie's finally asleep. Do you want a cuppa? We could sit on the deck where there's probably fewer germs."

"Sounds good. So, is Millie okay?" Bridget takes the pot I was holding, and I follow her through the house to the kitchen, where she puts it down on the counter and flicks the switch on the kettle.

"I'm pretty sure it's viral. She's got a runny nose and a non-productive cough. She says her ears aren't sore. If she gets worse, I'll get her seen by the GP." Bridget pours the boiling water over tea leaves in a pot for her and a jasmine tea bag for me.

I really like Bridget. She's changed a bit from the first time I met her when I visited Brisbane with Boyd and Emily when I was sixteen. She'll soon be a qualified obstetrician and gynaecologist and is a great mother. Looking at her with Giles gives me a glimpse into the future I can imagine with Boyd.

Sure, I'd love more than two children, but I want the family Giles and Bridget have created. As much as I think medicine isn't the be all and end all, I like that Boyd and I can debrief at the end of the day, and we have some sense of what the other is going through. With Bridget off today, I can imagine it's extra busy at work, and I can see why Boyd only sent those few words to me before.

I don't know a lot about Bridget pre-children. As a teenager, I was swept away with her and Giles' love story, but I watched it from afar. Now Bridget is someone I aspire to be like. I want to be the mother and the doctor.

We move outside to the deck and sit around the large table. "So, you've got a good GP then?" I ask as I pull the tea bag from my cup, push it against a spoon, and squeeze the last goodness out of it.

"We go to Cassowary Family Medical Centre. Dr Nat's great with the kids." Bridget pours her tea into a cup.

"Is she good with adults too?" I ask, hoping my voice sounds neutral and well-paced. I'm a ball of nerves on the inside and can't even look at Bridget.

Seeing a doctor means something is wrong, and I don't know if I'm ready to accept something isn't as it should be. My own medical training should make this easier, but it doesn't prevent the anxiety. If anything, it adds to it, as I have a greater understanding of all the things that might be wrong.

"I think so." Bridget takes a sip of her tea before placing it back on the table. "Are you looking for someone?"

"Yeah, I mean, I've been seeing Dr Vincent Wang since I was a kid, but he's getting ready to retire, and I turn twenty-five soon and need to have cervical screening and stuff." The words fly from my mouth as I wave a hand in the air.

"We still get referrals from Dr Vincent for women wanting to deliver their babies with us. He's still well respected."

"Bridget?" I put my mug down and clasp my hands tightly on the table. "Can I, uh, pick your brain?"

"Of course." Bridget sits back in her chair and crosses her legs.

"I've just got my period, and we haven't been using contraception since we've been married. I'm worried there's something wrong." A tear slips from my eye, and I wipe it away with the back of my hand. It's a relief to verbalise my fears.

Bridget takes a breath. "Most of us aren't as fertile as we would like to believe. I mean, if you look at a bell curve, the number of people who get pregnant from one session of unprotected sex is at one end, with rather small numbers."

I think back to the few times Boyd and I played roulette with skipping a condom. I felt I knew my cycle well enough to know when I'd be fertile, and the chances of conception were slim, but they'd still been there.

"At the other end, you've got people who try and try and try and don't get pregnant. The rest of us are in the middle."

"I suppose, from your professional opinion, is there something we're likely to be doing wrong?" I can't look at Bridget as I speak, instead choosing to pick at a jagged nail on my right hand.

Bridget stirs her tea, even though the milk is already dispersed. "I think you've been having sex longer than I have, and if you haven't worked it out—"

"Oh no, Boyd is, well, talented, if you get my drift." I wave my hand to the side and look skyward. "I mean, we've got the sex part down pat." My cheeks are reddening.

"Well..." Bridget pauses. She had a brusque manner at the best of times, and I wonder if she was trying to escape into doctor mode or family mode. "I've never specialised in fertility. I know at a conference last year, there was a speaker whose session I attended. They reminded all the usual things: sex at least three times a week, guy's pants shouldn't be too tight, make sure he's ejaculating into the vagina."

"I think we've got all of that well covered." My mug comes to my lips to hide my smirk. "I mean, we have plenty of sex. I don't think that's the problem. One thing though, I mean, Boyd's pretty, um, blessed, and I wonder if it gets too cramped down there sometimes."

"Could be." Bridget shrugs. "Wouldn't hurt visiting a GP and getting some tests done, just hormone profiles and sperm counts. That sort of thing. I assume your cycles are fairly regular?"

"Clockwork regular. Although this one is a day late," I muse.

"Well, Dr Nat does my cervical screening for me and has a good bedside manner. I've heard good things about Dr Trina at Riverview, too, but she only works part-time and is harder to get into. Not that Giles has been to the doctor in ages, but when he got the flu last year, he saw one of the other doctors who works with Nat and said he was thorough, too." It doesn't surprise me Bridget has researched as much as she has.

We sit and talk a bit more. Millie wakes up and comes and snuggles on Bridget's lap.

"Auntie Emily made us some soup, Mills. Would you like me to get you a bowl?" Bridget strokes her daughter's hair back from her face.

"I'll get it and let you snuggle with Mum." I make my way into the kitchen, grab a small bowl, and ladle some soup into it. It's still warm, but not too hot for her small mouth. I also fill her water bottle that was sitting on the draining board next to the sink and take them both out to her.

Poor Millie isn't well, but she manages a few spoonfuls of soup before she falls asleep in her mother's arms. I remember being sick as a child and wanting my mum. I yearn to have children of my own who would seek my comfort.

"Did you always want two children?" I ask Bridget as she strokes her hand down the sleeping Millie's arm.

Bridget takes a deep breath and kisses her daughter on the head. "We had a miscarriage before Millie." Bridget looks down at her daughter. "We never told anyone. I didn't want Hillary's sympathy. I mean, I know she means well, but she can be..."

"Intense?" I offer.

Bridget looks up at me and smiles. "That's one word for it, yes. We were in Brisbane, and I didn't want Hillary and Charlie flying down and making a fuss."

I uncross my legs and lean in to listen to Bridget.

"We wanted three or four kids," Bridget continues. "Mia's birth didn't go to plan. To cut a long and gruesome story short, she perforated my uterus, became distressed, I had an emergency caesarean, the doctor nicked an artery, and I ended up having an emergency hysterectomy."

"I didn't know." My voice was elevated. Bridget isn't a touchy-feely type of person, but I want to reach out and place my hand on her wrist.

"No one did." Bridget smiles a sad smile. "Giles had already said early on in labour that he couldn't wait to do this again. After it, he said he was glad I was still alive."

"Do you regret not telling people? I mean, Henry and Boyd are always having a go at Giles for not getting you pregnant again."

"My husband can look after himself." Bridget chuckles. "But, yeah, it hurts sometimes. We've been so blessed with Millie and Mia, though. I think it might have been different if it happened after Millie's birth." Bridget looks pensive as she gazes into the yard.

"I won't tell Boyd." I nod at Bridget as she holds Millie.

"And I won't tell Giles, unless..." Bridget trails off and looks at me with her eyebrows raised.

"I think I'll talk to Boyd and suggest we don't tell his family. I mean, I don't think I could cope with the inquisitions every week at the dinner table." Bridget might have said that Giles could cope with the ribbing his brothers gave him, but beneath Boyd's humour and bravado, there's a softer side that he rarely lets people see.

I leave Bridget with Millie. She says she's happy to sit on the deck and just be. I offer to grab her tablet or a book, but she tells me she's fine and will practice her mindfulness. Even though she tells me not to worry about our cups, I take them in and wash them, emptying the tea leaves from the pot into the compost and wiping down the bench. I place the soup in a plastic container and find space for it in the fridge.

As I wipe down the bench, I wonder if Boyd and I will ever have children.

I've never thought of a life without them and can't begin to imagine what that would look like. I've planned my career around raising a family and assumed it would happen. I've never paused to wonder what would happen if it didn't.

"Hey, wife." Boyd greets me with a kiss as he walks through the door and finds me in the kitchen. "Something smells amazing."

"Spinach and ricotta lasagne," I reply as he holds me in his arms and squeezes.

"I meant you."

Our apartment isn't big. It suited us as students because it was cheap and halfway between the university and the hospital. We've talked of moving closer to the hospital, but we can't decide whether to go for a larger apartment or an actual house. We still need to rent whilst we save a deposit, but I hope we'll be moving out sooner rather than later, although there seems little point when it's just the two of us.

"How was your day?" I ask as Boyd grabs a slice of cucumber from the salad bowl in front of me.

"Yeah, not bad." He kisses my cheek before heading to the fridge and grabbing a can of Coke. "Gynae ward was a bit of a shit show with three post-op infections from caesars that were performed on the same day. Someone else is investigating that one." Boyd grabs knives and forks from the drawer and lays them on the breakfast bar where we eat.

"Not Bridget?" I ask as I take the lasagne from the oven.

"Nah. Bridget was off sick today. Or one of the kids was or something."

"Yeah, I took them soup."

I tell Boyd about my visit. I also mentioned Bridget's advice to visit a doctor for some preliminary tests as I plate up our dinner before we take a seat at the bench where we usually eat.

"Fuck." Boyd runs his hands down his face, clearly concerned. "I get why you talked with her, but now Bridget will tell Giles, Giles will tell Henry, and Henry will tell the whole fucking world."

"I don't think so." I take a mouthful of our dinner and smile as the flavour dances on my tongue, making me proud that it's better than my mother's version. "I'm almost certain she'll keep it to herself. Does that mean though that you don't want to tell your family? I mean, you wanted to put not having to use condoms anymore into our wedding vows," I remind him playfully.

"Yeah." Boyd puts down his fork. "I'm almost glad I listened to you about that. I mean, it's awesome fucking you bare, but if they knew we'd been trying, they'd all be giving us advice. Even Henry, who I don't think has ever been with anyone with a uterus."

"Bridget suggested we could wait a few more months and see what happens. I mean, we're both young." My voice is soft and tentative. As much as I need reassurance from a doctor, I'm also worried they will find something wrong with us, and we will be told we'll never have children.

Boyd turns to face me and places his hand on my thigh. "I think if we get things checked out, and they find something there, then great, we'll do something about it, but otherwise, we can wait a little and see if next month is any different. What do you think?"

"Yeah. Sounds like a plan. I don't want to see Dr Vincent, though."

"Shit, no," Boyd splutters as he takes a sip of his drink. "I mean, he plays cards with my father each week, and it might be, well, weird."

"Bridget suggested someone at the practice she and the girls go to." I grip my right thumb with my left hand. I'm not sure why I feel so nervous talking about this.

"Bridget would only recommend the best. You know what she's like." Boyd smiles as he finishes the last of his dinner. I've lost my appetite. "See if you can get an appointment for when one of us is off, and the other can take a sick day if we need to."

I smile my agreement and lean over to kiss his lips. Even though I have lots of theories about what could be wrong, I keep them to myself, and I suspect Boyd does, too. We'll visit a doctor and get some answers. Together.

Emily, Age 17

Boyd and I fucked up. Like, really fucked up. Last weekend, Val had a debating thing down in Sailor's Bend, so Hillary and Charlie went down to spend the night. Boyd invited me over, and I knew I was going to stay the night. I meant to pick up more condoms, but I forgot. Boyd usually carries one in his wallet, and I thought there were plenty in his bedside drawer. Turns out there were only three. Like in total.

Well, we used them all Friday night. Saturday morning, I woke up and Boyd was spooning me. It felt amazing feeling his morning wood press into my arse. I rolled over, and we started kissing. Neither of us were wearing any clothes. Boyd kissed down my neck. I'm getting shivers just remembering it. He has this way of sucking on my nipples that just sends me into some other plane. I mean, I've told him so many times now that I think I could come just from him playing with my breasts. He says we'll try it sometime.

I grasped at his cock and started stroking it. I was going to go down on him, but he was too keen on playing with my tits. In hindsight, we should have tried sixty-nining, but we were just both so worked up. Maybe it was lack of sleep from all the sex the night before, maybe it was hormones. Whatever. We ended up having sex without a condom, and Boyd came inside me. Apart from the weird feeling of having his semen dripping from me, I think it was the visual of seeing what we'd done that made the possible consequences of our irresponsible actions sink in.

He suggested the morning-after pill, but I did some reading, and I had an important chemistry test that I didn't want to be unwell for. I mean, I did the maths, and I was due to ovulate yesterday, five days from when we had sex. I know it's unlikely the sperm would live that long, but I might have ovulated early. Maybe my body recognised there was sperm there, and the egg popped out early?

I've been freaking out a lot about it. It's my last year of school, and if I was pregnant, I'd be due in late February. All the Hartman kids are February babies. There's probably something super fertile about Hartman men's sperm that makes them pop them out then.

Boyd and I had a chat about it. He's taken this year off and is working in childcare. He loves it, even wiping the babies' bums and changing them and feeding them and everything. The kids seem to love him, too. I can imagine he will be the perfect father. I mean, he has Charlie as a role model, and Charlie is pretty amazing, but we're so young. Boyd says we'll cross that bridge when we get to it. He said that if I want to investigate an abortion, he will support me. There's no way I want to abort a baby of Boyd's.

I alternate being excited about the prospect of being parents with Boyd and worrying that we are far, far, far too young. I'm not eighteen until next month. I've got exams. What if I get morning sickness? I could have fucked everything up. One moment of passion. That's what they told us in sex ed. I didn't listen.

Last summer, I went to see our old family GP, Dr Vincent. I wanted to ask him about going on the pill or getting the implant or depo injection. He started the appointment by telling me how thrilled he was that I had 'taken up' with the young Hartman boy and that he'd heard we were both going to study medicine. He then said something about beating Charlie at cards. There was no way I was talking about sex with him, or contraception. I even tried to say I had heavy periods and wondered if the pill might help, and he said I should avoid hormonal contraception if I could. Not sure why, and I was too embarrassed to ask. I might Google it.

Boyd's sitting next to me reading some romance book Val left next to the couch. Hillary asked if I was staying the night. They're cool with me sleeping with Boyd. Not sure they would be if they knew I might be pregnant. I wanted to say yes, but I said I had to get home to study for my exams. Then I spent the evening on their couch with my computer writing this. Maybe if I get it out of me, then I'll be able to concentrate on studying. I did okay on my chem test last Monday, but I could have done better.

I just hope I haven't fucked up our lives. I mean, we want kids, we really want kids, but perhaps not yet.

Chapter 5

Boyd

My leg taps up and down as I sit in the waiting room, eager to see Dr Nat. Bridget recommended her, and I believe her judgement, but it's still nerve-wracking. Emily's period arrived again. Another month where I've failed to knock her up.

I did some googling. It's not unusual to go up to twelve months without conceiving. Don't get me wrong, I'm loving all the sex. Sex with Emily is always amazing. Right from the get-go, we've been great together, and it's only ever gotten better. It's like our bodies are made for each other, which makes it even more astounding that we haven't managed to get the whole pregnancy thing happening.

"Do you think I'll need scans?" Emily whispers in my ear as I tried to read a poster about being respectful to the staff.

"Maybe. I'm probably going to have to wank into a pot, aren't I?"

"Shh..." Emily says louder than I thought I'd spoken. "I might be able to help you with that." She offers me a nervous smile.

"They might not let you." I grip her hand and lay it in her lap. I'm trying to stay upbeat, but I'm concerned something is wrong with me. "What if I fuck it up? What if I fail?"

"Emily and Boyd?" a cheerful voice sounds from the back of the waiting room. We stand, and I kiss Emily on the cheek as we follow the doctor down the corridor to her room.

It feels like a corridor of doom. I have no idea what to expect, but my usual cheery, joking self is nowhere to be found that morning.

"Hi, I'm Nat Asafa. What can I do for you folks?"

The doctor is calm and friendly and puts me at ease. She has long dark hair that she has messily piled into a bun, which has two pens poking out of it. If I had to guess, I'd put her at younger than my parents, but older than Giles. Maybe early forties? She has a photo of a boy about Millie's age hanging upside down on a monkey bar in a playground on her desk. She wears baggy multi-coloured harem pants and a T-shirt that says 'I found this humerus' with a long bone pictured next to it. I like how comfortable she looks as she sits on her desk chair with one leg curled under her bottom.

"Well." Emily clears her throat as she looks at me and grips my hand tighter. "Boyd and I have been trying to get pregnant for a while, and it doesn't seem to be happening."

"A while?" The doctor's eyebrow rises.

"Since December."

"So, seven or so months?"

"Yeah." Emily nods. "And it's not like we don't have sex. I mean, we have lots of sex, like—"

"More than three times a week?" Dr Nat interjects.

"We'd go three times a day if we didn't have to work." Emily laughs. I love that sound, and I realise I've been hearing less of it each month we haven't been successful in our pregnancy quest.

"And what do you both do for work?" Nat is jotting down notes on her computer, her wireless keyboard tilted towards us and away from her screen.

"We're both junior doctors at the hospital," I offer. "My sister-in-law, Bridget, recommended you."

"So, you are that Hartman family. I didn't want to assume." Nat smiles.

"Bridget knows." Emily looks at me with a creased brow. "But no one else in the family knows we've been trying for a baby."

"And they won't hear it from me. Don't worry."

Nat goes on to ask several questions about our sexual history. She offers no judgement and remains totally deadpan as we answer her somewhat invasive questions. I knew they were standard, and she needed to follow the same questions for everyone, even though we were doctors, but yes, we were aware which hole was the vagina and knew when Emily's fertile time was likely to be.

"What I suggest..." The doctor puts down her keyboard and untucks her leg from under her. "What I would suggest is some basic tests. Bloods for you both to check hormone levels. Emily, I suggest we do a day twenty-one progesterone test to see that you have indeed ovulated, and maybe have an ultrasound mid-cycle to check your ovaries."

Emily nods.

"Boyd." Dr Nat swivels her chair to me. "We might as well check your testosterone levels, too. It wouldn't hurt to do a full STD screen, too. I mean, I know the likelihood for both of you is extremely low, and Emily, I wouldn't be too concerned about possible tube damage." I'm relaxing more around this doctor, who somehow makes me feel listened to. "So, Boyd. Do you know how to do a sperm test?"

"I have a fair idea." I smirk.

"So, two to three days, but no more than five of no ejaculation, then—"

"Wait, what?" I splutter. "I can't usually go three days without coming in my wife."

"I've had my period for four days..." Emily reminds me with an eye roll. I have no problems with period sex, but we've both been busy at work, and it has been a few days since I've been inside any part of her.

"Yeah, but in the shower, this—"

"I get the picture," Dr Nat laughs. "The lab in the city has special kits with the right sort of lube to use. You can perform the test at home and transport it straight to the lab, keeping the sample at body temperature—so in your pocket. Don't put it in the fridge or leave it in the car or anything."

Dr Nat prints off forms for blood tests and medical imaging for Emily's ultrasound. "I'll see you two in about a month. I won't patronise you by telling you to relax or anything. Personally, I know how stressful this can be. Just be kind to each other, okay?"

"So, you've..." Emily grasps her hands in her lap, stroking her thumbs together.

"Now, I know you both know how unusual it is for the doctor to share their history with the patient, but yes. It took me and my partner eight years. Parker's now four, but the memories of that time are pretty fresh. Now, I'm not saying it will take you two eight years, but it might. We'll see what these tests say, okay?"

I HATE to say Emily has it easy, but she doesn't have to have blue balls. From what I've read, I need at least forty-eight hours of no ejaculation to get an accurate sperm count. Some places recommend three days.

Emily bought what she described as a granny nightie to wear to bed. She thought it would turn me off her, but if anything, it had the opposite reaction. I wanted to slip my hands underneath it and feel the treasures that lay beneath it. Sunday, we spent the day in bed. We both had the day off. Emily reassured me it was early in her cycle and there was virtually no chance withholding for a couple of days would hurt our chances of conceiving that month.

I even went as far as contemplating spending a couple of nights at my parents' place, but it would mean they'd ask questions, and I don't want them to think there's anything wrong with Em and me, let alone explain that I was there because I can't keep my hands off her or my cock out of her.

"Do you think I can do the test and then get hard again and fuck you before I drop it off?" I ask Emily as we lie in bed on Tuesday night.

"Idiot." Emily laughs as she strokes my chest. It was nice lying there holding each other, even though my cock thinks it's an invitation to take things further. "You'll need to drop it off as soon as possible. Do you want me to help you in the morning?"

I know what Emily is suggesting. "Well, I have to wash my hands and my penis and ejaculate straight into the cup. I hope it's big enough."

"Honey, even I don't think you could fill it up." Emily chuckles as she continues her stroking.

"No, I mean to fit my cock in. What if it squirts everywhere? What if I can't catch it all?"

"Then you'll have to do it again." Emily shuffles up the bed, trapping my arm under her, and places a gentle kiss on my lips. "Whatever the test shows, you're still all man to me."

But what if I wasn't? What if there is something wrong? The fears I've tried to push down are surfacing, and I worry it's all my fault that we aren't pregnant yet. We could use donor sperm, I suppose, but the thought of someone else's spunk being inside my wife makes me shudder. I was born slightly premature and have a droopy right eyelid that was put down to my prematurity. *What if it had also affected my balls?*

"You're thinking too hard." Emily turns off the bedside lamp, and I snuggle into her.

I'm hard as a steel pipe and want nothing more than to show her how much of a man I can be to her. *One more sleep.*

It's a night of broken sleep. I keep waking up and checking the clock. The lab doesn't open until half six, and I don't start work until eight. At five, I decide I'm not getting back to sleep. Pulling on my running gear, I set out for my usual morning run. This time, I won't be getting home and climbing back into bed with my wife, though, because I'll be wanking into a plastic cup.

I use the five kilometres to try to clear my head. It hasn't bothered me that I'd been on the maternity ward for the last week. Sure, I've seen people having babies in less-than-ideal circumstances, and it was painful seeing child services arrive at the hospital to inform a mother that she wouldn't be taking her newborn, who was in the special care nursery being monitored for drug withdrawal, home. It all seems so unfair. Why couldn't Em and me conceive?

When I get home, I jump in the shower. My cock swells as I think of Emily's belly round with my baby. It's a fantasy I've had for years. We've had a couple of scares over the years where we'd either forgotten a condom or one had broken, and I'd secretly hoped that Emily might be pregnant, even though we were both so young.

After drying myself, I wrap the towel around my waist and make my way to the kitchen for a glass of water. The clock on the stove tells me it isn't yet six. I probably should wait. It won't take me long to wank. I figure I could have it wrapped up in a minute or so. It's been over two days, after all.

The kit stares at me on the kitchen bench. It's in a brown paper bag, so it isn't obvious what it is, but I know. I open the bag and take out the pot and sachet of lube. I wouldn't need that. The plan had been for Emily to help me by just being there. No doubt she would play with her tits for me. God, I love her rack. It's perfect. Grapefruit-sized tits that hover over her chest, their pale brown nipples just poking out in front. There's no sag, not that it would have worried me if there was, and they fit perfectly in my hands.

Shit, thinking about my wife's breasts has me hard. I unscrew the lid on the pot and drop the towel to the kitchen floor. A few long strokes feel amazing. I imagine fucking Emily's tits, sliding between them as she pokes out her tongue, waiting to receive my offering.

I don't want to draw this out. It's a medical wank. I've read stories online of men going to cubicles at testing centres and finding porn mags to wank to. I have Emily to think about. Sure, we watch a bit of porn from time to time, but there is no way I need porn this morning.

It's the thought of Emily's pregnant, swollen belly that tips me over the edge. The cup almost slips from my fingers as I angle my cock to it, but I catch all the jizz. I was expecting at least half a cup, but it's a couple of tablespoons max; seeing it sitting in front of me like this makes me question if it's enough.

Emily's still asleep, so I throw on some sweats and a T-shirt, grab my car keys, phone, and wallet, and make my way to the lab.

The roads are empty, and I still have ten minutes to wait with the sample sitting in my pants pocket. There's a man sitting at the entryway on his walking frame, no doubt waiting for an early morning blood test. I don't think he's here for the same reason as me, anyway. Glancing at my watch, I see the doors should be opening in a minute or two, so I climb out of my car and move towards the chap who's also waiting.

"Checking your sugars too, lad?" The man tips his hat at me.

"Something like that." I don't want to make small talk.

"Morning, Rodney." One of the nurses opens the door and starts helping the older gentleman inside. I follow.

"I'm dropping off..." I hold up the brown paper bag.

"Thanks." She removes the cup from the paper bag with her gloved hand and places it inside a plastic one, holding it up for the world to see. Fortunately, there were only the two of us present, Rodney having been ushered into a room to have his blood taken. "Your doctor will have the results in the next day or two. Have a nice day."

Have a nice day. I mean, really?

I walk out, shaking my head, and climb into my car. I wasn't sure what I was expecting. *Did I want her to comment on the quantity? Did I want her to comment at all?* I think it was the holding it up and having a look that got me. Sure, she was probably just checking I'd filled in the label correctly, but I was a doctor used to taking lab specimens. I know what is needed. I don't want to fail this test, and I've done my best to prepare. No one was going to accuse me of going in half-cocked. Well, I mean I had to be fully loaded to do the test. Jesus, my brain is going around in circles. It must be lack of sleep. Lack of sleep, or lack of being inside my wife.

Emily's favourite bakery is open, so I grab us some chocolate croissants and head home.

SHE'S STILL IN BED, the alarm having not yet sounded. The glow from the light that sneaks into the room from beneath the curtain makes her look almost ethereal. Sure, others may see the drool on her pillow or her hair sticking every which way, but to me, she's just perfect. I strip my clothes and climb in next to her. The way she snuggles into me as she sleeps made my cock take notice. Sliding my hand up her leg and under the ugly nightie I like far too much, I feel her stir.

"You've got to do your thing," she croaks as she rolls onto her back.

"Done it. It's all delivered and everything." I nuzzle against her neck.

"So, you didn't need me, then?" I think Emily sounds hurt, but it could be her morning voice.

"I used memories of these amazing tits to get myself off. I was going to wait, but I was standing in the kitchen, and I started picturing the most gorgeous breasts I've ever seen, and I just couldn't stop myself."

"Tell me more about these breasts." Emily pushes her chest out as I undo the buttons on her nightgown, exposing her chest.

"They're round and soft, and so, so lickable." I take a nipple between my lips and apply firm suction, listening to Emily's moan. "They're sensitive, and they sit on the chest of the woman who's my always and everything. The one I adore. My best friend. My soulmate." I pepper kisses over them, Emily's hands running through my hair, pulling strands out from my hair tie, still tied back after my run.

"Fancy making another deposit?" Emily murmurs as she pushes me onto my back.

The question is rhetorical. She almost rips the nightie over her head as she climbs on top of me and sinks onto my cock. *Twice before work? Best day ever!*

Emily, Age 18

I'm loving the uni life. I'm certain I've made the right decision studying medicine. At school, I got frustrated in classes where teachers would slow things down so that everyone could keep up. Here, it's fast-paced and aimed at us all being high achievers.

Boyd and I are in the same classes. I felt bad today though. Simon, who looks as though he's maybe Korean, asked me where I was from. I gave my standard response that my mum's Italian and my father has Scottish heritage. I don't see myself as Chinese Australian. My Chinese parents didn't want me, probably because I was a girl, and they wanted a son. I was five months old when my parents adopted me. It's not like I have memories of China.

One of the stipulations for overseas adoption when I was a baby was that my parents would keep me close to my culture. I didn't want to study

Mandarin on Saturday mornings. Lunar New Year was fun, but I never really understood the significance as a child. Mum tried to help, but Dad was adamant that I was Australian.

It wasn't until Dad left that I started exploring Chinese customs a bit more. I don't think I missed out as a child.

Priscilla and I talked about this a lot in my sessions. She noted my jasmine tea addiction and how it was the only hot drink I enjoyed and had since I was a child. We talked about me visiting China. My parents adopted me from an orphanage in Shanghai, but I could have come from anywhere in the country. I know I could do one of those DNA tests and see if I have blood relatives, but I don't want to.

Mum is my mum and always will be.

I've moved into the Hartman house. I thought Hillary and Charlie might clean out Giles or Henry's room for me, but they're cool with me sharing with Boyd. I enjoy being near Val, too. Even though she's younger than me, apart from Boyd, she's my bestie.

She's kind of seeing a boy from school. She's not that keen on him, but he's infatuated with her. It's funny to watch. Michael came over tonight for a movie night. He's quiet, and it took him to the last ten minutes of the movie to put his arm around Val as they sat together on the couch. She leant forward as the car chase heated up, and we willed the FBI agents to shoot the baddies. I think Michael was expecting a romantic comedy.

Hillary told Val that if she wants to have Michael stay over, he can, but Val scrunched up her nose and said no way.

I worry that she reads so many romance books, that she might have a skewed idea of what things can be like. She's told me that she expects a guy to give her an orgasm. I'm probably lucky in that Boyd always gives me one. I know from girls at school and uni, though, that this isn't always the case.

I hope Val gets what she wants. She thinks it's cool that Boyd and I are together. I know some friends would feel icky about their bestie sleeping with their brother, but not Val. It just goes to show how close the Hartmans are.

Chapter 6

Emily

"Come here, my *principessa*." Nonna cups my cheeks with her bony fingers, her smile wide and a tear in her eye. "*Tanti auguri*."

I turned twenty-five during the week, and Boyd and I have taken the one-and-a-half-hour drive to Sailor's Bend to see Nonna to celebrate. It is nice having a weekend off together.

"Thanks, Nonna." Her hands drop from my cheeks, and we squeeze each other tight.

"Now, what did your husband give you, apart from his rooster?"

Boyd's grown up knowing Nonna, but she's still able to make him blush. I'm sure if he had a drink in his vicinity, he would have spat it everywhere.

I couldn't tell Nonna he took a sperm test for me. "He framed a photo from when we were in Venice. It's him and me sitting in a gondola together. I didn't even know it had been taken, but he arranged it with the gondolier."

"And you worked on your birthday?" Nonna leads us from the entryway to the lounge room, where we sit on the comfy, old, threadbare couch. She perches next to the chair that Nonno always sat in. It's still strange seeing it empty when I have so many childhood memories of him just being present with his enormous laugh.

Yes, I worked, but I also spent the day with a condom-covered ultrasound probe up my vagina, confirming there was one beautiful looking follicle on my right ovary that looked like it was ready to erupt and send an egg down to await Boyd's sperm.

"Yeah. We both did, Nonna, but Boyd grabbed a Thai takeaway, and we spent the evening in bed."

"*Accipicchia*," Nonna exclaims as she stands and sways her hips from side to side, her apron fluttering from the movement.

It was an amazing birthday. I showed Boyd a photo from my ultrasound, and he told me he hoped it was our baby's first photo. We made love that night. I mean, we always show love to each other, but this was more tender. Our eyes locked, and I swore I could see into Boyd's soul. We moved as one and timed our climaxes perfectly so we came together. We were silent for ages afterwards, unable to stop our fingers from grazing over each other.

Thinking back to our appointment with Dr Nat, I can't imagine waiting eight years to have a baby of our own. I knew I was impatient, but surely Boyd and I shared enough love that the universe would recognise we were going to be amazing parents.

I don't know a lot about my parents' struggles to become parents. I know Mum had endometriosis, and it had scarred her tubes. They'd tried IVF, but it hadn't worked, so they adopted me. That was back when adoption was easier than it is now.

"Lunch is done. It's soup. You hungry?" I hadn't noticed Nonna had left the room. I was so stuck in my thoughts.

"We can wait a bit." Boyd looks at me, and I nod as he speaks.

There's such comfort from sitting with Boyd like this. I love Nonna's house. Some would call it kitsch with its figurines and lace doilies everywhere, but everything has its place. There is a story behind each ornament, and many were gifts from Nonno.

"Tell me about work." Nonna sits, leaning forward with her hands resting in her apron.

We can't tell her much, but there are a few stories we share. Boyd is a natural storyteller, making you believe you were there. I am sure some of it is embellished, but it's entertaining to listen to.

Eventually, we move to the dining room. Lunch is perfect. The soup is as comforting as being in Nonna's presence. It's been months since Boyd and I have been down to visit. We need to make more time to visit more often. Nonna wasn't getting any younger.

After lunch, Boyd leaves Nonna and me alone and goes outside to trim some overhanging branches in her driveway. Nonna makes herself a coffee, not caring that she uses the instant stuff. She's even bought some jasmine tea just for me.

"What is it, my *principessa*?" Nonna asks as we sit again in the lounge room. "He looks like he treats you well."

"He does. He treats me like a princess. He's so loving and thoughtful and caring." I pause. We've said we aren't going to tell family, but perhaps that just meant the Hartmans. "It's just... we've been trying to get pregnant, and nothing's happening." I wipe a tear from the edge of my eye.

"It will happen if it's meant to." Her voice is so soft. She places her coffee cup on the side table and reaches for my hand. "I had your mother and wanted more. She adopted you. Both of us would have liked more, but it wasn't meant to be."

I had wondered why Mum was an only child. It isn't the sort of thing I feel comfortable talking about with Nonna.

"We're having some tests done and will take it from there." I shrug.

"Your Nonno had tests. He had one ball that didn't come down right and only half the seeds. We were blessed with Rosa, but alas, no more."

Nonna has a tear in her eye now as she grips my hand. She and my grandfather had come to Australia over sixty years ago as newlyweds. Nonno had worked on a sugarcane farm before he moved to the mill and became a manager there. The smell of molasses in the air was one of the things I adored about visiting Sailor's Bend. It reminded me of Nonno.

It wasn't fair that the two women in my family who I loved and who loved me without question struggled to grow their families.

Boyd and I are good people. We'll provide a stable, loving home for a child. It's not fair that it isn't happening for us.

"THANKS FOR HELPING with Nonna's garden." I kiss Boyd as I open the door to our apartment. He's weighed down with a large tub of soup with the leftover cake from lunch balanced precariously on top.

"You know I enjoyed it." We take the four steps from the front door to the kitchen, and I grab the cake, unwrapping the foil Nonna wrapped it carefully in, and place it on a board before cutting us both a slice. Boyd places the soup in the fridge. "It's one of the downsides of living in an apartment, not having a garden. I saw Giles and Bridget have some overgrown bushes at their place I could hack into."

"Please don't talk about hacking into your sister-in-law's bush." I laugh as I flick on the kettle.

"Your bush is the only bush I want to be up close to." Boyd wraps his arms around me from behind and kisses the top of my head. "And I don't care if you trim it, let it run wild, or deforest it."

"Did you have a good chat with Nonna?" Boyd asks as he loosens his grip on me and steps to the fridge to grab a can of Coke.

"I told her." I look down as I pour boiling water into the mug. My voice is soft, and I'm not sure how Boyd will react.

"Good."

I look up and see Boyd's smile. "Really?" I scrunch my nose, and my brow furrows.

"Yeah. Really. Now let's shoot some zombies." Boyd throws his already empty can in the box for recycling in the corner of the kitchen and rubs his hands together.

I love playing video games with Boyd. It's relaxing sitting between his legs, leaning against him, as we shoot zombies, race cars, or do whatever the game of the hour needs.

We play for a while until I throw the controller across the room when I'm killed and Boyd apologises for not having my back. He has my back, though. He's always there for me and will defend me as needed. I love how he's helped me grow so that I can stand up for myself, too. He sees the importance of me having a voice.

For a while, after Dad left, I sank in on myself. I was quiet and reserved. I can remember so many occasions at school and throughout uni where someone would say that I was Boyd's girlfriend, only for him to remind them that he was Emily McIntyre's boyfriend.

It is like he has me on a pedestal, except I never feel like I'll fall from being on a plinth high above the ground. I don't need catching, but rather, he's there with me, standing beside me as I fight my battles.

Playing video games takes my mind off me not being pregnant. It allows me time to be in the moment. I remember that Bridget is big on mindfulness and practicing being in the moment, although I don't suspect shooting zombies and seeing blood splatter everywhere is exactly what she means, but it works for me.

While lunch with Nonna was calm and relaxing the day before, lunch with the Hartmans is anything but. Not that I'm complaining.

Most weekends, we'll gather at Charlie and Hillary's or Giles and Bridget's for brunch, lunch, or dinner. Henry and Ken both play cricket, but their match this week was on Saturday, so we decided that Sunday lunch it would be. It was also one of the few weekends where all of us are off. In a family full of junior doctors, this is a bit of a miracle.

"Here they are. Trust the newlyweds to be late." Henry stands in my in-laws' kitchen chopping herbs as Ken hovers over the stove where he loves to be.

Every week, he and Henry declare they needed to get a bigger place so they can play host.

"Here they are." Charlie appears from the spare room with a few bottles of wine, stopping to kiss me on the cheek before he puts them down on the bench and embraces Boyd in a hug.

"I think they've been in bed all morning." Henry smirks at Boyd.

"Not all morning." Hillary breezes into the room, fastening an earring, clearly not understanding that the jibe was not directed at her. "Just most of it. But what can I say? My husband's a DILF." Hillary greets us all with hugs.

"What's a DILF?" Millie and Giles have snuck in without us hearing, Millie picking up on her grandmother's comment. "Is that like when you call Mummy a MILF?" She turns to her father.

"Mia won't get out of the car, and Bridget's decided to argue with her." Giles changes the subject.

I love meals with the Hartman family. They are big and busy, but full of the love the family lives by. Love is a verb, and everyone goes out of their way to make sure everyone is taken care of.

It's this very fact that makes me question whether or not we should tell them about trying to get pregnant. I know they'd be supportive, but it could also be smothering, and I'm not sure we need the extra pressure.

As if Boyd senses my inner musings, he passes me a glass of water, wraps his arm around my waist, drawing me to him, and plants a kiss on my head.

"Lukey, Lukey, Lukey." Mia is out of the car now that Ken's sister, Dipti, and her children Luke and Sarah are here.

"I baked a Love Cake for dessert." Dipti places the container on the bench and starts greeting everyone.

"Now, where's Rosa?" Hillary asks as she fusses around Ken, who tries to shoo her away from the stove.

"Running late, as usual." I shrug.

"She'll be late to her own funeral." Hillary laughs just as Mum walks in. "Speak of the devil."

"Sorry, sorry." Mum places a bottle of wine on the bench and throws her bag on a seat. "Were your ears burning, Boyd?"

"Nah, I expect people to be talking about how amazing I am," my husband replies, letting go of me as Mum embraces me in a hug and squeezes tight, just as she has done for as long as I could remember.

"I was on the phone with Mama, and she was raving about the work you did in her garden yesterday." Mum gives Boyd the same hug she's given me.

"I had fun." Boyd seems incredulous that it is such a big deal.

"Always welcome to help out at ours, Boyo." Giles slaps his brother on the back on his way to the fridge to grab a beer.

Ken bans us all from the kitchen, telling us lunch isn't too far away. Most of us gather in the dining room. In the centre of the room, there's a long table that easily sits sixteen, although there've been times when there were at least twenty people around it. Eclectic art hangs on the walls, from anatomical drawings of the heart to paintings by local artists, and photos of the Hartman family. The large glass doors at the end of the room open to the garden and the pool area where we held our wedding.

I love thinking back to that day. It came together exactly as we planned. I never wanted a fuss or fanfare. It was an opportunity for our family to share our love in the house that showed me what love meant.

I let my mind wander as I look around the room. My parents had what I thought was a happy marriage until my father decided it wasn't. They never really argued, but perhaps that was their problem. They had their set roles, and it was quite traditional. Mum stayed at home and cooked. She sewed and sometimes took some of her kids' clothes range to the markets. Dad was a financial planner. Mum's never said anything, but I was sure he screwed her over in the divorce settlement. I'm not sure why I think this, because I look at my childhood as being idyllic. However, seeing him that evening telling us he was leaving, I saw a different side of him.

We sit together to eat, and lunch is amazing. Ken outdoes himself with a variety of curries whose flavours danced on the tongue long after they were in our bellies. I pretend to sip the glass of wine, not swallowing a drop. This is the month I am sure I will be pregnant. I can feel it.

Emily, Age 18

Boyd and I went to the medical centre on campus today. Together. We've been using condoms since we started having sex, and as much as Boyd tells me he doesn't mind using them, I want the freedom to be able to have spontaneous sex without having to stop in the middle of it all to find one.

The nurse went through all sorts of different options. We agreed we wanted something that was almost fail-proof. Over and over, Boyd said he didn't mind taking responsibility and if there was a pill he could take, he would. A vasectomy seemed rather drastic, especially as we both want kids one day.

In the end, I said I'd try an IUD. The doctor was able to fit it during our appointment. Well, try to.

She was lovely to begin with. She explained what would happen, and I signed the paperwork. She even let Boyd stay with me.

They took us to a procedure room, where I was put in what looked like a medieval contraption, complete with stirrups to put my feet in to keep them out of the way. I'd stripped down and was wearing the scratchiest of paper gowns. Fortunately, Boyd was there holding my hand.

She put the speculum in without warning me and opened it. I almost hit the roof and let out a scream when she pinched some skin. She apologised, but I was quite anxious at this stage. I mean, I'd only ever had Boyd inside me. We'd talked about getting some dildos to see what it felt like to have something other than his penis in me, but if it was anything like that plastic speculum, then I wasn't that sure it was a good idea.

I was told my cervix looked healthy, which was good, I suppose, but I wasn't sure why it wouldn't look good. I saw the metal torture device before she tried to insert it. It was to test the length of my cervix and the depth of my uterus. I knew I was tense, but I didn't know I could tense my cervix.

The pinch from the speculum felt like a caress from a lover compared to this awful, painful thing. I screamed and tried to pull my legs from the stirrups. With one leg free, I almost fell off the bed as I tried to roll onto my side. I kicked the tray of instruments, sending it to the floor in a loud clang.

It was Boyd who said he didn't think it was going to work. The doctor ripped off her glove and said she knew of women who had to have their IUDs inserted under general anaesthetic. There was this look in her eyes like she was judging me. She'd decided I was a wimp. I felt bad enough that I hadn't been able to go through with it; I didn't need to be further reminded by someone who should show compassion.

I doubted she would have tolerated the pain. Boyd and the nurse comforted me. I was embarrassed on top of it all. I'd been the one who complained about using condoms, not Boyd, and here I was unable to go through a tiny medical procedure to help us out.

Would childbirth be like this? At least then I knew I could get an epidural.

All the way home, I kept telling Boyd how sorry I was that I was such a wuss. He tried to reassure me. I really thought it was all me, but Boyd assured me the doctor was a cow. It was my first experience with a doctor like that. I'd heard and read of women not being taken seriously by their doctors and being passed off as being emotional when there were medical things wrong with them.

I vowed then and there not to be like that when I was a GP. This experience will be one I'll use to help others. I tried to bring up going on the pill with Boyd, and he wouldn't hear of it, telling me he didn't want me to artificially mess with my hormones. I even did the whole 'my body, my choice' thing, but he said he would still use condoms just to show that he was prepared to take responsibility for contraception.

Looks like it's going to be condoms, but not for the next few days. I'm not letting anything near my vagina after today.

Of course, Boyd recounted the experience to his family over the dinner table tonight. I should call the Hartman house home, because I've moved in. Val's told me I can have her room at the end of the year to store stuff in when she moves to Brisbane.

She's such a good friend. After dinner, we lay on her bed together, and I recounted the full story of my clinic visit and how nice the nurse was. She told me she'd never let a guy come inside her without a condom. She had this thing with Michael from school, but I think it's fizzled out. I know she's hell-bent on moving to Brisbane to study law at the end of the year. Bridget's due to have their first baby soon, and I think Val wants to be close to them. I get that.

Hillary's told us we are all going down once the baby arrives, even me. It's just accepted that I'm part of this family, and I really like that. Part of me says Boyd and I should just say fuck it and stop contraception and start a family now. I know we're young and are living with his parents, but we could get kids out of the way and then work things out. I know I want to be a doctor, but I could wait and go back later. There's a lady in one of my classes who's studying part-time with young kids at home. I've never really spoken to her, but I might, just to see how she does it.

I mean, if someone told me I had to choose between being a doctor and being a mother, motherhood would win hands down. Despite people thinking otherwise, Boyd and I are the real deal. He's it for me, my always and forever. I really am the luckiest girl alive to have him in my life.

Chapter 7

Boyd

It was almost déjà vu, sitting in the waiting room waiting for Dr Nat. Except this time, she was running late. We both left work on time for once and made it to the surgery for her last appointment of the day.

"How was your day?" I try to hide the anxiety in my voice as I pull the waiting room chair closer to Emily's and reach for her hand.

She's had a rough week. Once again, her period arrived on the day it was expected. I suggested she take a sick day from work, but she assured me she'd be better off at work taking her mind off things. Her cycle was regular. She didn't experience debilitating cramps like some women. Yeah, she was uncomfortable, but it didn't hint at endometriosis or anything.

One thing about only ever having been with each other meant the chance of sexually transmitted infection was virtually nil. I knew Emily took her period arriving hard. I mean, it wasn't hard not to. For me, though, it slants things further and further to my side of the equation.

Perhaps I should mention my concerns to my wife, but I'm sure she thinks about them, too. The likelihood is I am shooting blanks. I was born prematurely, the smallest of Mum and Dad's babies. I suspect it was my dramatic entrance that caused the four-year age gap between me and Val. There was never any explanation for my early arrival. One minute, Mum was doing rounds, the next, her waters broke, and the four other doctors present turned their focus to Mum instead of the patient in front of them.

I've heard this story so many times. The way Dad was nearby, also rounding, the way no one could find a wheelchair, so they put Mum on a commode and wheeled her to the lift and up three floors to the maternity ward, the way I arrived seven minutes later and spent a month in the special care nursery.

I'm the only one of us that Mum didn't fully breastfeed. She'd tried, but the shock of everything took its toll. She told me earlier in the year, when I was doing my gynae and obstetrics rotation, that it was one of her biggest regrets. I've pointed out that I ended up healthy and that was all that mattered. Not that me being breastfed would help sperm production, but no doubt Mum will use it to blame herself.

"Yeah, not too bad," Emily replies with a sigh. "Discharged one to the hospice and another two home. I'm getting used to talking about death more. It surprises me how philosophical so many patients are."

"Yeah?" I reply absentmindedly, still thinking about how I am about to be told it is my fault Emily isn't pregnant.

"How about you?" She squeezes my hand. Her strength astounds me.

"Pretty shitty." I sighed. "Twenty-five-year-old with a dodgy heart had her sixth baby, and once again, it went straight into care. She was there all alone. No Mum to sit with her. No friends. No partner. It's just not fair."

It isn't fair. But then again, life isn't. Emily is working with people with cancer, people facing their mortality years before they should. I'm working with people having babies, most of whom couldn't comprehend what it is like to want to be pregnant and find themselves unable to conceive.

We are the only ones in the waiting room now. The sun has almost disappeared, and I can see the streetlights outside have come on.

"Emily and Boyd," Dr Nat calls from the back of the waiting room.

"I love you," I whisper to Emily as we stand. Her hand squeeze, smile, and kiss on the cheek show me she loves me, too. Whatever happens, we will do this together.

"Sorry, I'm running late," Nat says as she closes the door behind us, and we all take our seats in her room. "How have you been?"

"Another dud month." Emily half smiles at me, tears glistening in her eyes. "But we had some amazing sex."

I can't help but laugh. My perfect wife had broken the tension beautifully.

"Good." Nat nods as she stretches out the vowels. I feel like she wants to tap us both on the knees to praise us. "You know, couples who experience infertility often say their sex life suffers because they are so focused on making a baby, they forget to make love to their partner."

I couldn't ever see this happening to us. No matter how long it takes, sex with Emily is never a chore, and she instigates it just as often as I do.

"Well, I've got good news for you two." Nat clicks some buttons on her keyboard and pulls up our results. "Emily, your hormone levels are exactly where we want to see them at the different stages of your cycle. Your scan showed a lovely follicle, and there's nothing wrong with your uterus, according to the ultrasound."

Emily smiles and once again squeezes my hand. This is where the bad news is coming. I suck in a deep breath and prepare myself.

"Boyd." Nat smiles. "Your sperm count was right up there. The morphology, or size and shape of the sperm, was great, the motility was what was expected, and the sample size and consistency were all normal."

This is meant to be good news. I wanted the tests to show something wrong. I wanted there to be an answer why, after eight months, we aren't expecting a baby.

"So, there's nothing wrong?" Emily asks in a soft voice.

"Nothing that we can see from these tests, no." Nat uncrosses her legs and leans closer to us both. "It's only been eight months. I can't diagnose infertility until you've been having regular unprotected sex for twelve months."

Emily nods, and I can sense she's close to tears. I wrap my arm around her shoulders. She smiles up at me and squeezes my thigh. I can't help but love this woman.

"Come and see me in the new year if you still aren't pregnant, and I can then refer you to the local clinic. I'll warn you though, there's about a six-month waitlist to get in to see them at present for the under thirty-fives."

Her words hit hard. I feel like we've always been discriminated against because of our age. There is the expectation we won't make it as a couple. I've known from the start that Emily is my person. Whatever happens, we'll do this together, and we'll get through this together. We are an unstoppable unit.

Hiking has always relaxed me. I love nothing more than spending time in nature listening to the sounds of the birds and insects and smelling the clean air of the local rainforest.

Emily was the one to suggest a hike this morning. Usually, we ask Henry and Ken to join us, both being keen hikers themselves, but we needed to do this together, just the two of us. It's been a couple of months since Emily and I had been out together, and I need this time to recharge and regroup.

We haven't said a lot after the appointment with Nat. I know we have to wait twelve months for a definitive diagnosis of infertility. As much as I want a reason for us not being pregnant yet, part of me is relieved there was nothing wrong so far, and it gives me hope we might still manage to conceive over the next few months. The other part wants time to speed up so we can see a specialist now. I imagine it will require more tests, probably even an exploratory laparoscopy for Emily to check her tubes. There's no reason for them not to be working properly, but it seems the most likely explanation for our failures now we know everything else is normal.

I still feel like a failure. What sort of man can't manage to knock his wife up, especially with the amount of sex we're having?

A riot of kookaburras breaks forth into their raucous laughter as Emily holds a branch aside, and we climb over a fallen log. We're hiking one of our favourite paths beside a local creek that leads to a waterfall. It's one of those paths that only locals know about and manage to keep out of guidebooks and tourist information. It always takes a few hours to get to the top of the trail, but the views are worth it, and there are small pools of water you can laze in to cool off.

It isn't unusual for us to hike in silence. Henry always says he enjoys hiking with me because it's the quietest he knows me to be.

My thoughts are filled with making a family. If we'd conceived on our honeymoon, like we'd planned, we would probably have been spending this weekend decorating a nursery and preparing for our baby's arrival.

As much as I love hiking through the rainforest, the moment we break through into the clearing and see the views down towards the coast always takes my breath away.

I take off my cap and swipe my arm across my forehead to wipe away some of the sweat. Tugging the elastic out of my hair, I hold it between my teeth as I smooth it with my fingers and gather it in another ponytail.

Emily takes off her backpack and places it on the ground. Her face is flushed with exertion, and her hair is as damp as mine. Stepping behind her, I wrap my arms around her neck and draw her to me, passing her my water tube to drink from.

"We need to do this more often," Emily says softly as she brings her hands to mine, holding them in place. "I like the way I get to think when we hike."

"Hmmm," I hum into her hair. I'm not about to disagree with her.

"We haven't really talked since the appointment." Emily breaks my hold and turns to face me, her left hand holding her right bicep and her head turned down.

"Hey." I tilt her chin with my finger and see the tears in her eyes. "So far, there's nothing wrong, so there's no reason we shouldn't have a baby in the next twelve months. Sure, it might not be to our original timing, but we'll make it work."

"Would you mind if I told Val?" Emily's eyebrows crease as her eyes meet mine.

"Of course not." I give her a hug. "She's your best friend, and I'd be more worried if you wanted to keep things from her."

"But we spoke about family, and..." Emily trails off as she bends down and starts pulling the containers of sandwiches from her backpack.

I lay out the small blanket we brought so we can take in the view.

"Giles would probably go as far as saying Val's not really family, as she's not studying medicine." I try to inject humour into the situation, but it falls flat.

"She's going to be an amazing lawyer." I sit, and Emily lies next to me, both of us propped up on an elbow as we open the plastic containers.

"What about you?" Emily asks as she bites into her sandwich.

"What about me?" I reply.

"Who are you going to talk to?"

Emily is so caring. It's one of the things I love most about her. Swiping away a strand of hair that hangs across her cheek, I lean in and plant a tender kiss on her forehead. "I'm alright. I don't need to talk to anyone. My sperm are super swimmers, and it would only make my brothers jealous if I boasted about it."

My tone may be jovial, but the reality is I don't really have any friends. Emily has always been my best friend. I've had acquaintances through medical school, but no one who I share things with. If anything, Val was as much of a friend of mine, despite being four years younger than me.

Maybe I should find someone to talk to, not a professional necessarily, but someone who might understand. We're putting a lot of pressure on ourselves. I can only imagine how much more intense it will get if we haven't managed to conceive before we see Dr Nat again in the new year.

I've spent years focussing on both my career and my relationship with Emily. I love being a doctor. I'm keen to train as a paediatrician and am due to hear in the next few weeks if I've been accepted into the program next year. That would lead to six years of study before I could call myself a paediatric consultant. It was unlikely that I'd be accepted straight up. Most junior doctors had to do a second intern year, but I was hopeful.

Emily's path to general practice is easier. She'll do a year or two more at the hospital, then be a registrar in a GP practice for two years. There's further training she can do, and I have no doubt she will, but she'll be a GP long before I'm a specialist. I've told her time and time again I want to take time off when our kids are born. She argues that I'll be closer to forty when I became a consultant if I do that, but I don't care. Maybe I should slow down a bit, find a hobby, learn a new skill, meet new people.

I push those thoughts aside. Hiking with Emily is precious, and I love that it's just the two of us. We can just *be* together. As much as I let my thoughts drift to work and getting pregnant, Emily is the most important part of my life, and spending time together is so special.

Fuck, I love this woman. Sure, we may have a few more months of trying to make babies, but at least it will be lots of fun.

Emily, Age 17

I'm sick and tired of people trying to tell me that Boyd and I won't last. I get the comment at least every other day. It's also the reason I've stopped seeing Priscilla.

I tried to tell her that I felt like things were going so well, and I was busy with my last months at school, but really, it was her constant questioning about what I had in my life apart from Boyd. I mean, really?

It was two sessions ago. I hadn't dared tell her about our unprotected sex. I've never been so relieved to see my period show up, but at the same time, I was a little sad that we weren't pregnant. We're in a committed relationship. I'd marry him today if I could. Anyway, Priscilla was going on that I was placing too much emphasis on my future with Boyd and not enough on my career.

My career is important, but it's not going to define who I am. Sure, I want to be a great doctor, but I want to be remembered as being kind and caring and thoughtful to everyone, not just my patients.

Priscilla asked me what I'd do if Boyd and I broke up. I told her it was never going to happen, and she basically said I was being naïve. That even the strongest relationships can fail. She had the audacity to suggest that my mother never thought her marriage would end. I don't swear a lot, not like Boyd anyway, but in my head, I was calling her all manner of slurs.

Sure, I get it's her job, but I felt she wasn't listening to me. I decided then and there that I didn't need the therapy anymore. I wanted to stop today, but I decided I'd do two more sessions so she didn't register that it was her criticism of my relationship with Boyd that did it.

Last session, I just rambled on about school and my hopes for medicine. I told her how I want to be a GP because it will give me the variety of patients and it can also give me a greater work-life balance so I can do the things I want to do. I didn't dare tell her that the things I want to do involved a family with Boyd.

Henry shared a hiking trail he enjoyed with Boyd, and we went last weekend. We've been on a couple of hikes together now. My boots are worn in, and I no longer get blisters, which is great. This one was through the rainforest up to a waterfall area that also looked out over the city. Boyd followed me on the way up there, and I might have swayed my hips a little extra in parts, just for his benefit. I insisted he lead the way on the way down. I didn't get to see as much of his gorgeous bum, but I saw enough.

He's growing his hair. It was long and looked a bit like a mop when he was at school, but it was above his collar, which is the school regulation. Now he can almost tie it back. It feels great to run my fingers through it.

I had long hair as a kid, but I chopped it when I started high school. I like it shorter. I really want to bleach a section and dye it something funky, like purple or green. It would look cool against the black. I'll have to wait until I finish school though, as Mrs Carmichael would have a fit.

See, Mrs Carmichael's another one. She saw me in the corridor today and asked me if I was still seeing "that Hartman boy." She seemed surprised when I said I was. I think she thinks he went straight to uni and is living it up with all the girls his age there. He's not. I know one of the girls he works with tried to ask him out for a drink, but he told them he was taken.

I can see why he gets hit on so much. I mean, he's gorgeous. It's the blonde hair, blue eyes that get me. And his smile. Swoon. He has an everyday smile and what I now call his Emily smile. My heart feels like it's going to explode when he looks at me like that. His smile covers his entire face, and his eyes just light up.

He's taking me away for the night for my eighteenth birthday next week. I would have been happy with a hike and camping, but he has arranged a bed-and-breakfast in the hills. He's been reading Val's dirty romance books. He told me it's to get ideas for our sex life, but I think he enjoys them. I'm the one who benefits, so I don't complain. His dirty talk game is amazing, and it always turns me on.

I can't wait to see Mrs Carmichael or Priscilla in twenty-five years and throw it in their faces that Boyd and I are living our happily ever after. We'll show them. I know we will.

Chapter 8

Emily

I SHOULD HAVE PERFECTED LEMONADE RECIPES BY NOW, seeing I've had so many lemons thrown at me over the last few months. We still aren't pregnant. Boyd hasn't secured a training program in paediatrics. We knew it was a long shot, but it's still disappointing.

There are limited places in paediatrics in Cassowary Point. I told Boyd I'll move to Brisbane if that's what it takes. I mean, I hate the idea of living in Brisbane, but I'd do it for him. He said we should wait, and that he's been told off-record that he was almost guaranteed a position in twelve months' time.

"You okay?" Boyd squeezes my hand as I stare out the plane window looking at the farmland below me.

We're flying to Brisbane for Val's graduation. She has no idea we're coming. She even told me not to come, as she knew how much I hate being in the big smoke. It isn't Brisbane, per se. It is that it is where my father and his new family live, and I am always worried I'll bump into them. Yes, it is a big place, but stranger things have happened.

"Yeah." I smile, but I'm sure Boyd detects it's forced. "It will be great to see Val, and I can't wait to surprise her."

Val and I have been chatting regularly. She really is living her best life. When she first went to uni in Brisbane, we'd have regular movie nights together where we'd watch the same movie and talk about it over FaceTime. These have become few and far between, especially since Henry moved back to Cassowary Point, but we attempted to have one at least once a month. She has the most active social life. She went out less when Henry lived with her, now she seems more liberated and is exploring what the big city life has to offer.

This last year, they've been almost nonexistent until I rang Val and burst into tears one Sunday afternoon, telling her that we weren't pregnant and that we'd been trying. She was empathetic and said the right things, but I don't think she had any idea what Boyd and I were going through. No one did. And we weren't technically infertile yet. We still had ten days until our first wedding anniversary, and then it would be twelve months. Like clockwork, my period arrived.

Our movie nights have been more regular ever since then though, and it had been so hard last night to not sign off that we'd be seeing Val today. We watched a superhero movie. Val and I agreed that the main actor was hot as sin, but I later told Boyd that I still preferred his looks and body. This morphed into a conversation about whether I was missing out by not experiencing more penises in my life. Boyd pooh-poohed the idea that he was missing out by not experiencing more vaginas, saying none could be as good as mine. He didn't like it when I used that argument about him and his gorgeous cock.

At the back of my mind, I wonder if I'm enough for Boyd. If we had any idea before we married that we might not have children, I wonder if he would have gone through with marrying me. He can claim he loves my pussy all he likes, but my body doesn't seem to be doing what it's meant to be doing.

Our flight this morning meant an early start, but seeing the sunrise out the window of the plane makes it all worth it. We took off in darkness and now can see the peeks of yellow, red, and orange creep along the horizon. Hillary and Charlie flew down yesterday and had an early dinner with Val after she finished her shift at the bookshop before the two of them went to see the ballet, leaving Val free for the online movie with Boyd and me.

With only hand luggage, we make our way from the plane through the crowded airport quickly. It seems we aren't the only ones with the idea of a long weekend in the lead up to Christmas.

"I'm peopled out," I huff as someone else bumps into me with their luggage. "The train will be busy, so let's catch a taxi."

If Boyd responds, I don't hear him. I hate crowds of people. Being short, I feel trapped. I can't see around me, and I hate not knowing what's going on. He simply grabs my hand and leads me to the taxi rank.

"Hey." Boyd sits next to me in the back of the cab, his arm around my shoulders stroking my hair. "Great idea to catch a cab."

We didn't have to wait long, and fortunately, the driver wasn't chatty. Even though I've told Boyd I'll do it for him, I dread the day we'll need to move here. When Boyd gets on the training program, he'll need at least eighteen months down here as part of his path towards becoming a consultant. He'd suggested we try another city, but we'll only be further away from Mum and Nonna.

"Sorry, I just..." I start stroking my pinkie finger up Boyd's thigh nervously.

"It's okay. I know you hate crowds, and I didn't realise it would be so busy this morning. It will probably be busy on Sunday evening, too. Do you want to move our flights?"

"No." I snuggle into this amazing man. I know I'll be much better going home. "We've got late checkout on Sunday, and I have plans for you."

"I like the sound of that." Boyd nuzzles into my neck, and I try to push him away when I notice the cab driver smiling at us in his rearview mirror.

"Val and I are going on an adventure tomorrow morning, but she doesn't know about it yet." I've calmed down a lot on the drive towards the city and can hear the playfulness in my voice.

"Can I come?" Boyd kisses along my jaw.

"You will after, I promise."

"You booked what?" I'm sure Val's shriek can be heard in Cassowary Point.

"A Brazilian. It's an early anniversary present for Boyd."

I've been confident that this is a great idea until I watch Val slapping her thigh, doubled up with laughter.

"You've never had one?" Val asks, wiping away tears. *I'm not sure what's so funny.*

"Um, no." The inflection at the end is one of nerves, but Val takes it as a question.

"Not even for your wedding?"

"Boyd says he doesn't mind, and it wasn't high on my list of priorities before now." I blow the air out through soft lips, making a rumbling sound. "You don't think it's a good idea?"

"I think it's a great idea if you want to do it, but you aren't exactly tolerant of pain." Val is still laughing as we walk down the street from her apartment to the salon where I booked the appointment.

"I'm getting better, plus, I Googled it, and it said it's not that painful." Val leans over and pinches a hair from my forearm. "Ow," I cry as I draw my arm back to more laughs from Val.

"This is going to be so much fun. Wait until I tell Henry." Val is wiping tears with her index finger.

"You don't need to tell anyone, especially not your brothers." I really am second-guessing my booking now.

We arrive at the salon. On the outside, it's sleek and white. The name is stencilled across the bottom of the window in gold calligraphy. A small bell jingles as I open the door. Immediately, I'm greeted with the smell of lemongrass and the sound of panpipes. I think it's meant to be relaxing.

"Welcome to Serenity by Shaaan." A tall blonde woman appears wearing a tunic that looks like something a dentist would wear.

I wondered if the signwriter misspelled the name of the salon on the window with the three letter A's in the name, but apparently not. Shaaan is listed as one of the consultants, along with Steffannee and Soosette.

"I'm Emily, and I've got a waxing appointment." I try to sound cheery, but my body shakes with nervous energy.

The blonde moves the mouse and makes some clicks, typing something into the computer in front of her. Another woman in the same uniform as the blonde in front of me comes out from the back with a stylish woman with the longest fake nails I'd ever seen.

"Stef, this is Emily, your next appointment," Blondie says without looking at either me or her colleague. "I'll fix up Cecilia for you." The blonde smiles and bats her eyes at the other client.

Val sits on an uncomfortable-looking chair and picks up an architecture magazine. I want to ask her to come through with me, but it's probably not the done thing.

Tentatively, I follow Stef, who I assumed is Steffannee—with all the double letters—to a back room. "When was your last wax?" she asks as she slides the door closed behind me.

The room is also minimal, with a large timber-framed mirror on one wall reflecting the stark white interior. The bed is covered in white towels. The lighting is soft, and the same panpipe music flows through the space.

"It's, um, my first." I bite my bottom lip between my teeth, closing an eye and scrunching my nose.

"Oooh, a virgin." Stef sounds excited as she pulls what looks like tongue depressors from the drawer hidden in the cabinet. "Well, bottoms off." She opens a door that hides the wax pots. "You don't want disposable panties, do you?"

Did I? I have no idea. If Stef doesn't think it's a good idea, then no, I don't. There was nothing on Google about disposable panties.

I climb onto the bed before Stef asks me to get down as she places some butcher's paper for me to sit on. I suppose she doesn't want wax on the nice-looking towels. I've half a mind to ask how they keep them so white, but I also think I probably don't want to know.

"Oooh, nice bush." Stef trails a glove covered hand over my mons. It isn't at all sexual. "Do you want a landing strip? I mean, you've got enough for a heart or an arrow, or I can take it totally bare."

"Um, maybe the heart?" I planned on a small strip, but the idea of a heart appeals.

"Oooh, great choice." Stef sprinkles powder over my labia, and I close my eyes. "So, new boyfriend?"

The first bit of wax is applied to my lips. It feels warm and comforting. *This might not be so bad after all.*

"No, my hu— Jesus Christ on a fucking bicycle," I scream as Stef rips the wax off.

"Oooh, come on." I want to slap Stef for her constant oohing. "It doesn't hurt that much."

Before I can tell her to stop, she's applied more wax to the other side.

"Could you—" Another scream comes from my mouth as she rips off more hair. I've never felt pain like it. It's as if pins are being inserted individually along the strip of skin. Perhaps this is what it would feel like to sit on an echidna or a porcupine.

Stef doesn't even react to my screams. The rooms must be pretty soundproof, because no one comes to check if I'm alright. Perhaps this was a common occurrence, though. Maybe the panpipes hid the sounds of the screams of other women.

"Oooh, have you never shaved before? They're coming out so nicely." More wax is applied. It's no longer warm. It's no longer comforting. It forebodes what's coming. And what's coming is more pain.

I'm more prepared this time, as Stef creates some traction before ripping away. There's no sound from my mouth, but my hand flaps in front of me.

"Oooh, you're doing well. New boyfriend, did you say? Did he ask you to do this? If he did, withhold blow jobs. Works every time."

More hair is yanked out. I want to sit up and see how much more she has to go, but I can't move. I'm paralysed by the pain. My vagina is burning up, and I know there is no wax going near the vagina, only the vulva. *What if some has dripped in though?*

"You aren't dripping wax in my vagina, are you?" I ask in a high-pitched tone.

"Honey"—I'm surprised to hear that Stef can start a sentence with something other than an ooh—"we're waxing your vagina."

"You're waxing—" More hair is ripped out. I never realised how much was down there. "My vulva. If you're waxing my vagina, there's something wrong." I pant, wondering how I ever thought I could get through childbirth if I can't manage a Brazilian wax. Perhaps I could major in anaesthetics and provide epidurals for women like me who want to wax their bits, but don't like the pain.

"Vagina, vulva, same thing." Stef waves the wooden spatula in the air as if I were the crazy one. "Now, do you want a big heart or a small one?"

"Just a landing strip." There is no way I can sit through Stef working out angles and shapes. A strip would be easier for both of us.

"How was it?" Val is trying not to laugh as I gingerly walk out the door of the salon.

"I am never doing that again." It feels strange. I'm glad I've worn cotton undies, as anything else might have caused static. "She wanted to wax my anus," I whisper as Val leads us into a nearby café.

"You didn't let her?" Val is giggling again.

"Of course not." My voice is so high, I'm surprised the dogs tied up outside aren't listening in.

"You tell me you're someone who doesn't swear, but hearing 'Jesus fucking Christ on a bicycle' in your high-pitched wail really made me laugh. I just wish I could have recorded it."

"Oh my gosh. I didn't think anyone could hear." I press my hand over my mouth.

"They turned the music up after that. I don't think blondie was impressed." Val has tears streaming from her eyes from the joy she's experiencing at my expense.

"Well, at least I never have to go back there." I laugh to myself as we're shown to a table.

"Janet does her own with sugar. She makes like this toffee, and she and Penny get down, and... yeah, I think it's foreplay for them."

Janet is Val's uni friend, who was also her housemate. Penny is from Cassowary Point and moved to Brisbane after a breakup before falling in love with Janet. I've met Janet and Penny a few times when they've been to Cassowary Point. They're lovely people, but I don't want to think about sexy times involving hair removal from the root. There's no way I'm going to plant that idea in Boyd's head.

I SHOULD HAVE PLANNED my lingerie choices better, but I hadn't factored on feeling so different after my wax job. The lace of my thong rubs against me, creating friction I'm not used to. I splurged on a new dress when I was out with Val this afternoon. It is a deep violet with fluttery sleeves and wraps around me, creating a true hourglass look. I twirl in it to show it off to Boyd, further allowing my underwear to rub.

Boyd isn't letting me head back into the bedroom area though, instead ushering me out the door.

"Wait, I need—" He holds up my phone and my purse and hands them to me. I'm seriously contemplating removing my thong altogether, but Boyd won't let me into the room. It's been a long time since my early lunch with Val, and we're probably both starving.

We've booked dinner at a popular local restaurant that Hillary and Charlie rave about. They, along with Henry and Ken, were the real foodies of the family. I love eating, but I can't really differentiate between all the flavours. I just know if I like it or not. We head down the elevator and out the glass doors of our hotel. Boyd hails a cab, and we both climb into the back seat for the short ride to the restaurant.

As soon as we enter, I can see why Charlie and Hillary would like it. I'm still irritated by my underwear, but the ambiance of the restaurant does help take my mind off it. Starched tablecloths, polished silverware, and crystal glasses adorn the tables, with a real candle burning in a hurricane glass that is surrounded by some foliage. The lighting is soft and the music unobtrusive.

I couldn't tell you what we eat, but it's been delicious. Our conversation has been light and jovial, picking apart the movie from Thursday night, and Boyd is telling me about some of the people he bumped into when out shopping.

We don't mention work; we don't mention babies. We talk about where we want to travel; I pick Bali. Boyd says he wants to see parts of Africa. I was expecting him to say the US. I know he doesn't because it's been a childhood dream to visit Disney, and we said we wanted to take our kids there one day.

It truly is a magical night. Boyd and I make the waiter laugh when we fight over who is paying the bill. We have a joint account anyway, so it doesn't really matter.

A couple of glasses of wine have me almost forgetting about the underwear situation. Maybe I'm just getting used to it.

We stroll from the restaurant along the riverbank towards our hotel. Boyd holds my hand. It's a perfect early summer night. Pausing near a busker who is playing Christmas music, Boyd holds me tight and whispers in my ear how much he loves me. He doesn't need to tell me. I feel it every day.

Emily, Age 20

If you go by tradition, I will become an adult tomorrow. I turn twenty-one and get the key to the door or something.

I've already got a key. We used the uni break to move into our own place. It's tiny. I'm making good money playing piano at the casino, and Boyd flips burgers on the weekend and tries to get a shift or two at the childcare centre each week.

In an apartment block, ours is a corner one that I think was an afterthought. It's up a flight of stairs, which doesn't bother me. You walk in, and there's the world's smallest lounge room. I think you could possibly put a fold out bed there if you were desperate, but only just. We've got a ratty secondhand couch that Hillary and Charlie's receptionist wanted to get rid of. It's grey and looks like the former owner's cats have used it as a scratching post. But hey, it's comfortable.

Boyd splashed out and bought a new television. It's not a big name brand one, but it serves its purpose, which for us, is to plug our gaming console into. When you come in the door, it's like, there's the lounge, and it's, like, three steps until you're in the kitchen. There's a counter with two stools. You can't have more than two people in the kitchen at once, as there's simply no room.

Charlie called it a small house and said it should be on one of those small house programs that he and Hillary like to watch. I actually wonder if some of the small houses on that show are bigger than this apartment.

There's one door from the lounge that leads to the bathroom, not that there's a bath in there, which is a shame, as I love a nice long bath. Then there's the bedroom. It fits our queen-sized bed with room for a bedside table.

It's annoying that there are so few power points, but I've draped extension cords and power boards around where we need them. At least there's a built-in wardrobe in the bedroom.

The walls are this boring beige. Well, there's exposed brick in the lounge and our bedroom. But none of it matters. I've shacked up with my boyfriend, and life couldn't be better.

We're having a birthday dinner at Hillary and Charlie's this weekend. I don't want a huge party. Val's busy with uni, so she won't be here, and I told Giles and Bridget there was no point in them coming up. Bridget's due to have their second child in the next couple of months, anyway. Henry's doing his intern year and says he can't get time off work. I'm honestly fine with it.

The Hartmans can be a lot sometimes. It will be Hillary, Charlie, Mum, Nonna, Boyd and me. Nonna wants to see our apartment. Mum says Nonna has some old crockery for us. What we're using at the moment came from a secondhand store.

People have told us we can't live on love, but I think we're making a good go of it.

Chapter 9

Boyd

I know I spend a lot of time with Emily. I mean, we work in the same hospital, but the administrators have been pretty clear that they won't give us rotations on the same teams. There are days when one of us is working, and the other isn't. If it's me who's off, then I find things to do. I play games; I visit my nieces; I clean the apartment. But I always miss her.

I love spending time with my wife, even if it's in silence, with both of us reading or watching a movie or something. Her presence seems to calm me.

My mum would say I was a hyperactive kid. I was inquisitive, always wanting to know how and why about things. It wasn't ADHD or anything, just that I'm curious. Emily calms me. If she'd been with me on my shopping spree today, then I wouldn't have bought as much as I did.

I'm well aware that Emily and I are different from most of our peers. In an age where promiscuity outside of a relationship is assumed and, rightly so, accepted, we've only had each other. And I don't care. I mean, look at someone like Giles, who was an absolute manwhore when he was at uni. He thought he'd never settle down and that he would be hopping from woman to woman for the rest of his life. And then he met Bridget.

Despite how much I love her and how perfect we are for each other, I'm worried Emily will come to the realisation that I'm not enough for her, and she wants more. She'll figure out I'm too intense or inappropriate and decide there is someone better out there for her.

I wouldn't blame her if she decides she wants to experience what another cock feels like. I mean, I'm pretty confident in my abilities, and I'm all about bringing her pleasure, but what if it's not enough? I could never share her. It would kill me to know another guy had tried to give her the same pleasure I do. But another guy might be able to get her pregnant.

Yeah, I know I might be thinking out of my arse, but it's a concern. We talked about it the other night, and Emily laughed me off, telling me I'm being stupid. I try not to think about my sister's sex life, but apparently, she's told Emily that it's not the cock that brings her pleasure, but the guy it's attached to. I've got no doubt that Emily loves me as much as I love her. Val got me thinking though, and perhaps I can satisfy Emily with a cock that's attached to my hand.

Which is how I find myself in a sex shop. Emily's dragging Val shopping, and for some secret mission that I'm not allowed to know about. I figure I might as well have a secret mission of my own, too.

I'd browsed sex toys online, but I don't know the difference between six inches and eight, let alone the different girths of dildos. I tried to line up photos online, but they were taken from different angles. The descriptions didn't help either.

I know I'm blessed in the cock department. Perhaps Nonna is right, and it is a rooster. Emily claims it's relative to my long fingers. Us Hartman boys all have long fingers, but I've never wanted to think about my brothers' schlongs. Bridget and Ken seem happy, and that's all that matters.

At eleven in the morning, I figure the shop won't be that busy. I hadn't factored that this would mean the sales assistant was free. She looks scary with her long black hair, numerous facial piercings, and black lipstick. Tattoos of serpents and flowers adorn both arms, with what looks like a spider web disappearing from her neck to her PVC bra. Her legs are covered in more tattoos, this time different symbols, including a skull, a dagger, and a pentagram.

I find the dildo section and am browsing. A few silicone cocks would be a good idea, I figure. I didn't realise some would be floppier than others, or that there would be glass ones, too.

"For you?" I hadn't noticed the assistant come up beside me.

"Ah, no." I clear my throat. "My wife."

"This one's popular." She pulls a beige-coloured cock off the wall. "It's average, and most women say it gets the job done when their partner's away."

"Yeah, no. It's for when I'm there. I want her to experience what different sizes would feel like and maybe we'll work up to, I don't know…" I'm never usually this embarrassed talking about sex. "Maybe DP with a toy in one hole."

"Well, if you'll be in her pussy, I suggest a plug."

I never got the assistant's name, but she's good, and I leave with four dildos—including a glass one—and a set of three plugs of various sizes. I also grab a feather on a stick that I planned to use for pleasure. In the past, I've slapped my hand against Emily's arse, but never hard. I wasn't about to start suggesting I whack her with a riding crop or anything. Maybe it's something we can talk about, though.

As I sit in a burger place for lunch, I want to text Emily to see how she's going, but I stop myself. It's important she's able to do things away from me. I hope my sister isn't leading her astray. Val hates shopping, so I doubt they'll spend the entire day browsing boutiques, but with my sister, you never know.

When Val was eighteen, she got a nose piercing. It suited her. One night when she was home and we were having dinner, it fell in her soup. It was during her vegetarian stage, and she decided that the soup was no longer solely plant based, so she refused to eat it, despite what we told her about the nose ring coming from her body. I think she was just picking a fight.

But that nose piercing had been spontaneous. I love the idea of spontaneity, but I often fail at the execution. I go in half-cocked and fuck things up. Maybe Val will drag Emily along to do something spontaneous today, or maybe Emily will drag Val shopping. I doubt it will be the same shopping I've done.

Emily needs more spontaneity in her life. Our lives are currently focused around a twenty-eight-day cycle. Spending time with Val is great, and I'm all for it. I know Emily doesn't really want to move to Brisbane, but she would do it for me, but if we did move down here, she'd have someone to go to the movies with and catch up for coffee.

We rely on each other so much, and I don't think that's necessarily a bad thing. I know Val's always been one of my biggest cheerleaders, and she'll always remind Emily how awesome I am. On the other hand, if Emily decides I'm not enough for her, she'll need someone like Val to be the friend that I may no longer be. I mean, I hate to think about that, but Emily may decide that she will be better off with a guy who can give her children, and that guy may not be me.

When I get back to our hotel, I take my purchases out of the packaging and lay them on the bed. I like the look of the massive purple dildo. There's no way you could get your mouth around it to blow it. I might have tried—just for research purposes—and it would take some working up, but I was pretty sure I could get it inside Emily, and she could feel what it would be like to be really stretched. My cock reacts to the idea.

I hear the door handle turn and manage the get the toys back in the bag and stow it next to the bed.

While Emily takes a bath she won't let me join her in, I line up the dildos on the table next to the bed, along with the bottle of lube the sales assistant threw in. They're all ready for later, I just wish later was now.

I wonder how Emily will react when she sees them. It could go either way. Emily could laugh, and the few hundred dollars I've thrown down in the shop would be wasted, or we'll have a night to remember. Maybe I should have talked to her before I went shopping, but it's too late now, and they're out of the packaging.

Emily's been all secretive in the bathroom. She took bags in with her and told me she'd get dressed in there, allowing me to use the bedroom. I'm tying the laces on my shoes when I hear the door slide open, and I rush to block her from entering the bedroom space.

I almost cancel our dinner reservations when I see her in a new purple dress. She looks stunning. My cock recognises it, too, and stands to attention. She is the most beautiful woman I've ever met, and I'll do almost anything to make sure she keeps choosing me.

DINNER IS AMAZING. Sure, the smells and tastes are great, as is the ambient sound, but it's the touch of Emily's hand and the way she looks that makes the night special for me. We smile and talk about how different Val's graduation was to ours, which, of course, circles back to our wedding.

"I'd marry you again, over and over." Emily strokes my palm as I finish my glass of wine.

"Ditto," I say as I reach for her other hand. "I wish they'd bring the bill."

Dropping Emily's hand, I look around for our waiter. She appears a minute later with a small leather folder. Both of us fight to produce our bank cards, arguing that we've got it and making the waiter laugh. I win in the end, and Emily reluctantly places her card back in her wallet. I open the folder, a smile hitting my face as I close it again before passing it to Emily.

"What?" she asks as she grabs it from me. Emily wipes a tear from her eye when she opens it and reads the note inside aloud. "Happy anniversary, lovebirds. Love, Mum, Dad, Mum, and Nonna. PS- you should have had the lobster." Emily frowns. "But it was a set menu."

"You know Mum. I'm surprised she didn't bet us five dollars there was extra dessert back at our hotel."

"She's probably sick of taking your money." Emily laughs.

The walk from the restaurant to the hotel takes us along the Brisbane River. It's a gorgeous night, warm enough to not need a jacket, but not too warm that we're sweating buckets. We watch a busker play Christmas music on the cello, and I stand behind Emily, my arms around her belly as I hold her to me.

Emily turns her head as we listen and places a kiss on the edge of my mouth. Her lips aren't plump, but they're soft, and I always love the way they feel across my body. Just standing with her, watching her enjoy the music, sees blood flow to my cock. I wriggle so she can feel it against her bum.

At first, I think Emily is pulling away from me, but she simply turns around and wraps her arms around my neck, drawing her lips to mine. I forget we're in public with families around us. The tenderness at which our mouths meet sends shivers down my spine. Emily's tongue probes my lips, and I open, our tongues duelling to be closer to each other.

The music and the scenery don't matter. I just feel. Emily's breasts push against my chest, and my arms draw her closer. The moans that escape my wife's lips only encourage me to continue. I nip at her bottom lip before our mouths press together again. I know enough about where I am to not consider undoing the tie that holds up Emily's dress and pulling down the cups of her bra to suck on her amazing breasts, but the thought has crossed my mind. I'm as hard as I can ever remember, my cock pressing painfully into the zipper of my pants.

"I think I need to get you back to our room, husband," Emily whispers in my ear before she sucks on the lobe, sending me into more of a frenzy.

I don't care that her lipstick is all over my mouth, or that people can no doubt see the tent in my pants. The need to get her back to a place we can be alone is all I care about.

Our stroll turns into a quick walk that almost breaks into a run. I'm glad Emily isn't one of those women who wears insanely high heels, even though it would have brought her to my height. It means she can keep up with me as we move.

When we finally arrive back, we stumble into an empty elevator in the hotel lobby, and I manage to swipe our key to press the floor we need.

"Your beard, my clit." Emily is peppering kisses along my jaw and down my neck. She often tells me how much she likes my facial hair.

"Baby, I'm going to have you seeing stars tonight. You will be drunk from orgasms from my fingers, my tongue, and my cock, plus maybe some other surprises," I whisper. The shudder I feel as she hears my words shows me she needs this as much as I do.

Emily's dress is untied as I open the door to our room. Her purse is dropped on the floor, her dress falling on top of it. In my mind, I was going to take things slowly, but our bodies haven't got that message. A black lace cup is dragged under her breast as my lips attach themselves to a nipple. I suck and lap as Emily reaches behind herself to unclasp the bra before sliding it down her arms.

Taking a few steps towards the bed, I slide my hand down her stomach, under the elastic of her lacy thong. It feels strange, different. I pull away to see Emily smiling down at me, her lip between her teeth.

"You like?" she asks as my hand stills.

I almost tear the lace as I yank it down her legs. "Fuck." My voice fills with amazement. Most of the hair is gone, save for a strip pointing towards her clit. Emily has gone stiff. "Is this what you did with my sister?" I murmur as I stroke through her folds, feeling her slickness cover my fingers.

"So, do you like it?" Emily pauses, her face scrunched as if she thinks I'll be upset at her actions. "It hurt like a mofo, and I'm never doing it again, but—"

"No buts. I love it. I mean, I love your pussy covered in hair, and now waxed bare. Fuck, I love your pussy full stop. How does it feel?"

"Smooth." Emily laughs. "It still feels strange when I walk, and it rubs against my knickers, but it's nice, I suppose."

"Nice? Fuck, babe, it's more than nice."

Lifting her, I throw her onto the bed before crawling between her legs and diving in with my mouth. Emily has the sweetest pussy, and I love the tang of her juices. My tongue takes its time learning the contours of her folds without hair, spurred on by her moans.

I suck on her clit, flicking my tongue across her sensitive nub. Glancing up, I'm pleased to see her playing with her breasts as she stares down at me.

"Keep going," she pants. "You've got the best tongue and the best lips. Fuck, you can eat a pussy."

I slide two fingers inside her, reaching up to find her pleasure spot. I want to reach for one of the toys I've bought, but they're too far away, and I'm not stopping until she comes. Emily writhes under me, her thighs pressing against my head. I'm aware I'm still fully dressed, my cock straining to be set free. But this moment is all about her, about making sure she comes and enjoys herself.

Emily's breath hitches as I sweep my tongue against her again before bringing her clit between my lips and attempting to suck her entire body into my mouth through the precious bundle of nerves. Her thighs grip my ears like a vice before a moan so beautiful escapes her mouth, and her pussy convulses around my fingers. Her fingers are white as they grip the sheets, as if she's trying to tether herself here, making sure she doesn't fall into an abyss. I keep a gentle sucking motion going and flick her G-spot with my fingers before she lets go of the sheets and tries to push my head away.

"Too..." Her breath hitches again. "Too much."

I lift my head and trail my soft kisses across her belly, over both breasts, and up her neck before pausing just in front of her lips.

"I bought you some presents," I whisper as I rub my chino-covered cock against her core, knowing the dark fabric will be visibly covered in her juices.

Emily starts undoing the buttons on my shirt. "Can we just get to the part where you stick that massive cock in me and fuck me senseless?" she mutters as she undoes my belt.

"You mean this massive cock?" I reach for the side table, hold up the purple monstrosity, and wave it in the air.

"Fuck, Boyd," Emily exclaims, her eyes widening. "That could do some damage."

"Maybe this one, then?" I hold up a blue-and-pink dildo that looks like a tentacle.

"How many..." Emily starts.

"Or I'm sure you want to see what this feels like. The glass gliding in and out of your pussy. I mean, I could put it in the fridge and get it nice and cold. Would you like that?" Emily doesn't reply. Her pupils are blown and her mouth is slightly open to let out the rapid breaths she's taking.

"I'm going to start with this one." I hold up the beige five-inch dildo that boasted realistic veins on the packaging. I'm not sure how veins in a cock could be unrealistic, but I'm not a marketing guru. "Is that alright?"

Emily's eyes are wide as she nods rapidly. "Yes," she whispers quickly. "Yes, please."

She pushes herself up so she is resting on her elbows. As I grab the tube of lube, I place some pillows behind her. I don't think she notices, her eyes on the dildo that's lying on the bed between her legs.

After slicking some lube over the tip, I pause with it at her entrance. It slides inside her easily, her natural juices aiding its way. I lie next to her on the bed, half undressed, my cock aching to replace the silicone inside of her.

Even though Emily was adamant the other night that she doesn't need to experience any cocks apart from mine, I want to give her the option without her feeling she can do it without me. I mean, sure, I won't care if she uses the toys when I'm not around, but the thought of her with another man makes me feel sick, and I already feel sick from not being able to get her pregnant.

"How does it feel?" I whisper in her ear.

"Yeah, different." Emily rolls her hips as I slide the toy in and out. "It feels strange having something inside me and feeling your cock against my side."

I'm beginning to think we should have talked about toys years ago, but I put that down to us being so young when we got together. We're learning as we go along, and I just hope Emily wants to keep learning with me.

"But you like that idea, don't you?" I latch onto a breast, flicking the hard nipple with my tongue. "Two cocks at once. One in your pussy and one in your mouth, or even..." I pause as I switch to her other breast. "One in your pussy and one in your arse."

The small gasp and the way Emily's hand reaches for my head, pushing it harder against her breast, tells me I'm on to a fantasy of hers. *I can never share her with anyone, but with a toy? Sure.*

Emily flails under me, lifting her hips to meet the thrust of the dildo. To be able to look at it slide in and out of her, seeing something that's not me, and the way her body flushes in reaction makes me almost come in my pants. I'm leaking so much precum, and I don't think I've ever been this turned on. It takes some coordination to be able to suck and play with her breasts while keeping the artificial cock moving, too. I can sense from her breathing that she is close to another orgasm. My cock is pissed that it isn't involved in the fun. It's desperate to be touched, but the excitement in seeing Emily come undone like this is worth it. With the hand that controls the dildo, I push it in, holding it still, and reach my finger across to strum her clit.

A keening cry escapes Emily's lips as her body shudders with orgasm. We lie in stillness for a minute before I remove the dildo, causing Emily to open her eyes as I bring it to my lips and lick her juices off the tip.

"Would you suck a cock?" Emily asks innocently as she runs her fingers through my hair, pulling out the elastic that holds it back from my face.

"No. It's not something I feel I've missed out on. I just love your taste." I shake my head.

"And I love yours." Emily pushes me down on the bed so I'm lying on my back, removes the dildo from my hand, and places it on the bedside table, before standing and moving to the end of the bed so she can pull my trousers down. She throws them to the ground, my boxers following as my cock almost shouts hallelujah from being released from its confines.

Emily gives the best blow jobs. I mean, I've never had one from anyone else, but I can't imagine anyone else could bring me undone like she can.

"I can count on one hand the number of blow jobs I've given you since we've been married, and that changes tonight," Emily purrs as she positions herself over me and licks the large bead of precum that has gathered on the tip of my cock.

She's right, but I want every drop of cum to be inside her, giving it the chance to meet with a willing egg. Anal, too, has been a regular part of our sex lives, but we haven't tried it since Venice.

My mind tries to focus on Emily's ministrations on my cock. Her lips feel amazing as they suck in the tip, and her tongue, well, that's an expert in tracing the realistic veins that run up the side of my cock. I remember back to the first few times she tried to blow me and how she'd gag. Her mouth recognises my cock now, and she's able to take me all the way down her throat. It isn't something we do every time, but Emily is determined tonight is going to be one of those nights. I can see it in her eyes as she lies between my legs, my cock in her mouth.

"That's it, baby." I let out a low groan. "Take that cock. Fuck your mouth with it."

I know Emily hates when I place my hands on her head when she's sucking me, so I feel for my own nipples, rolling them between my fingers.

"Oh, yeah..." I groan as the pressure in my balls increases.

The back of her fingers trail up my thigh until she finds my aching scrotum. There's something about the forceful way she sucks my cock whilst gently playing with my balls that almost fries my brain.

I've no idea where my brain is, because usually, I can tell when an orgasm is approaching, but this one hits me like a freight train I hadn't seen coming.

"Jesus. Fuck me dead. Jesus. Whoa..." Strings of words escaped my mouth as Emily swallows every drop of my release down her throat. She licks and laps at my cock, gently this time, cleaning it with her mouth, drawing the foreskin back with her hand, and placing a kiss on the covered head before climbing over me and lying next to me.

It's been one of the best blow jobs of my life. I had plans to spend all night fucking Emily, but I'm too drained from her mouth. Emily must be equally tired, as I look over to find her eyes closed and her breath even. So much for pillow talk.

"I love you." I kiss her forehead, and she mumbles something back.

I grab the spare comforter from the wardrobe and lay it over her before removing my shirt that never came off during our lovemaking and climbing in next to her.

There's no doubt I am the luckiest man alive to have this woman in my life.

Emily, Age 17

I finally finished a blow job with Boyd. I mean, it's not like I'd been blowing anyone else, so, naturally, it was Boyd, but, well, you know.

He's always been the one to give me pleasure. He's learnt where to put his lips, tongue, and fingers to really make me detonate. We've tried so many different positions, some great, some, well, let's just say that we've given up on trying everything in the Kama Sutra. I mean, it was a web page we stumbled across, so I'm not even sure how accurate it was, but even the diagrams looked bizarre, and we couldn't get our legs and arms in the right place. In the end, we were laughing so much that the mood was broken.

Today was different, though. I start my final year of school next week. It's been a lovely summer break. Boyd and I spent a week with Nonna at Sailor's Bend. Nonna still goes to mass every Sunday, but she didn't care that we shared the same room. She's so funny. She kept talking about Boyd's rooster, even though she knows it's a cock.

Even though it was hot, she pumped up the air-con and showed Boyd how to make pasta, rolling and laminating the dough. This was all interspersed with stories of her and Nonno. I wish Boyd knew him better. I mean, he met him a few times over the years, but Nonno never knew Boyd was it for me. Well, maybe he did. Nonna seems to think so. She says that Boyd and I have always been destined to be together like her and Nonno. He was her one true love.

I wonder about Mum and Dad. They started out as a wonderful love story. Mum was working in a bakery, and Dad would pop in for a coffee, as his office was nearby. Mum would throw in an extra cookie for him. I remember him always telling Mum he loved her cookies. They'd laugh and joke, and we'd do things together as a family. I thought it was perfect. Well, until it wasn't.

Anyway, Boyd had today off, so we spent it at mine. I'd got myself killed in the game we were playing, but he was in the middle of fighting this weird zombie monster. I mean, it had five limbs and tentacles. I told Boyd I couldn't cope if he had an extra arm, as my body would combust from all the attention. He told me he was sure I'd be able to take it.

He tried to swat my hand away when I trailed my fingernails up his thigh towards the hem of his shorts. I swirled them through the hair he has there before lightly dragging them over his fabric-covered cock. It was hard not to giggle when I felt it jump. I could see Boyd was torn. He was so keen to kill this monster he'd found, and yet, I wanted to play with him.

In the end, he held up his hips and let me slide his shorts and jocks down. His cock wasn't fully hard until I licked up the side of it. I've blown him before, but he's never finished in my mouth. It's always been a precursor to him getting inside of me.

So, I did the swirly thing with my tongue that I know he likes, and I took as much in my mouth as I could. I know from experience that when it gets to a certain place in my mouth, I gag, but I was prepared for that today. Taking it slowly, I sucked as much as I could until it reached that spot, then I eased past it, willing my gag to go away and felt him right at the back of my throat. I wanted to swallow it down until my nose was buried in that small patch of hair at the top of his dick.

I had no idea what was happening on the screen. Boyd was relatively quiet. There were the sounds of the buttons on the controller being pushed, but not in the same frenzied way they had been before I started. The sound of the monster laughing—a deep evil belly laugh—told me Boyd had lost. Instead of throwing the controller away like he usually would, though, he placed it on the arm of the chair and started playing with my hair.

It was taking everything to ignore the gag that was dying to come out. It was like my throat knew that it wasn't usual to have a cock down there. I was so close to taking that last inch and pressing my nose against him when I felt pressure on my head as Boyd tried to push me further down.

All bets were off. I was gagging and spluttering. Trails of saliva coated both his cock and dribbled from my mouth as I tried to gain my composure. Boyd apologised profusely. He wanted to stop and told me he wanted to fuck me. I told him I needed to get back on the horse, and he does have a horse cock, and simply asked him not to touch my head again.

It went better when I focussed on the head and the first couple of inches. I found a rhythm again, and Boyd was hard as diamonds. He dribbled precum into my mouth, and I lapped at it as if it was nectar and I was a bee. When I started playing with his balls, Boyd moaned. It was one of those moans that showed both satisfaction and desire. He jumped when I must have pressed too hard on one ball, but he recovered quickly.

Perhaps it was a testament to my blow job skills, but he lost the ability to form words and tried to pull me away by my shoulders when he was close. I took him deeper and listened as his breath hitched and the first jet of semen hit my mouth. It tasted, well, weird. I read somewhere that I'll have to feed him lots of pineapple. I mean, it could only improve the taste, surely? It was not like I read in Val's books. It wasn't sweet and salty. It wasn't bitter, and it also wasn't the first choice of thing to put in my mouth. Not when there was chocolate in the world.

Boyd slid off the couch onto the floor in front of me and pulled me to him, smashing our mouths together. He would have tasted remnants of him in my mouth, but he didn't care.

So yeah, semen 4/10, deep throating 6/10 and climbing, having my head held 0/10, but the satisfaction of knowing I'd pleasured Boyd and the feel of his cock in my mouth, a definite 12/10, probably higher. Will definitely do it again.

Chapter 10

Emily

"Come in, come in." The salt-and-pepper-haired specialist appears more like a salesman than a doctor, wearing what looks like an expensive suit and a silk tie emblazoned with the fertility centre logo. "I'm Dr Sherman. Now..." Boyd and I sit down on the ornate chairs with carved wooden arms the doctor has pointed to across from his large timber desk. "Referred by Dr. Natalia Asafa I see. Gosh." He looks over the top of his laptop at us. "You're both so young. Typically, I see women in their mid to late thirties."

We've filled out extensive paperwork. Dr Nat had explained that there was only one fertility clinic in Cassowary Point, and the specialists came up from Brisbane to consult and perform treatments. Because of this, there was a waitlist. Nineteen periods have arrived since our wedding. Nineteen cycles of hope dashed.

It didn't scream medical centre when we walked in. It was opulent, with carved chairs covered in soft florals dotted around the small waiting room, and I didn't get the impression one would be made to wait hours to see the doctor here. There were photos of babies in gilded frames on the walls. Instead of a counter, there was a desk we were directed to where we paid the out-of-pocket fee for the consultation. A fee we recognised we were privileged to be able to afford. This type of service would be out of the reach of so many people.

The woman who checked us in left the room, the sound of her heels loud against the marble tiles, before returning with glasses of iced water with a slice of lemon. These weren't any glasses either. I recognised them as Waterford crystal and was amazed at how heavy they'd felt in my hand.

We hadn't waited long at all before Dr Sherman called us back to his office.

"Ah, doctors I see." The doctor looked up from his screen and gave us a weak smile. "Specialising in?" He went back to his computer before we could give our response.

"I'm going into paediatrics." Boyd shuffled his chair closer to mine and reached over to rest his hand on my thigh.

"Hm…" He kept typing away at his screen.

"And GP land for me," I offered, trying to sound saccharinely sweet.

"Not planning on making the big money, then." It is a statement as he looks up from his screen, weaving his hands together and laying them on the desk.

"Well, we can afford to come here, so we're doing okay," I reply as I glance at Boyd, who looks like he wants to be anywhere else but here.

"Touché." Again, we're given a fake smile. "So, unexplained infertility, then. I see your swimmers are just fine, Boyd, and you seem to be cycling regularly, Emily. Any family history of anything that might give concern?" I shake my head. "Right, right. Now, I don't like to presume, but you aren't cousins or anything." He chuckles, almost implying we might actually be related and hadn't contemplated that this might impair our fertility. I feel dirty. This guy gives me the creeps.

"Look, I'm sorry"—Boyd presses two fingers against his forehead and rubs—"but Emily and I would like to find out why we aren't falling pregnant. We're all doctors here, and I think Em and I both have some rudimentary understanding of genetics. Should we be checking Emily's tubes or something?"

"I mean, we could." Dr Sherman sits back in his chair. "But even if we did, and they're clear, then you're no closer to finding answers, and if they aren't, we head straight to IVF. Now, our clinic has the highest rates of success in this state, if not the country. You're young enough to use your own eggs, so that's good. One of the nurses can explain it to you, but basically, you inject hormones every day, we monitor things, and retrieve the eggs under sedation. Boyd, you'd give your sample, and then we'd implant an embryo and wait a couple of weeks to see that it takes. Now..." The doctor moves back to his computer and taps away at the keyboard. "Your last cycle... See, we're only here for a week each month, so we need to time cycles, but it looks like yours will fit in nicely. We can start in a couple of weeks if you like. Candice, my nurse, will explain things to you more."

I don't know what I was expecting from the consultation, but it wasn't this. I'd thought we'd talk about some of our history, that I'd need to hash out my adoption and not knowing about my family of origin. Boyd assumed they'd want another sperm sample. Their website explained that many tests would be conducted, but it seemed the only test they were worried about was that we can afford their services.

"Questions?" Dr Sherman looks between Boyd and me and places his hands on the table as if he's going to stand.

"Do we have to start next month? I mean, can we leave it a bit?" I ask, my voice soft and wary.

"Well, you can, but the sooner you start, the sooner you'll have that baby in your arms. Now, let's go and meet Candice, and she can explain more."

I can't believe we've paid several hundred dollars to spend around five minutes with this doctor. I thought we were meant to have half an hour. On one hand, I'm angry, but on the other, I can't wait to get out of that room. Dr Sherman was more of a salesman than a doctor. Sadly for us though, his currency was babies, and that's what Boyd and I want.

The receptionist from earlier meets us in the hallway and ushers us into the next room to wait for the nurse.

"That was..." Boyd lets out a long breath.

"Yeah," I reply. "I mean, I get it's a business, but..."

"I think he assumed because we're doctors we filled everything out correctly." Boyd sits back in the chair and shakes his head. "Perhaps I should have written we have sex twenty-six times a week or something."

"I'd like to see that, oh husband of mine."

"It can be arranged." Boyd laughs as a tall, slender woman enters the room.

She wears the same white crepe dress that the receptionist had worn with the company logo embroidered on the right side of the chest, but her heels were only three inches tall instead of the five inches the receptionist preferred. Like the woman we'd met earlier, her hair is slicked back in a bun, and her makeup is immaculate.

"Hi, I'm Candice." She carries an electronic tablet, which she places on her knee as she sits across from us on yet another ornate chair. "So, IVF next month then." There's no question in her voice.

"Maybe." I clear my throat, as it feels dry. I would love another glass of water. "I mean, we'd like to talk about it a bit."

"You've got questions then?" Candice crosses her legs and leans towards us.

"I think what my wife means is that we'd like to talk about things together, Em and me." Boyd has once again moved our chairs together and placed an arm around my shoulders.

"I can give you five minutes if you like." Candice makes no attempt to show she's going to leave the room. "But I'm not sure what you need to discuss. We can arrange a payment plan if money is an issue."

"How much are we looking?" I ask, remembering the figures on the website.

"Out of pocket for the first cycle, you're looking at a little over three grand." Candice smiles, as if everyone would have this sort of money lying around. I mean, Boyd and I do, but we've been saving for a house. "We have the greatest first cycle success of any clinic in this state."

"And who are your usual clientele?" Boyd asks as he lays his foot across his knee.

"We have a lot of single professional women who don't have time to find Mr Right. Quite a few same-sex couples too, as well as, well, people like you who haven't been able to do it on your own."

The nurse's words are like a punch to the gut. Technically, I know there's nothing they've been able to find wrong with Boyd or me. I can't take their figures seriously though if they're having success with women who haven't necessarily gone month after month without a pregnancy despite actively trying.

"It won't be next month. I've got a conference interstate," I lie.

"Oh, lovely." Candice's lips turn up, but I don't get the impression it's a genuine smile. "I'll get one of our receptionists to email you the dates for the rest of this year."

Candice uncrosses her legs before standing and opening the door.

We haven't seen any other people apart from the staff during our appointment. The door to the room we saw Dr Sherman in is closed, and I hear laughter coming from behind it; no doubt the people after us.

Boyd grasps my hand and squeezes as we follow Candice down the hallway, and she opens the front door to the centre for us. "I'll see you when we're retrieving those eggs. All the best." Candice grips the tablet to her chest.

I was so glad to be out of the place. If anything, I feel our quest for a child is further away than when we'd entered. Sure, we've been given the option of IVF, but I felt so out of place in that clinic. It's not the sort of medicine I ever want to practice or be subjected to.

"Tell me it's not just me." I turn to Boyd as we wait to cross the street.

"Oh, hell no." Boyd drops my hand, wrapping both arms around my neck and drawing me to him. "That was a sales pitch. It wasn't medicine."

"I can't believe we both took a day off for this appointment." I want to cry into Boyd's chest, but I'm too numb.

Perhaps I've been naïve to think that Dr Sherman would be able to find something that Dr Nat, Boyd, and I have missed. I've pored over journal articles over the last few months looking for answers. I haven't learnt anything new. Based on our ages and Boyd's quality swimmers, I know that there's between a four and five in ten chance of getting pregnant in the next twelve months with no intervention and a six to seven in ten chance of getting pregnant with IVF. Whatever path we take, it isn't an impossible dream. The waiting and endless disappointments though, the hurt each month when we don't make a baby together, it makes that dream already seem so distant. Although I desperately want a child, I don't want to be pressured into it by the slick sales-like tactics employed by the fertility centre. But if Boyd wants to go ahead now, I will.

WE PULL APART as the lights change.

"Burger Bonanza for lunch?" Boyd asks. It's his favourite. If he could live on burgers, he would.

"Sounds good," I reply, reaching for his hand and bringing it to my lips for a kiss.

We make the short walk there in silence.

"Ah, docs." Bruno, the owner of Burger Bonanza, looks up when the bell over the door tingles as I open it. This is more to us than a flashy medical clinic. The place is spotlessly clean, but shows its age with scuffed marks on the linoleum floor, and cracks in some of the vinyl chairs that have been lovingly patched with fabric tape. It has been a Cassowary Point staple for almost forty years. Technically, Bruno's daughter, Heidi, runs it now, but Bruno insists on coming in each day and greeting each customer. "Day off?"

"Yeah." Boyd takes the hand of the older man, who draws him in for a bear hug. "How's Cheryl?"

"You know my wife. She's looking after grandchildren today. Did you hear? We're going to be great-grandparents." The old man beams. "Lulu, I think she's a bit younger than your sister, right? Well, she's nineteen and swears they were using condoms, but..." The man shrugs. "He's no good for her, and I don't think he'll stick around. He wants to go and work at the mines. But hey, we're all happy for them."

I swallow the pool of saliva that has gathered in my mouth. I have nothing against Bruno and Cheryl, who are lovely people, but hearing of a teenager getting pregnant despite using condoms... and yet here are Boyd and I.

"You two will have to get started soon. I mean..." Bruno laughs as he slings a tea towel over his shoulder and hoists up his trousers over a round stomach. "I know you've got careers, but there's nothing like the joy of children. Don't leave it too long. Hey, Boyd." The man's belly shakes as he laughs. "If you need some tips to do it right, I'm your man.

I mean six kids, sixteen grandchildren, and a great-grandchild on the way. I must have done something right."

Boyd pats Bruno on the back and walks us to a booth at the back of the restaurant. It's how I imagined a diner, with stools along a bar-like area, tables in the middle, and booths at the back. The tables are rimmed with chrome, with old style serviette holders and condiments that include Cheryl's famous barbecue sauce.

"Hello, you two." I'd been at school with Mandy, our waitress, who hands us menus. She's Bruno's youngest daughter. "I can't believe you're still together. Wow! Drinks?"

"Just water." I put down the menu. We know it back to front, anyway.

"Coke for me." Boyd reaches for my hand across the booth. "Yeah. We've been married eighteen wonderful months now. How about you? Still with... was it Jason or Jarred?"

Both Jason and Jarred had been football players at school.

"I went south with Jason, yeah. I was going to do hairdressing, but it wasn't for me. So, I had a baby. Jonaquin's five and just started school. I mean, things didn't work out with Jason. I then met a guy at a bar and found myself pregnant again. So, Shanny's three, and she's a real handful. Anyway, none of the baby daddies were interested in their kids, so Mum suggested I come back here, and I did. I bumped into Jarred at the races last year, and we hook up as you do."

Mandy presses her pen to her notepad as she tells us her story.

"As you do." Boyd winks at me. "And how's your mum?"

"Yeah, good. She looks after Shanny three days a week, and I started working here last month. Dad's lovely to work with, even if Heidi can be a bitch. Sisters, hey? Plus, you meet lots of hot guys."

"I'll have the grilled chicken burger with peanut sauce." I push the menu towards Mandy.

"Oh. You're ready to order." She writes it down on her pad, despite us being the only customers ordering.

"Double beef, bacon, and beetroot." Boyd is a creature of habit. I wouldn't mind betting Bruno already told the kitchen we were here, and they've started on his meal.

Mandy reads our orders back to us, spins around, and leaves.

A tear escapes the corner of my eye, and I lift my hand to wipe it away.

"Hey." Boyd grabs a serviette from the holder and comes around to sit next to me. "It's okay." He holds me tight as the tears flow.

"It's not okay." I hiccough as he strokes the back of my head.

"We're together. We're in love. We've got each other. I just wish I could take the pain away." Boyd holds me as my tears slow.

Mandy must have been back and placed our drinks in front of us.

"It's just not fair." I blow my nose into a serviette. "Bruno's grand-daughter, Mandy… they can get pregnant at the drop of their under-wear. Do you think we're not doing sex right?"

"Em"—Boyd chuckles, a huge smile on his face—"I'm happy to sex you up however you want, but I think we know that tab A has been inserted into slot B enough, and you turn me on so much that I've left so many deposits."

"I expected a lecture on lifestyle this morning at the appointment." I take a sip of my water.

"What do you mean?" Boyd asks, confusion in his voice.

"You know, perhaps we should be totally clean eaters, with no processed food and no caffeine or anything."

"I'll give up Coke if you think it will help." Boyd pushes his drink away with the arm that isn't around my shoulders.

"No, not you. I mean, your sample was amazing. You've got great swimmers. It has to be me." I sigh as I admit this again to my husband.

"You can't blame yourself." Boyd presses a gentle kiss to my lips.

I know Boyd never says anything he doesn't mean, but his words are of little comfort.

Mandy is walking over with our lunches, and I try to pull away from Boyd, but he's having none of it.

"So, you're both doctors then, Dad was saying." She places our burgers in front of us, along with a basket of fries we hadn't ordered. "He also says it must be hard having people die around you and the like, and he said that carbs cure everything, so the fries are on him."

People assume work is hard and full of challenges, but life is more challenging at present. Work is simple. I'm in a great rhythm. Currently, I'm in a general medical rotation and see so many varied diseases and illnesses. I work with a great team. In a few weeks, I'll be moving to psych. Henry and Ken are so excited and say they'll make sure I have a great time there. I know it's unlikely that I'll be working with them directly, but spending time with them won't be a hardship. If anything, work takes my mind off babies and infertility.

"Thanks, Mandy, and please thank Bruno for the fries." Boyd smiles at Mandy as she turns and leaves us. "So, what's this conference next month?" Boyd changes the conversation as he picks up a slice of beet-root that has fallen from his burger, placing it back between the buns.

"It's a conference with your cock." I take a sip of water.

Boyd almost chokes on his lunch, and I have to pat his back as he coughs away. "I thought I'd missed you telling me about it, but it was just to put the doctor off?" I nod as I pick at a fry.

"So, you're not keen on IVF?" he asks as he finishes his glass of Coke.

"That's the thing, I am. That hasn't changed," I admit with a sigh. "But there's still almost a 50 percent chance we could fall pregnant without intervention over the next twelve months. I know I really want a baby with you, but maybe we should keep trying for a bit?"

"I really like that idea." Boyd tucks a strand of hair behind my ear, a look of hunger in his eyes. "Fuck, all that sex we're going to have. I want to count your orgasms. I want to give you five hundred."

"Only five?" I bat my eyes at him.

"Six hundred it is, and we're going to start counting them this after-noon. I love you so much, Emily Hartman. Let's get out of here. My cock's got a date with your pussy."

Emily, Age 23

I can't believe it—we're in Thailand. Like, we've left Australian soil. It was our plan for finishing our fifth-year exams. We chose Thailand because both of us love Thai food. Boyd has perfected his chicken pad Thai at home, but tasting it in an authentic café off the beaten track was something else.

There's poverty here I wasn't expecting. I mean, there are tourist areas that are just lovely and places that are opulent and luxurious. We're not staying there, though. We're staying in a little hostel on the edge of a poorer part of Bangkok. Mum was worried we might not be safe, but we both commented last night that we feel really safe.

Today, we took a taxi and visited different markets. My heart smiled so much when Boyd bought bunches of flowers and gave them to people he came across, from someone we found sweeping out the toilet area to our taxi driver to take home for his wife.

Our hostel has a kitchen, and we bought things to throw together for dinner. Neither of us were that hungry after we'd been shown more off the beaten track areas to taste authentic Thai food. It was nothing like the Taste of Thai restaurant back home we often got takeaway from.

The satay skewers are something else. I could live on them, or at least live on the sauce.

Tomorrow, we're visiting a temple that was recommended by our guide today. It's a couple of hours outside the city, and we'll see some other areas. Then on Friday, we'll head up north a bit into some jungle area where we're going to do some hiking. I can't wait.

One more year of uni left. Boyd and I had a great chat last night. Neither of us want a big wedding. We're going to see if we can do it in our uni break midyear. Just a small event with family around the pool at Boyd's childhood home. Boyd thinks his parents mentioned something about a conference in the US they want to go to, but he can't remember if that's in June or September. We also don't want an engagement. We know we're it for each other.

We also talked about family. We both know we want lots of kids. The GP training program is shorter than paediatric training. We're going to try for a baby straight away. I hate the thought of people thinking we're getting married because we're having a baby. I know it's none of their business, but the pressure so many people put on us wondering if our relationship will last. I mean, we both know it will.

If I get pregnant in July and am due in March, then I probably won't start my intern year. If we have to delay the wedding until December (I think Hillary told me the conference is in June/July) then I can start and take twelve months off. I'm not keen on working full-time with kids, but I'll need to for my intern year. It sucks, but we'll get through it.

Boyd likes the idea of calling a girl Layla, which I didn't mind, and I liked Hugh and Eddie. None of these were family names. Sure, we both like the idea of naming a baby after Nonna, but we'll just wait and see. I joked with Boyd that we were probably jinxing things talking about baby names, but he disagreed and fucked me harder. I must admit, I can't wait to be done with condoms.

I really am the luckiest woman alive.

Chapter 11

Boyd

I LOVE SEX. WELL, PERHAPS MORE ACCURATELY, I LOVE SEX with Emily. I mean, sex with myself can be okay at times, but sex with my wife, it's always been phenomenal. Seeing Emily writhing in pleasure is such a turn on. The way her body arches and comes alive as her climax grips her, well, it will never get old.

Twelve months ago, we saw Dr Sherman at the flash fertility clinic in town. It wasn't like a medical practice, but more like how Mum described the day spa she dragged Dad along to for a couple's day earlier in the year. Neither Emily nor I could see the appeal in the lush surroundings of either the clinic or the day spa.

I may have wanted to give her six hundred orgasms, but I suspect I fell a little short. It's not my fault. For three months at the end of last year, they sent me to Sailor's Bend Hospital. They have two wards and an emergency department. It meant that for a few nights a week at least, I'd stay with Nonna. Although I missed Emily something fierce, I appreciated Nonna's wisdom and insight, and, of course, her cooking.

She knows we're trying for a baby. There were one or two nights when I stayed with Nonna, but Emily was due to ovulate, and I hated the idea of missing a cycle. I made sure I got some deposits in early, and once or twice I actually drove the hour and a half home to see her, only to turn around and head back the following morning. Of course, it never mattered. Like clockwork, her period arrived, and her cycle started again.

At first, it was a disappointment that greeted us each month when we realised we hadn't been successful. I hated the days I was in Sailor's Bend and couldn't leave. I wanted to hold her as she cried over missed opportunities.

Emily's taken to reading. Val always has a book in her hand. I sometimes joke that she came out of the womb holding one. She doesn't just read romance either. She's been on a mystery kick recently. Emily was trying to explain the thriller they read last week, which both she and Val hated because, apparently, the serial killer was the least likely out of all the characters and not even a suspect. I thought this would have made a good book, but apparently not.

Movie night chats have made way for book chats, and seeing I don't have time to read, I sit and listen, usually trying to catch up on work. I'm loving the paeds training program, plus it means I'm stuck in Cassowary Point for a while. Emily's chosen to do another year at the hospital. She could have found a job as a registrar in a GP practice, but she said that would be added stress, and she knows what she's doing in the hospital setting.

For Emily, I think reading is a distraction and can take her to worlds that help her forget our infertility. It sparks bizarre conversations between the two women that I often hear part of. Recently, they were talking about phrases and words they think are overused in the books they read. Emily isn't a fan of moist, but Val says the word doesn't worry her. Both hated a book where the author used the term digits for fingers. They laughed and laughed about the female being digitised instead of fingered. I made sure to tell Emily how moist she was and that I loved sticking my digits in her later that night. Yeah, it dulled the enthusiasm somewhat. Lesson learnt.

Some of the things that Emily thinks are far-fetched are more realistic than I think she realises. The phrase that both of them hate is when the character lets out a breath they hadn't known they were holding.

Not being a reader, I have no idea how often this occurs in real life, but it's happened to me when Emily was referred by Dr Nat to a local gynae-cologist, who suggested an exploratory laparoscopy to check her tubes wasn't an unwise move.

Seeing Emily being wheeled away in the blue gown with the mesh hat on her head was frightening. I don't usually experience anxiety. I brush things off as jokes and get on with life. It's too short, after all. But seeing her go through the theatre doors was confronting. Seeing her return to the ward was a relief, but the breath I hadn't known I'd been holding was released when the doctor told us that all looked clear inside my wife.

There were no adhesions, no signs of endometriosis, and her tubes were clear. Emily read in one of the papers she downloaded about inves-tigations into infertility that sometimes the dye they sent through the tubes clear out microscopic particles that might have impeded fertil-isation.

That hasn't happened for us.

"Happy birthday, wife." I kiss Emily's head as she stirs. I've been awake for an hour. Holding my sleeping wife is never a hardship. She looked calm and peaceful, and she fit just right against me.

"You remembered." She rolls towards me, trailing a finger down my cheek, and gives me a gentle kiss.

The morning wood I woke with that disappeared is replaced with a full-blown boner.

"Of course I remembered." I kiss her back before peppering kisses all over her face. "Now, would the birthday girl prefer my tongue on her clit after I've feasted on her gorgeous tits, or is she too horny and wants a good, hard fucking?"

"Yes." It comes out breathy and as three syllables as she hisses the vowel at the end.

Making love with Emily is still no hardship, but it reminds me that as pleasurable as it is for both of us, it hasn't had the desired effect, and we are no closer to picking out colours for a nursery or even choosing names for a baby that hasn't materialised.

At times, I think I'm putting on a brave face, but I try to remind myself that Emily is my everything, and although I still think a baby would enhance our relationship, I believe we can still have an amazing marriage without a child of our own. It's becoming a little harder to believe at times. I've always believed the glass is half full, but I fear the water level is dipping, and sometime soon, I'm going to have to face our reality that we may never become parents.

I'm not going to do that today though, I'm going to celebrate my wife and how much joy she brings to my life.

ONE OF THE senior registrars at work recently became a father for the first time, and he keeps complaining that his sex life is nonexistent. He always looks haggard and moans the baby never sleeps. Emily and I went to their wedding just over a year ago. It's hard hearing him be so ungrateful, knowing what Emily and I are going through.

I'd been bitching about the injustice of it all one evening when Emily suggested we try IVF. Emily was almost overjoyed when she rang the clinic and was told that Dr Sherman was on leave, and we'd have to see Dr Singh. I'm happy we're taking this next step, but it adds a new level of anxiety with it. There will be medications and hormones that might affect Emily's mood and could even make her quite sick. I feel like I get the easy path, and it's my responsibility to remain upbeat and supportive of Emily as she navigates this new adventure we're about to undertake. I'm the duck floating on the pond, looking as if I don't have a care in the world, when no one can see just how fast I'm paddling beneath the surface.

Emily thought I hadn't noticed it was her birthday. And so, here we are, sitting once again in the opulent waiting room.

"Boyd and Emily, come on through." A woman of about Emily's height greets us with a huge grin, her dark brown hair messily tied on top of her head with tendrils escaping from almost every direction. She wears navy scrub pants and a white scrub top with the company logo on it. It's hard to judge her age, but she does nothing to hide the lines around her mouth and eyes that show her propensity for smiling.

"Take a seat and bring them closer together." She closes the door behind us. It's the same room we'd seen Dr Sherman in, but she's brought the chair around the desk and sits opposite us. "Now, I'm Jacquie." She crosses her legs and leans towards us. "I must ask, are you related to Charlie and Hillary?"

"They're my parents." I shrug my shoulders.

It was hard being known as Charlie and Hillary's son. There were expectations that you'd be as good, if not better, than them. Add Giles and Henry into the mix, and I should have felt the weight of the world on my shoulders. I've been lucky though. Studying up here had been right for me, and I was always seen around the hospital as a medical student and not part of the Hartman family. Even though I looked a lot like Dad and had his height—or lack thereof—I didn't look like my older brothers as much and probably got away with much more than they ever did.

"Ah." Jacquie smiles and claps her hands together. "I was a couple of years behind them at medical school. I went to a Women in Medicine breakfast about, what, ten years ago now where your mum spoke. One thing I remember is she was very proud of her kids. Not that you're a kid now, of course."

"Give them a call," Emily offers, a smile on her face. I'm so glad she seemed more relaxed at this appointment.

"I might just do that, but I won't mention I've seen you both, of course." Jacquie's smile is warm, and she seems in no hurry to carry on with our consultation.

"Have you always worked in fertility?" Emily asks.

"Not really, no." Jacquie laughs. "I thought I was going to be an emergency physician, but in my first year of training, I discovered I was trying to make sure I saw the women who came into the department with miscarriages, and I caught a few babies when the mum didn't make it to the birth suite. So, I changed to obstetrics and gynaecology. I worked at that for a few years before I got sick of getting up every night to deliver babies and then working the next day, and I almost fell into this."

She pauses, the smile on her face showing she is recalling a happy memory. "A colleague was going on maternity leave, and I took her patients. They were mainly women who had issues ovulating, so I did a lot of work on that side, and then a job came up in a fertility clinic in Brisbane, and I took it."

"Do you have kids?" Emily asks.

"No." Jacquie takes a breath. "I've never been married or in a long-term relationship. If anything, I've been married to my job. I've got three nieces and a nephew, though. But!" She claps her hands together. "We're here to talk about the two of you. Now, you've been trying to conceive for two and a half years now?"

The consultation took more than an hour. Jacquie answers our questions about how the IVF cycle will work. She said that, statistically, we were 80 percent likely to be pregnant after two cycles, but that included any transfers of frozen embryos. For the first time in a long time, I feel hope. Sure, I'm worried about the effects it will have on Emily's body, but we're doing something, and something is better than nothing.

As a doctor, I've given lots of injections. Probably not as many as your average nurse, but still plenty, but I'm so glad Emily is giving herself the hormone injections, though. Yes, it's a tiny needle that goes into her stomach, but she takes them like a trooper. She says it doesn't hurt, but I still don't want to be the one inflicting further pain on her. The emotional toll is enough already.

She's been poked and prodded, literally. We've had two early morning ultrasounds where they stick a probe inside her vagina to check her ovaries for follicles, making sure there are eggs maturing in her ovaries. They were pleased with the half dozen that seemed to be developing. These were accompanied by blood tests to check her hormone levels. Everything is great, apparently.

Thirty-six hours ago, she was given the trigger injection to bring on ovulation. Having the initial sperm test seems so long ago, but I need to abstain again. It's easier this time, as Emily is in a small amount of discomfort, and even she admitted the last thing she could think about was sex. I'm trying to show her how much I love her by bringing her cups of tea and cooking her favourite meals, but I want to do more, especially when I can see her unease. I feel useless. I just hope this works, because I can't imagine having to go through this again month after month.

At night, I hold her. I stroke her sides and try to remind her how amazing she is. I picked up some flowers after work last night, pink tulips, which I knew she loves, and gave them to her. I even let her win our game of *Mario Kart.* Her smiles show me how much she appreciates these small actions, but they feel hardly enough. I feel hardly enough. Giles seemed to knock Bridget up pretty easily, and Mum and Dad had four kids without help. Why can't I do it?

ONCE AGAIN, we have made an early morning pilgrimage to the fertility clinic. Just as people of faith who attend places of worship on a regular basis believe there is a higher being controlling their life, for Emily and me, it is a team of doctors, nurses, and scientists who seem to hold our future in their hands.

I hold her hand as we wait for her to be called through for her egg retrieval. She'll be sedated for the procedure. Whilst she is doing that, I'd be in another room wanking into a jar.

"It's not how I imagined our kids would be conceived," I whisper as Emily sits next to me in her white hospital gown. I think it's the first time I've been so honest with her, and it actually feels good to voice it and put it out into the universe.

This room is also luxurious. It's small. I suspect they have many individual waiting areas so you can't see who else is here. This morning, though, I've seen another woman walk past our room in her gown.—I presume on the way to her egg retrieval, too.

"At least you get an orgasm out of it. I don't think my body could perform." Emily lays her head against my arm.

These chairs are uncomfortable. They look nice, but there is no way I can have Emily sit on my lap like I want. If our bodies can't join to make a baby, then I want to hold her and show her how much I cherish and adore her. I want to remind her that no matter what happens, I'll love her and that she is the most important person in my life.

"I love you so much, Emily Hartman." I kiss the top of her head and pull my arm around her shoulder. "We may not be making love to make this baby, but he or she will be born out of love."

I have to believe this. It isn't how we wanted it, but at least we have a chance of becoming parents, which is all either of us cares about.

"Emily." A nurse in scrubs appears in the doorway. "I'll be back for you shortly, Boyd." I give my wife a kiss and watch as she leaves.

I want to crack a joke, but I can't find humour in the situation. There's nothing funny about watching your wife become bloated and emotional. They warned us about mood swings, but even without the extra hormones, the emotional toll meant we've both been on edge for over a week.

"Boyd." The same nurse is back.

I follow her down a hallway to the last room. She opens the door and ushers me inside, staying in the doorway herself.

"Now, take your time. There's no rush. Push the button on the handle to make sure the door is locked. Your cup is on the shelf over there." She points behind me. "Wash your hands before you start. When you've finished, come back to the waiting room you were in."

There's no asking if I have any questions, which, fortunately, I don't. I've been wanking for years. It's yet again another palatial room with black-and-white stylised photos of female bodies on the wall. An unlocked computer tablet shows an offering of porn. Yet again, there's one of these damn carved chairs, this time all timber with no fabric trim. Easier to clean, I presume with a wry chuckle.

There's no way I'm sitting on it though. Other dudes have had their bum cheeks on it. I wonder how many guys have been in here before me. This must be called the wank room. Actually, because this place is so posh, it's probably called the Masturbatorium or something.

The issue is, I don't feel turned on. I don't feel sexy. I shouldn't be making a baby by myself. Not that that's what I'm doing, I'm just providing the spunk, and I don't even get to inject it into my gorgeous wife's pussy. It's just another difference in how I imagined life would be. My shoulders sag, and I let out a long sigh.

I stand at the table in the middle of the room. The tablet is sitting there, daring me. Do they leave it on the porn the guy before me was watching, or is there a generic landing page? I open it up. It's part way through a scene with two female porn stars. This definitely isn't the amateur stuff I prefer. Both women have massive fake tits, lips full of filler, long blonde hair, and fake nails and eyelashes. It doesn't look sexy to me. It looks as fake as this whole situation. I know I'm dawdling. They must have an egg or two by now. There were only six follicles on the scan, but they were happy about that for a first cycle. Imagine if we get six embryos. We could have a large family, after all. My cock twitches at the thought.

Ever since we stopped using condoms, sex has been about creating a family. Sure, it's still about love and connection, but family has been our goal. But this really isn't how I imagined it happening, and it reminds me that, until now, we've failed.

The porn is doing nothing for me. I go to the search bar. I read on the internet that some mythical rule thirty-four states that if there is something in real life, then there must be porn made about it. I've never tested that theory. Might as well give the next guy in here a laugh.

It's tempting to find something outrageous to shock the guy who's coming after me—like, literally—but I don't want him to curse me for putting him off his game. He probably feels the same way I do, a loser who can't knock up his partner, like almost every other man before us. It may not even be his first time, and he might be used to this. I'm not sure I will ever get used to wanking into a cup to make a baby.

God, I'm never going to get hard thinking such morose thoughts. Where has the old Boyd gone? The joker who wants to make people laugh. There's nothing fun about this room.

I hope he doesn't have any phobias when I type circus porn into the search tab. The first clip that pops up is perfect. Full clown makeup, big red shoes, a frilly shirt, and a pretty impressive cock. The woman looks like she's meant to be an acrobat. She has a gymnast's body, but enough wrinkles that she doesn't look like a teenager. Yuck. I'd never do that. I don't care what they're up to on the screen and pause it when a guy dressed as a ringmaster enters.

At least I might get a 'what the fuck' from the next guy in here. He can then switch back to the fake girls playing with each other.

I'm not here for the next guy in here, though. I'm here for Emily.

For us. I take the two strides over to the shelf where the plastic cup I need to deposit my sample in sits, glaring at me, almost daring me to fill it.

I think back to the first time Emily and I had sex. It was a first for both of us. Not that I was holding out, but I knew I only wanted to have sex with her. I made great use of my hand until that time. Teenage Boyd needed to be quick, though. I'm glad I've trained myself to last longer these days.

Mum and Dad have always been open about sex. They're still horn bags, even at their age. I must have been about thirteen when we had one of those family dinners that evolved into sex talk. Val was at Emily's for the night, and Giles was getting ready to head off to uni in Brisbane. Dad gave us a monologue about how amazing masturbation can be, and how it can take your mind to places you haven't dreamt of, creating anticipation for when you are with your lover.

Thinking of Dad pulling one off was gross at the time. Hell, it still is, but I need to hold on to that anticipation now. I doubt Emily will be up to sex when we get home. Just holding her will be amazing. Stroking her hair, playing with the short strands on her neck, running my hand down her side and over her hip. We could watch a movie or play a video game. Heck, if she wants to read, I might even pick up a book.

Now we're getting somewhere. I can feel some blood has rushed south. Nowhere near enough to make me fully hard, but enough to start things off. There's a small window in the corner of the room. I pick up the jar and wander over. We're on the top floor of a six-story building. There are apartments beneath us, holiday rentals mainly. I don't need to think of people being around me. The window faces the hills behind the city, the same ones Emily and I like to hike.

I chuckle as I remember the walk we went on when we were at uni. I bent Emily over a log and fucked her so hard, she had splinters in her belly. She refused to let me take her to the emergency department, so I sat at home with a pair of tweezers and eased out those buggers.

Undoing my jeans, I pull my cock from my pants. There are so many sexy times I could draw on to bring it to life. Our first time. The trip to Brisbane where I bought all those sex toys, and we had to pay for checked baggage, as Emily was too embarrassed to take them through security in her carry-on. The time I got to use a toy in her ass as I fucked her pussy.

There are other moments, so many times I've woken up to find Emily stroking my cock. A few times, I've woken up with it in her mouth.

It's not the memories of sexual exploits past that get a raise out of little Boyd, it's the thoughts of future exploits, embarrassing teenagers by having loud sex, just as my parents did, grabbing a quickie at a family function when others are minding the kids, like I know Giles and Bridget have done.

I'm not thinking of sex, though. I'm thinking of the day when the doctor or midwife hands a baby to us, the radiant look on Emily's face as she holds our son or daughter to her breast and I gaze at them like the doting father I'll be.

Little Boyd is hard enough to grip tighter and really start to work. I don't bother with lube. I just want to get this over and done with. It's the image of Emily's amazing breasts nurturing a baby that gets me off in the end. It's not mind blowing or earth shattering. I would have expected more after a three-day abstinence, but it's enough, and there's spunk in the bottom of the jar.

"Swim well," I whisper to the jar. "Go and do your job, and I'll see you in nine months."

This has to work, I tell myself. *There's no way it won't.*

Emily, Age 20

One hour. That's all we got on infertility. I'm enjoying the compulsory gynaecology subject this semester, but I think the syllabus was designed by a male. I had a rant to Boyd after the lecture, and he even agreed with me.

We spent three weeks on the menstrual cycle, including pubescent changes and hormone levels, and next week, we look at menopause. It feels like we're skimming the surface. Sure, I get that we need to do our investigations and learning, but I just expected more.

It's probably because it's Mum's story. She always had painful periods.

I remember her scrunched up on the couch in agony for at least a day a month. I was eight when she had a hysterectomy. At the time, I remember thinking that all women must have had their uterus removed when they finished having kids. I'd dreamt of a baby brother or sister until then, but even at that age, I knew that I'd be an only child.

And yes, I knew I'd been adopted. I mean, I look rather different to both my mother and father, after all. I wonder what it felt like for Mum trying month after month to have a baby. The physical pain she experienced when her period arrived would have been compounded by the knowledge she wasn't pregnant.

In many ways, I'm glad we aren't genetically related. I have regular cycles, with little to no pain each month. There's no reason to expect I'll have any trouble falling pregnant.

They touched on hormonal disturbances in the lecture. PCOS was mentioned. Jemima at school was open about her PCOS. When boys would tease her for being slightly chubby, she'd ignore it. She wore makeup to cover the acne, and she told me how she waxed her arms because otherwise they were covered in dark hair.

It will be women like Jemima I see as a GP. I need to know more about things like PCOS and endometriosis than a few minutes in an undergrad lecture.

Hillary had four kids, but I know the first two were easier than Boyd and Val. Boyd was premature, and it took them twelve months to fall pregnant with Val. I only know this because I overheard Mum and Hillary talking years ago.

Infertility shouldn't be secret women's business though. We didn't even get to talking about sperm counts or mobility or whatever. One in six couples will experience infertility, taking over twelve months to conceive. I looked around the lecture room and figured a few of my colleagues might be in that position one day.

Boyd is such a horn dog himself that I'm pretty sure he'll just have to look at me, and I'll be pregnant. To be honest, I can't wait for that day. I can't wait to make him a daddy.

Chapter 12

Emily

I'M GROGGY WHEN I WAKE UP FROM THE SEDATION, BUT I know to lift my hand and see the number written on the back. We were told before the procedure that they'd write the number of eggs retrieved there so I could see it when I woke up.

There has to be a mistake. There were six follicles, and there's only a number two written there in black marker pen.

There's no pain or discomfort from the procedure. I'd expected there to be some, but they've either dosed me up with pain relief, or my body doesn't mind what it's been through.

I glance at my other hand, hoping there's a higher number written there. Perhaps they wanted me to do some maths? But my other hand is bare, save for my gold wedding band wrapped in nurse's tape. I could have taken it off before the procedure, but I'm so used to seeing it there that I feel almost naked without it.

"Ah, you're awake, Dr Hartman." The nurse walks over and presses a button, causing the blood pressure cuff around my arm to inflate. "Did you see your number?"

"It says two." My mouth is dry, and I croak out the words.

"Two's okay." I feel like I'm being scolded for wanting more. "It only takes one, after all."

The cynical side of me wonders if that's how the clinic plans it—fewer eggs means fewer embryos and more cycles for them to get more dollars from us.

"Is my husband..."

"I think he's finished. I'll call and get him sent in here." She moves to a desk, satisfied with my blood pressure, and asks for him to be sent through.

This room looks slightly more clinical than the rest of the place. It looks like a recovery room with oxygen and suction ports behind the bed and a monitor displaying my vital signs. There's room for two beds in here, but I'm the only patient present.

Sometimes, I think it might be nice to see someone else here, to know that there are other people going through what we're experiencing. Then again, it could be someone we know, and that could be awkward.

Last week, I found a local infertility group on Facebook. I don't use my real name or photo, and my profile is locked down—not that I share a lot, anyway. I don't want my father snooping on me, let alone patients. In the end, I was glad of the anonymity.

There were only a handful of people regularly communicating, and even then, it was more bitchy than not. They complained about this place and its prices, with one person arguing that you get what you pay for, and they have great success rates.

I never introduced myself. There was a long rant by one woman about how doctors are only in it for the money. Her sister's friend or something in Brisbane knew Dr Sherman's ex-wife number three and gossiped that he wasn't making the trip up here anymore, as he had knocked up one of the staff members here.

I've got enough drama in my life without worrying about others. The thread descended into a pile on about all doctors, with someone criticising various GP surgeries in town for not being able to drop everything and see them when they want.

"Hey, babe." Boyd walks in and rushes to my bedside first, planting a kiss on my forehead before pressing our lips together. I hold up my right hand to show him the number on the back. "Two? That's okay. One now, and a sibling in a couple of years. Are you okay? Any pain?"

"I'm okay." I smile, feeling so much better now he is here with me. "I'm just thirsty."

"Can my wife have some water, please?" Boyd looks over at the nurse, who is typing something on the computer she sits behind.

Lowering the bed rail, Boyd sits down next to me and tucks my hair behind my ear. Water comes, and I take a large sip, grateful to feel it lubricating all the way to my stomach. The blood pressure cuff inflates again. The nurse presses more buttons, saying nothing.

"How did you go?" I asked Boyd, passing the water to him.

"It was hard." He sighed.

"Well, it had to be, didn't it? Hard and thick."

Boyd chuckles and shakes his head. "You should see the room. I'm calling it the Masturbatorium. There was another carved chair, this time all timber, but I wasn't putting my butt where other dude's butts had been. There were these stylised black-and-white photos of naked women on the wall, but they only showed the outline of the breasts. Then there was the tablet."

"Porn?" I ask.

"Yeah. I put circus porn on for the next sucker who goes in after me." Boyd smirks, and I laugh.

Someone appears with a tray of food for me. There are dainty sandwiches that look like they belong on a high tea stand, a chocolate chip cookie, and a plate of sliced fruit artistically arranged. A bone china teacup contains steaming jasmine tea.

"Today's sandwiches include a French poached chicken in a light mayonnaise with slivered almonds on rye, and a brie and cranberry on artisanal sourdough. Enjoy." The lady who brings the tray wears the same white dress that seems popular in these parts. She nods at Boyd and me before leaving the room.

"Artisanal sourdough. Well, la-de-dah." Boyd puts on his poshest English accent. "I would have expected a cream cake, perhaps a scone with jam and cream."

I reach for the tea and take a sip. It's perfect. For all the money we've laid out for this cycle, I suppose it needs to be.

"But you got the job done?" I ask as I place the cup back on the saucer and pick up the chicken sandwich. I'm not sure what French poached chicken is, but it smells alright.

"Eventually." There is a tray of food in front of me, but Boyd gazes into my eyes. "I just had to think of you and us. Do you think they've joined them yet? Do you think our babies are sitting in a dish waiting to get inside your gorgeous body?"

"You've got a one-track mind." I smile as I taste the sandwich. It's delicious. "Oh my god, taste this." I hold the sandwich to Boyd's mouth as he takes a bite.

"Yeah, not bad. Better than the sliced cucumber and plastic cheese they give you where we work."

I share the other sandwich with Boyd and give him most of the cookie. I'm not that hungry. All I can think about is our potential babies. It is August, so I will be six or so months pregnant at the Gala next February. I know Mum will be able to sew a gorgeous dress to show off my bump.

"Hello again, Emily, Boyd." Jacquie comes into the room, removing her scrub cap and placing it in her pocket. "So, you've seen your number?" I hold my hand up again and nod. "I'll be honest, I would have liked more, as we had six fantastic looking follicles, but you only need one. The embryologists are doing their bit now, and then we'll keep monitoring your embryos and let you know if we'll transfer on day three or day five."

"When will you decide when to transfer?" Boyd asks as he grips my hand.

"I lean towards day five," Jacquie explains. "You can see the embryonic development better and choose the healthiest looking one to transfer. But we'll be in touch. Any other questions before I let you scoot out of here?"

"You'll still only transfer one?" I ask somewhat apprehensively.

"It's what I recommend. A singleton pregnancy is much easier to manage than a multiple."

I nod. It makes sense, despite how tempting it is to have them transfer two. Getting this far though gives me renewed hope that one day I might hold a baby of my own in my arms. I like Dr Jacquie and her no-nonsense attitude. In some ways, she seems out of place in this pala-tial clinic, but she says it how it is, and in many ways, I put my hope down to her.

"Hi, Emily?" I duck out of handover when my phone rings the following morning, the display indicating it is the clinic.

"Yes," I blurt.

"It's Scott, the embryologist here. Can I confirm your full name and date of birth?"

I rattle off my information. My heartbeat quickens, and I feel my palms go sweaty.

"So, we've got one good-looking embryo this morning."

"But there were two eggs."

"That's right, but only one has fertilised." Scott has a calm, soothing voice, but I'm still on edge.

"Oh." It's all I can manage. I try not to cry as I stand in a public corridor. Fortunately, it's deserted at this time of morning.

"It only takes one," Scott reassures me. "I'll call you tomorrow morning to keep you updated."

I look at the time on my phone. Boyd is probably in handover, too. Even so, I sit on a windowsill and write out a text.

> Hey. Just heard from Scott, the
> embryologist. We've only got one.

People file out of the handover room as I stand, waiting for a reply from my husband. I know he's probably busy. I'm not usually this emotional. It must be the hormones. I keep reminding myself it will all be worth it, but at the back of my mind, I know this cycle will be a bust. A tear runs down my face, and I swipe it with the back of my hand.

"Emily, hey, are you okay?" Fred, one of the senior registrars from our team, finds me in the corner.

"Yeah. Just some family news." I try to smile and hope he doesn't get too compassionate. I don't need compassion. "I'll be fine."

"You can go home if you need to, but I understand if you'd rather be here keeping your mind off things."

I already had a soft spot for Fred, but his kindness in this moment means more than he could ever know. I needed to keep busy, though, to keep my mind off things.

"I'd like to stay." My voice is back to its usual pitch, and I've wiped away all the tears.

"Good. Care to scribe?" Fred squeezes my upper arm.

He's given me a job that means I can listen to what's happening on rounds and type away at the computer. I can do this with my eyes closed. Sure, I'll need to concentrate, but I won't need to ask questions, and it will help keep my mind off things. The intern below me who usually scribes will think all his birthdays and Christmases have come at once, as he never fails to make it clear he hates the job.

I jolt away from my conversation with Fred at my phone vibrating in my hand.

> HUSBAND
>
> Hey, it only takes one, remember? I love you
> so much.

I know Boyd doesn't have the increased hormones racing around his system, but he's his usual calm self. I'm almost surprised he didn't make a humorous quip. Last night, he was going on and on about how IVF was giving all his sperm a chance they wouldn't normally get, as he argued the first spurt was usually the strongest and that would catapult the best swimmers straight into my uterus, and the poor guys that dribbled out at the end would die trickling down my legs.

The way he talked about it had me in stitches, which was what I needed. He tries to hide behind humour, but I know this cycle is just as stressful for him.

Walking behind my team to the first ward we were rounding in, I'm glad I stayed. Sometimes, I wonder if general practice is what I want, as I do like the hospital environment. Then I get rostered on nights and can't wait to get out of the place.

I get to the ward and unplug the workstation on wheels. My password is entered, and the charting program we use fires up. *Let's get this show on the road.*

I'm out of the shower and throwing on my hot-pink scrubs the following morning. I stayed up too late reading last night and will pay for it today. It's a book Val recommended that's a mystery with a twist. I had to know how it ended and was so satisfied when it finished. I can see why she liked it.

Boyd loves it when I wear the pink scrubs. I'm of the opinion scrubs look like the least sexy pair of pyjamas you could wear, but my husband thinks I look hot in them. I didn't stir when he woke and went for a run this morning.

We haven't had sex for five days, which is really unusual for us. It's not that I think he doesn't find me attractive, I mean, he did suggest I join him in the shower when he came into the bathroom and stripped out of his running gear, but I was already dry and was doing my hair. The stress and all these extra hormones floating around my body causing reactions I'm not used to might explain our lack of sex, but I know we need to rectify the situation. I told him tonight was a sure thing, and he winked at me. Now I'm in the kitchen watching that our toast doesn't burn. We really need a new toaster, but I keep forgetting to make time to buy one. My phone rings. It's the clinic.

"Hello, it's Emily," I answer, my words fast and tumbling out of my mouth.

Boyd appears in the doorway to the bedroom, a towel wrapped around his waist, water still dripping from his hair down his chest.

"Emily, it's Scott—"

"Emily Hua Hartman..." And I rattle off my date of birth, desperate to hear how our little embryo is doing.

I put the phone on speaker, and Boyd places his hand on my lower back as we listen.

"You're eager." He laughs. *Yes, I am.* I mean, it's our baby he's calling us about. "It's divided as we expected, and I've spoken with Jacquie. She's going to do the transfer tomorrow."

"But I thought we'd know more if it gets to blastocyst stage." I look at Boyd, who has an unreadable expression on his face.

This is one of those times where knowing a bit about medicine probably doesn't help.

"True," Scott replies, "but we want to give this little embryo every chance it can have. Can you be here at six? I know it's early, but Jacquie said to put you first on the list, as you start work early or something."

For all the lavish surroundings of the clinic and the brashness of Dr Sherman, I like Jacquie and Scott. They're right. I can probably make it to work on time if I have an early transfer.

Boyd doesn't say much as I hang up. He tosses the toast I made in the bin, as it's burnt, and he puts on two fresh slices before grabbing the blender to make himself a smoothie.

The day passes, not in a blur but a bleugh. My mind is everywhere but at work. I feel nauseous, but I know it's a mix of anxiety and hormones. I don't get lunch, but I'm thrilled when Boyd pokes his head into the doctor's room where I'm writing out prescriptions for patients being discharged and brings me a salad from the cafeteria.

"Fuck, I love you." I throw my arms around his neck and pull him close. "You smell sour."

"Yeah, a baby on the ward vomited down me. I changed my shirt and wiped it up, but I must have missed a bit."

"It will be our baby one day, won't it?" I ask almost tentatively, as he holds me close, glad we have the room to ourselves.

"I believe it will be, yep." To anyone else, Boyd would sound convinced of this, but I can hear the slight tremble in his voice. He kisses the top of my head just as Li, another doctor, enters the room.

"I can..." She points to the door, but I tell her she can come in.

"I'll see you tonight." Boyd tips my chin and places a gentle kiss on my lips. "Do I really have to wear the nurse costume again, though? I was hoping I could be the doctor this time, Mistress Emily."

"You idiot," I laugh. "I might have to bring out the whips and chains, though."

SLEEP ELUDES ME. All I can think about is our embryo sitting all alone in a Petri dish. I'm all yawns as we sit in the damn carved chairs in the waiting room at the clinic. Boyd and I are both dressed in scrubs, ready for work. I've gone for the plain navy, whereas he's wearing a top covered in butterflies.

"Emily, Boyd. Come through." Jacquie's lips move as if to smile, but it doesn't stretch past the lower part of her face. "I think you've spoken with Scott on the phone."

Scott's nothing like I imagined. He's an older man with almost white hair, but I suspect he's gone grey prematurely, as his skin still has a younger feel to it.

"It's not good news. I'm sorry." Jacquie leans against her desk as she indicates for Boyd and me to sit. Scott stands in the background. "Your embryo hasn't divided anymore."

It's Boyd who wipes the tears from his eyes. I think I'm more in shock. I feel numb and think that I should be the one crying, not Boyd. Deep down, I never expected this cycle to work, but I'd held out hope. Hope hadn't been our friend since we started trying though, and I feel almost foolish for thinking I could trust it now.

"So, it's my eggs then?" I ask softly, looking between Jacquie and Scott.

"Not necessarily," the doctor says as she crosses her ankles and leans back. "We'll give you more hormones next time to try to create a few more follicles and hope to get more oocytes."

"Sure." I can hear the tension in my voice. I want answers. "But maybe I'm not releasing eggs each month, or our embryos in my body aren't viable. There's probably something wrong with me, isn't there?"

"No." Jacquie stands and then squats next to my chair as she looks up at me. "It's still unexplained. I know you want answers, and I wish I could give you some."

Jacquie pushes up to full height before moving back to the desk, clicking her mouse, and bringing up something on her computer. "I recommend taking a month off, and we can go again in October or November, if you like."

I nod and squeeze Boyd's hand. I hadn't even noticed he'd taken it, but I suspect he's been holding it since we entered the building.

"Any questions, get in touch, otherwise, I'll see you in a month or two."

Our first cycle failed even before we managed to transplant an embryo. Maybe it's just not meant to be, but I still feel the need to be a mother and the want to carry Boyd's baby inside me. Hope may be a fickle bitch, but I need to hold out a tiny bit and hope this was just a snag and not an indication that it will never happen for us.

"I love you." Boyd kisses my knuckles as we exit the building into the warm morning sunshine.

I love him too, but I hope that's enough. Love has sustained us until now, but I wonder if it's enough in the long run. IVF being hard was a given, but I never expected to stall at the first hurdle. I have to keep telling myself the next cycle will be different, even if I can't really believe it 100 percent.

THE LAST SIX weeks have been a blur. Work, sleep, repeat. I volunteer to do a week of night shifts, knowing it leads into a week of nights Boyd's been rostered on to do. I don't think I planned to avoid him, but instead, my subconscious had other ideas. At the back of my mind, I try to push away thoughts that one day he'll wake up and realise I'm not worth it. I've never been one to volunteer to do extra, but I argue we need the money if we have to pay for another IVF cycle.

I love our apartment, but it feels tiny when Boyd's sleeping and I need to keep quiet in the next room. I need to flip my sleep schedule. It feels like the worst jet lag. I'm up and dressed, lying on the couch reading, when Boyd gets home from his first night shift of the run. Something tells me it hasn't been a great night. He looks like shit with big grey bags under his eyes. He left last night with his hair in a man bun, but it's now in a ponytail, strands having fallen loose and hanging limply around his face. Although he left for work in his favourite superhero scrub shirt, he's wearing a pair of hospital issue scrubs.

"Hey." He tries to smile as he greets me, but he simply looks shattered.

"Rough one?" I ask, standing and moving to him for a hug.

It's not the typical Boyd bear hug that I'm used to. I can see that he's had a rough night, but part of me is insecure, wondering if I've done something wrong.

"Yeah." He sighs as he falls onto the couch and toes off his shoes. "Five-month-old drowned in a bathtub. He was screaming, and his parents knew a bath soothed him. The mum was so tired, she claims she fell asleep on the bathroom floor, and her partner found the baby unresponsive, face down in the water. It was a mess."

I've grabbed Boyd a glass of water. Handing it to him, I sit next to him and curl into his chest. He pulls me closer, and my insecurities about him not wanting me dissipate somewhat.

"Then a kid on the ward started vomiting blood. The mum's been saying for days something was wrong, but no one could work out what." Boyd rubs his eyes with his fingers. "Naturally, Pete's away at a conference, and there's no locum cover."

I knew Pete was the only paediatric surgeon on their team.

"So, did you have to send them south?" I ask as I reach over and stroke the whiskers on Boyd's cheek.

"Yep. Which is such a hassle for the family. They've got two other kids at home and no family support." I feel Boyd kiss the top of my head.

"Finally, I was called back to ED." Boyd holds me tighter. "Nine-year-old fell out of a bunk bed and hit her head. The ambos tubed her on site before bringing her in. The scans weren't looking good. I left as Grace arrived and left her to tell the family that Brisbane won't take her because they've looked at the scans, and it looks like she's had a catastrophic brain injury."

I hate that he's had to deal with this. Work has been my place away from stress for the most part, and seeing Boyd so upset makes me want to make it better for him.

"I know you, Boyd." I turn and press a kiss to his cheek. "You're so talented, but even your skills couldn't have helped these kids."

"Hmm." He huffs, and I can't tell if he agrees with me or not.

"I prescribe sleep. I was going to bake a lasagne this afternoon. There'll be plenty of leftovers for you to take to work this week."

"I love you, Emily Hartman." Boyd unwraps his arm from my

shoulders and stands before heading to our room and shutting the door behind him.

Opening my emails, I see one from the clinic. They want bloods to check my hormone levels. I grab my bag and the book I've been reading and head to the pathologist next to the fertility clinic as directed.

Two other women sit in the waiting area when I arrive. One is dressed in a suit and keeps looking at her watch as she taps her foot. The other is dressed more casually, like me. She even smiles at me as I take a seat after checking in at the desk.

"Gina." A nurse appears holding the blood form, and I see the logo from the clinic next door at the top.

"Actually, this woman is in a rush. Can she go before me?" The casually dressed woman points her open hand towards the woman in the suit. The nurse rolls her eyes before coming back and taking the other woman, who is really grateful.

"That was lovely of you," I say as the door closes behind the woman who's gone to have her tests before us.

"Thanks. I get it. I've got the day off and don't need to be anywhere. I'm Gina, by the way."

"Emily. I saw the logo at the top of your form. You're from next door too?" I hope I haven't overstepped.

Gina appears older than me, probably in her early thirties. She has dark, curly hair and an infectious smile.

"Yeah. You too I guess?" I nod. "We're starting our fifth cycle."

"Oh, wow. So, no kids then, I presume."

"No." Gina presses her lips together in a flat smile. "I've taken this term off school. I'm a teacher, and I've well and truly exhausted all my sick leave with egg pick ups and transfers and needing mental health days when cycles haven't worked."

"So, how long..." I ask.

"Three and a half years of IVF. Two years by ourselves before that. My hubby's away a lot for work, and we just assumed we weren't doing it enough to get pregnant. Once, when I was at uni, I had a one-night stand with a guy. I mean, he was the nerd of our class and did the whole 'This is my first time, you're so special' thing, so I let him go bare. Looks like I must have picked up an infection from him, as my tubes are scarred."

"That sucks. Hey, do you want to grab a coffee after this?" I ask as the suited woman walks past and once again thanks Gina for letting her go first.

"Oh, I'd love that." Gina really smiles now. She is such a beautiful woman with a cherubic face. "I'll wait for you."

Gina is called and follows the nurse towards the blood draw room. It looks like I might have a friend.

Emily, Age 19

Val flew out to Brisbane for uni this morning to start her uni adventure. Whereas her brothers all started school a year later than they should have, Val started a year early. She was more than ready.

We had dinner together last night, and Charlie tried to lecture Val on being responsible, seeing she's only going to be seventeen. I'm pretty sure she's got a fake ID, though.

She's going to be living with Giles, Bridget, and Millie. I'm kinda jealous. Bridget announced when they came up for Christmas that she's pregnant again. Millie is just the cutest. She sat, and we played together, and a few times, she fell asleep in my lap. I can't wait until it's me being pregnant.

It's been a really lovely summer. Boyd's been putting in lots of hours at the childcare centre again. I've been playing piano a fair bit, but I decided that it would be lovely to just spend time with Val before she heads south.

We spent hours painting each other's toenails, even though Val complained about it. She's had a couple of boyfriends now. It's strange talking sex with her, knowing I'm having it with her brother. We laughed when Val said she was going to get an arrow tattooed on her, pointing to her clitoris.

It made me glad that Boyd took time to learn about me and my body and what turned me on. Well, he still does. We still discover new things.

Our uni breaks this semester aren't in the same week, so we won't really be able to catch up. Val's hoping to get a job down there. I've helped her send off lots of letters applying for things. She even sent one to the manager of a bookshop she loves to visit, telling them they need to employ her. I wouldn't put it past Val to just turn up and start working there and force them to take her on when she sells so many books.

I'm really going to miss her. We had lots of deep conversations about things these holidays, too. She understands why I don't want to contact my dad and meet my brother. We even talked about doing a DNA test to see if I have any biological relatives around.

It's not something I'm keen to do. Mum's done it, and it shows she's got lots of relatives in Italy. It was hilarious—she took the results to Nonna, who said that she recognised a lot of them, and they rang her brother to confirm.

They're my family. I don't feel Chinese, even though I look it. I'm not sure I feel Australian half the time either, because I look different. It's so weird. Dad's parents died before I was born, and he'd been an only child.

It's hard having all these really lovely childhood memories of my father and then he went and undid them all with what he did. He broke my mother's heart and mine along with it.

Val says she still doesn't believe it, because she has the lovely memories of him, too. It's strange to see how he had us all fooled.

I cried when Val left this morning. She didn't want me to come to the airport. Charlie and Hillary are heading down for the week to settle her in.

My mind's all over the place this afternoon. Val's been my bestie for so long, and now we'll be living in different cities. She's promised me we'll still text each other every day, and one night a week, we're going to watch a movie together online and critique it.

There are some people I get on alright with at uni, but I wouldn't call them friends. I couldn't tell them about my father and his evil ways. They don't know me like Val does. Boyd told me he'll be my best friend. I mean, he's already one of them. I'm not going to go looking out for someone to replace Val. I mean, that's not even remotely possible, but I might go for coffee with some of the other med students once in a while.

Oh, man! I just got a text from Val—she forgot to pack her laptop charger and wants me to post it. She really would forget her head if it wasn't screwed on right. I really am going to miss her.

Chapter 13

Boyd

I'm angry. In fact, I'm fucking fuming. I want to throw things and punch things. We should be parents by now. Fuck, we should have had our second baby if things had gone right. Emily and I are good people. We haven't killed kittens or been playground bullies. We're both kind and caring individuals who are pretty talented doctors, even if I say so myself.

I feel medicine is failing us. It's much easier to blame that than to think there might be something wrong with either of us.

We should have gotten more eggs at the retrieval stage, and we should have had more embryos develop as they should. And yes, we definitely should have had one transferred and be pregnant.

But we're not.

So many should haves.

So much disappointment.

I've chosen to work with sick kids, but that means I spend a lot of time working with deadbeat parents. We had a kid this week who was really sick with pneumonia, and her parents left her for the day in the hospital so they could see a movie and have dinner together. Like they saw the hospital staff as free babysitters.

Sure, I get that it's important to maintain your relationship when you're a parent, but when your kid is sick, you drop everything for them. Well, that's what I'll do.

I have to keep telling myself it will work sometime. Dr Andrews, my new consultant who still tries to get me to call him Kevin, told me this week I seem a lot more mature recently. I think it's because I know I have to be more grown up to be a dad. Sometimes, I consider it's the universe telling us we aren't ready to have kids because we act like kids ourselves.

Then I treat a kid whose mum was a kid when they were born. It's just not fair.

Emily and I have had a few scares over the years. There was one time when we were really irresponsible and had sex without a condom. I'd run out. I wasn't going to fuck her, but hormones took over. My sperm was probably pretty weak by this stage, as I had already come several times over the previous twelve hours.

We would have made the most of it, though. I would have delayed going to uni to look out for a family. Another time, we had a condom break. It was a few days before Emily's period was due, so we thought little of it, but if it had happened in a fertile window, we would have again relished the opportunity to welcome a baby into our family.

It's like the universe looks at us now though and laughs. It's telling us we aren't good enough. I want to be good enough. I want to make Emily the mother she's always dreamt she'd be.

"Hey, you're home early." Emily walks in the door and dumps a bag of groceries on the bench before heading over to me on the couch, leaning down, and giving me a kiss.

I want to look down her shirt at her tits, but I stop myself, telling myself I need to be more grown up.

"I'm home on time for once." I laugh as she returns to the kitchen to put the groceries away.

"Were you reading?" she asks as she places fresh bananas in the fruit bowl.

"No, just thinking." I try to force a smile. Fortunately, Emily is focussed on putting away groceries.

"How was work?" She grabs the rice cooker from the cupboard next to the stove and places rice and water in it before hitting the cook switch.

"Yeah, not too bad. I was in clinics this afternoon, which was a pleasant change." I get up from the couch and move behind her in the kitchen as she grabs a chopping board and a head of broccoli. "I thought I was cooking tonight."

"Yeah, sorry." Emily doesn't stop to lean back into me like she always does. Instead, she keeps chopping and adding the broccoli to a small bowl before peeling and mincing some garlic cloves. "I stopped at the shops to grab bananas, and the broccoli was on special, and I knew we got the beef out of the freezer, so I thought I'd cook beef and broccoli. I mean, I know how much you like it."

It's true. I do.

"I can cook it. How about you sit down and relax?" I reach for the ginger, but Emily pushes me away.

"No, I'm good." Emily looks anything but good. I mean, she looks as fantastic as she always does, but she seems tense, her shoulders tight and movements jerky. "Fuck."

Emily rarely swears. I look down to see blood on the chopping board. I guide her to the sink and run the tap, rinsing the small cut. I find a plaster in the bottom junk drawer and wrap it around her finger, placing a tender kiss on top of it.

"I hate to tell you, but nothing in the literature says a kiss helps heal wounds," she snarks as she snaps her hand away and moves back to the board.

"Emily." I twist her to face me, my arms on her upper arms. "Let me cook dinner, okay? I wish we had a bath you could soak in, but why don't you go and sit on the couch and watch me work? If you're lucky, I'll try to flex my muscles for you."

I know why she's snarky. She starts her hormone injections tomorrow. This cycle has come around quickly. I hoped beyond hope that, somehow, magically, she would conceive last month. Her period was even late for once, but I suspect her natural cycle was thrown out from the hormones the month before.

"Look, I know you're trying to help, but I need to keep busy, okay?" She turns back to the chopping board.

"Then shoot some zombies, or call Val or Gina." I move her away from the bench, and she takes the few steps before she flops onto the couch and grabs a remote for the gaming console.

The soundtrack to the game and the exploding squelch I know is zombies having their brains blown out is almost relaxing as I prepare the rest of the ingredients needed for our meal.

"Take that, motherfucker," she growls. I smirk as I look over and see her engrossed in the game. I'm hoping she can let out some aggression. We're both angry and uptight, and that's not like either of us.

Emily met Gina a couple of weeks ago, and they've caught up for coffee a few times. This weekend, we're going on a double date with Gina and her husband, Damo. Apparently, no one calls him Damien, apart from his mother. I'm glad she's got someone she can share the trials and tribulations of IVF with. It seems like Gina and Damo have had a rougher time than us. Let's hope this cycle works for all of us.

We eat dinner in silence, sitting on the couch. Emily is still playing her game, forking food into her mouth between her aggressive moves on the screen. Usually, I'd be turned on watching her like this, but I know she's doing it to escape and to get out of talking to me.

It's not like we really ever fight. Seriously, this infertility shit is the first bad thing that's happened to us as a couple.

Emily finishes her dinner long after me, held up by the game. I'm glad she has something to distract her, but at the same time, I'd love to hold her. She moved away when I first sat on the couch and swatted my arm when I tried to put it around her shoulders.

With dishes washed and leftovers packed away to take to work for lunch tomorrow, I head to the bedroom to catch up on some journal articles. I grabbed a quick shower when I got home, as I always do, but Emily is still sitting in her scrubs. I hear her cuss at the television and cheer when she clears a level.

Usually, this is a game we play together, but tonight, it's just her. It's been a few days since we've had sex, which is really unusual for us. I've tried to rationalise that our rosters have been all over the place, but deep down, I'm worried about the toll IVF is taking on our relationship. I'm looking forward to this weekend though when we both have two days off together. Maybe we'll be able to spend Saturday in bed. Fuck, I love the idea of that.

I WAKE up alone in bed. Reaching over, Emily's side is cold and doesn't look slept in.

Flinging my legs over the side of the bed, I stand and yawn. It wasn't the best night's sleep. I look at my watch, and I still have time to go for a run. In my mind, I know it's the right thing to do and will set me up for a good day, the rush of endorphins and stuff, but I'm really lacking the enthusiasm.

As I open the bedroom door, I see Emily asleep on the couch, still dressed in her scrubs from yesterday. The television is still on, which means she's been playing most of the night, as it turns itself off after two hours. I take a deep breath and try to calm myself. Sure, I'm pissed she stayed up gaming all night, but we've both been so stressed, and me going off at her won't help the situation.

"Hey." I brush a strand of hair back from her face as I kiss her forehead. She barely stirs. "You planning on going to work today?"

"What time is it?" she mumbles, her voice sounding hoarse, no doubt from yelling at zombies for most of the night.

"It's just gone six. I thought about going for a run, but I'd rather take a shower with you." She pushes me away as she goes from lying to sitting. I'm trying to be supportive and not read anything into her actions apart from exhaustion and stress, but it's bloody hard. "How was the game? You looked like you were really into it."

"Yeah." She yawns. "I finished it." She stands and walks to the bathroom. No kiss for me, and no real greeting.

It's so unlike Emily. I mean, sure, she's super stressed. We both are. Each cycle of IVF costs a lot of money, even though the government subsidises part of it through the national health plan. I don't think either of us was prepared for the emotional stress we'd be under. Getting pregnant and having a baby was meant to be easy, and this is anything but.

I hear the shower running and go to open the bathroom door, but it's locked. We never lock the door. Confusion bubbles through me as I wonder what Emily is thinking as she stands under the running water.

Emily has Gina now to talk to, but I have, well, no one, really. I don't want to talk to Giles or Henry about our struggles. They won't get it. I don't think I'd get it if I wasn't going through it. Ken's lovely, but he'll only tell Henry, and it would be a disaster if the Hartman family found out what we were going through. I can hear the jokes now, and Mum would be placing these stupid bets that the next cycle would work.

Dad might understand, but he'd tell Mum. They share almost everything. I'm still surprised he didn't tell her about our wedding.

There are no eggs in the fridge, otherwise, I would have cooked breakfast for Emily. Instead, I make a larger than usual jug of smoothie, adding in lots of bananas and blueberries, as I know she loves both.

She strolls naked from the bathroom, and my cock rises instantly. "I'm going to call in sick. I haven't slept enough to be safe." She takes a sip of the smoothie I push towards her and leaves it on the bench as she grabs her phone from next to the couch. Her fingers fly furiously across the screen as she types a text to her boss. "Night." She hardly looks at me as she goes into the bedroom, and I hear the rustle of the sheets as she climbs into bed.

My cock doesn't get the message that she's gone to bed to sleep, though. I head to the shower and end up tugging one off as I think about my wife, her lips wrapped around my cock as she kneels in front of me. Shit, it's been ages since she gave me a blow job. I have plenty of memories in my spank bank though, and I call up plenty of them.

The water sluices over my back as I tug faster and faster, fisting my cock harder. I grunt as I watch the ropes of cum flow down the drain. There's a relief of sorts, but it's not the relief I'm after. I know I get greater relief if I come knowing Emily has gotten off, too. Solo sessions aren't the same anymore.

Emily's out cold in bed as I dress and head off to work. I leave a Post-it note next to her bed asking her to text me when she's awake, as I want to make sure she has lunch delivered. For a brief second, I contemplate taking the day off to spend with her, but I want to keep my sick days for our IVF cycle.

I close the door softly behind me and head to work early. There's always something I can do to catch up on things. Things that might help me take my mind off my wife and what we are going through. Things that will stop me wondering what will happen if we have another failed cycle. Things that will make me not focus on the fact that we may never have kids at all.

> **WIFE**
>
> Texting as directed. Who says I want lunch delivered? Presumptuous much?

Fuck. Her mood hasn't changed. I've never known her to be so snarky. I have to convince myself it's the hormones and this isn't a side of Emily she's been able to hide for all these years. Even when her dad left, she didn't talk to people like this.

> Hey. Hope you slept well. I didn't think you'd want to risk being seen in town. I thought I'd get a laksa delivered from that place we like.

> **WIFE**
>
> I was going to head out and have lunch with Gina.

I pause. She's been so volatile over the last day. I know it wouldn't help to tell her she needs to be saving her sick days in case we need more IVF and she needs more time off work, but even I know that won't help. Being seen at a café in town having lunch with a friend when you are supposedly sick could cause warnings at work.

> How about I order lunch for her too?

> **WIFE**
>
> Hold on.

I wait for a minute, glad I'm just catching up on notes and not in the middle of seeing patients. I shake my head and can't really believe she's being so selfish. This is not the Emily I know and love. I signed up for better or worse, and this is definitely the worst we've experienced in our relationship.

WIFE

She'll have a chicken laksa and said she'll pick them up on the way.

I love you. If you want me to come home early to help with your needle, I will.

WIFE

I'll be fine.

I hate text messages. I couldn't read the tone behind them, and Emily knows how much I hate the word 'fine,' as it rarely means you are indeed okay. But I couldn't spend any more time checking what was wrong with her, because I was at work and needed to focus.

"Hey, Hartman." Dr Andrews appears in the doorway to the room where I am working. "Your sister-in-law's delivering twins, and I'm the second paed in there. Thought you might like to come, too."

"Don't let Bridget hear you talking about delivering twins—you'll get her pizza lecture." I chuckle as I log off the computer.

I'm in two minds. When a consultant offers you an opportunity like this, you grab it with both hands, but the thought of seeing someone giving birth, knowing it wasn't my wife, isn't high on my agenda for the day.

"I just need to order some lunch for Emily. She's off sick today," I say as I order on the app on my phone. "I don't usually sit on my phone all day."

"I know that, Boyd. You're doing well. Is Emily okay?"

"Yeah, she will be." I had to hope she would.

"Dr Hartman." I nodded my head as we walked into the operating room where the woman had been moved to deliver, causing Bridget to shake her head.

"Well, hello, Dr Hartman." She laughs as the labouring mother pauses between contractions.

"Is that your husband?" the partner of the woman asks, wiping his partner's face with a damp cloth.

"No, brother-in-law. My husband's a cardiologist, and I don't think Lou here will need his services. Is that another contraction? Right, bear down again, Lou. You're doing so well." Bridget coaches as her consultant stands behind her.

I look around the room. There are six doctors here and three midwives. This poor mother.

"We've got a head, Lou, and it's bald like its daddy." The man squeezes his partner's shoulders as she grips his hands. Would this ever be me supporting Emily like this?

"That's it, one more push." The baby appears, small and covered in vernix, which looks like white goo, but it's crying, and Bridget seems relaxed as she clamps the cord. "Right, Dad, do you want to cut?"

I'll never forget the tears in his eyes as he separates his son from his wife. The baby cries and is handed to his mother, who is also in tears.

After a minute, the other paediatric team takes the baby and starts their checks.

"Right, so twin two, who must be our little girl, is exactly where we want her, Lou. You're going to be just fine, and so is she," Bridget announces after examining Lou.

It doesn't take long until the second twin arrives, but this time, it's blue. Dr Andrews steps in and takes the baby, suctioning its nose and mouth and putting some oxygen over them once they are clear. It doesn't take long to pink up and a loud scream erupts from its lungs, causing Mum and Dad to hug each other and cry even more.

"You hand him to them." Dr Andrews smiles as he passes the baby to me.

"Um, unless you've got another one in there, it looks like the sonographer got something wrong." I pass the baby to his mother.

"It's... it's a boy." She looks shocked. "How could he have hidden that penis in the ultrasound?"

"So, not going to be a Grace then?" Bridget asks as she delivers the first placenta.

"No. Twin one will still be Harrison, but we didn't have a second boy's name." The father holds the second twin as the mother holds the first.

"There are a few men in the room to give you inspiration." Bridget looks at us. "There's Duong, who was one of your midwives, and Kevin and Boyd, who looked after twin two."

"What about Jack, after Dr Jacquie? I mean, she really made this all possible." Lou turns to her husband, and my ears prick up.

I never considered that these babies weren't conceived naturally.

"I like that." Lou's partner kisses her before placing a kiss on baby Jack.

"Are these your first children?" I ask as Kevin finishes up some paperwork that I could have done.

"Yes." Lou beams. "We've been trying for three years. This was our fourth IVF cycle. We had to argue about having two embryos implanted, but they were our last two. I think they were both meant to be."

I didn't realise how much I needed to hear this. Sure, it had taken four IVF cycles, but this couple hadn't stopped, and they'd been blessed with twins. I had to hold on to hope that things would work out for Emily and me.

Convinced both babies were well, Kevin leads me away from the delivery room and promises someone will be there to see the babies in the morning—probably me.

I STOP at the florist on the way home from work. I bought Emily a plant once, but we killed it within a month. If plants are going to die under our watch, I might as well grab flowers that will meet a similar fate. I didn't dare tell Giles about buying a plant, as he still raves on about the damn plant he bought Bridget when they were going out that thrives in their lounge room.

There are no tulips today. There's a single sunflower in a vase, but it looks huge, and I'm not sure it will fit in our small apartment. My eyes land on a bunch of mixed gerberas. Their bright colourful petals scream sunshine and happiness. There's red, yellow, orange, and pink in the vase on display, and I decide to take it as is, vase and all.

The florist wraps cellophane around the vase and ties a large bright-yellow ribbon around the arrangement. She's tipped out most of the water already, and she places the vase in a box, propped up with packing materials, so it will make it home in my car. I still drive carefully. It would be just my luck to brake suddenly and for the flowers to go flying and end up crushed.

This evening can't be worse than the last. Perhaps we were lucky last cycle that Emily didn't really seem to react to the hormones she was on. I know they're going to increase the dose a bit this month in the hope of growing more follicles and harvesting more eggs, so there might also be more side effects.

I don't know what's going to greet me as I slide my key in the door. I take a deep breath and exhale it slowly, before turning the key and pushing open the door.

The smell of lasagne greets me as soon as I enter. Emily bursts into tears as she sees me entering, hiding my face with the flowers. I place them on the kitchen bench before taking my wife in my arms. She feels like she belongs here, and I hope she realises this. I'll let her hit and punch me both with her fists and with words if it helps her get through the pain and suffering an IVF cycle throws at us.

"Hey, it's okay." I stroke her hair as she sobs into my scrubs. I don't think there's anything gross on there today, but working with kids, you never know.

"I'm such a bitch." She sobs as she grips me tighter, as if I'm going to run away.

"No, you're not." I tighten my hold too, to help her realise that I'm not going anywhere.

"Last night though." She sobs again, and I can feel her tears have seeped through my shirt to my chest. "I didn't even give you a kiss."

"Relax, woman." I try to sound upbeat, but as soon as the words escape my mouth, I'm ready for her to explode again.

"I'm going to try." She gives a solitary chuckle, and I'm glad she doesn't take offence.

"Yeah? How was Gina?" We still stand in the lounge room, holding each other tightly.

"Yeah, good. She says thanks for the laksa and looks forward to meeting you tomorrow night."

"Here." I pull away from her and place the vase in her hands. "They didn't have tulips, but these looked nice and bright."

"They're beautiful." Emily leans around the flowers and kisses my cheek. "Would you mind if I put them next to the bed?"

"Does it mean you'll spend more time in there with me over the weekend?" I ask, wiggling my eyebrows.

"That could be arranged." She laughs as she takes the vase into the kitchen and fills it with water before heading to our bedroom.

I let out an enormous sigh, glad that some semblance of the Emily I know is back.

Emily, Age 24

I'm getting married tomorrow. Finally, I'll be Dr Hartman legitimately. Well, I've been legitimate for the last six months, not that we've told anyone. I wanted my graduation certificate in the name Hartman, and I knew that couldn't be done unless we were married, and we weren't getting married until a couple of days before graduation, so I changed it legally at the courthouse.

I would have married Boyd whilst we were there, but I know our families would have been disappointed. I think I would have been disappointed, too. When we marry tomorrow, our family will be there witnessing our love for each other.

In the morning, I'm dragging Val to Gloria's salon. She's been around Cassowary Point for years and does relaxing pedicures, amongst other things. I'll tell Val when we're there about the wedding and how we want her to be my bridesmaid. Boyd still hasn't worked out which brother to ask to be his best man. Knowing him, he'll make them earn it.

From early on, I knew I was going to marry Boyd. We hardly ever fight. If we do, it's over trivial things, and we make up on the spot. I can't think of one major disagreement we've ever had. There are so many people who've doubted our love over the years. They don't believe in childhood sweethearts or something, but they think we'll fail.

I can't wait to show them. We'll be the ones in the old age home together reminiscing about the people who thought we'd never last.

It doesn't worry me that I'll have the same penis forever. Boyd's penis is exceptional, after all. Fuck, he knows how to use it so well. Our honeymoon is going to be epic. With the pressure of final year, we've had fewer sexy times than in the past, but I'm pretty sure we'll be fucking like rabbits for the next while at least.

Plus, super exciting that we won't be using condoms. We both want a baby. I don't care taking time off from my intern year. It's a quicker path to general practice, and I can do it part-time to raise a family at the same time.

To think that this time next year, we might celebrate our first anniversary with a baby. It's so exciting to dream about. I know it might not happen the first month, but it wouldn't surprise me if it does. I'm sure Boyd has the most amazing sperm, and they can't wait to swim inside me and impregnate me.

The thought of baby making sex is really arousing. Boyd's already told me he's going to clean me up after he comes in me.

I think Mum suspects something. I got her to sew me a stunning red dress. It's floaty and ethereal, with red chiffon trailing behind. I figure I might alter it to wear to one of the Hartman's galas one Valentine's Day. I wouldn't be able to do that with a white wedding dress.

The plan was to change out the purple streak in my hair for red, but I ran out of time. Purple goes with red, after all.

We fly out to Italy next week. It will be a long flight, but it will be exciting. I'm looking forward to meeting members of our Italian family. Nonna has been talking with her brother, Gio, and he has arranged so much for us. We'll spend Christmas with them and then New Year in Venice. I know, romantic, much?

I probably won't be drinking, because I hope to be pregnant. Even so, fireworks from a gondola with Boyd next to me—sign me up.

We're going to have the best life together, Boyd and me. I can feel it. He loves me, and I love him. If something pops up, then I know we'll handle it together. He says I'm his always and forever, but he's also my forever and always.

I can't wait to be his wife and to experience how wonderful life together will be. It will be amazing, of that I'm sure.

Chapter 14

Emily

Until now, I've never been subjected to cyclical mood swings. Well, fuck my life. Or perhaps more pertinently, I'm fucking the lives of those who come into contact with me. I had to start this cycle by taking the pill for ten days. Just popping this tiny tablet every morning screwed with me. I shouldn't be taking contraception in order to become pregnant.

The night before I started my hormone injections, I acted like an absolute bitch. Poor Boyd. He tried to calm me and encouraged me to shoot some zombies, but I got carried away. I mean, it's probably not a bad thing my mind was taken elsewhere, but it meant I got little sleep, determined to finish the game once and for all.

I finished it somewhere around five. It was stupid of me. I had to take the day off and use up a sick day that I might need later on. The guilt from calling in sick was only marginally less than the guilt of making Boyd put up with my sourness the night before.

This morning, I'm sitting again at the damn fertility clinic. The chairs are uncomfortable, and I feel so bloated. My blood's been drawn, and I'm waiting for the ultrasound to count the follicles. There had better be more than six.

Gina's coming in later. It's been lovely getting to know her. Boyd and I had dinner with her and Damo last Friday night. I'm not sure about Damo. I put it down to the hormones, but I thought he was staring at me for too long on several occasions. Then he kept knocking my leg under the table and not even apologising. Boyd thought he was nice enough, but I can't see the two of them getting together and having chats about life, the universe, and stuff.

Damo seemed shocked when Boyd said he relaxes by playing video games. I mean, Gina's thirty-three, and Damo's a couple of years older than her, but he looked at both of us as if we were teenagers. He also stared in disbelief when Boyd said he didn't play golf, as if every sane person plays that stupid game. I must have been influenced by the hormones, because Gina loves him and keeps saying what a lovely bloke he is.

"Emily," a nurse in white scrubs with an immaculate bun and makeup calls me back. I haven't met her before. She saunters down the corridor as if she's on a catwalk, even though she's wearing Crocs. I feel like a slob next to her in my navy scrubs. The top has some faded spots on the bottom from where I tried to get something out of them with the wrong laundry product. I never got around to taking up the legs, and the backs are frayed from dragging along the ground. I need to do some laundry, which is why I had to settle for this pair this morning.

I'm led to a room where I change into the fabric gown and remove my underwear, and the nurse is back after a minute or two to take me to the ultrasound room.

"Morning, Emily. How are you feeling?" Dr Jacquie sits on a swivelling stool at the bottom of the chair I have to weave myself into so she can stick the probe up my vagina. She's placed a condom over the probe, and I laugh to myself, thinking it must look weird having a fertility clinic place orders for bulk condoms. But then again, I was on the pill for almost two weeks, and I'm trying to get pregnant.

"Bloated and emotional," I reply as I hook my second foot in the stirrup at the side of the chair. "Poor Boyd's been copping it all week."

"I see you're flying solo this morning." Jacquie raises the gown to my knees and spreads lube over the probe.

"He's got a clinic in Sailor's Bend this morning and had to leave early. The joys of being a registrar." I know I'm trying to make small talk, but really, all I want to know is numbers.

The doctor chuckles as she slips the probe inside me and clicks some buttons on the computer in front of her. "Uterine lining looks good. Now, let's see the right ovary."

It's not the most comfortable feeling being probed like this. The probe's wider than a tampon, but nowhere near any of the dildos Boyd and I own. It's been ages since we've played with any of our toys. I must remember to Google if it's safe to play with dildos when you're pregnant. Believing this is the cycle I will conceive is what keeps me going and makes the mood swings almost bearable.

"Right ovary is looking good." Dr Jacquie clicks some more buttons and takes some measurements. My untrained eye can see five follicles. That's almost as many as we had in total sides last time. The doctor moves the probe, and I think I see one that I didn't see before.

"I'm counting seven, but there's a couple more that might develop, too." The probe is turned inside me And it's similar on the left ovary. It's an immense relief to see my body reacting to the increased dose of hormones.

"There are plenty of follicles, but we need them all to develop. Honestly..." The doctor pauses as she removes the probe and strips the condom off it before passing it to the nurse to clean. "I'd prefer a few less to avoid hyperstimulation syndrome. Now, watch out for nausea, diarrhoea, and any abdominal pain. I'd also start a low-dose aspirin tablet each day. You'll be hearing from me later on today with your blood results, but I want to know if you get any symptoms of hyperstimulation, okay? I suspect when I speak to you later, we'll be lowering the hormone dose."

I nod. Jacquie might be concerned with the risk of ovarian hyperstimulation syndrome, but I'm just glad to see so many follicles.

It's a relief to get out of the gown and back into my own clothes. The thought of getting so many more eggs and potentially so many more embryos is exciting. As I leave the building and walk to my car, I text Boyd.

> Quite a few follicles on each ovary. The pain and mood swings will be worth it.

When I get to work, there's a message from Boyd.

HUSBAND

Great news, babe. See you tonight. I'm having lunch with Nonna, by the way.

> Give her a hug from me and tell her to keep her hands off my husband—I know she's got a thing for you.

HUSBAND

Yeah? Well, I've got a thing for you, and you only. What was it you read in that book that had you and Val laughing so much? Granny Fanny? I'll be on the lookout for suitable men. Of course, being the GP, you'll have to prescribe the Viagra. It would look strange as a paediatrician writing out a script for erectile dysfunction.

My heart is full as I walk into work. I'm even on time despite the early morning trip to the clinic. Today is going to be great.

I'M A MOODY BITCH AGAIN. I haven't dared tell Boyd that I've got diarrhoea or that my abdomen feels like it's going to explode because it feels so tight and every touch sends pain shooting through my body. Yesterday, I barely got through work, and I offered to complete discharge summary paperwork that no one enjoys doing for the afternoon so I didn't have to see any patients.

I haven't slept. Fortunately, egg collection will probably be soon, so Boyd is building his sperm reserves. He is asleep when I come to bed. He tried to snuggle on the couch, but I told him the medication was making me feel a little woozy. It was an understatement. I'm not sure how I kept dinner down. I don't even toss and turn, because that will be too painful.

It should be a scan this morning, trigger this afternoon, and egg collection the day after tomorrow. Acting has never been something I'm good at, but I will do almost anything to avoid letting on that something is wrong and that this feels like the symptoms Jacquie told me to watch out for. I know ovarian hyperstimulation syndrome can be a risk, but if I can just get to egg pick up, and they can retrieve the eggs, then they can be fertilised and frozen.

Boyd is blending a smoothie. The smell of banana sends me to the bathroom, and I dry retch, as there's nothing in my stomach. It's all come out the other end as water. I text work and tell them I won't be in. My brain's working overtime as I try to come up with a reason to take two cars to work when we usually carpool after clinic visits. Boyd would carpool every day with me, but at least one of us invariably gets held up at the end of the day, causing the other person to wait around when all we want to do is get home.

"You look pale." Boyd places a glass in front of me filled with his smoothie of the day, but I can't drink it.

"I think I'm just nervous. I didn't sleep well." I push the glass towards him, hoping he'll drink it. "Gina mentioned yoga tonight after work, so I might drive myself if that's alright with you?"

Boyd rinses the glass in the sink before he fills it with warm soapy bubbles and washes up the breakfast dishes.

"You sure? I don't mind dropping you off." Boyd empties the water from the sink, shaking the bubbles off his hands before wiping them on a towel. He comes around the bench and draws me in for a hug.

It's the worst thing he can do. My abdomen feels like it's going to explode. "Boyd." I push him away and reach for the bench to steady myself. I try to take slow breaths, but it's impossible. My abdomen feels like it's on fire. Beads of sweat are forming on my forehead, and I feel some dripping down my back.

"Emily, what's wrong?" Boyd places his hand against my forehead to feel my temperature. I don't think I'm hot, it's just pain.

"It's just a bit uncomfortable, that's all." I try to brush him off, but he knows me too well.

"Come on, we're going, and you're having a day off work." His words are forceful, and he grabs his wallet, phone, and keys before guiding me out the front door.

It takes ages to walk down the stairs. Each step puts pressure on a different place. I'm concerned that I've twisted an ovary or something. Boyd buckles me into the car before racing around and getting in his seat. I've suggested for years he invest in a new car, but he loves his old rust bucket.

Needing to distract myself, I think back to dinner with Gina and Damo. I'd driven, and my car is slightly more modern than Boyd's but not at all flashy. Damo drove up to the restaurant in his Audi as if he owned the world. I suppose it's the different priorities people have.

Boyd can be a careless driver, easily distracted by conversations or things he sees, but this morning, he's on his best behaviour. Luck is on our side, and he snags a park right outside the clinic. Sure, I know it's early, but usually, even these spaces are gone. Boyd rushes round to help me out and has one hand on my hip and the other on my elbow as he guides me inside.

The lift takes forever, but it finally arrives. A doctor I've seen around the hospital is leaving, obviously heading off to work. I forget that people live in this building interspersed with the holiday lets.

"Do you think he recognised us?" I ask breathily as Boyd presses the button for the floor we need. I'm in too much pain to really care if he did or not.

"Nah. He's stuck up as fuck." Boyd chuckles. "I doubt we're even a blip on his radar."

The lift doors open, and we walk down the corridor towards the frosted glass doors emblazoned with the clinic's logo. There's another lady waiting to be seen, and she looks at us with raised eyebrows. Usually we see no one else whilst we're here. A receptionist appears, a puzzled look on her face.

"I'm sorry." Boyd's brows are knit together. "We're early, but Emily's not well."

The receptionist calls a nurse who takes us down the corridor into a consultation room. My pulse is high, and my blood pressure is low. I'm not surprised. Anyone would be dehydrated from the vomiting and diarrhoea. The nurse manages to draw some blood and leaves to take it to the lab.

We wait in the room until they're ready for my scan. I change into the gown and am surprised to see the marks on my belly from where the elastic of my scrubs has cut in.

"So, when did this start?" Dr Jacquie doesn't look impressed as I climb gingerly into the chair for my scan.

"Um, yesterday," I mutter. I know I've stuffed up.

"And did you call?" I shake my head as lube is applied to the familiar probe. "And you reduced the hormone dose on Monday, as we discussed?"

"No," I whisper as tears fall down my cheeks. "I wanted all the follicles to develop."

The nurse passes me a tissue to wipe my eyes. Jacquie doesn't even click buttons to take measurements.

"You're a smart woman, Emily." The doctor removes the probe and hands it to the nurse before lowering my gown and placing a hand on my foot. "You need to listen to my instructions, though." She helps me release my feet, and I sit on the edge of the chair. I can't see Boyd, as he's standing behind the bed, but I bet he's angry with me. "I can't give you the HCG trigger. Usually, it's that which brings on hyperstimulation syndrome, but I'm concerned that if we give it and proceed to egg pickup, things will get worse."

"I'm sorry." My voice is strained, and I'm trying not to sob.

"Normally, I'd be sending you to ED, but I don't think you'll go, will you?"

I shake my head. Boyd kisses the top of it as he comes and stands next to me.

"C'mon, babe." Boyd wipes some tears away from my cheeks with his thumb. I see unshed tears in his eyes, but they are still so full of love. "I've taken the day off too, and we can play hooky together."

"I'll warn you both..." Dr Jacquie looks serious as she looks at both of us. "There's a lot of follicles there, and some may erupt. I'd advise against unprotected sex for the next few days, because the risk of multiples is just too high."

It's this that sends me into a full-on meltdown. The nurse directs us back to the room we'd been in and tries to say some kind words, but I don't hear them over my sobs. I should have reduced the hormone injections like I was told, but I was greedy. I wanted all the follicles, and all the eggs, and all the embryos, and then all the babies.

Infertility sucks.

"They won't mind?" I ask as Boyd pulls up in his parents' driveway.

"You've known my parents almost all your life and when will they mind that we are hanging out at their place? You can go for a swim, or soak in the bath, and we can raid their fridge." Boyd sounds so tender and loving. He should be angry with me for yet another failed cycle.

The icing on the cake as the nurse spoke to us is that they don't do full IVF cycles in December, just frozen embryo transfers. I'd go again next month, but Dr Jacquie wants us to rest and wants a scan to see that my ovaries have settled. She's sure there's no permanent damage, but I wouldn't put money on that not being the case. I've probably made things worse.

The idea of a bath sounds lovely. Boyd leads me upstairs to his parents' room. Everything here is white and fresh. I'd love to have a bedroom like theirs one day with a king-sized bed with lovely linen and lots of scatter cushions.

We both laugh as we enter the bathroom and see a clear silicone dildo stuck to the mirror. Boyd places the plug in the deep bathtub and turns on the water. Sorting through some drawers, he finds his mother's stash of bath products and grabs a lavender-scented bath bomb, telling me his mother won't even notice it's gone.

"I'm going to make you a tea, okay?" His eyes are full of concern. I really don't deserve this compassion.

He leaves the room, and I burst into tears. I should know better. I'm a doctor, for God's sake, and I didn't listen to the professional telling me to adjust my medications. If I were the doctor, I'd be pissed at a patient if they didn't listen to me, especially if they're supposed to understand how the medical system works.

Wiping my tears, I shed my scrubs and sink into the water that's half filled the tub. It's deep, and I hate to think how much water I'm wasting by filling it, so I switch off the taps. The scent of the lavender is calming. The nausea has eased, but I still feel like crap.

"Hey." Boyd reappears, his voice soft as he passes me a steaming mug of jasmine tea. He kneels next to the tub and strokes a finger down my jawline. The tears have dried up at least. "You haven't filled the tub."

"I left room for you," I respond, trying to sound much more upbeat than I feel.

"I..." Boyd takes his top lip between his teeth as he contemplates what to say. "I don't want to hurt you or make you uncomfortable, and I can only imagine how shit you're feeling, so I'll just sit out here and wash your back if that's alright?" The finger that stroked my jawline moves to my shoulder, and I lie back again in the water. "Want me to turn the tap back on?"

I nod. Boyd removes his phone from his pocket and turns on some music. It's Beethoven's piano sonatas. I know he never listens to these by himself, but he's playing them for me, as he knows how much they calm me.

It's been months since I sat on a piano stool. Mum tells me all the time I should head home and play, but I never seem to make the time. Work really is doing a number on me. I need to start applying to GP practices to get a registrar position for next year. Secretly, I've been putting it off, thinking that I'd be pregnant by now. It's been almost three years of trying.

I glance down at Boyd, who's lying on the bathroom tiles, listening to the music. His face is one of sadness, with heavy eyes and down-turned lips. I'm the one who's put that look there. It's easy to think that Boyd deserves better than me, but I know I won't find anyone better than him.

"You're thinking too hard, princess." It's been years since he's called me that. He used to use it as a term of endearment when we first started going out, knowing how much I hated it.

"I'm sorry." My voice is soft. "I should have listened to the doctor and reduced the dose. I just wanted more eggs this time."

"But, babe, it's your health." Boyd props himself up on an elbow as he looks at me. "I'd rather get a few eggs each cycle and have a happy and healthy wife, rather than risk your health and well-being."

The tears flow again. I really don't deserve his compassion, but it soothes me all the same.

The water is no longer hot, so I reach for the plug, and the tub empties. Boyd holds my hands as I step out, a fluffy white towel draped over his shoulder. Gently, he dries me, patting away the drops of water. His touch isn't sexual, it's more than that. This is the cherishing we exchanged with our wedding vows. I need to get back to showing him more of the same.

I'd already booked tomorrow off work for egg retrieval, but Boyd convinced me to take today off as well. He's working short shifts on the weekend, but he's been noncommittal about what we can do.

Memories of yesterday come back to me. After our bath, Boyd and I snuggled in front of his parents' large screen television and rewatched old *Firefly* episodes. We're both such geeks at heart. Boyd made popcorn and found a chocolate cake in the freezer, which he defrosted and we fed to each other.

He'd washed the towels we'd used in the bathroom along with our scrubs and found some old sweats in his old room, which we put on. We left a note for his parents telling them we'd been there, and we passed Hillary driving up the street as we were leaving.

Today, I'm at Mum's place. It's the house I grew up in and contains such mixed memories. I remember Dad reading me stories and listening to me play the piano. I felt like he was always my biggest cheerleader.

As I sit at the piano stool and play scales, I almost feel like I could turn around and see him sitting in his armchair, crossword in hand as he rhythmically tapped the biro against his chin, searching for the word that would fit whatever clue he was pondering.

My fingers are rusty, but I start with C Major and increase in semitones before I land back on C and start again, before moving to minor scales. I used to hate practicing scales, but it's the structure that has me reaching for them today. There's a predictability, the same tonal distance between each note, and they do what is expected of them.

From scales, I move to arpeggios, before moving to different chord sequences. I was classically trained, but I've dabbled in some jazz, and, of course, popular music when I played at the casino.

My sheet music is stored in the piano stool and boxes that are stacked next to the piano, but I don't reach for music. There are songs I know by heart. My fingers are rusty, but I let them do their own thing. Before I know it, I'm playing the opening bars of Billy Joel's famous hit 'Piano Man'. I remember Val tagging me online in a post where someone was arguing that it was a song about a gay bar. It might have been, but it might also have been a song of its time where men gathered in bars and women did their own thing at home.

Dad used to go to the pub on a Friday afternoon after work with his team. Sometimes, we'd join him for dinner. I can't think of the last time Boyd went out without me. I know he has in the past, but not for ages. It worries me he has no friends other than his siblings and me. I wish he had someone to talk with. Finding Gina has helped me so much.

Gina has her egg retrieval tomorrow. She told me she had a good number of follicles on her scan yesterday, and she was super hopeful they would get a decent number of embryos. Although I'm jealous her cycle is still going ahead, I'm also hopeful for her. I'm not sure how I'll cope if she gets pregnant and I don't, but I'll cross that bridge if I need to. For now, I'll simply hope for the best for her. She told me about the time she had ovarian hyperstimulation syndrome, but it happened after she had had the trigger shot, so they went ahead with egg pick up and froze the embryos.

My phone rings when I'm in the middle of the final chorus. I stop and look over at it, seeing it's the clinic.

"Hello, it's Emily." I put the call on speaker, the song continuing in my head as I trace my fingers across the keys without pressing them.

"Hi, Emily, it's June from the clinic. Just seeing how you are today." I don't know if I've met June. No one seems to wear name tags, and I have no real idea about who's who.

"Yeah, no, I'm feeling a lot better, thanks. My tummy's settled. I still feel a little bloated, but I assume that's to be expected." The song finishes in my head, but I simply start it again, wanting to distract myself from thinking about our inability to have a baby.

"Good, good." Her voice is saccharinely sweet, but I can't tell if it's real or something she's put on for the phone call. "Dr Jacquie wanted me to make an appointment with you for your next scan."

Yep, she's one of the receptionists. I sigh as I take my fingers off the keys and reach to grab my phone. "No, I'm on nights that week." I look at my roster and the dates for the scan June has mentioned. "I could come in on the Tuesday morning, say around half eight?" I suggest.

"Perfect. See you then." June hangs up, and I enter it into my calendar.

I switch my phone to silent before tossing it behind me onto the chair my father used to sit in. Turning back to the piano, the desire to play upbeat pop songs has vanished, and my hands move over the keys, playing Chopin's 'Funeral March'.

This is the piece I played over and over the year after Dad left. I still can't get over how upbeat Mum was, despite her world being as uprooted as mine had been.

Muscle memory takes over. It's something I haven't played for years, but my fingers know where to go. I don't need the music.

"I thought you'd forgotten this god-awful piece." Mum laughs as she opens the door, and Millie and Mia run towards me, yelling my name and fighting for hugs.

I feel a little guilty about not telling Mum I was coming over. It's Thursday, and I knew she'd be heading to Sailor's Bend to take Nonna shopping like she does every week. I planned to be out of here by the time she came back to pick the girls up from school, but I lost track of time.

"It's just melancholy." I shrug as Mia pushes me aside on the stool and sits next to me.

She proceeds to play 'French Folk Song', the latest thing she has been learning in piano lessons. Giles and Bridget have bought an electronic keyboard for her to practice on at home, but she loves coming here to play a real piano.

"Tea?" Mum asks as she heads towards the kitchen.

"Yes please. I lost track of time, sorry." I yawn.

"Did you have a day off?" She asks as I follow her into the kitchen. I hear the girls squabbling over who should be playing the piano. Millie took lessons for a term before she decided that piano was boring, but she is now more enthusiastic, seeing her younger sister take it up.

"Yeah." I pull the mugs from the cupboard as Mum fills the kettle and flicks the switch to turn it to boil. "I should have offered to take Nonna shopping. I'm sorry, I didn't think."

I feel guilty now. I knew it was shopping day, but I wanted to spend time with my piano.

"Nonna would love to see you. She's had lunch with Boyd a few times when he's had clinics down that way." I love that Mum's not asking questions, but I know she must be wondering why I'm here on a random Thursday when I'm usually at work. "Girls." Mum sounds calmer than she looks when the girls bash at the piano keys. "I've got your snacks. Now, wash your hands, please."

She's sliced up some apples and cheese, and I've helped myself to some, too. It's exactly what she used to do for me after school. Val would often come over here with Boyd whilst Giles and Henry headed home.

"Now, who's got homework?" Mum asks the girls as she clears away the now empty plate. Millie rolls her eyes before reaching for her school bag. She brings out her homework folder and opens the Velcro tab.

There's a reading comprehension task about elephants, which she completes in a few minutes. No one could ever accuse her of being an underachiever. Mia has some reading to do and asks me if she can read to me.

We go into the lounge room, and she points to my father's chair.

"Can I sit over here instead?" I ask, moving towards the couch.

"No. Here, please."

I daren't defy the six-year-old, so I sit on the chair I haven't sat in since, well, since Dad left. It's comfortable, and I sink into it as Mia climbs onto my lap. It no longer smells of him, but it brings back memories I'm not sure how to process yet. Mia's reading is excellent, full of expression and emphasis in the right places. I leave a comment in her reading journal, but she makes no move to get off my lap.

"Did you know Stevie in my class has seven cousins?" she asks, as if the idea is incredulous.

"No, I didn't," I reply, hoping this isn't going where I think it is.

"I've got no cousins. Mum says Uncle Hammy and Uncle Kenny might have babies one day, but they're both boys, and Auntie Val doesn't even have a boyfriend." Mia shakes her head as she sits up and looks at me. "Are you and Uncle Boyd going to have a baby?"

My heart sinks. There's nothing I want more, but how do I explain this to her?

"One day, Uncle Boyd and I would love to have a baby." It's not a lie.

"Okay." Mia shrugs. "I mean, if you don't have a baby, could you get a puppy? I'd love a puppy, but Dad says no. You could get one and call it Moose, and I could visit it like it's a cousin."

"Moose?" I ask, trying not to laugh.

"It's a good name for a dog. I'll ask Uncle Boyd when I see him." She jumps down from my lap and runs back to the kitchen to put her reading folder in her bag.

I might see a puppy in the future, but I'd much rather have a baby. It's hard to explain that logic to a child, though, let alone myself.

Emily, Age 15

I think I'd love a puppy. We've never had pets, but Mrs Hamilton next door lets me walk her dog after school. Boyd comes with me sometimes. Today, we took Rascal—that's his name, even though it doesn't suit him— and went to the local dog park.

Rascal's one of those dogs who's a bit of everything. He wouldn't win any competitions for the best-looking dog, but he's a real sweetheart. As we walked along the street the dog park is on, we saw a house for sale. It literally screams family home. I told Boyd it's exactly the type of house I want when we're married.

There's a large tree in the front yard and a tyre swing. I can see our kids playing on it. There's a swinging love seat on the front veranda, and I can see Boyd and me sitting out here in the evenings talking about our day once the kids are in bed.

The photos on the real estate sign out the front look gorgeous. There are four bedrooms, and the family that lives there at the moment must have a few children, as the three bedrooms apart from the primary suite are decorated with fun murals and have toy boxes in them.

Out the back, there's a large deck that overlooks a swimming pool. I'd love a pool. Mum doesn't have one, but the Hartmans do. I can picture it now, our four kids—or maybe five if Boyd has his way—a dog, possibly a Golden Retriever because, hello, they are hella cute, and a white picket fence.

We could have an outdoor eating area and have all the Hartmans come to us for Sunday lunch. I can't see Giles settling down anytime soon. He's happy playing the field, I think. Not sure about Henry. I think he'd like to find someone but hasn't yet. As for Val, well, who knows? I'd say we'll have children long before Val ever gets around to it. Boyd and my kids will probably end up babysitting Val's kids.

The house we saw is bigger than Mum and Dad's place. I mean Mum's place. I still think of it belonging to both of them, even though Dad doesn't live here anymore, and he signed it over to Mum. It looks like Mum's place, though, as it's in the same style. It's not as big as the Hartmans' place, but I don't think we'll need a house that big. I know they added to their place after they bought it as their family grew. Perhaps Boyd and I could do the same thing.

Rascal got in a scrap at the dog park, so we ended up leaving earlier than we thought. I know Boyd has homework he needs to finish. I'm up to date, but I could do some piano practice. Priscilla thinks I should play some more upbeat music. I think Mum told her about my fascination with the funeral march.

Ms Winthrop, my piano teacher, says I should play some Beethoven and start on the piano sonatas. I might do that. I've listened to them a bit, and they're pretty cool. Ms Winthrop says I could be a professional pianist, but that doesn't really excite me. I'd hate to be on the road away from my family and friends. Well, away from Boyd.

Whenever we get a house, I'll make sure it's on one level so we can get my piano in. Mum says it was an absolute pain having it delivered here with the steps up to the front door. Getting it out shouldn't be that much of a problem.

I've been practicing my signature, getting ready to sign Emily Hartman. I can't wait to get rid of my dad's name. I wish I could do it now. I can't understand why Mum kept it. I've told her she should go back to her old name, but she doesn't want to. It's hard. I think she still loves him, even after all he's done. I know I'll never forgive him, that's for sure.

It's just Mum and me for dinner tonight. Boyd headed home to finish his English assignment. He'll ace it, even though he complains that he hates English. The garlic is wafting through the house. I think Mum's made Puttanesca. I made the mistake of referring to it as slut spaghetti once. Mum reckons the story of sex workers making it between clients is apocryphal, anyway. To think, one day, I'll be making it for Boyd. Maybe even after we've had sex.

My body's ready for sex, but I'm holding off. I mean, I'm sixteen in a few weeks, maybe then. Who knows? I just know he's the only man I'll ever have sex with, and I like that idea.

She's calling me for dinner. Better rush.

Chapter 15

Boyd

I LOVE CHRISTMAS. IT'S THE BEST TIME OF THE YEAR—WELL, apart from Emily's birthday week. I mean, I love spoiling her then, too.

Family Christmases are the best, and this year, we will all be together. Giles and Bridget are now fully fledged consultants and have scored Christmas off. Somehow, Henry and Ken have swung it too, and Val's coming home, even though she'll be back for the Valentine's Gala in February. Emily and I both worked last Christmas and put in for Christmas Day off back in January. The roster gods have smiled.

One of my earliest memories is waking up Christmas morning and being so excited to see what Santa had brought everyone. It was the year Henry received his first cricket set. We spent hours in the backyard that summer playing with the tennis ball that Dad replaced the cricket ball with. It still went crashing through a window, though.

I would have been almost three. Val wasn't even born. I'm wracking my brain trying to remember what Santa brought Giles. It might have been the year he got the tennis ball on the pole with the coil at the top. I could never hit the damn thing, but Giles would stand behind me, holding the yellow plastic racket to help.

The weird thing with this memory is I can't even remember what Santa brought me. It was the atmosphere that made it special, that our family was together. Henry had been into craft and made everyone decorations to hang on their trees. They were paper angels or something that he coloured with pencils and stuck glitter on.

We spent that summer with Mrs Mac, as we called Mrs McIntyre. The three of us boys let Emily run around with us. We've even got a photo somewhere of the three of us with Santa. People laugh at it because I'm pointing off to the side, but I'm pointing at Emily. I couldn't work out why she wasn't in our family photo. To me, she should have been.

The following Christmas, Mum was pregnant with Val, and I thought I'd made that happen by asking Santa for a sister the year before, until Giles told me that Santa wasn't real.

These days, I miss not believing in someone who can grant wishes. I've never believed in a higher being. I've had talks with Nonna, who's been Catholic all her life. Lately, I've been wishing I did, and that I could ask them to bless me and Emily with a baby.

I'm at Cassowary Central, the main shopping centre in town, trying to find Emily the perfect Christmas gift. It's hard when I know exactly what she wants—what we both want—and I can't give that to her. The place is crowded, and piped music fills the air, singing about the most wonderful time of the year and dashing through the snow on a sleigh. If it wasn't almost a hundred degrees outside and the middle of summer in Australia, I might feel more festive.

Emily doesn't wear perfume. She doesn't need to, as she smells so sweet as it is. Her shampoo leaves her hair smelling like a citrus grove. It's alluring. She hardly ever wears makeup and has had the same purse for years, arguing that it serves a purpose and hasn't worn out yet. Not that a purse screams sexy Christmas gift.

We sleep naked. I mean, I could buy some sexy lacy nightgown, but it would only end up on the floor. Why cover perfection, after all? She buys books as soon as they're released and prefers to read them electronically, anyway. Her e-reader was a Christmas present last year.

In January, she starts at a GP practice as a registrar. She left it late applying around Cassowary Point, hoping she'd be pregnant. She's not, of course. The job is at the practice here in the shopping centre. Why anyone would want to go to a major shopping centre to see a doctor when they're sick is beyond me, but it's attached to a pharmacy.

I haven't met Dr Doug, the GP she'll be working under. Emily says he seems nice enough, even if he appears to dye his hair and has plenty of facial fillers. I've seen his Aston Martin driving around town complete with personalised plates that actually say 'Dr Doug.'

When I asked Emily what she wanted for Christmas, she told me a new sunhat. I mean, boring. Sure, it was after a gust of wind blew her old one over the side of the hill when we were hiking recently, but it's not romantic.

I'm drawn to a stationery shop. Emily is mainly digital, like me, but I know there will be lots of paperwork as a GP. There's a display of trays and magazine holders in gold at the front of the store, but they're a bit too flashy for Emily. The displays are separated by colour. There's a black-and-white set, and on the bottom of the in-tray is written in a flowing script 'If this is empty, your work is done.' Pretty meh, if you ask me.

Hidden down the back is the end of range or misfit section. Not matching sets, but items that have had their matching bits sold without them. There's a deep-purple set of three trays and a penholder with a rooster on it. It makes me think of Nonna and her name for my cock. There's a set of three magazine holders that are labelled 'Stuff,' 'More Stuff,' and 'Stuff that wouldn't fit in the other two.'

Neither of us is the most organised, so it makes me smile. A silver marker is at the register, and I grab it to further, um, decorate the gift. She may think she wants a boring hat, but I'm about to have to put up with not having her around the hospital with me every day. It's not like we grab lunch together or anything, but I love knowing she works in the same building as me.

The sales assistant offers to wrap my purchases and looks at me as if I've got two heads when I write on top of the in-tray before she does.

As I leave and continue to wander looking for more gift inspiration, I pass the tea shop I know Emily loves, and I eye a large mug with a rooster on it. Must be the season for them or something. I head inside and grab a small tea pot and some jasmine tea leaves and have them bundled together as a gift.

Emily's at work. We've planned to come back here again tomorrow to buy for Millie and Mia, and Ken's sister, Dipti's, kids, Luke and Sarah. The kids are spoilt at Christmas. Us adults make do with Secret Santa, meaning we only buy for one person. Initially, I drew Emily's name, but Mum made me put it back. I've now drawn Dipti. Emily has Giles to buy for.

Mum and Dad have an enormous Christmas tree in their lounge room. You can tell where the kids have decorated the lower limbs as the top has evenly spaced baubles, and the bottom looks like a box of decorations exploded over it. I know Millie, Mia, Luke, and Sarah had fun, though. Mum told us at lunch last weekend. Millie even found some of the handmade decorations we made as kids and scattered them over the tree. Can't wait to tease Henry about his angels.

As I'm about to head for my car, a small, raggedy looking tree catches my eye in a discount store. It's so kitsch. I mean, you plug it in, and lights on the end of the branches flash. We really don't have room in our apartment for a tree, but I can't walk by this monstrosity. I grab it and a box of mixed decorations and head for home.

Sure, I love shopping for presents for my wife, but I hate it when Emily and I can't spend the weekend together because one of us is working. From next year, it will be me working weekends, as she'll be Monday to Friday with no nights and no weekend shifts. I hope it will be easier to avoid long stretches without seeing each other due to us being on opposing night shifts. Just another hope that may not come true.

When I get home, I assemble the tree, and by that, I mean take it out of the box. The branches fall into place, and I plug it in, only to find that half of it isn't lighting up like it should. It adds to the appeal. It's a bit broken, like Emily and me and our inability to fall pregnant.

I toy with the idea of pulling it apart and looking at the electronics, but I've got some zombies to shoot. Ever since Emily finished the game, I've been trying to as well, but this one level just stumps me. I can see Emily is dying to tell me the secret to solving it, but I want to figure it out on my own. I'm still battling it when she gets home at five.

"What in the absolute hell is that?" she asks when she sees the tree in the corner. Her nose is scrunched, and she looks disgusted.

"It's Christmas cheer," I reply, closing off the game before she's tempted to spill the tea on the trick to beat the zombie, who's three times the size of the rest of them. I swear, every time I come back to the game, it's gotten bigger. Must be from eating all my brains.

"It's hideous." Emily laughs. "But it's growing on me. Why are there only lights on the top half of one side and the bottom half of the other?"

"Because it's broken. I could take it back, but I like it." I smile as I stand and walk over to her for a hug.

"There are presents under there." Emily looks under my arm at the tree again. "Did you get something for Dipti and Giles?"

"Nope. Just for you."

"Boyd Edward Abraham Hartman." Shit. She's full named me, knowing I hate the Abraham. "They don't look hat shaped."

"You should be a detective, my beloved." I try to distract her by holding her face and planting kisses all over it.

"But we said we'd save money for the house, and, well, stuff."

I know exactly what stuff she speaks of, too. She means IVF. It isn't cheap.

"Look." I get her to look at me. Her eyes aren't full of rage, and I think she's secretly pleased I want to spoil her. "They aren't big. I mean, they're not expensive, like a new car or diamonds or anything, but I enjoy spoiling you."

"I want to be angry with you, but I love you too much for that. Wait here." Emily pecks me on the cheek and rushes into our room, returning a few seconds later with a small box tied up with orange ribbon.

"Now that looks too small to be a water bottle." I look at her as she places it under the tree.

"I'm not getting you a water bottle for Christmas." Emily huffs, shaking her head. "You'll only lose it like the three you've lost this year."

"The nurses have stolen them." I draw my lips between my teeth and make my eyes bulge as I sprout this lie.

"Bullshit. I know if I headed to ED, I'd find them in the box of water bottles that collects in the corner."

Emily was right. "Do you think we can open our gifts now?" I ask, one eye now closed and my nose scrunched up.

"No." She laughs. "It's a week until Christmas, and you're going to wait. And no peeking either. Santa will know, and he'll bring you coal."

"See, I like to think Santa's all hip and environmentally conscious, and I'd at least get a solar panel." I laugh as I again draw my wife in for a hug.

"You're an idiot, Boyd Hartman, but you're my idiot, and I love you for it."

God, I love her, too. Even more, I love being able to banter with her without having to talk about IVF all the time.

"Hey, what's up?" I emerge from the bedroom to see Emily sitting on the couch, a mug of tea in her hand, her head thrown back.

"It's nothing," she says in a tone that tells me she's lying.

Taking the mug from her hands and setting it on the coffee table, I slide in next to her and drag her to my lap. The tea is well and truly cold, and I sense something has been on her mind.

"Want to try that again? Good morning, my gorgeous, sexy, amazing wife. What's up?" I intersperse my words with kisses.

"Look, I adore Millie and Mia. You know that, right?" I did. She would do anything for those girls. "And Luke and Sarah, I mean, they've had a rough few years, but they're gorgeous kids."

Luke, Sarah, and their mother had escaped a rough home life peppered with abuse and were doing so well in Cassowary Point.

"I know you do, and they all adore their Auntie Em, too."

These kids were all older than any kid of ours would be. I was almost grateful that Henry and Ken hadn't talked kids and that Val was adamant she was nowhere near being in a committed relationship to consider kids. With both of their girls at school, I doubted Giles and Bridget would go back for more, but who knew?

Unlike me, Emily wasn't surrounded by babies at work. We were fortunate that we were still this side of thirty and none of the friends we studied with were thinking of kids. Sure, there's been a registrar on her team who was excited that his wife was pregnant, but Emily said he hardly shared anything, and it wasn't like he was flashing ultrasound photos around or anything.

It was still hard, though. For three years, we'd been trying to conceive. Almost forty missed chances. Statistically, things were due to fall in our favour. Well, that's what I tell myself each month.

"We should have shopped online for them all." Emily snuggled under my chin. I loved how she fit in my lap and was like my own weighted blanket.

My hand strokes along her side. I'd thrown on a pair of boxers when I woke up and discovered Emily was already out of bed. She's dressed in shorts and a tank top.

"Yeah, but nothing will get here in time. We could do a click and collect. What do you think they'd like?"

"See." Emily huffs out a breath. "I haven't thought at all about what they'd like. I mean, Dipti was saying she was getting a PlayStation or Xbox for them, so we could grab a game, I suppose."

"That kinda screams fun aunt and uncle, I suppose." I give Emily a squeeze.

"Don't lie." Emily almost chuckles. "A video game doesn't scream fun aunt and uncle. And what about Millie and Mia? Giles would have a fit if they started playing video games."

Giles and Bridget had set rules about Christmas presents. Their girls received something they want, something they need, something to wear, and something to read. And the want usually something educational.

Last Christmas, Ken and Henry had bought Mia a nail salon kit, complete with stickers and some neon polishes. For weeks, Giles had a painted thumbnail that he let his younger daughter play with on the weekends. Millie had received a child's makeup kit and spent hours dolling up her sister. It made me laugh that it was Giles who was more uptight about these presents than Bridget.

"I always wanted to be the fun uncle who bought my nieces and nephews drum kits." I laugh as I kiss the top of Emily's head. It is lovely sitting here like this, even though I really need to pee.

"We could always go to the music store and buy tambourines and harmonicas and, like, loud instruments for them. You know, educational, like Giles and Bridget espouse and all." Emily sits up, a glint in her eye as she bites her bottom lip.

"I'm loving the way you're thinking." A deep chuckle escapes my mouth. This could be fun.

"I think I've been avoiding shopping for them because I don't want to be reminded that we aren't shopping for our own kids," Emily admits, her smile fading and her head dropping as she lets out a huff of air.

My mind swirls with dozens of possible responses to my wife, but this seems like one of those times when words won't help, so I hold her tight for a while until we both stand and leave the safety of the four walls we call home.

"Merry Christmas," I yell as I open the front door to Mum and Dad's. Everyone's cars are outside, and we're definitely the last to arrive. Even Rosa and Nonna are here before us.

Emily had to drag me out of bed in the end. As much as I love my family, it would have been the perfect Christmas just spending it in bed with my wife. Now Emily's recovered from the last disastrous cycle, our sex life has improved a lot. It's not totally back to the old days, but more and more, we're having trouble keeping our hands off each other, just how we both seem to like it. It feels like we've found a new normal, and that normal involves sex, so it's a huge win in my books. The blow job she gave me had me seeing stars, and it surprised me she wasn't walking funny after I pounded her from behind.

Millie and Sarah appear at the door in the guise of helping carry things. They just know there'll be presents.

"It's a ball?" Millie shrugs, taking the largest of them all.

"Don't shake it, or it might break," Emily yells at them as they run down the hall, each carrying a couple of gifts to put under the tree.

It wasn't a ball. I'd spent ages wrapping the damn tambourine in bubble wrap to look like a ball and to try to tamper the tingling sound. I think I almost managed.

"Careful, Mia." She grabs the last box and gives it a shake, the maracas inside singing the song of their people. There was no way to hush them.

"Is it a puppy?" she asks with her big blue eyes.

"It better not be." Giles appears, and Mia runs down the hallway with the gift. "Here, let me."

Giles takes the bowl of salad Emily and I had made last night, and we make our way towards the kitchen, where we know everyone will be gathered.

"You have a glow about you," Mum says as she kisses Emily on the cheek. "Anything you want to share?"

Fuck you, Mum.

"Your son gave me five orgasms this morning." Emily shrugs as she looks at me. It is a look of both pride, but also fear, knowing what Mum was getting at.

"We've been up since four thirty, and the girls have not left us alone." Bridget yawns as she gazes at her husband.

"Fucking cock blockers," Giles mutters just as Mia enters the room.

"What's a cock blocker?" She reaches for a handful of diced cheese that's laid out on the kitchen bench.

"Five? Your brother gave his partner five." Ken smirks as he stirs something on the stove, Henry beside him.

"Quality, not quantity, babe." Henry bites at Ken's lip before Val yells at them to get a room.

"Gramps, can we do presents?" Sarah looks at Dad, who has just cracked open a bottle of champagne.

"That's an excellent idea." Dad kisses the top of her head. "Get your brother away from that game he's playing and let's all gather around the tree."

The next hour oozes happiness. It is what Christmas and families are all about. For a brief moment, I can forget it's not our children we're spoiling with gifts, and having them open presents we'd consider wildly inappropriate.

Giles and Bridget have gone the sporting route with Luke and Sarah and bought them a cricket and totem tennis set. Dipti promises we'll all head outside after lunch to play. Dipti almost cries when she opens the large box that contains a gift certificate for a spa morning at a local resort.

Santas were meant to be a secret, and we always tried to throw each other off. Henry opens a gift containing a pillowcase with Ken's face printed all over it. It's the sort of gift that has my mother's fingerprints all over it, but I see Bridget smirk in the corner and elbow her husband.

Nonna receives the apron she demands every year, but this one has Millie and Mia's faces on it. I suspect Giles and Bridget got a printing deal somewhere. Rosa oohed and aahed over the new teapot, and she spent ages just sniffing the tea that came with it.

Fortunately, the kids are too busy painting fingernails with the new nail polish Ken and Henry gave them all—even black polish for Luke, which he grinned at—to see Mum open a book called *The Complete Idiot's Guide to Blow Jobs*.

"Well, she doesn't need that." Dad snickers from next to her as he opens it and finds an interesting illustration. "But perhaps we could try this one afternoon."

Dipti bites her bottom lip as Val opens her gift and is genuinely excited to receive premium movie passes. She loves going to the cinema.

Ken blushes when he opens the box he's been given, quickly placing the lid back on it before Henry has a look.

"Yeah, that ring looks too narrow for your fat rooster." Henry laughs, and I glance over to see Rosa and Nonna sharing a conspiratorial wink. I don't want to think about that one.

Giles looks at his gift suspiciously. Emily has my arm gripped in anticipation. When he opens it and shows Bridget, they both start laughing. Bridget often teases Giles about needing to learn the entire periodic table, as he apparently recites it in bed. Whatever floats their boat, I suppose. Emily found him a Perspex model that is etched with illustrations that represent the elements.

"Too clever." He laughs. "Thanks, Santa."

Charlie opens an inflatable pool toy that will make him look like he's lying on an absolutely ripped dude's body. It's so wrong, but it suits our family perfectly.

"C'mon, you two, you've been sitting on your presents watching everyone else," Mum chides Emily and me.

My family loves to joke around, but I'm scared they'll have given us something triggering. It would be easier in some ways if we shared our struggles with them, but that would lead to another set of issues with unwanted advice and too much sympathy.

"Bridget's waiting, too." Emily's voice is high-pitched, and I suspect she's also anxious about our gifts.

"I just love watching everyone." Bridget's lips form a flat smile. "I never had this growing up, and it's just so special."

Mum is sitting on the other side of Bridget on the couch and wraps an arm around her shoulder, giving her a hug. The mood dissolves when she opens a gift containing a sweatshirt that says 'Obstetricians: offering takeout and delivery.'

The tears of wistfulness that threatened to escape my sister-in-law's eyes come as tears of laughter. We've all heard Bridget's rants about the language of birth and how she hates being told she's delivering a baby, but the shirt is perfect none the less.

All eyes in the room, well, apart from the kids who are still busy painting nails, are on me and Emily.

"Shall you go first or will I?" I turn to Emily and kind of jokingly ask.

"The kids haven't opened their gifts from us, and we might have to make a runner after that, so perhaps we should go together?" Emily bats her eyelashes at me.

"Whatever you got them can't be worse than nail polish." Giles laughs. "Emily first."

Emily's gift is floppy, like clothing. My breaths come faster as she slides her finger under the tape, hoping it isn't a T-shirt that talks about babies or something. A pop of purple emerges from the wrapping paper. Shit, it's a shirt.

I feel like things move in slow motion until I see Emily open it, scrunch it up, and let out a chuckle before holding it against her chest. 'I haven't hiked everywhere, but it's on my list'. Under the shirt in the wrapping is a purple wide brimmed hat with a drawstring, so it won't fly away. Emily places it on her head and I see what's printed on the back—'Stop staring at my arse, Boyd'.

Pulling it off her head, I show it first to Emily, then to everyone gathered around. "What? Her arse is perfect. It's like..." A rumble escapes my mouth as I picture Emily riding me backwards this morning. "Like a perfect peach, and so succulent and juicy, and—"

"Yeah, we get it." Henry throws some balled up wrapping paper at me.

It's my turn. It's a box that's bigger than a shoebox, but something is rattling inside. I'm not gentle. The paper comes off as if it's being attacked, and I throw it on the ground. I open the box and can't help but laugh.

"Yeah, yeah." I bring out the drink bottle and show everyone. On one side is printed 'Cassowary Point STI Clinic. Please don't come again.' And on the other 'But if you do, wear a fucking condom.' "Well, I'm not taking this one to work."

"I can't see the nurses stealing it." Emily shakes her head, a wry smile across her mouth.

"Right, kids." Giles gathers up the wrapping paper that covers the floor like a patchwork quilt. "Last presents are for you."

Val has given each child some books. She is convinced everyone should love reading. I'm just glad she didn't give me one.

"Cool," Luke screams in excitement as he opens the present from Emily and me. "It's a harmonica. I always wanted one of these."

Dipti shakes her head as she looks at us both. Sarah opens some maracas and a wooden click thing. I told Emily we should just get coconut halves, but no, she thought these would be appreciated. They are.

"Am I going to kill you, brother?" Giles blows out a breath as Mia opens a tin whistle and starts blowing it. The sound is awful. "Just you wait. Henry and Ken, the nail polish is such a thoughtful gift. Thanks."

Bridget is laughing.

"They got instruments, and I get a ball." Millie looks as though she's about to throw the unopened gift from the window.

"Do you really think Uncle Boyd, your favourite uncle in the whole wide world, would get you a ball?" I ask her as she looks at me with suspicion in her eyes.

She removes the paper to find the bubble wrap. As she unwinds the meters and meters of wrap, the tinkling sound of the mini cymbals chimes.

"It's a tambourine," Millie shrieks as she jumps up and down on the spot, the instrument held above her head shaking and making a god-awful din.

"See, best aunt and uncle ever, hey?" I offer as she runs towards us and throws her arms around us, the tambourine clanging as it hits the ground.

"You're my only aunt and uncle because Henry's got Ken, who's another uncle, and Val doesn't have an uncle yet." Mia picks up the tambourine and shakes it from side to side.

Seeing the joy on everyone's faces as we exchanged gifts made me remember that families come in all shapes and sizes. Emily and I might not have kids of our own, but we have nieces and a nephew. Dipti, Luke, and Sarah may not have formally been adopted into the Hartman fold, but they belong here as much as anyone else.

Emily and I are surrounded by love.

It's not just Christmas Day that we're surrounded by love, it's all the time. Love is a verb for my parents, and they've shown it all day, every day.

Giles has the kids picking up wrapping paper, and Bridget tries to hide the instruments away, but Millie is watching.

I stand and help Emily up from the floor where we've been sitting.

Once she's standing, I turn. "I love you, Mum." I wrap my mother in a hug and squeeze her tight. "You've made my life awesome by modelling love, and I don't thank you enough."

"Oh, my baby boy." Mum's voice almost cracks. "Funny water bottle. Of course, if you and Emily want to stop using condoms, or whatever contraception you're on, I'd love more grandbabies."

And just like that, the spell is broken.

Emily, Age 17

Best. Christmas. Ever. Well, at least since before Dad buggered off. We spent the day with the Hartmans, of course. Giles and Henry are back from uni, and Giles brought Bridget with him. Giles is so different with her. I don't think Bridget knew what to make of Hartman Christmas, though. It's a lot.

They've taken to doing Secret Santa, which means you only have to buy a present for one person. I got Val and gave her a new bikini. I know Charlie was dying to say something about how it was too revealing, but he held it in. It must be hard for him seeing his baby grow up. I have to laugh though when Val tells him he's being a misogynist. I don't think he is. I mean, he's protective, but he also wants what's best for his kids. He even told Val recently that he knows he's treating her differently to how he treated his sons, and he's trying.

Boyd gave me some thong underwear. Not in front of his family, of course. I've never worn that style before. I wore a pair today, and they were the most uncomfortable things to have ever graced my bits. Don't worry, I told Boyd, and he suggested I put them on when he wants me to take them off. Makes sense, I suppose. He said my arse looked amazing in them. One minute, he's telling me he can't get enough of my tits, the other, he's all about my arse. Well, perhaps I'll get him some, and he can feel like his bum crack is being flossed all day.

For Secret Santa, I was given a case for my new phone. It's purple and luminescent and has E hearts B on the back. Whoever drew me must know how much I love purple. And Boyd. Boyd drew Henry and got him a book about some cricketer. It was funny because he was convinced it came from Val because she's the reader. Sneaky!

The food was amazing. I love how the Hartman's combine tradition with new things. So, we had rolled turkey, ham, and porchetta, but with salads. Val's really gotten serious with her baking efforts. She made a Christmas log that looked and tasted so good.

After lunch, we lounged around the pool. This really is the best time of year. I love the heat of summer, the holidays, and all the festivities. We're going to spend New Year's Eve here as well. The pool deck looks down towards the city and out to sea. It's stunning. You can see the fireworks in town.

I can't wait to do my last year at school and then head off to university with Boyd. He starts at the childcare centre that he's got a job at in mid-January. Nonna said we should head down and spend a week with her at Sailor's Bend. We might just do that.

It's not that I've forgotten about my father. Sometimes, I wonder what he's up to. I can only hope he experiences the same pain that me and Mum went through when we discovered what he'd done. I mean, I always thought I had an idyllic childhood. Hearing the stories of how much my parents wanted me that they travelled to China to take me out of an orphanage where I'd been dumped made me feel so wanted and cherished.

Mum and Dad's tales of trying to have a baby and nothing working, then finding me, I thought it was perfect. Then Dad went and ruined it all. Priscilla thought there will always be things that don't go well throughout life, or things that could go better. I don't think anything could be as bad as your father telling you he's moving out and moving to the other end of the state with another woman.

I can't get over Mum's resilience, though. She's dusted herself off and gotten on with life. I just wish she'd find someone to share it with, but I know Dad burned her.

Chapter 16

Emily

It's the look on Boyd's face as his mum told him on Christmas Day that she wanted more grandkids that makes my heart so sore. I wanted to grab him and run away, somewhere far away from his lovely, but somewhat meddling, family. But running away would mean running away from Dr Jacquie.

I've grown fond of our fertility doctor. She's a straight shooter who doesn't hold grudges. She's never brought up again that I didn't follow her directions on our last cycle. My period arrived last week, which means we're starting our third IVF cycle. Maybe this one will actually get further than the last two.

When I think back to our last cycle, I feel sick. In my desperation, I put my health at risk. Boyd's never pushed me about it, but I've promised him over and over that I'll stick to the instructions this time.

"Thank you, dear. You've been so helpful. When I couldn't get in to see Doug, I'll admit, I was concerned. I mean, he's been my doctor for almost twenty years now." I stood at the door to my new consultation room, trying to get Mrs Buchannan out. She could talk underwater with a mouth full of marbles. "But when I saw you were Asian, I knew I was in excellent hands, as you people always study so hard."

"Thanks, Mrs Buchannan. Now, don't forget to make that appointment." There was no point telling this almost eighty-year-old woman how racist she was being. She thought she was being kind.

"Oh, I've got the appointments booked. I didn't know you could get an indifferent referral."

Indefinite, I wanted to scream at her. I've heard all about her daughter, who is a teacher, the son who runs a highly successful business in town, and her grandson, who is training to be a paramedic. I've been here for over a week now and was trying hard to stay on schedule, but it is hard when I have patients like Mrs Buchanan who love to talk.

Dr Doug is reading the newspaper when I enter our small break room, but he makes a point of checking his watch as if to tell me I am running behind. He likes to schedule our breaks at the same time so we can discuss patients if we need to. It makes sense, even if I'd rather eat alone sometimes.

After sticking a tea bag in a mug and filling it with water from the urn, I turn to face him. "I've just had my ear chewed off by Mrs Buchanan. Apart from her telling me she trusted me because I'm Asian, she refused to take new prescriptions because she still had a month left of medication and will 'just make another appointment'." I lean against the bench after removing the tea bag and throwing it in the bin.

"She was widowed young and has raised three kids by herself." Doug is precise as he folds the newspaper and leaves it on a pile of magazines on the table next to where he sits. "No doubt she told you about Kylie and Shawn?"

"The teacher and businessman?" I nod, huffing out a breath. "Yep, heard all about them, and the grandson who's training to be a paramedic."

"She wouldn't have talked about Neil. He's in the secure mental health ward under a forensic order. He's got schizophrenia and raped Shawn's wife, what, ten years ago now. Mrs B looked after Shawn's kids from when they were babies, but after the trial, his wife cut all ties with the family and moved interstate." Doug rests an ankle across his knee as he leans back in the chair, his arms crossed over his broad chest.

I still don't know how to take Doug. He refuses to let me call him Dr Doug. "It's just Doug," he told me on my first day. He seems like a competent doctor who is loved by his patients, but he sometimes gives me the creeps. There's a look he gives me, almost a smirk, with a look of hunger in his eyes. I've tried to describe it to Boyd, who told me I was being paranoid, but he then told me he wouldn't put it past any man not to get hard when I was around. When I told him that must include his father, he changed his tune.

One good thing about running behind is I can pick up my tea and retreat to my room to finish it between patients. My next patient is either running late or is a no show. I'm pleased with my little consulting room. It is the smallest in the surgery, but it suits my needs. It's big enough to have an examination bed, and I can still sit at my desk with the curtain closed if I pull my chair right in.

My degree is framed and hangs on the wall. Bridget gave me a plant, which I'm proud to say I have kept alive, if only because one of the receptionists is plant mad and told me she'll care for it. I'd laughed on Christmas night when we finally got home from the Hartman celebrations and opened our gifts to each other. I love the stationary he bought me, especially the handwritten message in my inbox. My inbox was never empty, but I love lifting the papers in it and seeing the message 'If this is empty, head home and see your husband.'

I smile as I run my fingers over the rooster mug Boyd also gave me for Christmas. Several patients have asked me if I liked chickens when they see the rooster-covered paraphernalia dotted around my desk. I always say they bring me joy. Well, Boyd's rooster does.

As I glance to the left of my monitor, I see the framed photo of Boyd and me on a gondola in Venice over three years ago. It amazes me that Boyd still looks at me the same way, even though I haven't been able to get pregnant.

Now that I'm done with shift work and have the weekends to myself, I hope getting pregnant becomes easier. Stress can affect things, and shift work is very stressful.

I took my first hormone shot of the cycle yesterday. As a bit of a joke for Christmas, I gave Boyd some orange silk boxer shorts. Somewhere online, I read that orange is the colour of fertility. I know his spunk is good quality, but giving his balls more room and surrounding them in orange might help. I joked that I wanted to get him an orange thong, but as we both tried thong underwear as teenagers and hated it, I knew he'll never wear them.

My eyes are drawn back to the flashing on my screen showing my next patient is waiting. It's a two-year-old, and from the date of birth, it was probably conceived around the time Boyd and I were in Venice.

Taking a deep breath, I walk out of my room and down the hall towards the waiting room. "Lateesha? Lateesha Harrison?" The ragged-looking mum stands and grabs a small girl, who is talking to an older man. The mum looks heavily pregnant. In my head, I count to ten. I can do this, I know I can.

"AND HOW ARE YOU FEELING?" Jacquie asks me as she removes the probe from my vagina and hands it to the nurse. Being probed like this is second nature now.

"Yeah, good. I'm bloated, but I'm so much better than last time," I reply, feeling upbeat after seeing at least a dozen good-looking follicles on the screen.

"Good to hear. I'll double-check your hormone levels when the bloods come back, but I'd say it will be trigger tonight, egg pickup Friday." The doctor offers me a hand as I stand.

"Sweet." I smile, feeling all sorts of confident as I head to the room to get changed.

Sitting on the stool after slipping on my shoes, I text Boyd.

> Me: Looking good. At least a dozen follicles. You can jab me in the bum tonight.

HUSBAND

> But I have to abstain for the next few days until I make my deposit. Don't offer me your bum like that when you know I have to refrain from coming.

> Dork!

HUSBAND

You're a dork! I'll be home on time. I hope to gently massage your poor glute after I jab it with a pointy thing. Not the pointy thing I want to jab it with, though.

> If you're fucking the muscle, you're doing it wrong.

HUSBAND:

Have a great day, babe. Kevin wants to see me in his office. He's been cool, and I don't think I'm in trouble, but maybe I missed the cues?

> You'll be fine. I'll see you tonight.

It's a short walk from the clinic to the shopping centre where the doctor's surgery I work in is. I'm over an hour early for work, so I decide to stop for a tea.

> Hey, if you're running early, I'm having a very mediocre tea at Cassowary Coffee at Central.

GINA

Can we do lunch?

I haven't really caught up with Gina since I started my new job. She's talked about joining me for lunch, but our plans have never panned out.

> Course we can! Want to meet at the food court?

GINA

Can I bring stuff, and we eat in your office?
I'd love to talk.

> Sounds like a plan.

My morning goes well. It's still school holidays, and some parents have brought their kids who are heading off to school in for their vaccinations. Practice policy is that a doctor sees them first to check they are fit enough for a jab. It's really so the practice gets more money for the service, but I don't complain.

I've seen four kids this morning for vaccinations and an eighty-seven-year-old man who wanted Viagra, as he's met someone at the bowls club. He was so sweet and told me he hadn't even looked at another woman since his wife died eight years ago.

I did a medical for a woman going for her pilot's licence and saw a man who finally plucked up the courage to talk to someone about his depression.

The variety is amazing, and I know I'm doing what I've dreamt of for years.

"Ah, Emily." I make it to the break room first for our morning tea break. Doug places his mug under the fancy coffee machine spout and presses the buttons to produce what he always calls the perfect brew. "I see we've both got an opening straight after lunch, so I thought I'd take you out, away from here."

He stands at the coffeemaker, that smirk is on his face again making me feel grimy. He's a good-looking man who clearly still works out, but his face is filled with plastic, and I'm pretty sure he dyes his hair. I mean, good luck to him, but he's probably old enough to be my father.

"I can't today. I've got a friend meeting me for lunch." Taking the single seat at the head of the table to avoid my boss, I inwardly sigh when Doug pulls a chair closer to me.

"Can you put them off? I was looking forward to getting to know you more." His knee touches mine, and I jerk out of the way. "When's that husband of yours next working nights? We could do dinner. Have you tried Chez Philipe?"

I know of the restaurant, as it is Hillary and Charlie's favourite. They're always going on about the romantic atmosphere. It's the last place I want to go with my boss.

"Um, Doug." I take a large gulp of tea and try not to cough as it threatens to go down the wrong hole. "You know I'm happily married, don't you?"

"Oh, Emily." Doug places his hand on mine, his stubby fingers nothing like Boyd's. Bile rises in my throat. "I just want to be friendly, that's all. No one really understands the pressures put on general practitioners, and you'll need someone you can turn to when things get hard. Remember, I'm here for you."

I planned on telling him I needed Friday off, but there was no way I could ask now. Everything seemed like a bargaining chip with him, a tit for tat, and he's been very suggestive that he wants my tit for any tat I asked for. I tip the rest of my tea down the sink and rinse out my mug before heading back to my room without even a glance in Doug's direction.

MY DESK PHONE rings as the last patient before lunch leaves. Fortunately, I haven't been thrown any curly scenarios of diseases or symptoms I know little about, and I didn't have to ask Doug for advice. We passed in the corridor as we walked patients back to our rooms, but he simply smiled at me as if nothing was wrong. He may feel like it's situation normal, but I feel physically ill whenever he looks at me.

"Hi, Dr Emily, it's Carol on reception," a voice announces from the other end of the phone. "There's a Gina here for lunch with you."

"Thanks, Carol. I'll come and get her."

I so need a catch up with my friend and am excited to share my morning ultrasound news and find out how hers had gone. I was hoping we'd be sharing this cycle and then a pregnancy together.

"Hey." Gina's eyes look bloodshot, and for once, she's wearing no makeup. I've never seen her like this. "Come through."

As soon as the door to my room closes, Gina dissolves into tears. "Hey." I draw her in for a hug and let her cry on my shoulder. "Did you have a bad scan?" I feel her shake her head as she pulls away.

"I..." She sobs. "I cancelled my cycle."

"You cancelled it? Not Dr Jacquie?" I ask as Gina sits in the chair and blots her eyes with tissues.

"Both—" Gina starts before there's a knock at the door, and Doug pokes his head in.

"You coming to lunch, Emily?" he asks, ignoring the scene in front of him. He sounds upbeat and cheerful, and I just want to punch him in the balls.

"I'm busy, and I already told you I'm unavailable." I shoot him a glare that I hope conveys he needs to back out and fuck right off.

I want to punch him when he rolls his eyes and lets out a small huff as if I'm inconveniencing him by not kowtowing to his demands.

"Sorry about that," I say after he closes the door.

"If you've got plans..." Gina stands and grabs her bag.

"I have no plans, apart from having lunch with you. Doug's a creep, and I'm regretting taking the job here. Do you want to talk, though?"

Gina nods and grabs her water bottle from the bag she's lowered to the ground next to her chair. "I brought sushi." She produces a small cooler from her bag, which she unzips, and places the containers on my desk. I'd love to know what else is in her bag. It seems bottomless.

"I'm not that hungry," I admit, as I push the containers to the side.

"Same." Gina nods. "So, last week, at my first scan, Dr Jacquie noticed some strange discharge coming from my vagina. She ordered some tests, and I came up positive for gonorrhoea."

Gina has stopped crying and lets out a long breath.

"But you were treated for that when you first started treatment, weren't you?"

"Yep." She shakes her head, almost contradicting her affirmation. "And Damo was convinced I'd given it to him. We were both treated."

Treatment for gonorrhoea was usually effective, and, besides, I knew she had screening tests after her antibiotics that confirmed it had cleared.

"Jacquie called me yesterday and asked that I come and see her at the clinic by myself. I mean, Damo was away until last night, anyway." She's talking with her hands, both of which are clenching tissues she pulled from the box on my desk. "Jacquie told me the results and said we could pick up eggs and freeze embryos, but I couldn't have any implanted this month, which makes sense, I suppose. She then asked me if I'd slept with anyone other than Damo, and I laughed." Gina pauses, and I can see the pain in her eyes.

"That fucking bastard," I say, not usually one to swear, but I can feel my pulse rise as anger builds in my chest.

"Literally. A bastard who's been fucking around." Gina again shakes her head and huffs out a breath. "And he didn't deny it, either. He told me I'd never be enough for him, and he needs it... how did he term it? Oh, yeah, 'rough and hard from women who know what they're doing and don't want to be made love to'."

Gina and I have talked sex, and she's told me how jealous she is that Boyd isn't averse to trying new things in the bedroom. She complained Damo wanted to treat her like a princess and would only do missionary or cowgirl with her. "But he told you he hated hard sex and didn't want to break you?"

"Oh, the irony, hey. He literally told me last night that you make love to your wife, but you fuck other women. He has no shame. Oh, and it gets better." Gina drops a tissue into her lap and reaches for her water bottle. "Turns out he's paying child support for a six-year-old I knew nothing about, and the kid goes to my school. I could have been her teacher. She's living in this town, and he never sees her."

"Hasn't he heard of condoms?" I ask, still trying to get my head around things.

"He says they're uncomfortable. So, yeah, turns out he probably gave me the clap which caused my infertility. I mean, I took him at face value when he told me he was clean and had just been tested when we first got together, but I don't think he was ever tested before we rocked up to the fertility clinic. I was the one who had to give the phone numbers of the two boyfriends before Damo, so the public health people could contact them and tell them that a former partner had tested positive for fucking gonorrhoea. He said there was just me, and he charmed them to believe he'd been tested, too."

I felt sick for my friend. She was due to start back at school in a week and was looking forward to being back with 'her kids'.

"So, what are you going to do?"

"I left last night and stayed at a hotel. I told Mum this morning, and she said I should head back to Brisbane and do relief teaching for a bit. It's tempting. How was your scan, by the way?"

"Yeah, it was good." I lean across and place my hand on hers. I can't imagine what she's going through. I wish Boyd and I had space to put her up, but our place is too small. We chat for a bit longer before she stands to leave, and I plan to check in on her tomorrow.

Not only has my first appointment after lunch been cancelled, I see they've been moved to see one of the other doctors at the practice, and the one after that doesn't show. I do some reading up on gonorrhoea and confirm my original thoughts that this is indeed a reinfection for Gina. There's another tap at my door, but it sounds different from Doug's tap, and the door doesn't open.

Tentatively, I pull the door towards me, flinging it open when I see my husband standing there. "Fuck, am I glad to see you." I throw my arms around him and bring his lips to mine just as Doug walks past to collect a new patient. "What a fucking morning."

I close the door behind us, and both of us sit up on the examination table in the room. He shakes his head as I tell him about Gina and Damo.

"Jesus. I'm sorry. I wish I could say I'm not surprised. I mean, he was always a bit full-on, but I never got creeper vibes from that Damo," Boyd says as he scrunches his nose. The same way he never got creeper vibes from Doug.

"So, to what do I owe the pleasure?" I ask eventually as I cross my legs and lean into Boyd.

"Well." He blows out a deep breath. "So, I told you Kevin wanted to see me."

"Yeah."

"So, I haven't said yes or anything, and I told him I had to discuss it with you." Boyd bites his upper lip as he looks at me, clearly nervous at what he's about to say.

"Spit it out. You look too excited to have been fired." I laugh.

"Okay." He takes another deep breath. "So, you know I'll need to do at least six months in Brisbane as part of my training at the children's hospital?"

I knew this, and it was something I always brushed over. I nodded.

"So, the doctor who was working with Professor de Jong and doing a project on kids from the regions who have to spend extended time in the city at the big hospital, well, she's pulled out at the last minute. Her mum's sick or something, and Kevin put my name forward, even though I'm not an advanced trainee yet."

The hits kept coming. I was dreading moving to Brisbane. I'd told Boyd that perhaps he should spend time in Melbourne at the Royal Children's Hospital there. There's no way I'd bump into my father in Melbourne. He must see the look of shock on my face.

"Look, it's just something to think about. I mean, I know this cycle is going to be the one, and I know it will suck having a baby in Brisbane with your mum and Nonna up here, but Val's down in Brissy, and she's made it clear she doesn't plan on coming back up here anytime soon." It's clear Boyd is excited about this prospect from the way he's bouncing with energy and talking with his hands.

"But what if this cycle isn't successful?" I ask, needing to be the voice of reason.

"Well, Kevin said I'd be here until early April, so if we need to, we can fit in another cycle or two."

I've been working here for two and a half weeks. Whilst I love the patients, I can see Doug becoming a problem. "You know I love you and want what's best for you. I may hate the idea of Brisbane, but only because I'm scared I'll bump into my father, but I could never hold you back. It's still only one rotation in Brisbane though. We won't have to go more than once, will we?"

"No, just this one. It might be until the end of next year, but you can be a mummy or do more training down there." Boyd had planned this out. I could see this. His enthusiasm is contagious, and with Gina probably moving back to Brisbane, I will know a couple of people at least.

"Tell Kevin and the professor to lock it in." I take his face in my hands and kiss him.

Two taps sound at the door, and it flies open. "Oh, Emily, still busy I see."

"Hey, Doug. Sorry, can't keep away from her." Boyd places a hand on my thigh.

"Sorry, Doug. Can I help you?" I look at my watch and see I've still got four minutes before my next consultation.

"I wanted to arrange a time for dinner, that's all," he says, one lip lifted in a grimace as he stares at me.

"Cool," Boyd says as he jumps down from the bed. "You know my roster, babe. You bringing your wife, Doug?" Boyd asks as he moves towards the door.

"I'm not married at present," Doug sneers.

"Well, you should meet Emily's mum. She's a hottie, just like Emily, and has been single for far too long. I don't think she minds older men, either. See you tonight, babe." Boyd winks at me as he pushes past Doug and leaves the surgery. Doug is beet red as he turns and storms back to his room. *God, I love my husband so much.*

"So, we're going to implant this one," Jacquie says as we look at the image of a clump of cells on the screen. "And then tomorrow, we'll hopefully freeze the other two."

We harvested ten eggs at pick up and eight had fertilised. The report this morning was we had this one grade one embryo, grade one being the best, two grade two embryos, and two grade three embryos, and the rest had failed to develop.

"Is it an option to put one of the grade three's in too?" Boyd asks from over my shoulder.

"It may seem tempting"—Dr Jacquie draws out her words, causing us both to listen—"but the grade threes aren't good enough quality to freeze, and we really want to get this amazing embryo here inside you and give it the best opportunity for developing."

Boyd holds my hands as the doctor guides the pipette containing the blastocyst inside me. All five embryos looked pretty good on day three, and we let them develop into blastocyst form before transfer, as this usually produces better results.

It's not as painful as it was when I tried to have an IUD inserted when I was at medical school, but it's not comfortable either. I'd much rather be having sex. Boyd strokes my hair and kisses my forehead as Jacquie is the one up in my vagina. It seems quite surreal.

"You're off to work?" The doctor claps her hands after she snaps off her gloves and rubs them with alcohol.

"Don't I have to rest?" I ask. "Like for half an hour or something?"

"No." The doctor smiles. "You're good to go. The embryo won't fall out. I'll talk to you in nine days after your blood test to see if the cycle's worked. Be kind to each other, alright?"

"Of course." Boyd pulls his head back, as if he is surprised anyone would think he would never be kind to me. "But, um, no sex, right?"

"You can if you feel like it." The doctor looks between us. "Some studies have shown contractions from female orgasm and the prostaglandins from the semen can aid implantation. It definitely won't hurt."

I have to laugh as Boyd fist pumps the air, as I climb off the bed and walk towards the change room. As I get dressed, I don't feel any different. It's strange. I pull out my phone to text Gina. She came over for dinner last night and flies out to Brisbane today.

> Hey, safe travels. One embryo, safely implanted. Well, ejected into my uterus. Now we have the longest nine day wait in history.

GINA

> I have good feelings for you, too, plus, you'll be in Brisbane before long. I can't wait to meet your sister-in-law. She sounds like a hoot.

Val has agreed to help Gina with her divorce. Damo had actually promised he'd wear condoms, but he couldn't promise he wouldn't sleep with other women and got angry with Gina when she told him their marriage was over. She is well rid of him.

"HOW ARE YOU FEELING, BABY MAMA?" Boyd takes me in his arms, his lips brushing mine as we wait for the lift to leave the clinic.

The kiss reminds me of our wedding day and the way he consumed me then. I love that despite everything we're going through, he still adores me.

"Nine days to wait to see if I'm a mother." I hold his hand as the doors open, and we enter the lift together.

Boyd stands behind me, his hands clasped on my stomach. "Whatever happens, we saw the procedure on the ultrasound, and an embryo was inserted into you. That makes us parents in my books, even if it is only for a matter of minutes, hours, or days."

I hadn't thought of it like this. I bite my lip, and a smile breaks across my face as I take in Boyd's words. His philosophy is sound and demonstrates how he is a glass half full kind of guy.

Last week, I told Mum we were doing IVF on the proviso she not talk to Hillary about it. We talked about her experiences with IVF, and it amazed her how much had changed and how much was like when she was doing it thirty years ago. She told me about the dreaded two week wait after transfer and am glad I only have to wait nine days instead of fourteen.

However long I have to wait, I know it is going to be long and stressful. Add in the preparations for the Gala Ball in two weeks, and things could get very stressful. Every five years, Hillary and Charlie host a Gala Ball to raise funds for the cardiac ward at the hospital. It also helps celebrate major wedding anniversaries for them. Helping Hillary plan it would help me take my mind off things, and surely, she'll know how to instruct people to hang the fairy lights by now.

"Well, baby daddy." I kiss Boyd again as the doors to the lift open. "Here's hoping it takes, and our little group of cells grows up big and healthy like its parents."

I have to believe we wouldn't fail. I mean, we've been through enough already, haven't we?

Emily, Age 23

Fifth-year exams are a killer. They can test us on anything knowing these are the last exams we'll sit, well, until we have to sit specialist exams, but that could be years from now. Boyd has cards stuck all over the walls of the apartment. Behind the toilet door, he has so many mnemonics that he thinks help him remember things.

It's our final exam in the morning. Bridget has really been mothering us. She had a breakdown during an exam in fifth year and tells everyone about it and how she'd been told at the time the results of the exam would mean nothing several years down the track, and how true this was. She drops off food every other day, even though I know she's busy at work. Henry brought around his old notes from his fifth-year revision, but he writes like a doctor, and I can't understand any of them. Boyd suggested he type them out for us, but he told us he was too busy for that.

Charlie offered to go over the heart with us, but I think we're both fine with cardiac stuff. Giles keeps quizzing us, anyway.

I know Bridget keeps saying that it won't matter if something happens, and we fail, but failure isn't an option for me. I want to graduate with Boyd. If one of us passes and the other one doesn't, we'll be separated and graduate apart. I couldn't think of anything worse.

On one hand, I've got Bridget telling me that it won't matter and will make success later on all that more sweet, and on the other, I've got Boyd telling me Hartmans don't fail. But I'm not a Hartman yet. What if I get in there and freeze?

Chapter 17

Boyd

I used to think school days went slow. Not that I hated school, I just found it boring. But nothing has dragged more than the last nine days. It's the Gala Ball tomorrow night, and I long for it to be a celebration for Emily and me. It's an event that screams love, and I can't wait to hold her knowing she's carrying our baby.

The signs are there that Emily's pregnant. I mean, I know she's been on hormones after the transfer, but her tits are super sensitive, and she had to gulp back a burp yesterday that I thought was nausea.

Perhaps I'm just wishing and hoping beyond hope that our struggles are behind us. It's been over three years, and I'm sick and tired of waiting. I want to be a dad. I want to hold a baby that Emily and I made and was born from the same love my family has always showed.

I don't know why I'm sitting with her, waiting for a blood test. It's not like we're seeing a doctor or anything, but I need to be close to her. We've both taken the day off to help Mum with the Gala preparations. The marquee looks amazing as always, with Mum and her team decorating it with an 'Under the Sea' theme for their coral anniversary.

Rosa has sewn Emily a stunning coral-red dress. I haven't seen it on her, but I know she will look a million dollars. Val flies up this morning. We're picking her up from the airport after the blood test.

"All good?" I smile as Emily makes her way out of the room where they drew her blood.

"Yeah." Emily's brow is furrowed and her voice is low. "I just, I mean, I just feel like my period's on its way. Yesterday, I was sure I felt nauseous, but today, I just feel bloated and a little crampy."

"Come here." I pass my arm around her shoulders as we leave the pathology centre. "You know your body, and whatever happens, we'll get through it together."

It was good to see Emily roll her eyes when I opened the car door for her. She hates when I do things like that, reminding me she is an independent woman. Secretly, though, I know she appreciates it.

The drive to the airport is quiet. Neither of us speaks, allowing Nora Jones to serenade us softly in the background. I don't know how long it will take for Dr Jacquie to call us. The results shouldn't take that long, but the doctor was probably seeing patients or something.

"She's landed and is grabbing her case, but she said not to park, and she'll be right out." Emily reads Val's text message as I turn into the airport.

I drive around twice as Val and Emily text back and forth. It appears Val left a bag on the plane and has to go back for it. I'm not surprised. She's always forgetting things. Finally, she comes running from the airport towards the car, just as the guard is about to tell us to move on.

Emily jumps out of the car, and Val throws her arms around her. I smile at the joy the two of them have in seeing each other after only a matter of weeks. Being closer to Val in Brisbane will be good for Emily, and maybe we'll convince my sister to move back up north to be closer to us all. If only she hadn't landed her dream job, as she keeps describing it.

"Stinky." I wink into the mirror as she gets in the back seat, knowing how much she hates her childhood nickname. "What did you forget?"

"Shut up. I left the bag with my dress on the plane, so I went back for it." She laughs as if it's a typical thing to leave things behind. Well, for her, it is.

"You know Mum would have whipped you up a dress." Emily

places her hand on my thigh as she looks over her shoulder at Val. I like the contact.

"I know," Val sighs. "And I hate shopping, but I found this dress last year, and I wore it to the Law Ball, and I want to wear it again. It's got a slit right up the thigh."

Giles' reaction to this will be interesting. He enjoys playing big brother and has trouble believing Val is all grown up. He's always going on about how she should have studied medicine, but secretly, I know he's proud of our sister for forging her own career away from the rest of us, as much as he moans about it.

Emily and Val fill the car with chatter. Val shares a case she's been working on where the husband accused his wife of cheating, something she strenuously denied, only to post on social media ten months later that he spent an amazing year with his new girlfriend.

"And she's an accountant." Val shakes her head, her voice rising with incredulity. "I mean, it's just basic maths."

"Yeah, well, not every guy's as good as a Hartman. Bridget, Ken, and I have all hit the jackpot. I wish you'd find someone nice." Emily's care is genuine, her voice full of the same compassion I'm sure she gives her patients.

"True." Val gazes out the window as we head towards Mum and Dad's. "I must admit, dealing with marriages ending in my work life and knowing the stats about divorce doesn't endear me towards settling down. I mean, I'm glad my brothers have all found love, and, well, Mum and Dad are the poster kids for happy families, but maybe it's not in my cards."

I'm just about to reply when Emily's phone rings. "Um, hello." Emily sounds hesitant as she places the phone on speaker.

"Emily, it's Jacquie Singh from the fertility clinic. Is it a good time to talk?"

We've just pulled into Mum and Dad's drive. Val goes to get out of the car, but Emily signals for her to stay.

"Um, yes." Emily's voice is clipped, and her hands shake as they hold the phone. Val has leant forward from the back, a hand on each of our shoulders.

"Good. So, I've got the bloods in front of me." Emily's nodding even though the doctor can't see down the phone. "It's come back showing you're pregnant."

"Oh my god, baby. Oh, my god," I scream as I clasp Emily's face in my hands.

"Boyd." I hear Dr Jacquie almost shout down the line.

"Sorry, I'm just a little excited." Both Emily and I have tears streaming down our faces.

"Okay, I just wanted to warn you." She takes a deep breath that I can hear down the line, and my brow furrows. "The level is below one hundred, and that usually means there's a one in four chance that it will be a biochemical pregnancy."

Fuck. Her words hit me like a kick to the guts. We have a positive pregnancy test, but we may also have a very early miscarriage, usually because something is wrong with the embryo.

"Sorry, it's Val here, Boyd's sister. So, there's a three in four chance that things will be okay then? That's good, isn't it?"

"It is, yes. I just want Boyd and Emily to be prepared."

I've had a few conversations with parents when they've had sick kids, not wanting to give them too much hope because things might still go wrong. I know what our doctor's doing here, but with everything that's gone wrong, I feel that for Emily and me, the three in four chance really is that something bad will happen.

"Have you got any questions?" Jacquie asks.

"So, another blood test then?" Emily is blinking away the tears that previously fell in joy, my hands clasping hers.

"Yes, on Monday. Look, it's great news that we've got to this stage, and things really might be fine."

"Thanks for warning us, though. It's appreciated," I reply, my voice trying not to crack.

Emily ends the call, and we sit in silence for a few seconds before jumping when there's a tap on the window.

"What are you three up to? Gossiping? I need help, please. The lights won't hang themselves," Mum speaks through the window. I turn off the engine, and Val leaps out of the car to give Mum a hug.

"Em's just going to help me take my stuff up to my room." Emily and I have climbed out of the car, and Val is trying to distract our mother from paying too close attention to us.

Val hands Emily the bag carrying her dress, and I want to tell her to not carry anything. She has precious cargo on board. I just want to run away for the day and spend it with my wife. Every night since transfer, I've whispered things into her tummy, promising our little bean that I'll be the best dad I can be. I have to believe things will end up alright. I have to be strong and know that what will be, will be. It's hard though.

THE MARQUEE IS SET, and the lights only had to be restrung twice in one section before we got it how Mum wanted it. It's Dad's birthday. Hen and Ken are in Brisbane at a wedding. We'd usually go out to a pub for dinner, but Bridget suggested fish and chips on their deck. Dipti did an amazing job helping in the marquee today, but she declined the offer to join us.

"You seem chipper tonight." Giles hands me a beer, and we clink the necks of the bottles together.

"I love the Gala." I take a swig of the amber liquid and remind myself not to say anything about the pregnancy.

It's so hard not to. I want to shout it from the rooftops.

Mia has Val and Emily entranced in a story about what happened at school and how she thinks her teacher, Miss Lilly, is so pretty and so lovely and so kind. All this because it was Mia's turn to lead the student line on the way to music class.

Giles tries to make everyone stay where they are as he clears away the butcher's paper dinner had been wrapped in. Val and Emily help him, and I go to stand when Millie asks me if I want to hear her play her tambourine.

"You know I'd love nothing more, Princess Millie," I tell her as she pumps her fists and runs inside to fetch it.

"Boyd," Bridget says firmly as she shakes her head. "The correct answer is no. You never want to hear that damn instrument again."

"It could have been a drum set." I shrug as Millie reappears, Mia behind her with some ribbons on a stick that she waves through the air, and the two of them put on a performance butchering either a Taylor Swift or Katy Perry song. I can't actually tell what it's meant to be, and the words make no sense.

Giles rejoins us outside and joins in with Mia as she hands a ribbon to him, and he twirls it over his head. Emily and Val must still be inside. Despite protests from Bridget, Dad encourages the girl to give us another song. I think it's meant to be Jingle Bells, but, again, it's mashed up with other classics, and we get lines about no room for a bed, and a dish running away with a spoon.

The scene is perfect. Giles is hamming it up, and I can't wait to do that with my kids one day. I smile, knowing I'm going to be a dad. Emily is carrying our baby. At the next Gala, it might be our kids putting on a performance for their grandparents, aunts, uncles, and cousins. I can't wait to give Millie and Mia cousins.

I look at Dad, who's laughing at the performance. He looks so content. He's in his late fifties and has done the best job as both a dad and grandfather. If I can be half the dad he's been to me and my siblings, then my kids will turn out alright.

"Right." Bridget claps and stands as they finish, taking the ribbons from Giles and Mia, and the tambourine from Millie. "It's bath time. Come on."

"I want Daddy." Millie grabs her father's hand, and Giles bends down and gives it a kiss.

"Nope, it's Mummy's turn tonight. Daddy can read you a story, though, and if you ask nicely, Auntie Val might even read you one."

The thought of their father supervising their evening ablutions is long gone, and the girls race inside.

Bridget appears a minute later and places a hand on my shoulder, leaning in to tell me that Emily isn't well.

Excusing myself, I make my way inside, expecting her to be lying in the lounge room, but instead, she's sitting on the toilet with the door open, Val on her knees beneath her, grasping her hands. Her cheeks are wet with tears, and she's struggling to take in an uninterrupted breath.

"Auntie Emily's sad." Mia appears from her bedroom, and Bridget shuffles her back, telling her she can shower in the morning.

"Hey," I whisper, my voice a higher pitch than usual.

Emily looks up from Val and starts sobbing, more tears appearing.

"She wouldn't let me get you," Val says as she stands, and I take her place. The squeeze on my arm provides comfort, I think, but my brain is still sitting out on the deck, reflecting that I'm going to be a father.

Emily's skirt is covering her knees, but her knickers are in a pile next to the toilet. I can see them covered in blood. My wife can't form words, and my brain finally catches up. I want to cry, but no tears come. I need to be strong for Emily. It might just be some spotting.

"Do, um, do you want Bridget?" I ask, trying to sound soft and soothing but feeling loud and angry inside.

Emily just nods, and I hear Val walking down the passage to the girls' room, knocking and entering.

Bridget comes over and tries to kneel beside me, but there isn't a lot of room. Emily looks at me with glassy eyes and nods as if she wants me to talk.

"So, um." I let out a breath, willing myself to stay strong. "This morning... no, we just did our first IVF that led to actually transferring an embryo. Nine days ago. And this morning, Em did a test, and the doctor rang and said she's pregnant, but it was lower than a hundred, and she warned us that it might be a chemical pregnancy."

"And you're bleeding." It's not a question from Bridget, she knows. Emily nods. "Is it spotting?"

More tears come as Bridget passes her a toilet roll to wipe her eyes.

"It's..." Emily's voice hitches in a series of breaths. "It's too heavy. There's... there's no way." She's shaking her head.

"I can get you seen by a colleague this evening at the hospital, but you'll need to go via ED," Bridget offers, rubbing Emily's knee.

I feel like I've frozen. I should be the one comforting her. I should be the one telling her everything will be fine, and she'll be alright—that we'll be alright.

"No." Emily is firm. "I'm not being triaged at the hospital. It's Gala weekend, and people will know. I don't want anyone to know."

"Are you cramping?" Bridget asks, and Emily nods. "I've got some oxycodone I can give you. It's probably out of date, but it will still be effective."

"Thanks." Emily tries to smile, but it's merely a slight movement of her lips.

Bridget walks away, and I try to lean in and hug Emily. I'm shocked when she flinches away. "Please, Boyd, no." She holds her hands in front of her, and I back away.

Bridget returns and hands Emily a tablet, which she swallows with the glass of water offered. "I don't have sanitary items, but I can get you some clean knickers," Bridget offers.

"Val says she's got some." Emily gives a single chuckle and shakes her head. "She said she never remembers when her period's due, so she carries them with her all the time."

I return to the deck to say goodnight to my brother and parents, telling them that Emily's not feeling very well. Mum, Dad, and Giles are talking about work, and I don't think they noticed we've been gone for a while.

When I get back inside, Emily is being hugged by Val. I try to take over, but Emily pulls away. Bridget accompanies us outside, and Emily is quick to open the car door and strap herself in before I can help.

"Be gentle with yourselves," Bridget says as she kisses me on the cheek.

Gentle? I feel anything but. I want to punch someone, but I don't know who. I want to turn back the clock to when we were told Emily was pregnant. Theoretically, I know women can experience a fair bit of blood loss without miscarrying, but Emily seems certain, and I trust her to know her body.

We drive home in silence. Emily has her belt off and is out of the car before I can switch off the engine. She's left the front door open for me. When I get to the top of the stairs, I find her in the kitchen, filling the kettle with water.

I walk towards her, but, again, she holds up her hands, silently telling me to stay away.

"Em, please?" I know she's hurting, but I am, too.

"Boyd." It comes out short as she stands up tall, arms by her side. She can't even look at me. "I think it's best you go to Brisbane by yourself."

I laugh, incredulous at her words, and I open my mouth to speak.

"No." Her hand is up again, and this time, she looks at me, tears in her eyes. "I need to get this out." Her breaths are shallow. "I'm broken. There's either something wrong with my eggs, or my uterus, but you need to be a father. You need to raise kids. I saw you with Millie and Mia this evening. You need to forget about me and find someone who can give you what I can't."

She pours water over the tea bag in the mug in front of her. "People were never expecting us to last, and no one will be surprised when they hear we're getting a divorce. You can move on. Hell, you might even love Brisbane and stay down there with Val."

I can't believe these words are coming out of my wife's mouth. Can't she see we're stronger together and that I don't want to be with anyone else? It's always been her, and it always will be her, forever and always.

Emily, Age 16

Unbelievable. I got a B on my piano exam. I've never gotten less than an A, usually an A+. The prick wrote on the report that my scales were sloppy, but the pieces were played with precision and finesse. Who wants to listen to me practice scales? It's not like I'm ever going to have people say 'Hey, Emily, can you play E flat harmonic minor, two hands, in some stupid rhythm for us? It's my favourite scale.' I mean, come on.

My teacher says she thinks the examiner was harsh, but he was harsh on everyone. She also said he was partially correct with my scales, and they could be sloppy. I didn't need to do this exam. It's not like I want to get into uni and study piano, even though I could and I might even enjoy it. I wanted to push myself and show people I could do it all; you know, get the straight As at school, be the best girlfriend for Boyd, and the best daughter and granddaughter for Mum and Nonna.

Last week, I got a call from the manager at a posh hotel in town. They've got a piano in the atrium that's never played, and he asked if I'd be interested in playing for a few hours on Friday and Saturday evenings. My teacher had mentioned something, and I'd told her she could give out my number. Apparently, there's two of us my teacher recommended, so it's not like I'd have to work every weekend.

I just hate the idea that I didn't do my best in my exam. I'm better than that. Failure isn't an option for me. As much as I want to just stop playing piano, the money from the hotel gig will be nice. It's so hard. I want to give up, but at the same time, there's still a pull. Sometimes, I wonder if I don't give up enough and keep going with things, even though I'm unsuccessful with them. I never carried on with Italian, even after taking lessons for five years, and there's no point learning how to bake when Mum, Nonna, and Val are all excellent in the kitchen.

Perhaps I need to make a stand though and anything in my future that I'm not good at, and I've given an effort to being good at, I just cut it out of my life. Perhaps I need to set a time limit. I like the number three. So, three weeks or three months it can be. Maybe for harder things, I might give it three years, but that seems excessive.

And yeah, Boyd was right. That examiner wouldn't know his elbow from his arsehole.

Chapter 18

Emily

I LIKE TO THINK I REMEMBER GOOD THINGS, BUT THE terrible memories from my life take over. I remember the pale-pink pyjamas with the thin white stripe that I thought were the chicest things ever to grace my body and put them on straight after school. They'd been my favourite thing ever until I was wearing them when Dad said he was leaving and tore our family apart.

I probably won't remember the navy skirt I am wearing today, but I will remember Boyd's face as he knelt in front of me as I sat on the toilet sobbing. Sure, I sobbed for the loss of the baby, but I also sobbed for the loss of us.

It wouldn't surprise me if Boyd's forgotten my fascination with the number three. It seems almost fitting that after three years of trying and three IVF cycles, I decide I need to let Boyd move on with his life.

Boyd was born to be a father. He adores kids and works with them every day. He's a big kid himself. It's not fair to take his dreams of fatherhood away from him. As much as it hurts, and I know I'll never find anyone else, he needs to move on and find a woman who isn't broken. One who can give him a baby.

Maybe I'm being a bitch and I know he wants to comfort me, but I need to make a clean break. The Gala tomorrow night will be hard enough. I can't not go. I couldn't do that to Hillary and Charlie, so it can be my and Boyd's last hurrah.

After I tell him it's over, Boyd stands in the lounge room, speechless. It's rare he's at a loss for words. I walk past him into the bedroom and throw a few things in an overnight bag.

"I'm going to Mum's," I say calmly.

I feel anything but calm, though. The cramping has eased, thanks to the tablet Bridget gave me, but the realisation that I was a mother for such a short period cuts like a knife. I know life's never been fair, but today, it seems like the world is out to get me.

"No, Em, please." Boyd is the one crying now. "Let's talk about this. I won't go to Brisbane."

"You will." I grit my teeth as I push the words out, hoping my voice doesn't crack like it's threatening to. I hate seeing Boyd like this, so broken, but I know he'll put himself back together again. "I'll be at the ball, and perhaps we can tell your family on Sunday, even though I know it will wreck your mum's birthday."

I never realised I have the strength to hold it together like I am, but as soon as I walk out our front door, the tears start again. This is the last thing I want. I know that, but I need to let Boyd do what's best for him, even if it means breaking me.

It's not safe for me to drive, but I don't care anymore. Being wiped out would solve a lot of problems. I'd never do it to myself, but if it happened to me...

Somehow, I end up at Mum's. The flickering light of the television shines through the gap in the curtains that have never fit the front window properly. I open the door and find Mum hand stitching the hem of a gown, probably one that someone will wear tomorrow night. There's a period drama on television. How much easier it would have been to live two hundred years ago and not have to worry about IVF. If I didn't get pregnant, there would be little we could do. It's not like they could have done scans or even blood tests to work things out.

"Hello," Mum says inquisitively.

"Oh, Mum." I drop my bag to the ground and slump to my knees on the floor, the tears once again flooding my cheeks. I know I've never cried so much in my life, not even when Dad left.

"Em, hey, what is it? Did you and Boyd have a fight?" Mum has thrown the dress over the arm of the chair and is on her knees next to me. There's a pin in her T-shirt that sticks into me, but it just adds to the pain I'm feeling.

"It's over, Mum." I wipe my eyes with the back of my hands.

Mum says nothing. She holds me tight, just like she did when I was a little girl, just like she did when Dad left. An ad comes on the TV for the fertility clinic with promises that they will help make all your dreams come true. Talk about false advertising. Eventually, I tell her about the miscarriage and how I've ended my marriage. Mum listens and offers sympathy, but she knows I'm not looking for advice.

Exhausted and emotionally drained, I put some distance between us. "I'm going to go to bed," I announce.

"I can make you a tea, or a hot milk?" Mum offers, kissing the top of my head. She knows I don't want to talk.

I shake my head and make my way to my childhood room. It doesn't look that different to how it did when I was eighteen and moved out to live at the Hartmans'. The sheets are still a pale pink with purple cushions strewn on the bed. I couldn't find a doona cover in the right shade of purple that I liked, so I settled on pink.

There's pain in coming to this room, though. It's the place Boyd and I first had sex. It hurts to think that Boyd will now have sex with someone else. Some other woman will get to experience what an amazing lover he is.

My phone beeps, and I half expect a message from Boyd. It's not him. Part of me is relieved that he is letting me go, and part of me wants him to fight for me, even though I know it's not in our best interests. It's probably best he isn't contacting me.

VAL

Hey. Just checking up on you. Hopefully, you're snuggled in your husband's arms (not that I really want to think of my brother like that, but I know he gives the best hugs—but don't tell Giles!) and don't reply to this until morning, but I hate seeing you hurt so much. It's just not fair. Love you xx

I want to reply. I haven't even contemplated that I'll lose Val in my divorce. I'll lose all the Hartmans. I feel sick when I think about how I fought so hard to break away from being Emily McIntyre, and now I'll no longer be Emily Hartman. Maybe I'll take Pucci, my Nonna's surname. What's in a name, though? Perhaps Shakespeare had it right.

I'm at Mum's. Boyd's going to go to Brisbane by himself. It will be an easy divorce. He can have our savings. We're going to be at the ball together, though, to save face and all.

I see the dots come and go, signalling Val is typing away and expect a long message. Maybe she'll offer me legal advice, maybe she'll try to tell me I'm being an idiot. Instead of staring at my phone and waiting, I head to the bathroom. I run a cloth over my face and brush my teeth. As I move to the toilet, I know any hope that an embryo might have survived is long gone, judging by the clots on my pad. Even though I feel numb from everything that's happened, it's a visual reminder that I'm no longer pregnant, and a heavy weight descends on me.

I move to the shower and let the water run over me, again seeing blood trickle down my legs. None of this is what we planned, and I never, ever thought I'd be in this position. I want to curl up in a ball on the shower floor, but I know I'll have no energy to stand again, so I turn off the water, dry myself, and throw my comfy dressing gown around me.

"She's in the bathroom," I hear Mum say. If she's let Boyd in, I'll scream. I swing the door open, ready for another fight, but I'm met by Val's arms being thrown around me.

"What are you doing here?" I ask, my voice once again faulting.

"I came to be with you. Not to talk, just to be." Val's voice is soft.

"But what about your parents?" I ask, not wanting to break from this hug.

"They're in bed, but they aren't asleep. I was about to head downstairs to get away from the 'Big boy' and 'Oh yeah, just like that, blossom' comments that I could hear from my room."

I laugh.

"I thought we could have a sleepover." Val places her hands on my shoulders as she breaks our hug. It seems strange she's here and not with her brother, but I won't complain. "You know I won't take sides, and I don't really want to talk about it all tonight, but you mean more to me than my brothers, and I hope you know that."

I laugh. I really laugh. Not that Val's that funny, but it's good to know she's in my corner. Well, I think she is.

"Here they are." Hillary beams as we walk into the salon for hair and makeup. We were meant to have mani-pedi's this morning, but Val cancelled them as I was finally asleep. I think I passed out after seeing the sun come up. "You still feeling poorly, sweetheart?"

Hillary looks at me with such kind eyes. Her words may be brash at times, but deep down, she has a heart of gold.

"She's fine, Mum." Val chastises her mother as I'm led away to the basin to have my hair washed. I get a wave from Trish, my usual hairdresser, who is busy with Bridget.

The apprentice washing my hair isn't a talker, for which I'm glad. I think the tears have dried up for now. Before we arrived here, Val begged me not to make any rash decisions and to wait a few days, but my mind is made up. It breaks my heart to set Boyd free, but he deserves to find someone who can give him the family he desires. It's that thought that keeps circling in my brain and what I need to keep telling myself so I don't falter and let him back in.

It will be hard losing Val as a friend, even though she swears I won't, and it will be even harder losing Hillary and Charlie, who have been surrogate parents to me.

I can't even move away to make things any easier. There's no way I can leave Mum and Nonna. I have thought I might see if the GP practice at Sailor's Bend needs a registrar. I could do some work at the hospital there until a position becomes available. Nonna will love it if I move in with her, and she could do with the help and the company.

I move on autopilot from the basin to the chair in front of the mirror. My eyes are bloodshot and red rimmed. The dark circles underneath them will need more than concealer to cover. Usually, I leave my hair in its bob around my chin. I'm flicking through a magazine, ignoring the conversation Val, Hills, and Bridget are having, when I notice the hairdresser playing with the side of my hair.

She's braided the part with the purple streak and woven it behind my ear. It looks badass, totally the opposite of how I feel.

"Sorry, I'm just playing," she says softly when she catches me looking in the mirror.

"I like it." I can't manage a full smile, but my lips move from the downturn they've been in since last night.

"Thanks, Nancy." Trish comes over, having finished Bridget's hair. "Ooh, I like this." She touches the braid on my still wet hair. "Are we keeping it, Emily?"

"Yeah, I like it," I say, my voice still flat.

"So, what's new with you?" Trish picks up the hair dryer. I had a cut and colour two weeks ago and filled Trish in on what a creep Dr Doug could be. "How's Dr Douche?"

"Same old, same old," I reply.

I turn back to the magazine. Some celebrity couple have separated, shocking everyone, except the nanny who he got caught shagging. Men are so predictable. Doug told me last week he's been married four times and complained that each time a wife took almost everything. He boasts that he's got five children 'that he knows of', as if this is a badge of honour.

Not all men are good and honourable like Charlie, Giles, and Henry. Usually, I'd add Boyd into that group too, but I know one day, if I don't let him go now, he'll do what my father did and wander. There's no way I'll be enough for someone as amazing as Boyd. He'll find a woman who can bear him kids.

Trish pulls at my hair with the brush as she dries the strands. My hair is so straight that we never have to use the hair straightener. We tried curling it once, but the curls didn't set, and it was straight again before I left the salon. Maybe I'll grow out my fringe. I'm not sure how it will look, but it will look different. I might even add some length to it so I can tie it back like I did as a child.

"Hi, Emily, I'm Moxie." The makeup artist pulls up her stool next to my seat. The hair dryer is still going, giving us some measure of privacy. "Now, Val mentioned perhaps waterproof eye makeup for you," she whispers into my ear. I simply nod and look over at Val, who has Nancy drying her pixie cut.

Val smiles at me, giving me confidence that is severely lacking at present. I've no idea how I'm going to get through tonight.

"I'll see you all tonight." Bridget slides her phone into her pocket and grabs her bag. She's been growing her hair again after one of her girls played hairdresser on her long locks. Trish has done an amazing job adding in curls, and Moxie has given her the most natural makeup look that really suits her. I know how much she hates hanging around the salon, but she does it for the Gala.

Hillary is also finished, but she makes no moves to leave.

"Well, Henry and Ken are back," she says, reading something on her phone. "And apparently, Boyd's in a foul mood. He picked them up from the airport, and Henry's amazed they got home in one piece."

Moxie is working her magic as Trish goes to put product in Val's hair and style it in the way only hairdressers seem to manage.

"Oh, and Charlie's been to the barber." Hillary looks down at her phone as if she wants to eat it. He's clearly sent her a photo, as she snaps one of herself to post back to him.

Once upon a time, I thought Boyd and I would end up like Charlie and Hills, snapping photos to each other, having loud sex that everyone else in the house could hear, and being, well, that couple still in love after so long. It's devastating to know that this isn't my future now, despite how much I love Boyd. Maybe I'll get a cat, even though I'm allergic.

"And how was your evening, Valerie? Are you bringing him to the ball?" Hillary raises one side of her mouth as she looks at her daughter.

"What?" Val asks as she waits for Moxie.

"Last night." Hillary chuckles. "I heard you go out, and you didn't come home. I assume you went for a hookup."

"Yeah, well, there were no orgasms." Val shrugs her shoulders, picking up a magazine to flick through.

I'm glad she didn't say she was with me. Her family knows her mantra that a guy has to give her an orgasm to get a second date.

"He still kept you out all night." Hillary smirks as she goes back to her phone.

"Nah, I spent the morning with Em. I don't see her enough, and, no offence, Mum, but you and Dad aren't exactly quiet. Most of my friends don't believe their parents have sex anymore, and yet anyone who stays at your place is subjected to the constant moaning and groaning from you both."

"You're just jealous." Hills smiles. "One day, you'll find a man who makes you as happy as Charlie makes me."

Val scoffs and shakes her head. I wish she would find someone she could be happy with. She has occasional boyfriends, but none of them last. I suspect none are smart enough to match her wit and keep up with her in the bedroom.

Moxie is doing an amazing job with my makeup. She can't do anything with the bloodshot eyes, but she's said she's going to put a big bold lip on and leave the eyes more subdued, so people are drawn down my face. I really don't care. I'll be seen at the Gala and then, after the speeches, I'll slip away. Dancing with Boyd won't be hard, because he's a good dancer, but it will be painful knowing this is where our fairy tale ends. In less than thirty-six hours, I've gone from being pregnant, to miscarrying and ending my marriage. After tonight, there's brunch tomorrow, where I'll tell the Hartmans that Boyd and I are no more.

I'm worried about Boyd. I hate hearing that he's in a bad mood, especially because I'm the one who's caused it. One day, I hope he'll understand that this really is for the best. There will be no more pain of IVF or miscarriages for him. He can move on and start afresh.

I just have to get through tonight.

It's a tradition that I get ready at the Hartmans' before the Gala. After the salon, I grab my dress and accessories from Mum's, and Val and I make our way to her house, the same place I called home for a few years when Boyd and I started at uni.

Boyd's car is parked in the driveway, and it doesn't surprise me that he's here early. I hope it means he's been talking to his dad, who will give him good advice. He must be looking out the window, waiting for us, because as soon as our car stops, he's out the door and running towards us. My tears start again, and I'm glad we went for the waterproof mascara.

"I can't do this," I whisper to Val, who opens her door and jumps out.

"Boyo, give her some space, okay? Just give her space." Val is firm with her brother, giving me a sense of how she is in court.

"I just want—" Boyd starts, his hand running through his hair, which has broken free from the hair tie he usually keeps it back with. He's still in a T-shirt and shorts, not dressed in his tuxedo. He looks as tired as I am, and I wish I could reach out and comfort him. It's going to take some time getting used to the fact that he's no longer mine to take care of.

"No," Val almost yells. "Inside. Now."

He turns and skulks inside, his feet dragging as they move.

"Come on." Val opens my door and helps me stand. She even passes me a tissue that's materialised from her bag. "You've got this. You're my bestie, who's strong and fearless. We'll get through tonight and take it one day at a time."

She takes me inside and up the stairs, fortunately avoiding Boyd, who has taken his sister's advice and made himself scarce. Val hangs my dress in her room and leads me to her parents' room where we enter the ensuite, and she turns on a bath.

It's the memory of Boyd doing this for me that has me undone again. The memory of how much he cared about me. I know he still cares, but as callous as it sounds, I tell myself he'll get over it.

"Mum's in the marquee, and Dad's who knows where, but I'm

going to be just outside this door, and I won't let anyone in here. You take your time relaxing, remembering your hair and makeup look stunning." Val squeezes my arm as I undo the buttons on the front of my dress and let it fall to the floor.

As I lay in the bath trying to relax, I hear Val whispering outside the door, but it doesn't sound like Boyd she's talking to. He tried to fight for me when we arrived, and I sent him away. Now I wish he was here fighting again. I'm so confused, and I tell myself it's only because Boyd means so much to me and I still care deeply for him. That's why I'm doing this, after all.

It's pure misery being here with so many wonderful memories, and before long, I pull the plug and reach for the plush towel Val left out for me. I dry myself carefully, wishing I'd thought to shave my legs. It's not like anyone is getting near them anytime soon, and my dress covers them.

With the towel wrapped around me and tucked under my arm, I open the door to find Hillary stepping into her gown and Val zipping it up.

"That's gorgeous, Hillary," I say, an almost genuine smile making it no further than my lips.

"Why thank you, Em. Your mother is a very talented woman."

Hillary's dress is a royal-blue chiffon number with wide shoulder straps and almost chiffon wings that come from the back and are clasped around her wrists. It looks ethereal.

"Nice bath?" Val asks, and I nod.

"The night is always darkest, just before the dawn." Hillary draws me in for a hug. I trust Val not to share things with her mother, but Hillary clearly can sense something is wrong. "Now, you two get dressed. Henry just texted, and he and Ken are on their way over. Bridget and Giles should be here soon if their daughters let them leave."

Millie and Mia had been demanding they come to the party too, but Mum's going to look after them and has brought in reinforcements in the form of Nonna. Those girls adore Nonna, partially because she always has sweets in her bag, and partially because she's just Nonna, and everyone loves her.

In Val's room, I reach for my dress. It has a built-in bra, and I wear my normal cotton knickers. There's no point wearing scratchy, lacy numbers when Boyd won't get to see them. I'm planning on staying at Mum's again tonight.

Wiping my eyes again, I'm amazed that the makeup hasn't budged. Val looks stunning in her black satin number. If she doesn't pick up someone tonight, I'll be amazed.

I tuck another tissue in the top of my dress, wishing I had taken my mother's advice to have pockets sewn into it.

"You got this." Val draws me in for a hug before she opens her bedroom door.

We make our way downstairs. Everyone's there waiting for us. Charlie and Hillary, Giles and Bridget, and Henry and Ken all have their arms around each other.

"You look stunning." Boyd's eyes are glassy as he stands open-mouthed, gazing at me. "If I wasn't so in love with you before, I'm, well, I'm even more in love with you now."

Hearing those words makes my heart sing, but I don't believe them. I'm broken. He knows I'm broken, and it's only a matter of time until he moves on. It's better this way. We just need to get through tonight.

I take a deep breath. "Let's go." I slide my arm into his, noticing how my heart hammers and I feel a sense of home in his touch. This could be a long night.

AFTER TWO NIGHTS of very little sleep, I feel like crap. I probably feel worse than crap, but I'm too numb to feel much. The Gala last night is a blur. It's like I was there in body, but I needed to distance my mind from being present.

I spent most of the night dancing. I remember that. It was hard being in Boyd's arms and not wanting to lean closer and take in his scent. The feel of his arms holding me like they wanted me there was hard, but they held me up and kept me standing when I just wanted to fall in a heap.

Hillary spoke of the ups and downs of a marriage. I remember that much, but I can't remember much else. Boyd was standing behind me for the speeches and had his arms around me, his chin on my head.

As soon as the speeches were over, I made an excuse and left, just like I planned. Val offered to join me, but I wanted to be alone.

I can still hear the music thumping in my head this morning, the songs about love and commitment and joy. Telling the Hartmans today will be one of the hardest things I've ever done. I know they'll be devastated. They need to know now though, so they can support Boyd.

Glancing at my phone, I can see it's just after nine. There's also a message from Boyd making me realise I need to change his name in my phone.

> **HUSBAND**
>
> Hey, can I pick you up to take you to Mum and Dad's? I really loved dancing with you last night. The image of you in that dress is burnt into my retinas—you looked stunning.

I hadn't looked that good. My eyes were puffy, and I don't think I found a smile all night. He sent the message just after six, and I knew if I didn't reply, he'd simply turn up here, anyway.

> No. I'll make my way there separately.

I knew I'd want to leave as soon as I told them all.

Mum's in the kitchen when I make my way in there to turn the kettle on. She's a step ahead of me and pours the freshly boiled water into the teapot containing my favourite leaves.

"I heard you in the shower," she says as she places two slices of bread in the toaster. I hope they aren't for me, as I know I won't be able to eat anything. "I didn't hear you come in, but then again, I was exhausted after looking after those kids."

"I was in before you got home. I left right after the speeches," I murmur as I flop into a chair at the kitchen table and pour myself a cup of tea.

"You're still planning on telling the Hartmans?" Mum asks as the toast pops up, and she removes it to a board and butters it before slathering it in Vegemite. She knows this is my favourite. She probably also knows I haven't really eaten for over a day.

"Yeah. I told Doug last week about Brisbane, and he knows I'm planning on leaving in a couple of months, and he's not happy about it, but if I can get a job in Sailor's Bend, I'll move down there with Nonna for a bit."

"Sounds like you've got it all planned." Mum slices the toast into triangular quarters and places it on a plate for me. It's exactly how I like it, with the right ratio of butter to spread.

I nibble at a triangle, leaving the crust. It could have been almost any morning of me growing up with Mum making toast for breakfast, but it felt different today. I did have it all planned. I was going to move on with my life as best as I could. Strength was what I needed, and I have to believe I have it within me to break away.

For once, Mum didn't comment on me leaving the crusts, both of us knowing that eating them would definitely not make my hair go curly.

She offers to drive me to the Hartmans, but I need to do this alone. Instead, she holds me in a firm hug before I climb into my car, and she tells me she'll be here for me if I need to come back. I don't know where she thinks I'm going. Of course I'll be back.

Boyd is waiting at the end of his parents' street. He pulls up behind me as I park out the front of the house I love so much.

"Hey." Boyd's voice is soft and full of love as he rushes up and opens my car door. "Can we talk?"

I sigh. Boyd holds my hand as I step out of the car, something I'm well and truly able to do without his help. I notice he has a gift wrapped for his mother. I'd forgotten it's her birthday, and I should have brought a gift from me.

"There's nothing to talk about, Boyd." I try to keep it together, but my voice cracks just as Val opens the door and comes out to greet us.

"Come on, you two. You're the last ones here, and they're all in there trying to argue their sex lives are better than yours, what with you running late."

I wasn't that late. This really is the last place I want to be this morning, though.

Following Val inside, I wrap my arms around my waist. Boyd places his hand on the small of my back as if to guide me. His touch still does things to me. It makes me feel alive and desired. I tell myself this is a Pavlovian response and my body was just programmed to respond to his touch after all these years.

"Happy Birthday, Mum." Boyd hands over the gift, and they give each other an enormous hug.

"Thank you both." She comes to me for a hug, and I try not to shy away. "Wasn't it the nicest ball? So many people, so much love."

I need to rip this Band-Aid off.

"Boyd and I are getting a divorce," I state, trying to sound so much more confident than I feel.

The room goes silent. Millie and Mia haven't come running like they usually do when we arrive.

"Good joke, Emily." Giles taps me on the shoulder as he walks past on his way to the fridge. From my face, others can obviously see this is not a joke, though.

"But why?" Henry appears confused as he looks between us. "I mean, the two of you are besotted with each other. The love is palpable and has been for years. What's changed?"

Val comes and stands between Boyd and me, her arms wrapped around both of us.

"I'm sure they do love each other—" she starts.

"What have you done, Boyd?" Charlie looks at his son, disappointment in his eyes.

"It's not Boyd, Charlie. It's me," I say.

"Don't lie, Em." I glance over to see Boyd shaking his head.

"Do you want me to tell them, Boyd?" I snark, both of us having made the decision to keep his family in the dark over three years ago.

"I think you should, yes." His voice cracks, and a tear runs down his face.

"Fair enough." I take a deep breath. "So, Boyd and I started trying for a baby as soon as we were married. Nothing happened, so we took some tests. They couldn't find anything wrong with either of us. So, we kept trying, and still nothing. Finally, we started IVF, and this last cycle was the first one where we could transfer an embryo. They told us

Friday morning that I was pregnant, but there was a chance it might not develop, and by Friday evening, the doctor's prophesy came true. Boyd deserves to be a father. He was born to be a father, and I'm setting him free so he can find someone to have a family with, because I doubt it's going to be me."

Whereas I'd expected his family to flock to Boyd to offer him hugs and sympathy, it was me they were concerned for. Henry jumps out of his seat and is hugging me, telling me how sorry he is for our loss. Giles pats Boyd on the shoulder, whispering something in his ear, before coming and taking over from Henry's hug.

Hillary sits with Charlie, tears trickling down her cheeks. "And what do you want, Boyd?" she asks.

"I don't want any of this. I mean, of course I'd love to have kids, but I only want them with Emily. I don't want to find anyone else, because I know they won't be as amazing as my brilliant wife. We may get a dog or a cat—or not a cat, because Emily's allergic—but Millie and Mia will always be in our lives, along with Luke and Sarah, and any kids Val may pop out in the future. I'm okay with being the fun uncle who provides the loud and unwanted by parents' Christmas gifts. But I'm not getting a divorce, and I'm not letting Emily push me away."

Boyd takes a breath and steps around Val, who is still separating the two of us.

"Em, baby, I adore you. I know you think you're doing the right thing, but it's not what I want, and I'm going to do my best to make you see we are so much better together, whether or not we have a baby. I'm going to fight for you, and I'm going to keep loving you. You're it for me, my always and everything. I'm not going anywhere."

"Right." Charlie claps his hands together. "Where are those girls? Now that this is sorted, I think we need to eat."

But it isn't sorted, is it? I realise Boyd is hugging me, and what's more, I'm hugging him back.

What the fuck has just happened?

Emily, Age 14

I was back with Priscilla after school today. Mum wouldn't listen when I told her it was a pointless exercise and Priscilla was a weirdo. She told me it will help me both now and in the future. That's a hard disagreement from me.

One of the things that's come from these sessions, though, is that I can write this crap, and I'll be able to laugh at it when I find it again in ten or twenty years.

So, today... she wanted to spend the entire session talking about my loser father. What did she want me to say? Of course I'm pissed at him that he would choose someone else over us and move a long way away from us. If anything, that's made it easier, because I don't have to see his ugly face, or have anything to do with her or their kid.

What sort of guy does that? What sort of guy chooses a woman almost half his age and leaves his wife and teenage daughter to start over again? My so-called father. I'm so glad we don't share DNA. Sometimes, when I wonder what my Chinese parents must have been like, especially to leave me in an orphanage like they did, I think that at least they probably didn't run off with another woman.

I can't imagine Charlie doing that. He and Hillary seem so devoted to each other. It's what I want. They have this love for their kids that I'm sure if any of them ever stuffed up, they'd be there to love and support them.

Charlie's a good-looking man, much better looking than my father. I've seen women try to throw themselves at him, which is kind of gross, because he's, like, old, but he ignores it. He only has eyes for his wife.

It's what I want with Boyd. It might be a little crush at the moment, and he hasn't definitely, like, told me he wants me, but he doesn't have a girlfriend, and he ignores the girls that hang around him and try to hit on him. He says he likes me, but does he like me as a friend, or is it more? He acts like it's more, but it's not like we talk about stuff like that. I think he just assumes that we'll be together. I mean, that's what I want, more than anything. A couple of years ago, he told me he's going to marry me, but he was just joking, I think.

I know Boyd will be the type of guy like his father is; you know, strong and dependable. He won't be the type who runs away with a younger woman.

Boyd is nothing like my father. Boyd's sweet and kind. He's loyal and supportive. Priscilla even suggested I talk with Mum about Dad. That's a hard no. I don't want to hurt her by bringing up him. She's fought hard to overcome what he did. I remember hearing her cry at night when she thought I was asleep. She really loved him, and then he went and did this. What a prick.

Chapter 19

Boyd

My mind is a mess. Henry and I had a chat before the Gala. I told him things were rough between me and Emily, and he told me we need to learn to communicate better. That's fucking rich coming from him. He almost blew things up with Ken because of his shit communication.

We communicate. We communicate really well in the bedroom. I know what he's saying, but we know each other so well. I've basically known her all my life. We don't have secrets—well, I have none that I keep from her. I think we know each other better than we know ourselves.

When she told me she wanted me to go and find someone else, it was like an out-of-body experience. There was no way she was talking to me. I mean, there is no one else I could find who would be any match for Emily.

The feelings that swam through me as I held her at the Gala as we danced reminded me how much I love her. It wasn't just the physical of having her in my arms as we moved to the music, but it was the way she hummed the tune or sang along to the band, something I doubted she even knew she did, that made the hairs on my arms prickle and rise.

I knew she'd been to the salon, and she'd used a different shampoo, as her hair smelt sweet like condensed milk. I could have inhaled her all night. And that dress. Her mum is an artist with the dresses she creates. Even though her eyes were puffy and glassy for most of the night, they did nothing to make me want her less.

Brunch has been, well, different. It's always fun when we get together, but today, there's an enormous elephant in the room. I didn't expect Emily to tell everyone about our infertility. I don't mind that she did either. In some ways, it will make it easier being open with them. Sure, there'll be some inappropriate remarks, I'm sure, but I know they won't be out of malice.

Emily is seated at the other end of the table next to Dad and Bridget, with Henry and Ken opposite them. I'm pretty sure she wanted to head out as soon as she dropped her bombshell, but Dad just said it was food time. He's not subtle, but I know he doesn't enjoy confrontation. It's why Mum seems to get her way so much. I'm at the other end of the table with Mum, Giles, and Val. Millie and Mia are in the middle of us all, creating a divide. I want to be down there sitting with her. I want to know what Dad and Henry are saying and why Ken is chuckling.

"Give her space," Mum says softly as she grasps my hand.

"I don't want to." My voice is high, and my brows are furrowed. "I want to be down there comforting her and telling her everything is going to be alright."

"But you don't know that," Mum replies as she lets go of my hand, pushes out her chair, and crosses her legs. She could be a counsellor, not a cardiologist.

Emily may not know that, but I have to think it and believe it. I need to make her understand that having kids is not more important than being with her.

"Bridget and I will probably suggest the same thing." Giles wipes his mouth with his napkin before also pushing out his chair to cross his legs. *What is it with these amateur shrinks?* That's Henry and Ken's job, and there's no leg crossing at that end of the table.

"And what will that be?" I ask, rolling my eyes.

"Therapy." Giles crosses his arms.

"Yeah, good luck with that." I chuckle. "You were at uni when Rosa made Emily see that shrink woman. Em hated it."

"I think she's at the right end of the table to be set straight." Giles smirks as he picks up some of the scraps Millie has pushed from her plate.

"She needs to make peace with what her dad did," Val says, draining the last of her mimosa.

"Her Dad's a—" I start.

"Ankle," Hillary interjects. "Lower than a CU Next Tuesday." She nods at the girls.

"They've heard the word, Mum." Giles rolls his eyes. "You know my mouth."

He doesn't even sound remorseful. Millie and Mia appear to have no idea what's going on, and Mia asks if they can go and play. I feel bad for ignoring them, but they don't seem to mind.

"So, yeah, we do this therapy thing. Then what? I mean, what else?" I need a plan. I need to know what to do to make sure Emily knows how much stronger we are together.

"Woo her." Mum shrugs her shoulders as if it's that simple. "Date her, show her how much she means to you. You know, all the things you never did as a teenager."

Perhaps I need to listen to my mother.

"Um, hi. I'm, um, Boyd." I'm making a mess of this. Mum, Giles, and Val are staring at me. "I, um, saw you at the other end of this room, and I had to come and speak to you. I mean, did it hurt?"

"Sorry?" Emily's brows draw together, and her head bobs backwards as she looks at me as if I'm an idiot. I am.

"When you fell from heaven. Did it hurt?"

"Oh, for fuck's sake." Henry pushes out his chair and throws his arms in the air. "I can't listen to this. You are so not a Hartman, baby bro."

Dad is chuckling, and Bridget has her eyes closed with her fingers splayed across her forehead. Emily's eyes are round, and she stares at me.

"Look, it's a beautiful day and, I mean, I love hiking. You get some amazing views, but I also like the foreshore in town. Have you been there lately? I thought I could take you for a walk down there, and we could get to know each other. Perhaps I could drop you home afterwards. I mean, at your mother's. Shit. Fuck. I'm not meant to know that, am I?" I'm so ballsing this up.

"See, I'm not used to this, and your beauty is putting me off." I know I should shut up, but I can't stop myself. "I mean, I've lived a really privileged life, and I've never really had to work for much, but I want to work to get to know you because you seem, like, well, awesome."

Everyone stares at us. I now wish Millie was here to tell me what a dickhead I'm being.

"Here, let me introduce you." Ken shakes his head, taking pity on me. "Boyd, you said?" I nod. "Okay, well, this is the charming Emily. She's a doctor and training to be a GP, but hates her boss and can't wait to leave the practice, even though the other staff seem alright. Now, Emily's just had her heart broken, so you need to promise me you'll be gentle with her, okay?"

"Yes." I nod at Ken, yearning to reach out and touch her.

"My best friend's flying back to Brisbane this afternoon, and I promised I'd drop her off at the airport." Emily looks at me.

I can't tell if she's trying to put me off or not. Val's already mentioned their plans, and I know anyone here would take my sister, but I suspect it needs to be Emily.

"Can we maybe meet at the playground at the top of the foreshore, near Cassowary Drive, at about three?" she asks. My chest swells with the fact she'll meet me, and we can actually spend time together.

"Yes," I blurt out all too quickly. "I mean, that sounds great."

I want to stay and talk to her... be with her, but I can't help but notice her fidgeting with her hands in her lap and not meeting my gaze. She needs space, and as much as it kills me to give it to her, I have to if I have any chance of making our marriage work.

Dad clears plates, and I jump in to help. There's almost three hours until I need to meet her, and I need to fill that time with things that help take my mind off her. Giles is in the kitchen rinsing plates before placing them in the dishwasher. It's a regular argument he and I have because I say that the dishes are going to be washed in the machine, and he thinks rinsing them helps. I always lose, because I don't have a dishwasher, and he and Bridget do. Big brother knows best.

Mum's putting leftovers into containers, no doubt already having decided who was taking what home with them.

"Let me do that, blossom," Dad says as he places his arm around Mum's shoulder and presses a kiss on the side of her head. "You're the birthday girl."

It's so domestic. It hurts that Emily and I may never have the same family dynamic with kids of our own, but the Hartmans are a unit. There'll be nieces, and one day, Val might even settle down and have a kid or two. I deal with kids at work, and I know how heartbreaking it is to watch them suffer. Our lives will still be full even if there aren't kids for us.

I'm early to the carpark at the playground Emily suggested we meet at. It isn't lost on me that we're meeting at a place where children gather. I set off early, but I'd had enough of Henry and Ken. They asked if I wanted to go with them to look at a townhouse they're thinking of buying. I didn't realise they've been looking for a while.

Ken let it slip that they were thinking of having a child themselves, just thinking, Henry emphasised. It would be great to have more kids in the family, but it brings home what Emily and I don't have, causing a shot of pain to shoot through my chest.

I went with them, but it was only slightly bigger than the place they're currently in and not what they're looking for.

I pull my hair from the elastic holding it in a ponytail, and place my ball cap back on my head. I nod towards a couple of nurses I recognise from the ward who are standing, gossiping, one with a toddler on her hip. There's no doubt I look like a creep standing near the gated entrance.

Emily pulls into the car park a few minutes later, early herself. She doesn't get straight out of her car, though. Instead, I see her with her eyes closed as her shoulders rise and fall with deep breaths. Eventually, she steps out, and the lights flash as she locks the car with the fob. Her beauty takes my breath away. She's wearing jean shorts and a plain pale-pink T-shirt. She's changed from the dress she was wearing this morning to brunch.

What really gets me, though, is when she pulls one of my old ball caps from her back pocket and places it on her head. There's usually one or two in both of our cars, but the fact she is wearing it means so much to me, regardless of the reason.

"Hi," I greet her, wanting to embrace her, but also recognising I need to let her come to me. "It's great to see you."

"Are we meant to know each other or not?" she asks as we move towards the path that goes along the foreshore.

"To be honest, I don't know if I can keep that up, and it might be pretty painful watching me try." I laugh. "I just... Fuck... Sorry..." I take in a deep breath. "We never really dated, not like other couples, and I want to get to know you again, if that's alright. Like, I mean, I'm assuming that this is alright with you. I don't want to get a divorce. I don't want anyone else. You really are my everything."

We take several more steps before Emily speaks. "Val said I should give you a chance," she says in a flat tone.

I want to fill the silences; I want to make her laugh, but I realise the silences help her get her thoughts together. It's killing me not to reach out and hold her hand.

"I mean, Val also said we should do marriage counselling or therapy or something, but you probably remember my experience of therapy last time." She looks at me, her bottom lip between her teeth.

"I'd be open to talking to someone, perhaps someone who has experience with infertility. Maybe Jacquie can recommend someone?" I suggest, stepping closer to her, but not touching her.

I feel like I need to put my hands in my pockets, but I know that if I do, there's no chance of us holding hands.

"Maybe." She shrugs, and I notice her hands aren't in her pockets either. "I'll be talking to her tomorrow. I'm going to get the blood test done, even though I know I'm no longer pregnant."

I don't want this walk to turn into a talk about infertility. It's not why I'm here. "So, tell me, Ms Emily, what's your favourite colour?"

"Is this going to be twenty questions?" She smiles, and I see her eyes sparkle as she looks at me.

My heart swells at the glimpse of the Emily I know and love.

"Maybe. Apparently, it's what you do on dates to get to know the other person."

"Well, it's purple." She chuckles.

"Nice. Why?" I ask.

"Because I also love blue and red, and when you mix them together..." She trails off, shaking her head as if it's a silly reason.

"I like that." I smile.

"What about you?" she asks as she steps in closer to me. Our fingers brush as we walk, making the hairs on my arms rise and my cock take notice. I will it down, telling it now is not the time.

"I like red. And yellow. I love the colours of the sun peeking over the horizon promising a new day." I've never told her this before.

"What's your favourite movie?" she asks next. I'm just glad she's getting into this as much as I am.

"*Toy Story.*"

"Which one?" she shoots back, knowing I can't choose.

"They all have their place." I spend a good few minutes arguing the merits of each movie and explaining why Mr and Mrs Potato Head are the best characters in the franchise. "I'm guessing you're a *Fast and Furious* fan."

She loves those movies. I suspect it's Vin Diesel, and I really can't blame her. He is pretty badass.

"Actually..." She slows a little. I look over and see her grab her arms as we walk, her brows furrowed. "I really love *The Sound of Music.*" She swallows and glances over at me. She's never mentioned this before.

"That's the one with the singing kids, no?" I think I remember watching it as a teenager, probably making fun of her and Val.

"I used to watch it every Christmas with Mum and Dad. It's Mum's favourite. We'd have popcorn in front of the telly, and Mum and I would sing along to all the songs. It's quite the romance, too. Val and I watched it again recently after a group online was going on about how Captain Von Trapp would have been a spanker and how much Maria would have liked it."

Holy fucking hell. I definitely remember this film through a teenage lens and need to watch it again if it gives off those kinds of vibes. I can't believe after all this time I'm learning new things about Emily. It reminds me that she can still surprise me in good ways.

We talk about pizza toppings, and our favourite foods, and how Emily loves eating cake but can't bake to save herself. I mean, these aren't new revelations, but small examples of things I love about her.

"So..." I take a large breath in and exhale, knowing I can't avoid the elephant that walks alongside us. "I'm not going to take the job in Brisbane if it means you won't come with me."

Emily says nothing. We walk along for a few more minutes. A Scottish Terrier ties itself around her legs, causing us both to laugh and the owner to apologise profusely. The electricity that shoots up my arm as I hold her hand as the dog gets more tangled trying to get away from its owner makes us all laugh even more.

Eventually, it's free, and we walk on, our hands still joined. "I'm quitting Dr Doug's on Monday." Emily doesn't look at me. Instead, she chews on her lip. I say nothing, wanting her to continue. "He's a prick. He's tried to manoeuvre it so that none of the other doctors get to talk to me, but I bumped into Nasan at the supermarket on Friday before we went to your brother's, and he asked if everything was alright and warned me about being alone with Doug."

If he's tried anything, I swear I will spend my life in prison rather than let him roam the earth. "Has he..."

"No." Emily is quick to answer. "I mean, he's made his intentions clear, but I've managed to ignore him. But me quitting might have affected my outburst and pushing you away. I mean, I don't want you to stay with me if you'd rather find someone to have children with." Emily's voice is low and soft. I want to throw my arms around her and tell her I would rather live with her and no kids than with anyone else.

"Our wedding ceremony was brief, but I meant it when I told you I want to be with you during good times and bad. I love you. I can tell you this until the cows come home, but I want to show you, and if this means wooing you and reminding you how much you mean to me, then that's what I'll do."

"I don't know what I want." Emily lets out a huff of discouragement.

"And that's okay." I squeeze her hand, glad she hasn't dropped mine.

"Perhaps the idea of some form of counselling or therapy could help." The inflection at the end shows the way she is questioning this, but I take it as a statement.

"I know you never really gelled with what's her face—"

"Priscilla," Emily interjects, her nose scrunched and her eyes rolling back in her head.

"Yeah, Priscilla, but we can try as many as you like until we find someone who we both click with." I hope the desperation I feel doesn't come through in my tone. If we see one or one hundred therapists until we find someone Emily gels with, then it won't worry me.

"I still keep journalling because of Priscilla, I suppose," Emily almost whispers.

I've seen her tapping away at her keyboard some nights and not questioned what she was doing, but I remember her reading me parts from her journal when we were first together.

"Do you have any plans if you're not working at Dr Douche— I mean Dr Doug's?" I ask. The sound of Emily's laugh is like music to my ears. Fuck, I've missed that laugh.

"Mia's piano teacher is having a baby, and I thought I might offer to take her classes for a month or two. It would give her time with her baby and keep some income coming in for her because I'd use her studio under her house and pay her for it."

It doesn't surprise me Emily is being so pragmatic about someone she doesn't really know.

"And you'll be alright hearing a baby cry and that?" I ask as we come across the marina in town, so many sailboats and yachts bobbing in the water, trying to break from their moorings.

"I think so." She sighs. "I mean, I see babies and kids at work, just like you do. It may not be in our future at the moment, but…"

She trails off. The way she mentions our future gives me hope that I haven't dared to have before now. Less than two days ago, she was telling me she wanted a divorce, now she's talking about our future.

"I'm meant to give two weeks' notice, but Bridget suggested I get a medical certificate from Nat and hand that in with my notice. You don't mind, do you?"

We've stopped as we look at a teenager reel in a small fish. He unhooks it and throws it back in the water. We're no longer holding hands but both leaning against the railing overlooking the water.

"I don't mind at all. If you don't want to be a doctor, I won't mind as long as you're happy."

"Happiness seems a fair way off." Emily chuckles. "But, maybe, I mean..."

I give her time to gather her thoughts. I hope I've made it clear I'm not going anywhere.

"I love medicine, and I love the idea of being a GP, but I think I need a break. I've... I've got a lot to work out."

As much as I think it should be simple, I know that I need to give Emily room to come to her own decisions.

"If you need to stay with your mum for a bit, I get it." Well, I like to think I do.

"Are you sure?" Emily turns and looks at me, her brows creased and her lip once again between her teeth.

"Baby, whatever it takes." I mean that with my whole heart. I'd rather we sort things out now rather than leave things hanging over us until the next major setback in our marriage. I'll hate sleeping alone, but it will make having Emily back beside me all that more special when it happens, and I know it will.

"Do you want to grab a pizza or a burger or something?" she asks, her hands rubbing at her elbows.

"Pizza sounds great." Anything that gives me more time with her sounds great. I'll even put up with damn pineapple on it to spend more time with her.

Emily, Age 15

Boyd is so hard to understand. He pretends he likes me, and he'll snuggle with me as we watch a movie and let Val tease him about it, even though Val doesn't care, and then he'll make fun of me for liking the movies I do.

Val and I watched The Sound of Music *tonight. I'm staying over at her place. Hillary and Charlie have gone out on a date to their favourite restaurant, and we've ordered in pizza. Boyd picked off all the pineapple. Philistine. He'll eat pineapple on a burger, but not on a pizza. It didn't really matter, because he simply popped his pineapple on my slices, so I got more.*

First, Boyd complained that if my mum had made him clothes out of old curtains, he would have refused to wear them. Knowing Mum, she probably did make clothes out of curtains she picked up at the thrift store.

I've watched this movie lots of times. It's Mum's favourite, and every Christmas, we sit down as a family, the three of us when Dad was still around, and watch it while we munched on popcorn. Val knows it too, and we sang along with a lot of the songs, with Boyd mimicking us. It was really mocking rather than mimicking, but we pretended it didn't matter.

It did, though. Deep down, it's one of my favourite films, too. I won't tell him that. I love the scene where Liesel sneaks out to see Rolf and the two of them sing in the pergola, him telling her he'll take care of her. Val rightly points out that it's not very feminist of her, but I kind of understand where she's coming from.

I don't want Boyd to take care of me, but I want him to desire me the way the Captain desires Maria. The look in his eyes as they dance together, and the way he snaps on his glove. Sigh! Then the wedding. Just that dress. Not sure I want a dress like it when I get married, but it's a love story, and I want a love story like that. A story where I'm desired and wanted and looked at like that.

Boyd made it clear he didn't appreciate the movie, so I doubt I'll ever watch it in his presence again. Perhaps it can be something Val and I do in secret. Who knows? Perhaps it is weird that I like a movie that's so old, but Christopher Plummer looks so hot in it. It's funny to see Charlie and Hillary's wedding photos displayed around the house, both of them looking so young, and then seeing them now. I mean, I know people get old and stuff, but Charlie still looks at Hillary like the Captain looks at Maria.

I wonder what Boyd will look like when he's in his fifties? Will he be grey like his father? He tells me he's going to grow his hair and grow a beard. I can't imagine him doing that, let alone him getting old. Time will tell, I suppose.

Chapter 20

Emily

I STARTLE MYSELF AWAKE; THE SUN IS STREAMING THROUGH the gap in my curtains, and it takes longer than it should for me to realise I'm in my childhood bed at my mother's. Glancing at my phone, I see it's gone nine, and I calculate I've slept for over twelve hours.

After sharing pizza with Boyd and watching people wander along the foreshore, we meandered back towards our cars. If this had been a first date, I'd be hanging out for a second. Boyd was everything I knew he was: caring and attentive, kind, sensitive, and perhaps most of all, a good listener.

Boyd listened to me rant about Dr Douche, as he refers to my boss. He listened to me rave about how awesome Val is. He even listened to me pontificate about the cyclists who had a perfectly adequate bike path along the foreshore, yet insisted on riding on the footpath.

I may have gone a little overboard about the cyclists, causing him to laugh, but he had dragged me out of the way of one, and it resulted in us walking with his arm around my shoulder for a good while.

It felt normal and natural and, well, nice.

When I told Boyd I thought we should divorce, I never expected any push back. I thought it sounded logical. The way he's acted, though, shows me why I'm so drawn to him. He is loyal, and he loves me. My reaction Friday night probably was a bit knee jerk. I hadn't really thought about it and just blurted it out.

I still came home to Mum's last night.

We've spent all our marriage trying to have a baby. Sure, the sex has been, on the whole, great, but it's been focussed on an end goal that we may never meet.

Val's been amazing, my rock, and shown why she's my best friend. I notice a text message from her from earlier this morning.

VAL

> Hey you. I'm in court this morning and will have my phone off, but send me a message, and I'll call you as soon as I can. You've got this.

I didn't necessarily know that I had it, but knowing I had Val's support was enough. She'd helped me draft a text to Dr Douche, telling him I wasn't well and would need some time off. He offered to pay a house call and check up on me, but I simply ignored him. If he goes to the address on my HR record, he'll get Boyd, and although I'd like to be a fly on the wall if that happens, I'm glad I won't be there for it.

His harassment has increased. He's subtle about it and acts like brushing past me is an accident. I'm sure he fiddles with my appointments and moves patients to other doctors so we can be free at the same time if he has a cancellation. I've taken to going to the food court in the shopping centre to have lunch, but he follows me and has sat at the same table with me. At least we've been in public, so he hasn't got handsy like I'm worried he might in the break room at the surgery, but it's off-putting.

Val agrees with me it's calculated behaviour and not enough for me to put in a complaint to the medical authorities, but enough to make me be on guard with him.

I hate he occupies so much of my thoughts. I want to forget about him and focus on something else, something positive.

Teaching the piano for a couple of months excites me. I'm catching up with Sue, the piano teacher, tomorrow. Small steps are what Val counselled. Small steps will mean getting out of bed, though. I can hear the whir of Mum's sewing machine. She was so busy leading up to the Gala that I thought she might take some time off, but it doesn't sound like it.

Val suggested I make a to-do list each day and mark off things when I achieve them. We wrote today's list yesterday before she left. I know I need to get the blood test, but I also need to book in with my GP for the medical certificate I'll need, and once I've managed to tick off my list, Val's given me a book recommendation, which I'm keen to start on.

It was strange making the list. So much focus has been on getting pregnant that everything else has sort of had to slot into the background. I've gone from the focus of finishing school, to finishing uni, to marriage and babies. Except where school and uni were a bit of a breeze, I've fallen short in the baby making department.

I call Dr Nat's surgery and am amazed when I can get in to see her this afternoon. At least I'm able to tick something off the list. I climb out of bed and head to the bathroom. My eyes aren't as puffy as they've been, but I still look like shit.

Standing in the shower, I take time to wash my hair and exfoliate my skin with body wash and a brush. It's a firm brush that is almost painful as I rub it across my skin, but I remind myself that I am feeling something after feeling numb all weekend.

Back in my room, I throw on shorts and a T-shirt. I grab my phone and my e-book reader and decide to get the blood test over and done with while I'm out.

"Morning, love. Cuppa?" Mum peeks up from behind her glasses as she hunches over her machine.

"No, I'm good. Are you quilting? I didn't know you still did that." I look at the patchwork of jewel tones cut into different shapes and arranged in piles around her.

"It's been a while, yeah." Mum smiles at me. "Have you got any plans for today?"

I love that she doesn't try to tell me what to do or berate me for not being at work. I know she wants to pry, but I don't think there's much to tell.

"I'm going to have that blood test, and then I've got an appointment with my GP this afternoon. Thought I might read in the botanic gardens for a bit."

"Why don't you at least grab some snacks to take with you? There's plenty of fruit and veg in the fridge. I could whip up—"

"No, Mum, you stay there and sew. You look like you're in the zone. I'll take an apple."

Mum's sewing nook is in the kitchen area, and she turns her attention back to her machine, patching fabrics together. I'm sure there's a pattern to what she's doing, but I can't see it.

"I was thinking I might ask Boyd if he wants to come over for dinner." I feel like I'm sixteen again, asking Mum for permission to see him during the week.

"That sounds like a lovely idea." She looks up from her machine. "I could grab some fish and cook a stew?"

"Send me a list of what you need, and I'll grab it whilst I'm out." I pick up an apple for now and shove another one in my bag, along with my water bottle. I walk over to Mum and place my hand on her shoulder as I plant a kiss on her head. "Thank you for being such a great mum. I love you, you know."

"I know you do." She pats my hand and looks up at me with such devotion in her eyes. "And I'm glad you and Boyd are working at patching things up."

I think I'm glad about that, too.

> I've just had the blood test. It will be good to have closure, I suppose.

HUSBAND

It doesn't make it any easier all the same. I've been wanting to message you this morning, but I just can't work out what to say that doesn't sound naff. I almost sent you a photo of my feet in the lift because I couldn't think of anything else to send you.

> You're crazy. But good crazy. I don't think I need to refer you to Henry or Ken just yet.

HUSBAND

I do wonder at times.

> I was wondering if you wanted to come over for dinner tonight after work. Mum said she'd make fish stew, the one with tomato sauce with bread and aioli.

HUSBAND

It's a date! But it seems awfully soon for me to be meeting your mum. I mean, we had our first date yesterday. Does this mean you see a future with us?

> Maybe. Maybe I just want my mother's input.

HUSBAND

I'll be there.

VAL HAS me reading a mafia romance, although there isn't a lot of romance so far. The female main character has been sold off to the male main character who just wants to dominate her. Little does the heir to the mafia empire realise, she is no meek and subservient handmaid who will kowtow to his demands.

The female is Asian American and described as being of Chinese descent. I'm loving the way the author describes the subtle racism from members of the man's team, who see her as being an Asian princess, even though she was born in America.

I'm up to a particularly spicy part where she tells him that if he can't satisfy her in the bedroom, then there's no hope for their arrangement, and she might as well just escape. Naturally, he's captivated by her spunk and does everything to ensure she knows just how capable he is at showering her with orgasms.

She's trailing her teeth down his cock, just gently grazing it to warn him of what she's capable of when my phone rings.

"Um, hello?" I almost drop it as I answer it, not realising how worked up I was over some words in a book.

"Emily, it's Jacquie Singh. Tell me what's been happening."

"Well, my period arrived Friday evening, and it was heavy and crampy, and I know the baby didn't make it." I don't cry. It's almost as if I'm not the one relaying the information to my doctor, but rather I'm talking about a patient of mine.

"I'm sorry, Emily, but yes, the bloods this morning show that the numbers have dropped. You can do another cycle next month if you like, or—"

"Actually," I interrupt, "I think we need to wait a bit. I, um, well, I told Boyd on Friday that we should get a divorce, and he should find someone who can give him kids."

"I see," Dr Jacquie says in a low voice. "Look, I've been doing this for a while, and I think that infertility brings couples into one of two camps: those for whom it strengthens their relationship, and those for whom it drives a wedge in their relationship that can't necessarily be mended."

"Boyd and I are going to work on mending things," I blurt. "I mean, we've talked about therapy."

"That's always a great idea. I know in Cassowary Point, we refer people to a child and family therapist called Priscilla—"

"No," I exclaim. "Anyone but her."

"Okay." Dr Jacquie sounds calm. "There's a few more to choose from down here, and I know they do video calls."

"We're, um, probably moving to Brisbane in a couple of months." Maybe, possibly, perhaps... I know Boyd needs to go for work, and I recognise I want to fight for our marriage.

"Okay, well, you aren't tied in to the same timetable we have in Cassowary Point, as there are many more doctors here at our Brisbane clinic. Let me know what you decide, and we can work things out when you get here. Meanwhile, I'll flick you through an email with the names and contact details of some couple therapists that you might like to check out. Does that sound like a plan?"

"It does."

I'm almost relieved that she didn't push us into starting another cycle straight away. We're fortunate that we can afford it financially, but mentally is another matter altogether.

"Emily, hi, I'm Amelia. I see Bridget Hartman recommended me to you. Now there's a blast from the past." Amelia set up a video call for us when I rang earlier in the week.

Bridget and I had caught up for breakfast, and she recommended the counsellor she saw in Brisbane whilst she was at uni. Fortunately, she's still practicing and could fit me in today.

"Yeah, Bridget's married to my brother-in-law. I'm pretty sure they named their second child after you."

"Yes, the second child." She chuckles, one side of her lips bent upwards. "Not worthy enough to have the first child named after me."

"Millie's a handful. Perhaps you should be grateful." I can't help but smile. I already like this woman. She seems forthright and no-nonsense, with a wry sense of humour.

"So, tell me the Emily Hartman story."

I start at the beginning, from being adopted, to a lovely childhood, to my father leaving when I was thirteen, to Boyd, to uni, to marriage, and then to infertility.

"Then I got it into my head last Friday, after I realised I miscarried, that Boyd would be better off without me and should find someone else who could actually give him children and make him a father."

I'm sitting on my childhood bed with my legs crossed, earbuds in, and a box of tissues next to me. I thought telling my story would be more painful than this.

"And Boyd said 'Gee, she's right, I better find someone else, because I'm only married to this woman I've known almost all my life because she can pop out a couple of kids'?" Amelia tucks her chin to her chest and looks at me over the top of her glasses.

"Not exactly." I chuckle. "He's decided he's going to woo me—his words—and we met and went for a walk last Sunday, and then he came around to dinner at Mum's on Monday, and then I went and spent a couple of nights with my Nonna, but we've been texting."

Nonna told me she said a similar thing to Nonno when they'd been trying to have a child for so long. He'd just laughed in her face.

"And you're still staying at your mum's?" Amelia asked, writing notes on an electronic notepad.

"Yeah. It's not something we've talked about, but we sort of moved in together as soon as I'd finished school, and we never really just dated. Initially, after I realised that getting divorced was really the last thing either of us wants, I thought I'd stay here, perhaps until we..." I pause and take in a deep breath. "I think one of the other reasons I told Boyd I wanted a divorce is because I don't really want to live in Brisbane, and he needs to work down there for a bit as part of his training." Originally, Boyd had been told six months. Now it looks like it might be longer.

"You don't like Brisbane?"

"No, it's just that. That's where he lives."

"*He* being your father?" Amelia writes furiously as she glances at me, her face expressionless. "Tell me about that night when you were thirteen."

Almost instinctively, I tug a tissue from the box and weave it around my fingers. "It was a Friday, and I was sitting in here doing maths homework."

I look around the room. The boyband posters that hung on my wall have gone, and the doona cover has been replaced, but the same purple curtains hang in the window, the same chest of drawers and bookcase.

"I'd heard Dad come home. He and Mum had been arguing all week when they thought I was asleep. I could never hear what it was about. Mum knocked on my door and asked if I could come to the kitchen, as Dad needed to talk with me. I can remember her phrasing, the way she said 'talk with me' even though when I got to the kitchen he spoke at me and didn't listen to me."

I look over at the bedroom door and can picture Mum standing in it. Her long dark hair only had a few silver streaks in it at that stage. She had an apron around her middle that she'd sewn from leftovers, so it was a patchwork of fabrics that didn't match, but waste not, want not was always her motto.

"Dad was sitting at the kitchen table, a glass of scotch in front of him. His hair was all over the place, like he'd been pulling at it with his fingers. He told me to sit down, and Mum sat next to me. I thought he was sick, that he was dying or something, but he was still dressed for work. I remember his words. 'Emily, I've been a stupid old man, and I'm moving to Brisbane'. I can still feel Mum's hand rubbing circles on my back as I told him I didn't want to move to Brisbane because my friends were here."

It's been years since I've told anyone this story. I don't think I even told Priscilla the full version.

"I remember telling him I wouldn't go, and I'd move in with the Hartmans. Val had a trundle under her bed, and I figured I could stay there. I didn't think they'd mind. He then repeated that he was moving to Brisbane, but this time, he added that he was going with Shona, his secretary, because she was pregnant. I didn't put two and two together for a while until Mum said that we were staying in Cassowary Point."

It's amazing that so many years later I can still feel the metaphorical punch to the gut when I realised my father was a liar and a cheat. That he'd knocked up his secretary and had been having an affair behind my mother's back.

Amelia is quiet for a bit until she realises I'm stuck in my thoughts.

"Did you go to Brisbane in the holidays to see him or anything?" she asks, her tablet lying on the desk and her arms crossed as she leans in towards the camera on her computer.

"He wanted me to, but I refused. He'd made his choice, and Shona and the baby were more important than Mum and me." I shrug my shoulders. "I thought I'd see him again before he left, but he left that night, and then on the Monday after school, Mum said he'd been and packed up his things and was gone."

"I can only imagine how hard that was for you, and it's definitely something we'll circle back to in future sessions, assuming you want to see me again?" Amelia looks up at me, and I nod. "Good. Now, are you and Boyd doing any couple's therapy?"

It's something we've talked about, but not arranged yet. Dr Jacquie sent me an email with some recommendations, but I've not looked at it yet. I have forwarded it to Boyd, though.

Amelia suggests a time for me to see her next week, and we end our call. I let out a sigh as I close my laptop, glad I didn't have to hold my phone for the last hour.

As heavy as it was reliving the night Dad tore our family apart, I feel lighter for sharing things with someone else, someone objective. No one can tell what the future will bring, but I don't think I'd survive Boyd having an affair, let alone impregnating another woman.

I need a cup of tea after that session. Sliding off the bed, I reach for my phone and see there's a message from Boyd.

HUSBAND

Hey you. So, tonight, I'll pick you up at seven. I've made dinner reservations. I thought perhaps we could go dancing afterwards or something.

You make us sound like geriatrics.

HUSBAND

Sure, but if we dance, I know I'll get to touch you and hold you.

That sounds quite nice. I have to pop over and grab a dress to wear.

HUSBAND

All good.

I hoped it would be.

IT FELT strange calling into our apartment, knowing Boyd wouldn't be there. I wanted to grab my purple wrap dress to wear to dinner tonight. Everything was neat and tidy, which shouldn't have surprised me. For all Boyd's childish antics at times, he enjoys order in things.

I didn't have an extensive selection of clothes at Mum's, and I was washing every day or so to have fresh clothes to wear. Today, I wore the lacy black knickers I wanted to wear to the Gala. When I bought them, I imagined them sending Boyd wild as he lowered my dress and saw I wasn't wearing a bra. I can't say I remember much about that night, even though it was only a short time ago, but it definitely didn't end in lowered dresses and panties being drawn down my legs by his teeth.

In possibly the most unlike-Emily thing I've ever done, I slip the knickers down my legs, glad I'm wearing a dress, and lay them on Boyd's pillow. I haven't decided how long I plan to stay at Mum's, but I grab a handful of other knickers along with another sundress and a couple of fresh T-shirts.

With my calling card left, I grab my things and head back to Mum's.

Mum is down with Nonna for the weekend. I know it's about giving Boyd and me space, but I don't mind at all. Spending a couple of nights with Nonna this week was special. She loves talking about family history, especially about her marriage to Nonno. To see how she misses him so much makes me question how I ever thought I could live without Boyd.

Except I am living without him. Driving back from Nonna's, I thought it would be easy to simply head home to our apartment and act like nothing's happened, but the last few weeks haven't been a dream. They've been the culmination of years of disappointment.

I don't regret not having any other relationships other than with Boyd. Once, I read an article written by a man whose wife had died from cancer. He spoke of how, at the time, he never believed there would be anyone who he could love as much as he loved his dying wife, but he's since learnt that there are plenty of other people with whom he's found a different kind of love. It wasn't like the romance books where a woman came along and drew him out of his grief, but rather that he experienced different relationships to his marriage, and they were just as valid as the love he shared with his wife. In the end, he found love with a man, something he never saw coming, and the two were planning their wedding.

There would be someone else out there for me, but the reality is I'm still desperately in love with my husband. Even though a week ago I wanted to set him free, I think I'm secretly thrilled he fought for me. For us.

The thoughts of separation and divorce have also taken my mind off our infertility. Mum and Dad were in their midthirties when they adopted me. I can't imagine adoption for us. I don't regret being adopted, nor being brought up in another country, but adoption is so much harder almost thirty years later.

I'd be lying if I didn't admit it was something I'd looked into, but most children being put up for adoption in this country have additional needs, and I'm not sure if Boyd and I could offer the care and support the kids would require. It probably makes me selfish. I recognise though that once I've finished my training and Boyd is further along with his, our priorities will no doubt change, and this may be something we can look at then.

I've tried to calm myself all afternoon with cup after cup of tea. It's meant I've spent the time I wasn't in the kitchen brewing the tea on the toilet, voiding it. Boyd and I have had date nights before. We've been out to dinner in Brisbane after Val's graduation. We've been to dinners up here and to movies. But tonight is different.

When we were at uni, Bridget kept trying to offer suggestions on ways we could relax and wind down around exam time. She gave us a link to a relaxation app that was supposed to promote mindfulness. It didn't work this afternoon. I kept looking at my watch and counting down the minutes until Boyd would be picking me up.

At one stage, I tried to sit at the piano and let the music sweep me away, but it didn't work either. Even playing scale after scale in tricky rhythms didn't take my mind off the fact that Boyd and I would be spending time together tonight.

He hasn't pushed for me to move home. In fact, he told me via text the other night that absence was making his heart grow fonder. I sometimes wonder if he swallowed a cliché dictionary with some of the sappy stuff he keeps telling me. From anyone other than Boyd, it probably would have sounded much cheesier, but he makes it come across with sincerity. He's always told me how beautiful he finds me and the different things he likes about me. The sappiness is just an extension of this.

The truth is, I miss him as much as he misses me. I miss hearing him mutter to himself in his sleep and waking up with his hair all over my pillow. Jacquie told us we could have sex after the embryo transfer, but we didn't, what with Boyd working late shifts and the stress of the wait.

The last three weeks have been the longest we've ever gone without sex, and I miss it.

Not living together, though, I miss the small intimate moments I've taken for granted. The small brushes of my lower back as Boyd reaches behind me in the kitchen, the foot massage in the evening as I lie on the couch reading a novel as he tries to concentrate on journal articles and research. The stolen kisses before and after work, and the way he'll try to catch me for a hug when he comes home all sweaty after a run, and I'm dressed to leave.

Somehow, I've passed the hours of the afternoon, and I find myself scrambling to get ready before Boyd rings the bell. My legs are shaved and my skin moisturised. I've even put on mascara and a bright-red lipstick. Pretending to be a hairdresser and attempting to braid my hair like last weekend was a disaster, so I brush it out and pin some of it back with an old hair clip I found in the chest of drawers. I'd forgotten about it, but seeing it made me smile and brought back some fond memories. I just hope Boyd notices I'm wearing it.

I'm just fastening the gold necklace Mum gave me for my eighteenth birthday when I see lights shine through the window as a car pulls into the drive. My hands shake as I snap a photo and send it to Val, asking if I look presentable.

> VAL
>
> Fucking hot! Now, have fun, but I don't want to hear about how much fun, okay?

> I'll try.

The bell rings, and I take a deep breath before opening the door. *Game on.*

Emily, Age 16

I can't believe it. I mean, it is school holidays, but it's my sweet sixteenth birthday, and Mum agreed to me going out on a date with Boyd. It's not like I'm sweet sixteen and never been kissed, but we haven't gone any further than that.

Usually, we get together as family for birthdays, often with the Hartman family. That they've agreed Boyd and I can go out together is really something. I'd like to think it means they accept our relationship. We've sort of fallen into one. I think I might even be falling in love with him.

After tonight, it's easy to see why. He brought me some red tulips when he came to pick me up. I love how he knew they're my favourite flowers. He told Mum we're going for burgers at Burger Bonanza. They do good food, and it was awesome sitting opposite him in a booth. I thought we might sit next to each other, but we held hands across the table.

Bruno, the owner, asked Boyd what the special occasion was, and when he was told it was my birthday, he brought us a chocolate brownie with a candle in it to share for dessert. We took turns feeding it to each other. Talk about swoon.

We had plans to go to a movie, but we just sat and talked. Boyd admitted he misses Giles and Henry when they're away at uni, but he forgets about it when they come home for the holidays, like they are at the moment, and use all the hot water.

Mum gave me some new hiking boots that I've been wearing around the house all day. I've still got blisters from them. Boyd suggested we go on a hike this weekend. Henry's been talking about some track that only locals know about. We might give it a go.

It was just nice sitting and talking. I realised Bruno had sat down and was reading the newspaper, and everyone else had gone. It was well after ten. Mum hadn't given me a curfew, and I was so embarrassed when she asked me if I needed condoms. I mean, tonight's really the first time Boyd and I have been out alone before. Val's usually with us, or we're hanging out at his place or mine.

Being together, though, was nice. I really, really like Boyd. Heck, I probably love him and am halfway towards being in love with him.

I apologised to Bruno for staying beyond our welcome, and he told us not to worry. He didn't even charge full price for our meals, and he wished me a happy birthday.

After dinner, Boyd drove down to the foreshore, and we got out and just sat on the grass. I could see he was concerned about something, as he kept scratching behind his ear. Eventually, though, he pulled out a gift for me. It was even wrapped in purple paper. He kept assuring me it wasn't much. I had to blink back tears when I opened it. It's a hair slide that looks like a piano keyboard with a pair of quavers at one end and a love heart at the other. I put it straight in my hair and threw my arms around him, tackling him back into the ground for a hug.

Just lying there, looking up at the sky, was perfect. There was a full moon tonight, and we couldn't see so many stars, but I felt like I was the centre of Boyd's universe, and it felt just about perfect.

Chapter 21

Boyd

HAVE I EVER BEEN SO NERVOUS? PROBABLY NOT. I'M standing at the front door of the house Emily grew up in gripping a bunch of mixed blooms in one hand and breathing into the other and trying to sniff my breath. I know I brushed my teeth and used mouthwash and a breath mint, but I'd hate to do anything that might put Emily off.

My toe taps on the doormat as I wait for her to open the door. I don't hear footsteps, and I wonder if she's standing there waiting for me, trying to work out an acceptable time to wait before letting me in.

Fuck. Perhaps she's changed her mind, and she doesn't want to go out with me. But then again, she left some panties on my pillow. That has to mean something, doesn't it?

I feel like I've been waiting here for hours, but it's not even a minute and I hear her heels moving quickly across the floorboards. I want to yell to tell her not to run, but secretly, I like she's in a hurry.

"Hi," she says breathlessly as she swings the door open.

"Hi," I almost whisper back as I take in her beauty.

She's wearing the purple wrap dress that has always looked amazing on her. She's never been a big wearer of jewellery, but she's wearing the heart pendant with the ruby, her birthstone, in it that her mum gave her for her eighteenth birthday. I blink back tears though when I see the musical hair slide I gave her for her sweet sixteen pinning her hair back.

"You look—"

"You look—"

We both speak at the same time and laugh.

"Here." I thrust the flowers towards her, my act robotic and something I should definitely have rehearsed.

"They're beautiful." Emily brings them to her nose and sniffs, a smile spreading across her face. "I'll just, um, come in. Um, water, vase."

It's almost a relief to see Emily is as nervous as I am.

"Is your mum—"

"She's at Nonna's for the weekend." Emily's words escape her mouth in a rush, and she almost drops the vase she's reached for in a kitchen cupboard.

"Emily." I place my hands on her shoulders as she fills the vase at the sink. "It's just us. You and me."

"I know." She sighs, leaving the vase in the sink and turning to wrap her arms around my waist.

It feels so good to just hold her like this. It feels right, and I know I've done the right thing fighting for her.

She breaks the hug and turns and places the flowers in the vase. "They're really beautiful, Boyd. Thank you."

"It's the wrong time of year for tulips, and, yeah, I wanted bright and cheerful, and, well, beautiful, because, yeah, well. Shit. Can we start over? I've never had to woo anyone before, and I think that's pretty obvious."

"You don't have to woo me." She grabs her purse and presses a kiss to my cheek. "I've been yours forever. We just have to work out how to make things work, seeing as our plans might have to change."

She's right, of course. We make our way outside, and I hold the car door open for her. It's not because she needs protecting or anything. I just want to be close to her for that bit longer.

The drive to the restaurant is in relative silence. I've had the car stereo playing the classical music station all week. It's not something I usually listen to, but it's soothing, and I've found some bangers that surprised me. Tonight, they're playing some violin music. I think it's from a film, and Emily seems to like it.

"Fuck." Chez Philippe is the local French restaurant and a favourite of my parents. It shouldn't surprise me that Dad's car is parked outside.

"Is that?" Emily turns her head as we drive past, obviously noticing the car, too.

"Yep." I pop the 'p.'

We're silent as I pull into a park a little further down the street. I look over and see Emily has her phone out.

"Hello? Yes, it's Emily Hartman here. My husband, Boyd, had a reservation tonight, but he's been called to an emergency. He's a doctor at the hospital, you see... Yes, yes. Oh, well, please pass on our apologies and tell Hillary and Charlie to enjoy their meal. You know it was their thirty-fifth wedding anniversary last weekend, and both of their birthdays... Oh, thank you, we'll let you know... Yes, bye." Emily turns to me. "Burgers?"

I laugh before placing the car in reverse and driving around the block so we don't have to go back past the restaurant.

"It was lucky I rang." Emily grins as she places a hand on my thigh. "They'd actually seated us together."

Burger Bonanza is on the other side of town, and we score a park a block and a half away. It means I get to hold Emily's hand as we walk there. We're both overly dressed for a dinner here, but it doesn't worry me.

"Boyd. Emily." Bruno greets us with kisses on both cheeks. "Where are you two off to all dressed up?"

"Here," Emily says as she squeezes my hand.

"There're no booths available at the moment, but if you take a seat at the bar, I can make sure you get the next one, unless you want a table?" Bruno looks around the crowded restaurant.

We nod to the bar, and then both of us take a seat. "What can I get you?" The Irish barman is new and hands us the drinks menu. "Beer? Wine? Cocktail? I do a mean Irish Coffee." He laughs, and it's infectious.

"Actually." Emily closes the menu and places it down on the bar. "I'd love a strawberry milkshake."

"And for you, sir?" There's a magical lilt to his voice as he takes away the menus he's just given us and spins a metal milkshake cup in the air.

"Actually, I'll have the same, thanks."

"So, to share then." One side of his lips trail upwards, and he wiggles his eyebrows.

"Why not?" says Emily, as she places her hand on my thigh again.

I want to reach out and place my arm around her waist, but I'm trying to play it cool, although I feel anything but. "You know, I wanted to share a milkshake when we came here for your sixteenth birthday, but I didn't know if it was the done thing or not."

"That was before you decided you liked strawberry milkshakes, though." Emily laughs, the sound like music to my ears. "You used to only drink vanilla."

"There's nothing wrong with vanilla." I try to sound wounded, but she merely laughs again.

"I'm glad your horizons have broadened past vanilla to things more" —she pauses as she takes her lip between her teeth—"spicy. Especially as we've gotten to know each other better."

Fuck me dead. Sixteen-year-old Emily would never have made such a suggestive comment. My cock swells in my pants, and I wonder if I need to cross my legs to hide it.

The barman brings our milkshake, and we both take a sip. I love being so close to her. I can smell the sweetness from her shampoo and want to take her earlobe between my teeth and tug at it.

"Here you go." Bruno ushers us to a booth from the bar. Despite the offer from one of the young waiters, I happily carry our drink.

We place our food orders and sit in silence. I don't know what to talk about. I wanted to keep tonight light, but we still have things we need to work out to move forward.

"What are you thinking?" Emily plays with some of the condensation that's dripping down the side of the milkshake cup. "And please, be honest."

"So much." I shake my head and sit back in the booth. I want to sit there and hold her hand and gaze into her eyes, but that won't get us where we need to be, back together as husband and wife. "Thanks for the email you forwarded from Dr Jacquie. I looked up the different people she recommended. There was only one that I thought would be a hard no because she also sells crystals and talks more about being a sex therapist than a couple's counsellor."

"I don't think we need sex therapy." Emily rolls her eyes, which makes me chuckle.

"Maybe we could learn something new. Her website said she uses a hands-on approach."

"Well, I'm not. I'm not that comfortable with the thought of anyone else putting their hands on you like that." Emily is playing with her fingers, picking at a cuticle that should probably be left alone.

My heart swells at her confession. I knew she didn't really want a divorce, but hearing her say this makes me realise how much she still loves me and is possessive of me and my body.

"Of the other three recommended, one is on the other side of the city, but they do telehealth consultations. The other two are closer to the apartment. That is assuming we're going to Brisbane." Shit, I hadn't wanted to bring this up.

"I think it's leaning that way." Emily swallows. "I, um, I don't really want to be apart from you."

Mum and Dad offered us the apartment they bought when Giles was at uni, but things have been up in the air. Val's been living in it since she moved to Brisbane, but she has been looking at buying somewhere closer to where she's working. I hate the thought of her buying down there and not in Cassowary Point, but if we're going to be in Brisbane for a year or so, then it will be nice to have her nearby.

"I've started seeing a therapist, too," Emily admits as she looks at the table. "She's someone Bridget recommended. I've never gotten over Dad leaving, and now, if we are going to Brisbane…"

There's a pause in our conversation, but I'm sure Emily can hear my heart beat for her.

"I know this is technically a first date or something, but, fuck, Emily, I love you so damn much. It's always eaten me up that you've never made peace with him leaving like he did." I want to jump across the table and take her in my arms, but I lean forward and hope she can see the intensity in my eyes.

I don't understand why he did what he did and could never imagine doing that to a woman I loved, but he wasn't my father. Since before I even realised what was happening, I've seen women hit on my dad. He's a good-looking bloke for an old man, but he's only ever had eyes for Mum. I don't think it's genetic, but he's set an example I know I want to live up to. He's always been a hands-on dad and taken time off work to come to sporting events and presentation days at school. He even took time off to look after us when we were sick. I hope I've been able to show Emily that I'm different to the lowlife who described himself as her father.

"So, what are the other two therapists like?" Emily asks.

"They're both middle-aged women who have rave reviews online."

"Can I leave it with you to find someone, then?" Emily asks. She has one eye closed, and her nose is scrunched up.

"Of course." I reach over and take her hand just as our burgers arrive.

Conversation moves to the piano teaching she'll be doing and how that will mainly be in the evenings. I talk a bit about work and complain I've got a run of nights coming up. She tells me about a new zombie game she's read about online, and we agree we should play it together.

We eat our dinner. I've never had a bad burger here. Even the time Henry convinced me to try the vegan mushroom and tofu burger, I was impressed. Emily has sauce dripping down her pinkie fingers, and I want to lean over and lick it off them. My cock's been hard most of the night, but seeing her tongue reach out and lap at the mixture of mayonnaise and ketchup sees me almost blow in my pants. I know she doesn't realise it, but it's so damn sexy.

I'm still only halfway through my burger when she finishes, as I've been too busy looking at her eat. She says nothing about my slow pace; she just wipes her hands on the paper serviette and starts talking again about what she's been up to.

"... And then Nonna says, 'I might be old, but I'm not blind, and these eggplants are as old and shrivelled as your *pene,* and I wouldn't put that near my mouth either'." Both of us are laughing as Emily recounts the trip to the market with her Nonna during the week. "So, needless to say, we didn't have eggplant parmigiana for dinner as planned."

"Mum and Dad used to fly to Brisbane every month to see Giles and the kids when they lived down there. Do you think Nonna would come down with your mum every so often?"

"Nonna hates flying, hates it with a passion, but we can ask, I suppose." Emily shrugs.

I know I'm asking a lot of Emily to come to Brisbane with me when she hates it down there, and she'll be away from her mum and Nonna, two important people in her life.

"Perhaps we could swing it so you could fly home, too," I suggest.

"It just gets expensive, that's all." Emily swallows a sip of water, and I wish we were sharing straws in the water glasses too, even though our milkshake is long finished.

I can read her subtext, though. IVF isn't cheap. We've spent thousands already for very little. We've saved, sure, and we're close to having enough for a deposit on a house, but I also want to travel. Mum and Dad won't accept rent on the Brisbane apartment, but we'll pay the taxes and fees required for living there. We'll have money, even if Emily decides not to work as a doctor.

The big thing is whether we continue with IVF. Part of me wants to, despite the heartbreak, because I know deep down there's no reason we can't fall pregnant. The other part of me, though, says that it's not worth risking my relationship with Emily, especially as it's her body going through it all.

There's no right or wrong answer per se, but I'm leaning towards having a break from it. The talk this evening about possibly moving to Brisbane has excited me. I won't lie, I want to work at a large children's hospital, if only for a year or so. What the last week or so has shown, though, is that I want Emily more. My bosses have been really understanding, and I don't want to push her to make a decision she'll regret later on.

I also want to ask Emily to move home with me. I want to ask her if I can stay the night with her. I want a lot of things. But most of all, I want to be us. I want to be together, talking like this and spending time in each other's company. Our life isn't all about sex. I mean, sex is amazing, but I need Emily to realise that there's more to our relationship than just sex or baby making.

"A brownie to share?" Bruno asks as he takes our plates and hands them to one of the young waiters. I don't think he does a lot of work around here, but the place wouldn't be the same without him.

"I'm full." Emily pats her stomach, and I beam, seeing her gold wedding band glint under the lights.

"Me too, Bruno. Just the bill, please." I bite my lip as I sit back and gaze at Emily. I am one lucky bastard having her in my life, and I want to make sure it stays that way.

Bruno sends one of the staff members over with the machine to swipe my card, and I slide out of the booth, reaching a hand to Emily to help her out.

"I was thinking of going dancing, but I've got no idea where to go," I admit as we leave the restaurant, still holding hands.

"I suppose there's the casino, but that's usually full of old people, and who knows if your parents might be there, too." Emily squeezes my hand as we slowly walk towards my car. "I mean, I love being seen with you, and you look hot tonight. I mean, you trimmed your beard, and your hair is in the perfect man bun, and you're wearing that stunning blue shirt that matches your eyes."

Emily sounds playful, but I could be reading her wrong. "I can sense a but coming on."

"No, no buts." With the hand not holding mine, Emily reaches over and grabs my upper arm as we walk along. "I mean, I could put some music on at Mum's, and we could dance in the lounge room."

The way her finger trails down my bicep as we pause in the middle of the path and look at each other does nothing to calm my already excited cock. I've told it that it's not going to see any action tonight, and then Emily goes and says these things and touches me like she is. I have to remind myself to go slowly. Dancing doesn't equal sex.

Holding Emily in my arms will be enough, even if I want more.

THE DRIVE back to Rosa's house is quiet. The classical music plays in the background. This time, it sounds quite modern and dissonant, but Emily doesn't seem to mind. It reminds me of how my brain is at present.

"That was Stravinsky's Rite of Spring," Emily tells me as we climb out of the car. "It was written for a ballet and is meant to depict the creative power of spring and, I think, from memory, includes the sacrifice of a young woman. Russian folklore, and all that stuff."

I love it when she spouts strange musical history to me. Her brain is full of it, from telling me about Beethoven's inspiration for various pieces, to the inspiration for 'Ticket to Ride' by the Beatles, which came from the way sex workers in Germany had to have a clean bill of health signed off before they could work.

"I can't imagine dancing to it," I tell her as she places the key in the door and pushes it open.

"Well, fortunately, I have some songs that we could slow dance to." I follow her inside, watching her hips sway as she places her purse on the couch after grabbing her phone out of it.

My mouth is dry, the moisture from there migrating to my palms, which have started to sweat. She turns on the lamp on top of the piano, adding an ambient light to the room, plugs her phone into the speaker on top of the piano, and presses buttons, looking for the music she's after. I have to chuckle as she kicks off her heels. Without them, she barely comes to my shoulder, but I don't mind.

The strum of a guitar heralds the Roberta Flack classic 'The First Time Ever I Saw Your Face'. I'm pretty sure she would have heard it plenty of times at my place growing up, as it's one of Dad's favourite songs.

"Em, I didn't come in to have sex with you," I blurt out. "I mean, I'd love to have sex, but I don't know if it's the best idea if I'm meant to be wooing you. So, I just wanted—"

Emily hushes me by placing her finger against my lips, grabbing one hand and placing it on her hip, and holding the other to the side of us as she brings our bodies together.

We danced at the Gala, but it had been forced. Emily hadn't pressed her body to mine like she was doing tonight. Her hand trails from my side, down to my bottom, squeezing it gently, drawing us even closer together. I feel like I should apologise that my cock is pressing right into her stomach, but she says nothing, simply swaying to the music.

The track changes to the INXS classic 'Never Tear Us Apart', and I wonder if she's gotten a hold of Henry's notorious playlist.

"You know divorce is the last thing I want, right?" Emily asks, her body gripping mine. "I mean, I said it because I thought you deserve to be a father."

"I don't think either of us is undeserving of being parents." I kiss her on top of her head. "And you should know I would never accept we were over just like that."

"I'm sorry I said those things and tried to push you away," she whispers as she holds me closer.

I reply with a kiss to her forehead. Her words of apology are special, but her body language has already told me she's forgiven me. Being apart from her this week has been hell. Dancing with her now feels almost perfect.

She hums as the music continues. More songs play, and we simply move to the beat. I'm careful not to step on her feet. During a more upbeat song that talks about loving you when I'm sleeping, she pulls back and looks up at me. Her eyes are glassy, the pupils blown, and her cheeks are flushed. I know this look on Emily.

I told myself we would not have sex tonight, but I know we both want it, need it, yearn for it. I hoist her up so her legs are wrapped around my waist, her arms flying around my neck as our lips smash together. It's not gentle or soft, it's possessive and shows the yearning that is deep within both of us.

An album worth of songs could have played, and I couldn't have told you what they were, as I'm lost in Emily. Our passion is broken as Emily's phone rings. I carry her to it, only to see it's my sister.

"Ignore her." Emily kisses my jawline, tugging on my beard with her lips as I silence her phone and carry her to her bedroom.

This is the same room we both had sex in for the first time. Over ten years of fucking, making love, screwing, and any number of other euphemisms for what we've done, and yet I don't think I've ever felt as desperate as I have tonight to be inside my wife.

I lower her to her feet as I reach for the tie that fastens her dress. Tugging the bow undone, I get no further as Emily pushes me back so I'm lying on the bed with my legs dangling over the end. She undoes the buttons on my shirt, kissing my chest as more is revealed. She's at risk of making me blow before I get my pants off with the way she straddles my thigh and rubs her leg against my extremely engorged cock.

Pushing my arms above my head with one hand causes her to travel back up my body, her cleavage almost in my face. She reaches for my belt, undoing it swiftly before pulling it from my trousers. I wonder if she's planning on binding my wrists with it, but she throws it on the ground and unclasps my pants, lowering the zipper tooth by tooth.

I'm doing all I can to try to hold myself back. Giles boasts he recites the periodic table. In the past, I've tried to think of paediatric drug calculations, but tonight, I'm having a hard time taking my mind from staring at Emily's beauty and longing to have my skin pressed against hers.

As her hand reaches inside my boxers, I have to stop her. "Honey, I'm so close already." I'm almost panting as I try to sit up. "I don't want this to be over before it's even begun."

Emily takes no notice, letting go of my wrists, which I could easily have broken free from, and trailing kisses again down my abdomen.

My breaths are coming quickly as she tugs my trousers and boxers to my knees. It's her fingers gliding over the underside of my engorged cock as it lies against my stomach that brings the hitch and the telltale feeling of fullness in my balls that tells me an orgasm is imminent.

"Don't worry, baby," she purrs, "I'll suck you 'til you're hard again."

It's her sultry tone that does me in. Either that or the way her lips gently slide over the head of my cock and she gazes into my eyes. I'm shooting more cum than I've ever shot in my life. But Emily doesn't choke. She swallows it down, using a finger to wipe up a small amount that escaped, before sucking it as if she was still sucking my cock.

I don't have time to be embarrassed by my lack of self-control though. Emily tugs at her dress, dropping it to the floor. She's wearing matching bra and panties, both in a vivid red. I can see her nipples against the lace, almost tenting it with their firmness.

"I'm going to have to take these off, because my panties are very, very wet." She sounds like a wet dream. I mean, I feel like I've died and ended up in Nirvana. My brain is short-circuiting as I try to catch up to her.

Fortunately, my cock is more than ready to keep playing. My eyes are on Emily as she reaches behind herself and unclasps her bra before holding it up with one hand as she slides the straps down her arms.

The sight of her nipples, hard and pointing towards me like bullets, tears my mind into action. I jerk up, my mouth latching onto a nipple, my tongue rolling over it. My hand toys with the breast neglected by my mouth, stroking the nipple and teasing it between my fingers.

She's rubbing her legs together, and I can see the wet patch spreading from the gusset to the lace, darkening it with her arousal. It's been years since I've spent so much time worshiping her breasts. They deserve better, and tonight, they're getting it. My lips and hands alternate between breasts. No set rhythm or time to their movements, just what makes her moan and groan in pleasure.

Her hands rest on my shoulders, and I want to bring my spare hand around to rub her clit. It's not needed though, as I feel her body tense and a loud "Yes, yes, yes, yes, yes," escapes her mouth as she comes.

I kick off my shoes and pants, managing to remove my socks by dragging them against the bottom of the bed. Emily has shed her knickers. Our lips have found each other again, and Emily is lying on me. If her breasts are hard enough to leave indentations in my chest, then my cock will also leave an indentation in her abdomen.

Our bodies are slick with sweat as I try to roll Emily onto her back. She has other ideas though as she helps me move up the bed so my head is on a pillow, our lips never parting. Emily swings a leg over me, and I feel the wetness from her cunt coating my cock as she slides against it. It feels like she's emptied a tube of lube down there, but it's all her. I want to lick her, to taste her and use my lips to devour her pussy, but she won't let me, rocking over me as my cock tries to find its way home.

He knows what he wants to do and where he wants to be, and it's not waiting for me to feast on my wife. I groan into Emily's mouth as she slides down onto me, taking my cock in one smooth movement. There's a tightness that I'll never get used to as her walls accommodate me. As she rocks her hips, I can feel the tension build in my body again.

I move my lips from her mouth to her jaw, kissing towards her ear, before sucking at the place just behind her earlobe that I know turns her on. I want to mark her, to show the world she's mine.

"Fucking perfect." I let out a breathy moan as she moves back and forth, taking my cock even deeper inside. I can feel her cervix and try not to bump it, but it's challenging not to.

Emily doesn't mind. "You like fucking your good girl, don't you?" She sounds so in control, whereas I feel anything but. I feel like I'm going to blow again, but I need her to come. I want her to come.

"You are a good girl. My good girl. You love taking my cock like this, don't you?" My voice is gravelly as I whisper into her ear, but it has the effect of causing her to gasp, as she sits upright and really rides me.

The look of her breasts swaying as she moves brings me closer to my second climax. My hands on her hips, I rock her back and forth, making sure her clit grazes my pubic bone. I can feel her body tense on top of me.

"You're going to come for me, aren't you?" I almost grunt as I feel my buttocks clenching. "You're going to come and draw the cum out of my balls so I can paint your walls and show everyone that you're mine."

This brings her over the edge, and I feel her pussy walls contract, squeezing my cock, bright lights flashing behind my eyes, my body tensing as I feel my cum erupt inside of her.

Emily slumps on top of me, and I wrap her in my arms, stroking the soft skin of her back as our breathing evens out.

"That was... that was... wow," she whispers. I simply hum in agreement.

Emily, Age 26

I faked an orgasm. Twenty-three months we've been trying, and this is the first time I haven't actually felt like sex. I ovulate tomorrow, and I know Boyd needed to make a deposit, but I just wasn't feeling it.

Perhaps I should have taken acting lessons. I think Boyd knew something was off. When he came to bed and started kissing me, I should have said no, but I figured we needed to do it in case it is the month we conceive.

I've made an appointment with the clinic again for next month, and it would be great if we can call and cancel it. Except now I'm worried that if I have conceived, it will be a lie, and our baby won't have been made out of love.

We did it doggy, so Boyd didn't have to see the disinterest on my face. I mean, I was happy to do it, don't get me wrong. I didn't feel coerced by anyone apart from me. It's just the knowledge that it's my fertile time.

He knows I faked it too, I'm sure of it. I mean, I clenched my muscles and faked a moan, but he asked me if everything was okay afterwards. I lied again and said it hadn't been a powerful orgasm. Yeah, because it hadn't been an orgasm at all.

He's always so attentive after sex. He grabbed a cloth to wipe me down and spooned me, telling me how much he loves me. It didn't take him long to fall asleep. I'm still awake an hour later, hence my entry here.

Is it wrong to hope I'm not pregnant? I feel so guilty. Sure, there have been times when I haven't come during sex, but they've been few and far between, and Boyd has always carried on stroking my clit and whispering all manner of dirty things in my ear until I climaxed. It's never been that sex is over because he's come, but tonight, I wanted it to be. I wanted it to be done with so I could get to sleep, except I'm still awake, feeling guilty.

I can't win. I'm pretty sure this will be the cycle I get pregnant, and I'll worry about this for the rest of my life.

Shit. Boyd's awake. I confessed to him, and he told me he knew. Of course he did. He thinks that it's an act of love regardless of orgasm, and the fact I was willing to do it even though I wasn't in the mood proved that. I'm not convinced. He also told me he thinks he owes me a night between my legs with his tongue. I'll probably hold him to that. He's so good at it, and I really am the luckiest.

Chapter 22

Emily

"Boyd, Emily. How are you both?" Pip's wide smile greets us through my laptop screen.

It's our third session with the marriage counsellor, and I think we're on to a winner. Boyd told me how he felt there was so much pressure to choose the right person. He looked at online reviews and mapped out how far away the offices would be from our apartment in Brisbane when we move down there. Then he flipped a coin because he couldn't decide. It was so Boyd and one of the things I love about him.

"Yeah, good." I turn to Boyd. We grasp our hands as we sit on the couch. I'm not even sure they're in view of the camera, but Boyd knows I'm holding him tight. "Boyd had Monday off, and we went for a hike, which was lovely. It's something we haven't done for a while."

We're trying to have at least one date a week where we get out of the apartment. After our week apart and our amazing date at Burger Bonanza—well, after the amazing sex that happened after the date—I agreed to move home, despite Boyd offering for me to stay with Mum for a while longer. There was no pressure, but it felt wrong to be apart from him. We both admitted we slept better that night than we had in ages and put it down the being close to each other.

After talking through things further with Amelia, I've even agreed to move to Brisbane.

"And Boyd, you're not coming off night shift again like last week?" Pip looks at me over her glasses, and I feel like I'm in the principal's office again.

"No." He chuckles. "I won't make that mistake again."

"It wasn't a mistake, I don't think. I feel it was a good session in the end, and you were both great at identifying the green flags in your relationship. Have you found any more?"

Pip isn't all about focusing on the positives. In our first week, Boyd identified how he hadn't really noticed how I was hating my job at the GP practice, despite him referring to my boss as Dr Douche. I also thought we'd be spending more time talking about our infertility, but it hasn't come up a lot so far in our discussions.

"I know we mentioned drama last week," I say as I glance between Boyd and the screen. "And how Boyd and I have had little drama in our relationship until now, but I think it's because Boyd is a genuinely nice person. I mean, he shows respect. He knows who the cleaners are on the ward and greets people by name. He makes people feel important."

"Good." Pip nods her head as she makes notes on a large notepad. She's different to Amelia, the therapist I see by myself, which I've decided is not a bad thing.

I meet up with Amelia early in the week and then Saturday mornings are our time with Pip. Boyd has had to make some roster changes, but no one seems to have minded much. He's always been the one to step in to help colleagues, so it seems almost right that they are now helping him.

Piano lessons have been going well. I met Sue's new baby this week. It helped that it was one of those alien looking ones with a scrunched-up face and wrinkles. When Sue started going on about how painful labour was and how she can't imagine wanting to do it again in a hurry and joked about not letting her husband come near her for at least eighteen months, I brushed it off.

It hurt hearing someone take their fertility for granted. I know she didn't mean it to be painful, but it highlighted how I might be more sensitive to others I might meet.

"Now, I know we've brushed on the upcoming move to Brisbane being stressful." Pip is flicking through papers in the manilla folder on her desk, probably looking for another worksheet for us. She loves her worksheets. "Have you thought of any ways that you might support each other through it?"

"Things seem to be falling into place," I offer as I smile at Boyd. "Nonna wants to catch the train down to visit us, which will be interesting. I don't think she realises how far it is. We've set up a new tablet for her so we can talk each week. Mum's also looking forward to coming down and visiting us, as are Boyd's parents."

"And I found someone at work who's been looking for an apartment and is happy to take over our lease, so we won't have to break it," Boyd adds.

He doesn't add that he's also got ads up around the hospital to sell his car, advertising it as the perfect vehicle to teach your kids to drive in. It's probably about the only thing his rust bucket will be useful for.

"So, I know the reason you see me is because of infertility, but I've been wanting to get an idea about the foundation of your relationship. You've shown me already it's strong. Now, you've got your notepads there, I hope?" This was one of Pip's things. She likes each of us having our own pen and paper, and when she gives us scenarios, we write things down so we can't change our mind once our partner has voiced their opinion. "If you went to bed tonight and when you woke up tomorrow, you found everything was perfect. There was nothing at all wrong with anything in your life. What would it look like? I'm not talking about world peace or ending starvation, but you as an individual. I'll give you both a few minutes."

I look at my notebook. It's an old one I've had for years that I didn't really have anything written in. I liked the purple cover, but it had been squashed between a couple of larger books once upon a time and has never been the same. Boyd was madly scribbling away. He has typical doctor's writing. I could almost understand it all, but only just.

What would my perfect world look like? I jot down notes about being with Boyd and knowing we were there for each other and a significant part of each other's lives. I then mention that I wanted to work as a GP, but not in a practice where I was harassed by others. Boyd puts his pen down and is sipping from his can of Coke. I keep writing, though, putting on paper about being there for Mum and Nonna and not letting my father's actions affect me so much. Finally, I admit I want to learn to live happily with the prospect that we may never be parents.

My tea is lukewarm when I take a sip, but it doesn't bother me. I surprise myself that I am enjoying therapy, both alone and with Boyd. It's nothing like what I experienced with Priscilla as a teenager.

"We'll come back to those thoughts at the end of our session, but first, I want you to tell me about your parents' relationships. Do you want to go first, Boyd?" Pip tapped her pen on her chin as she waited for Boyd to start.

He spoke of the love exhibited in his family, about birthdays and anniversary celebrations and about the Gala Ball that raised so much money to help people with cardiac conditions. He spoke of their values of fairness, tolerance, and understanding. It was clear from his words how much he adores them, and I knew they helped shape him into the man he is today.

"Do they fight?" Pip asked Boyd as she took notes, not even pausing to look at us.

"Yeah." Boyd nods. "They argue. It's usually over stupid things though, like Dad forgetting to pick up some ingredient Mum needs for dinner on his way home from work, or Dad complaining about Mum's knitting shit being strewn over the house."

"What about you and Emily? Do you argue?" Pip asks, this time looking at us.

"Not really." Boyd looks between me and Pip, almost questioning that it would be something we would consider. "I mean, sure, we forget to do things the others asked us, but there's no need to start World War III over forgetting to pick up toilet paper after work or running out of frozen berries for my morning smoothie. I think I get more annoyed with myself for forgetting to grab things and having to ask Emily for help in the first place."

Pip's lips turn into a perfect smile as she jots down notes. "And what about you, Emily? Tell me about your parents' marriage."

"I thought it was perfect. I thought it was what a family was like. They both cared for me and showed they loved me by providing for me. I mean, I didn't get everything I asked for, but I felt spoilt, I suppose. That's what pisses me off about my father. It was all lies. He was having affairs and then left us for his new family. I just never saw it coming." Boyd places an arm around my shoulders. I'm not crying though.

"I've spoken about this with Amelia, and she's questioned if I might have ignored some signs, or even if my mum tried to cover for my dad at times." I shake my head, knowing that the only way I'll get answers is by talking to my father. It's something Amelia and I have been discussing a lot.

"And what about Boyd? Do you get annoyed with him at times?" Pip asks, leaning towards the camera.

"Sometimes, I suppose, but it's easier to do things myself." I shrug, looking over at Boyd, who has removed his arm from my shoulders and placed his hands in his lap.

"So, you don't trust me?" he asks tersely, his brows knitted together.

"No, it's just easier to make sure I get the right things, I suppose." I place my hand on his knee.

"Is this about the tampons?" Boyd slaps his thighs.

"That was years ago." I can't believe he even remembers this.

"Yeah, and I'm sorry. I still think you've got a tiny vagina, and I thought the smaller size would be the most comfortable." He's spitting out the words, his eyes wide.

"And I shouldn't have laughed, but I fit your massive cock up there, so I think I can take a super tampon." I'm expecting Pip to interrupt us to bring us back to topic, but instead, she's sitting back in her chair intently listening to our tiff.

"If you asked me to get them again, I'd make sure I asked you what size you want. I didn't know there were different sizes."

"But I plan now, and I pick up some boxes as soon as my period's over so I've got them for next time." I'm making sense in my head, but I can see Boyd isn't convinced.

"What about last week when I forgot you were teaching late, and I was meant to be cooking and I prepared nothing, and then I stayed at the library at work, and when you got home, there was no dinner?" Boyd is beating himself up over this.

"You messaged me. It's just that I hadn't seen it. I think we had beans on toast or something, didn't we?" I grab his hand to stop him yanking it through his hair.

"But that's not the point." He's almost yelling. "I let you down, and I don't like letting you down. Just like I can't get you pregnant."

He pauses and looks at me, his eyes full of unshed tears. My arms reach instinctively for his neck, and I hold him as the tears flow. I hate seeing him so upset, but I can see how the different households we grew up in have shaped us, and in my case, not necessarily for the better.

Pip draws us back to the session, and we continue to talk about expectations and how these change. We don't necessarily talk about babies and fertility, but it's implied. We don't even get back to our earlier exercise about our perfect lives.

Our previous sessions have ended with Pip telling us to be gentle with each other. This one ends with her telling us to not be afraid to fight the good fight.

I'm exhausted. We had planned to spend the weekend packing. The Brisbane apartment is fully furnished after having members of the Hartman family living there for over ten years now, but we still need to pack our personal items and all our clothes. Mum suggested leaving things at her place, but the reality is, there won't be a lot. Our clothes will fit in the boot of my car. We'll take our gaming consoles and games with us, along with a few of our favourite kitchen utensils and pots, but we can donate the rest.

The doctor who's moving in here is happy to take the old furniture off our hands. We've told her the couch is lumpy, and the bed is old, but she doesn't care. It's one less thing to worry about.

"I didn't mean to bring up the tampons. I'm sorry." Boyd is still ruminating on our argument mid-session.

"It's okay." I stroke his cheek before standing and taking my empty mug and Coke can to the kitchen. "You know, it annoys me when you hang the toilet paper the wrong way. It's meant to come over the top, not underneath."

"Really?" His head juts back as he contemplates this. "Does it make that much of a difference?"

"Probably not, but it's just how I prefer it. I usually just change it over."

"Well, that's something I'll remember in the future." He follows me into the kitchen and draws me into a hug. "And do you think that in the future you can check to see if there's an open bottle of soy sauce before opening yet another one?"

"Sorry. Are there two open?" I try to look sheepish, but I know I often reach for the bottle in the pantry and forget there's probably an open one in the fridge.

"There's only two now. I decanted the remnants from the third bottle into the other two last night. So, please don't buy another one just yet." I can feel Boyd shake as he laughs as he hugs me.

His hugs are legendary. People talk of the safety they feel with a weighted blanket, but Boyd provides better than any blanket could.

"I'm tired after that session. Do you think packing can wait until this afternoon?" I ask as I pull away from the security of his arms and grasp his fingers in mine.

"Are you thinking sleep or..." His question dangles in the air as I lead him to our room.

I doubt there'll be much sleep at all, actually.

It's a long drive from Cassowary Point to Brisbane. We could have done it in two days, but we take our time, stopping off at various sights along the way. We've seen a big mango, a big bull, and a big pineapple. Not sure what the fascination is with big things, but if I hear Boyd say one more time that they should make a statue of his gigantic cock, I'll scream.

I know it's him trying to rile me up. He's been picking petty arguments with me, but only because he knows there'll be make up sex afterwards. No one had ever explained the concept of make up sex to me. Hilary laughed when I mentioned it at lunch last week.

The drive gives us time to really talk about some things. Dr Nat—or just Nat, as she's asked me to call her—put me in touch with a friend of hers who is a GP in Brisbane and was looking for a registrar after the one they took on at the start of the year went back to hospital work. Nat raved about how much fun Savannah was, and from the few times we've chatted via video link, I didn't doubt her. She introduced me to the other doctors in the practice already and said they were looking forward to meeting me.

Piano teaching wasn't for me. It was fun for a week or two until I realised so many of the kids didn't really want to be there and definitely didn't practice. Mia was one of the dedicated students, but she was a perfectionist and wanted to get everything absolutely perfect before she moved onto a new piece. She couldn't understand how she could leave something she hadn't mastered behind. She's a clone of her mother, that's for sure.

Giles and Bridget put Boyd in touch with a colleague of theirs from medical school, who's now a paediatrician at the children's hospital where Boyd will be working. Tommy seems like just as much of a big kid as Boyd is, despite being six years older than him.

Val's found a cottage she's fallen in love with, but she can't move in for another month. It's going to need a lot of work, but she thinks she can manage it. I can see weekends there painting and ripping out bathrooms and kitchens.

About two hours out from Brisbane, we finally start talking IVF. I told Boyd that I feel we both need to focus on work for a year or two, and it surprises me when he agrees. We're not going to do anything silly like use contraception, but we're also going to try to ignore my cycle. I know it's going to be hard.

Jacquie told us early on that as long as we're having sex every other day or thereabouts, that was fine. We've usually been much more frequent than that. If it happens, it happens. After I turn thirty, we're going to reassess IVF. I feel comfortable having a plan in place.

LAST WEEK, when we talked with Pip, we discussed future-proofing our lives, and we all agreed that me becoming a GP is one way to do that. Boyd's always been so encouraging with my career, and I know training as a GP will give me options in the future. Mum regrets never training to be a teacher, which is what she always wanted to do. I suspect she might have left Dad earlier if she felt she had options.

Now I'm doing something I should have done a long time ago. Instead of worrying I'll bump into my father unexpectedly, I've arranged to meet him for coffee.

I glance at my phone. He's late, not that this should surprise me. Gina's still doing relief teaching and has today off, so we're meeting for lunch. I won't wait around forever for him.

"Em, Emily?" He sounds hesitant as he grasps his tweed flat cap between his fingers. I'd forgotten he always wore that hat. "It's... It's... Wow. Look at you."

He leans in for a kiss, but I stretch out my hand to shake. I'm not entirely sure what's appropriate here.

It's a nondescript coffee shop at a shopping centre we're in. I take a sip of the worst cup of tea I've had in a while and don't even offer for him to order a coffee.

"Hi, Dad." My voice is low, and there's definitely no smile on my face.

He takes a seat, almost toppling it over and bumping into the person seated behind him.

"Shona said you'd come around." He reaches across the table for my hand, and I draw them away, placing them in my lap. "Hank would love to meet his big sister."

Dad leans towards me, his hat on the table, and tries to smile. I can imagine he's nervous. I was too until I saw him. He looks old, much older than Mum. I remember his hair had receded before he left, but now he's resorted to a comb-over. It doesn't suit him.

"I just want to know why, Dad. Why did you leave us?" I ask, crossing my arms across my chest. I don't care if it's a dick move or an aggressive position to place myself in.

"Well, as you know, Shona was pregnant, and she wanted to move down here to be closer to her mother, and I didn't want to make her have to do it on her own. You know, raise a baby and that." He runs his hand over his hair, smoothing it down, and I can see his fingers are shaking. I hope he didn't think I was inviting him here to pretend nothing has happened.

"But you left Mum to raise me?" I question, my head tilting to the side.

"Yes, well, I had a hard decision to make." He nods his head as if he's agreeing with himself.

"Perhaps it's a decision you should have considered before you slept with someone who wasn't Mum?" I want to slap him and see if I can get some sense into him, but we're in a coffee shop, and I don't want to make a scene. "She loved you. She did everything for you, and then you went behind her back and knocked up your secretary. What a bloody cliché."

"Well, she had a fine way of showing me how much she loved me." Dad crosses his legs and mirrors me with his arms across his chest.

"You mean by cooking your meals, cleaning the house, and doing all your laundry? Does Shona iron your shirts?" I'm not sure why I'm here. This isn't the father I remember. It's not the version I created in my childhood head.

"Shona got me into wearing polo necks for work. They don't need ironing." He nods again. "But your mother never worked. She had time to do all that."

I can't believe what I'm hearing. I take a deep breath. "Was it because I'm adopted, and Hank is biologically yours?"

This is the question that's always bugged me. The way my father drops his head gives me the answer I always feared.

"Was it the infertility that drove you and Mum apart?" I ask softly after a minute or two of silence.

"I think that started it, yes." Dad sighs. "I mean, your mother's never been a very intimate person. She always had one excuse or another. You know 'Oh, I'm in pain' or some such rot."

"She had endometriosis, Dad. She would have been in immense pain." I drop my voice to not make a scene, but the venom in it is clear.

"Yes, well, a man has his needs. I regret the way things ended, but..." He trails off, and I actually don't want to know any more.

"Have you been faithful to Shona?" I ask very matter of factly.

"It's not like she's been faithful to me." He sounds bitter, and I decide that there's no way I want anything to do with him. "When I had prostate cancer last year, she... Anyway, enough about her. I retired last Christmas. Gives me more time for golf."

He hasn't asked once about me or what I'm doing with my life. I always wanted to believe my father had a horrible choice to make, and he agonised over whether to leave Mum and me, but I don't think he's ever really thought about us. It's all about him.

"You know what, Dad?" I stand to leave, something he isn't expecting. "I came here today for answers about why you would leave our perfect family life, but it just made me realise that it really only ever became perfect after you left. You never came back for Nonno's funeral. You've never even sent me a birthday card. Mum has stood up for you for all these years and said what a stressful job you had, but I can see now that my life only got better after you left. It took me until I saw you again today to realise that. I don't want to keep in touch. I don't want to meet Hank or Shona. I wish nothing evil for you, but just know that I no longer consider you my father. You may have lived with my mother for the first thirteen years of my life, but that doesn't make you a dad."

It feels good to storm off like I do. A woman who is sitting at a table near us nods and smiles at me as I leave. As I walk away, I reach for my phone.

> Mum, it's me. Why didn't you ever tell me what a narcissistic arsehole my father is?

MUM

> I didn't want to cloud your judgement. I tried to protect you.

> But you never fought. I never heard you argue.

MUM

> There was never any point when your father 'was always right'.

> Are you happier than when you were married? I wish you'd find someone to see, even if it's just as a friend.

MUM

I'm so happy. I don't need a husband or
partner to be happy. I've got my friends and
my little business and my mama. And of
course, I have you.

I'll call you tonight.

Had I talked to my father sooner, would I have come to the same conclusions? Not once did he ask about me. He didn't ask if I was married or what I did for work. I'd held on to a memory that I'd perpetuated for years, never understanding why he left. It didn't hurt to know the truth now. No, it hurt realising that I could have worked this out sooner.

It worried me for years that Boyd would be like my father and leave me for someone else. He's nothing like him, though. If anything, Boyd doesn't think about himself enough, focussing on me whenever he can.

As I walk past a florist on the way to my car, I pull up a webpage on my phone and order a massive bouquet to be delivered to my mum, the best mum in the whole wide world.

Emily, Age 15

It's been two years this week since he left. Mum doesn't talk about him. I don't want to talk to him. Sometimes, I wonder about my baby brother or sister. I thought he might have written or something to let us know what she had, but he never did. The baby's probably a toddler by now.

Mum just smiles and says she's doing fine when I ask her if she's ok. I only found out this week that she and Dad divorced last year. I mean, I knew it was coming. Mum said it was all done through a lawyer, and she didn't have to go to court or anything. He gave her the house, and she says he pays child support each month like he's meant to.

He left because we don't share DNA. I know he did. Mum tries to hide it from me, but I'm convinced it's the case. I look back for signs that things weren't right, but I can't spot any. They never argued, like never ever. I've been at Boyd's when Hillary and Charlie have gotten into spats, only to find them making out in the kitchen half an hour later. It's hard to think that my mum and dad didn't argue and got divorced, and Boyd's parents argue and are together and seem pretty loved up.

Val argues with her brothers all the time, but I know they're all super close. She says that arguing is a form of love because she refuses to be a doormat. I don't think Mum and Dad were doormats. I don't think the arguing itself is a form of love either, but rather it's the talking and listening that is. Well, that's what I'd like to think.

This is not something I want to talk about with Priscilla, either. She had me painting with watercolours this week. I tried to paint a rooster because I really wanted to paint an enormous cock and balls because that's how I see her sessions. I used too much paint or water or something, and in the end, it was an impressionist blob of colour. Priscilla said it reflected the multicolour tapestry in my brain. I think she's smoking weed or something.

Last week, Charlie and Hillary got into an argument because Hillary grabbed green capsicums instead of red ones, and Charlie prefers red ones. I mean, they're just capsicums. What a dumb thing to argue about. Over dinner, they apologised, and Charlie said he'd had a rough day at work with a young patient dying.

When I hear stories like this, I wonder if I really want to be a doctor. It must be so hard sometimes telling people sad news and not being able to fix things. I'd like to think I'll make a difference. I can hope at least.

Chapter 23

Boyd

OUR TIME IN BRISBANE HAS FLOWN BY. ONE YEAR TURNED into almost two. It seems like only yesterday I came home to find Emily laughing hysterically when she saw me. Turns out her father's a narcissistic prick. Emily and Rosa have worked through a lot together, and I think my wife has almost forgiven her mother for hiding what an arsehole her father is.

We've done a lot of therapy over the last eighteen months. I've even found someone to talk to about work and the pressures around dealing with sick kids. Turns out humour is not necessarily the best coping mechanism all the time.

And Emily, well, she's thrived. In a few months, she'll be a fully fledged GP. I'm so proud of the work she's put in to get this far. It helps that she's been working with such an awesome team. Savannah is amazing, as are the other staff in the practice. If it wasn't for Rosa and Nonna, I think she'd consider staying here.

I've still got a few years to go until I'm a fully fledged paediatrician, but I'll get there. I passed my exams, so that's a step closer. Our plan originally was to head back to Cassowary Point at the end of the year.

There's a job for me at the hospital, and Emily has been putting out feelers. She won't be working with Dr Douche, that's for sure.

To celebrate her admission as a member of the College of General Practitioners, we've been planning a holiday—two weeks in China and a week in Hong Kong. Emily's done a lot of work with Amelia about cultural identity. She sees herself as Australian, but she acknowledges she also has history in the country she was born in. We planned to go to Africa for my thirtieth birthday a year back, but I left it too late to book leave. One day, we'll get there.

As I walk along the corridor towards our apartment—well, my parents' apartment—I can hear someone playing the electronic piano I bought Emily last year for Christmas. It sounds nothing like Emily, and I figure Mia must be here. Millie and Mia flew down by themselves to spend a week of the school holidays with Auntie Val. Apparently, Emily and I are chopped liver because Val lives in a cottage. To our nieces, it's as if she's Beatrix Potter herself, living in the middle of the countryside instead of in suburban Brisbane.

"Good afternoon." I open the door and hang my bag on the hook on the wall. "You're getting fantastic at that, Princess Mia."

I walk to where she sits next to Emily on the piano stool and peck her on the head before reaching around and planting a big kiss on my wife.

"You're as bad as Mummy and Daddy. They're always kissing." Mia keeps playing, ignoring our giggles.

"Mummy says I'm not meant to ask you when you're having a baby, but it's okay," Mia stops her playing and turns to us. I'm crouched down next to Emily, my arm around her waist. "Because Daddy's found a boyfriend for Auntie Val, and she's going to marry him and have lots of babies and move back to Cassowary Point. And he's a doctor, and Daddy says that Auntie Val should be a doctor, but she's a lawyer. Millie says she's going to be a lawyer. I'm going to be a hairdresser."

Mia stops her monologue and starts playing again. I stand, and Emily follows me towards the kitchen.

"Are you okay?" I lift her onto the kitchen counter and tuck a strand of hair behind her ear. "Mia doesn't mean to be insensitive."

"No, I'm fine." Her hand strokes my cheek, and I kiss her palm. "As we talked about with Pip, we can plan for the future, but plans may have to change."

I'm still disappointed we aren't pregnant yet. Pip says it's important to acknowledge that, even for the briefest of moments, we were parents, even though our group of cells that might have become a baby didn't make it. We never named our baby, but we often refer to it as Little H.

At the children's hospital where I work, they have a big charity drive each Christmas, and you can pull a tag from the tree that has the age and gender of a child and leave a gift knowing it is needed. Last year, we left one for a toddler, the year before, a newborn.

There's a knock at the door. We're expecting Mum and Dad. They have a key, but after walking in on Emily and me having passionate sex on this very kitchen counter last year, they now know to knock.

"I'll get it," Mia yells as the music stops, and we hear her soft steps across the tiled floor. "Gammy, Gramps!" Mia squeals as she greets her grandparents.

"Hello, poppet." I hear Mum's kiss on one cheek and Dad's raspberry on the other. "Where's Millie?"

"She's with Nonna and Mrs Mac. They've gone somewhere boring." I love the expressiveness in Mia's voice and can almost hear her eye roll from around the corner.

Rosa and Nonna came down on the train to help with Millie and Mia, as Val was in court yesterday and today. They're staying here with us, which is lovely, if not a little cramped.

"And Uncle Boyd and Auntie Emily are kissing. Again."

We aren't kissing, but we have our foreheads pressed together. I feel like we can communicate like this, without words, but with a touch that reminds each other that we belong together and will be together whatever happens.

"People kiss because they like each other." Dad walks around the corner with Mia, ruffling her hair. "I enjoy kissing Gammy a lot, too."

"Well, at school, before the holidays, we had human relationships education, and Mrs Bremmer said that when you grow up, you can choose to have sexual relations with people, but I don't think I'll choose to do that." I love the way she's scrunched up her face, as if she's being forced to eat the vegetables she hates the most.

"You might change your mind," I tell her as she runs away, shaking her head. The four of us laugh and know we'll lock that story away for her twenty-first birthday.

I hear the door open.

"We're back," Rosa sings out.

Millie gives a little wave as she walks past us all on her way to the couch, her head stuck in a book. I'm not sure if they walked around the city like that or not. Mia's at the piano again, practicing her scales.

"Sorry, we took our time. We got a call when we were out." Rosa looks at Nonna, who's smiling.

"I sold my house," she says, beaming.

"What?" Emily jumps down from the counter, a look of fear on her face. "But why?"

"Because I'm getting old, and it's far too big for just me. And I want to be closer to my daughter and granddaughter." Nonna grasps Emily's hands between her knobbly fingers. "My friends are either dying, or they've lost their marbles. Plus, the house has never been the same without your Nonno."

"We've actually signed off on plans to buy in a new apartment block. They're starting construction after Christmas." Rosa seems excited with the news, but I can see Emily is having trouble processing it.

"Are you selling too?" Emily almost shrieks at her mother. I walk over and stroke her back.

"No, honey," Rosa smiles as she strokes Emily's face. "That will become your place. You and Boyd. You can do with it what you like. Sell it, renovate, even add on. I know you hate the wallpaper in the lounge room."

"But..." Emily pauses. "But we've saved thousands."

"I know, and if you want to sell it and put the money towards your own place, that will be fine, too."

"I'm putting on the kettle." Charlie walks behind me and pats me on the shoulder.

"Wait, you knew?" I ask him, looking between him and Mum.

"Yes." Mum laughs. "It's a gorgeous complex, and the views rival those from our pool deck. Your father and I have also bought there."

"Wait, you're not selling?" I'm confused by all this real estate talk.

"No." Dad shakes his head. "We're treating it as an investment, but we will probably move there when we retire."

"We wanted to tell you now, though, so you can start making plans for when you move back." Dad pours water over the tea leaves he's measured into a large pot and leaves it to steep as he grabs cups from the cupboard.

This changes a lot of things, and it's something Emily and I will need to talk about. Whilst I hate that my family meddles, I realise they do it out of love.

"COME HERE, WIFE." I pull away the doona to allow Emily to slide into bed next to me.

We've been out to dinner with everyone, and this is the first time we've had alone since they dropped the whole housing bombshells this evening.

"How was your day?" I ask. Emily snuggles under my arm, and I can feel her breath against my chest. It's so comforting, and this cuddle has become part of our evening routine.

"Yeah, not too bad." She strokes my stomach. It's not meant to be sexual, but try telling my cock that. "Only had to call one ambulance."

"Don't tell me." I grin. "Older man who hasn't been to the doctor for years with a sore jaw and arm. ECG showed heart block."

"It's too predictable, isn't it?" She chuckles as she throws a leg over mine. "How about you?"

"Yeah. It was good." I rub my face with my hand. "It's still strange working in the diabetes centre named after Giles' mate, who died."

To be honest, although I've loved working at the children's hospital, I miss Cassowary Point.

"I saw you talking to your dad over dinner." Emily rubs her head against me as if she's a cat. I don't think she realises she does these things, but they make me feel so loved by her.

"Yeah." I sigh. "He suggested we move in with them for a few months. I mean, they've got the room."

"It's an option." Emily is quiet for a while. One thing we've learnt through therapy is that silence isn't always bad. Sometimes, it can be better to pause before we talk to each other. "It's very generous of Mum to give us the house. Are you okay with it, though?"

Emily props herself up on her elbow as she looks at me for an answer.

"I think we could make the place ours," I say honestly. "Perhaps we could turn that pokey third bedroom into an ensuite for the master bedroom or a walk-in closet. Or maybe even extend out the back and build a new master bedroom. It needs a new kitchen, unless you're fond of those brown tiles?"

"They're the first things coming out." Emily snuggles back into me again.

"Are you okay with it being something you remember about your father, though?" I ask as I rub her shoulder.

We talked a lot about him after Emily met up with him. Emily's also talked with Rosa, and whilst we can both see why Rosa kept his real personality from Emily, she did it out of love, and it gave Emily a chance to come to her own conclusions after a five-minute conversation in a suburban shopping mall. He's never tried to contact her again, and they both have the same phone numbers they did when he left.

It's his loss. Rosa's content on her own. She doesn't need a man in her life for companionship. I still find that hard to fathom, but she's not unhappy. It doesn't surprise me either that she's moving in with Nonna. In twenty or thirty years, she may move in with us, and I'll be cool with that. I'll just have to make sure Val has a few kids who can take care of their aunt and uncle in their old age.

"This may sound crazy." I look down to see Emily biting her lip like she does when she's nervous. "But we won't need all the house deposit money. How about we take longer off work and go to Africa after China?"

I've always talked about visiting Africa. It's not just the animals, but the way of life. One of my colleagues spent two months working in a series of villages helping stop a cholera outbreak last year. It sounded like fascinating work.

"That sounds like a brilliant plan. And then, if we're in Africa, we're almost on the same timeline as Italy almost, so we might as well pop up there and see your cousins." I'm holding her tight as different options fly through my brain.

"Savannah talks so fondly of her three-month stint in England when she worked for the NHS. It shouldn't be too hard to get work there if we want, too." Emily sounds so enthusiastic. "I mean, only if you don't mind pushing out your training program. They'll give you time off, won't they?"

I know they will. It will delay any further IVF plans, though. Strangely, I don't feel sad about this. One thing the last few years have shown me is that Emily and I are a strong partnership. Whilst we still agree that in the future we'd love to have kids, because it isn't happening at the moment doesn't mean it will never happen. Well, not necessarily. I mean, it might. We might hit forty and still be childless, but we can cross that bridge then.

It's such a fine line we've learnt to tread. I can tell there's still disappointment when Emily's period arrives each month, but it reminds us she has a regular cycle. There's a contentment there though. There are moments when we let ourselves rage about the perceived injustice of it all, but we still have each other.

"So, what, six, twelve months?" I ask as plans whir around my brain. We could go around the world and get to eat tacos in Mexico. My leg taps with excitement.

"We could start with six and extend," Emily says. "Even come home early if we need to."

I know what she's saying. If we find ourselves pregnant, then yes, we probably will want to head home straight away.

"Twelve months is a long time to be away from your mum and Nonna," I say as I smooth Emily's hair.

"We've seen more of them living down here than we ever did in Cassowary Point." Emily laughs. It's true. Nonna has mastered Face-Time, and she and I chat regularly, too.

"Where are you going?" I ask as Emily jumps out of bed. The sight of her tits bouncing sees blood rush south. She's so gorgeous.

"I was going to check airfares." She blinks her eyes at me.

We have a rule that our phones sit in the ensuite to charge so we aren't tempted to look at them overnight. It's something Pip suggested very early on. I know better than trying to stop her. I hear various oohs and a few disappointing sighs coming from the bathroom.

"Are you coming back to bed, wife?" I yell through the door. "This rooster isn't going to stroke itself."

"Goodnight, Boyd." I hear Rosa laugh from next door. *Fuck. I forgot my mother-in-law was here.*

"Do you really think we can travel?" Emily asks as she switches off the light again and walks back towards our bed.

"I think we can do anything we want, baby."

Emily slides back into bed, throwing a leg over me and leaning down for a kiss. I really am the luckiest man in the world having her as my wife.

Epilogue

Emily

THIS PLACE HASN'T CHANGED IN THREE YEARS. IT'S STILL uncomfortable chairs and staff in white dresses with pulled back hair and immaculate makeup. The same prints are on the wall, and the same fragrance disperses from the mister on the desk. It's ostentatious.

"Emily and Boyd, come through, come through." Dr Jacquie looks a little greyer around the edges of her hair, but her smile is still so comforting. "What's it been, three years?"

"A bit over that, yes," I reply as she ushers for us to sit on the new couch in her room.

"This is comfy," Boyd says as he wiggles his bottom in it.

"The chairs are revolting. I keep suggesting we get rid of them and fuck the aesthetic. Pardon my French." The doctor shakes her head, a lopsided grin on her face. "So, what have you been up to?"

"Well, we went to Brisbane, and I finished my GP training. Boyd spent some time at the children's hospital, and then last year, we travelled." I'm liking this couch because Boyd has his arm around my shoulders.

276

"Nice. Where did you go?" Dr Jacquie sits back in her comfy chair, her legs crossed, her arms comfortably hanging over the sides.

"We started in China, then Hong Kong. We spent a few weeks in India, which was amazing. I mean, the food was out of this world," I say, looking at Boyd.

"Yeah, except when you got explosive diarrhoea." Boyd laughs. "Then we went to Africa. First, South Africa for a bit, then up to Namibia, which was stunning. I got a call from a colleague in Brisbane about a cholera outbreak in Uganda, and we went and volunteered there for a month. It was... it was eye opening, that's for sure."

It was probably my most fulfilling month as a doctor so far. Not that I did much, but listening to the locals on the ground and seeing how limited the health infrastructure was to begin with made me grateful every time I complain that my patients have to wait a week or two to get in and see me.

"Yeah." I nod. "It showed us how lucky we are, I suppose. So, from there, we went to Egypt for a week, then Istanbul. Now that was gorgeous. Then, a month in Italy with family before we both did a five-month contract with the NHS in Edinburgh."

"How was that?" Dr Jacquie seems surprised.

"Different," we both say at the same time.

"And cold," I add. "But such a stunning place."

"We then spent a very expensive week in New York." Boyd bounces off me. It doesn't get old repeating our itinerary.

"And a week in New Orleans, which was a blast." Boyd and I look at each other, huge smiles on our faces as we remember this time.

"Then, Christmas in Mexico, eating tacos on a beach and drinking margaritas." Boyd leans over and kisses me. I know what he's remembering from Mexico. We had to explain to the front desk that we broke the bed after we both got a little too enthusiastic. Fun times. "We got back at the end of January and have been doing up our new place. It was Emily's parents' house. Em's working with Dr Nat."

"Yeah, it's going great." I nod. "And Boyd will be finished with his paeds training in about eighteen months. I'm doing a women's health diploma, too."

"It's great to see you both so content with each other. It's been, what, six or seven years you've been trying to conceive?" Jacquie crosses her legs after picking up her laptop and opening our notes.

It's hard to believe it's been that long. We sat on the beach in Mexico watching the fireworks heralding the new year and talked about IVF. The decision we agreed to was to do one fresh cycle a year for the next three years and then transplant any frozen embryos we might have, but to stop when I turn thirty-five. That will be over ten years of trying. I know at the back of my mind that there's nothing wrong they can find, and, who knows, we might be blessed later in life, but it's not something we'll count on.

We talked about fostering, but both of us work high-powered jobs, and I don't think I could take a child in and then hand it back after they'd lived with us. There's still a deep yearning to have a baby of our own, and I know when I hit thirty-five and if I don't have one, then there will be a lot of tears, but we've had to set our limits. Our marriage is too important not to.

I explain our plans to the doctor, who smiles and nods, agreeing with us.

"You know, I see lots of strong marriages fall apart over infertility. I see people pay thousands of dollars they don't have. Then I see couples like you who make such sensible decisions. I know last time I spoke with you, I gave you the names of some therapists. Did they help?" I feel so validated by our doctor.

"Yeah." Boyd shakes his head in disbelief. "Pip's been amazing."

"I hear she's good. Now, we'll run a few tests, and then we can start next month if you like?"

We both nod. We've got a plan, and we've got each other.

"ROOSTER. NO. DOWN." I laugh at Boyd's firm voice.

Rooster thinks it's a game. One of Henry's patient's dogs had a litter of pups. Henry, being the softie he is, paid to have the dog desexed and found homes for the three puppies. We only took one of them, and Giles and Bridget were very lucky not to end up with another one, but a nurse from the ward and a friend of Dipti's took the other two.

We got the badly behaved dog. It doesn't help that we asked Mia to name her after she sobbed when she found out we were getting a puppy and they weren't. You can't reason with a nine-year-old that Rooster is not a good name for a female dog, but she thinks it's hilarious. It's better than Moose, or whatever the other name was she had a few years back.

"But Nonna's always asking Boyd about his rooster," she says all innocently. I think Millie put her up to it. Giles chokes back laughter.

Boyd walks into our new kitchen. It's sleek and modern with not a brown tile in sight. Mum keeps threatening to move back in with us, but her new place is just as nice.

"She's chewed another pair of my runners." He sighs as he throws them in the bin.

"Did you think perhaps to put them away instead of leaving them outside when we went to the doctor?" I ask, drawing him in for a hug. He really gives the best hugs.

"I think my mind was elsewhere." Boyd holds me, his chin resting on my head. "I thought Jacquie might talk us into doing more cycles or something."

It was something I'd been concerned about too, but I knew I'd be able to stand my ground.

"Do you think we should take her for a walk?" I ask. She's had all her shots now, and I'm not as worried about having her around other dogs.

"I took her on my run this morning." Boyd is sulking. At least they were his old running shoes. It's about time he got some new ones.

"Perhaps we can tire her out, and it might tire us a bit too, and we may need to spend the afternoon in bed." I run my finger down Boyd's chest.

"Fuck, I love you." Boyd kisses me with a promise of more to come later on. "Rooster, we're going walkies."

I grab my phone, keys, and hat and meet them outside. Boyd's already forgiven the dog, and she's slobbering all over his face as he tries to fasten her lead.

"You're so good at restraining her," I whisper in his ear, "Perhaps you should try restraining me when we get back."

"Fuck, woman. You're making me walk with a fucking stiffy." I love seeing him try to rearrange himself and not be so obvious, especially as we know our nosy neighbour is in her yard.

It's a different neighbour to the one whose dog we used to walk when we were teenagers. I think back to my teenage self and marvel at how far I've come since the quiet, angry girl who couldn't understand why her father left her. I know now it wasn't me. Boyd shows me each and every day how special I am and how important we are to each other.

Whatever the future brings, I know we'll be okay. We're each other's always and forever.

Emily, Age 14

I saw Priscilla again today. Yep, our second visit. She wore these beige pants that gave her a camel toe. I mean, gross. I can't wait to tell Val. She's the one who explained to me what a camel toe is, after all. I told Priscilla I'm keeping my diary on my computer. There was no way I was telling her I kept it in a file marked 'Calculus Extension Work' because if anyone snooped, there was no way they'd look there. I haven't even told Val that I'm writing stuff down, let alone what it's called.

This week, I have homework. I'm meant to make a list of my life's goals. Not a bucket list of wanting to publish a book or drive a Ferrari. They were Priscilla's examples. Interesting to see what's on her bucket list, but real life goals. She said things like career and used words like fulfilment and stuff. She got so animated, her metal bangles clanged together. Apart from never wearing beige pants that give me a camel toe, I'm never going to wear jewellery that clanks together either.

I've only got one goal. I want to be happy. I want to live my happily ever after. And I will.

Please don't forget to leave a rating and/or review, they mean so much to indie authors. Bonus material can be found at jezabelnightingale.com

A Note from Jez

This has been nothing the easiest and the hardest book to write. Over twenty years ago, I was the one sitting through holiday celebrations feeling anything but celebratory. Even now, with children who are grown, Mother's Day is a strange day filled with mixed emotions.

I suspect that unless you have been impacted by infertility, then it can be hard to understand why people are acting as they are. I portrayed Emily and Boyd based on conversations with friends who had been through unexplained infertility. Not having answers made things all that much worse for them.

One thing I did differently with this book was to sit down and use software to plan the book. Chapter by chapter I wanted to capture the journey Emily and Boyd were on. I wanted to break the book into three sections- the honeymoon, trying, and success. At the end, it was going to be another family Christmas where Emily and Boyd were going to tell the Hartmans they'd been successful (using Christmas Crackers with baby items in there—just like a friend of mine did many years ago.)

Except, I thought back to my infertility journey and how I'd sought media to entertain me as I was experiencing disappointment after disappointment. One thing I remembered was the ending where they're pregnant and everyone was happy was not something I could relate to. Sure, it gave me hope, but it wasn't what I was experiencing.

So, I took the book on another path. More will be revealed in the last book of the series, and I'll leave it at that for now, except to add that as readers, we can journey through universes and, hopefully, see things that aren't necessarily on the page. I hope each reader can see into their own version of Boyd and Emily's future.

Acknowledgments

If you've come this far, you deserve more than my thanks. You deserve gratitude and warm fuzzy feelings that I can't put into words. So much for being a writer! Naturally, this includes the amazing ARC readers.

Seriously though, without readers, we do this for very little. I'm serious when I ask people to leave a review or rating, no matter what you think of the book, because that helps with visibility. I mean, if you love it, tell everyone. If you don't, tell me why, please.

My editorial team of Sarah and Cheyenne. You ladies are rock stars. I pour over the manuscript so many times before I send it to Sarah and she still has to ask me how Bob is getting Jane a drink from the fridge when they are both in the lounge/bedroom/outside etc. Cheyenne picks up the little things—the letters and punctuation in the wrong spot (imagine if I had left it as vermix instead of vernix. Having a baby covered in a uniform appendix was not what I meant!Yikes!) Both wonderful women make me a better writer, and I am better for having them on the journey with me. They also don't read this, hence all the exclamation marks :)

Kristin has helped me with another awesome cover, which I just love.

Thanks to those I talked to about their infertility experiences, especially B, S, and A. Also, the Supermums—we've gone from discussing peeing on sticks to toilet training, to school, to young adulthood and are still surviving. You are such an amazing group of women who I am proud to call my dearest friends.

To Dr Nightingale for believing in me and cooking dinner when I'm on a deadline. I don't think I've ever used our new washing machine, and it's almost a year old. You rock! And to my big babies, who helped ease the pain of infertility all those years ago. I love you.

Also by Jezabel Nightingale

The Hartman Family Series

The Heart Switch

A Meeting of Minds

Kidding Around

Fiction v Reality

The Bayview Monarchs

Tackling Love Once More

Lovemore Gap

Finding Love

Coming February 2025

Standalone Titles

Secret Santa

About the Author

Jezabel Nightingale is an emerging author of contemporary romance. She wears so many hats, including nurse, mother, wife, writer, and scholar. In her spare time, you'll find her cheering on AFL football, in the kitchen baking a cake, or reading a spicy romance novel. It is not unusual to find a gin and tonic in her hand, or something chocolatey in her vicinity. She will blame these vices for her overuse of exclamation marks and commas, because, why not?

She lives on the East Coast of Australia with Dr Nightingale, her spunkrat of a husband, her cats, and her kids who keep popping home, despite officially having moved out.

After publishing short stories online for several years, this is her third novel.

Manufactured by Amazon.ca
Acheson, AB

15879107R00166